MOON SHIMMERS

AN OTHERWORLD NOVEL
BOOK 19

YASMINE GALENORN

NEW YORK TIMES BESTSELLING AUTHOR

A Nightqueen Enterprises LLC Publication

Published by Yasmine Galenorn
PO Box 2037, Kirkland WA 98083-2037
MOON SHIMMERS
An Otherworld Novel
Copyright © 2017 by Yasmine Galenorn
First Electronic Printing: 2017 Nightqueen Enterprises LLC
First Print Edition: 2017 Nightqueen Enterprises
Cover Art & Design: Earthly Charms
Editor: Elizabeth Flynn
Map Design: Yasmine Galenorn

ALL RIGHTS RESERVED No part of this book may be reproduced or distributed in any format, be it print or electronic or audio, without permission. Please prevent piracy by purchasing only authorized versions of this book.

This is a work of fiction. Any resemblance to actual persons, living or dead, businesses, or places is entirely coincidental and not to be construed as representative or an endorsement of any living/existing group, person, place, or business.

A Nightqueen Enterprises LLC Publication
Published in the United States of America

ACKNOWLEDGMENTS

When I first started writing Witchling twelve years ago, I had no clue that the series would become so popular. It amazed me how much my readers took to the Sisters, and how rapidly the series gained traction. Eighteen books later, when my then-publisher decided to drop the series three books from the end of a very long run, I knew that I had to finish it on my own. I couldn't let my readers down, and I couldn't let the series down. So here's the first book in the last triad of the Otherworld Series. There will be more Otherworld stories—most likely in the form of novelettes—but this leg of the series, of their journey, will finish out.

I'm so grateful to my readers who've followed me this far. There has been quite a dropoff, I admit, but to the ones who've remained like glue to the adventures of the sisters—thank you for the love you've given this world of mine, and all my worlds.

Thanks also go to my husband, Samwise, who has been my biggest supporter as I've shifted my career to the indie side. And thanks to my friends who have cheered me on—especially Jo and Carol. Thank you to my assistants Jenn and Andria for all their help. And thank you to my fellow authors in my UF group, who have helped me learn what I needed to learn in order to take my career into my own hands.

A most reverent nod to my spiritual guardians—Mielikki, Tapio, Ukko, Rauni, and the Lady Brighid. They guide my life, and my heart.

And of course, love and scritches to my fuzzy brigade—Caly, Brighid, Morgana, and little boy Apple. I would be lost without my cats.

Bright Blessings, and I hope you enjoy Camille's book. For more information about all my work, please see my website at Galenorn.com, and sign up for my newsletter.

Brightest Blessings,
~The Painted Panther~
~Yasmine Galenorn~

Welcome to Otherworld

"You will rise to be a fearsome queen. Will you accept what this brings into your life?"

Then I saw. This was the end of dillydallying. The time had come. I saw the raging of demons, as I led the Knights into battle. Blood spilling on the ground like water over the falls. A harsh and terrible light and then, the image of Shadow Wing filled my mind. I had never seen him—none of us knew what he looked like. But there he was, rising like a winged demon, taller than a giant, with coiling horns and ruddy-red skin and flaming eyes. He wielded a sword and he was looking right at me.

I could barely breathe. Evil bled off him like sweat, and everything that he touched became tainted and vile. I tried to break away, tried to hide but there was nowhere to go. He could see me, as clearly as I could see him, and he knew what I was doing. He knew I had come for the diamond, and soon he would have a rival he never expected. I would be flanked by my Knights, but still—when it came time to face him down—I would be there, on the front lines, standing between him and the world.

Map of Otherworld

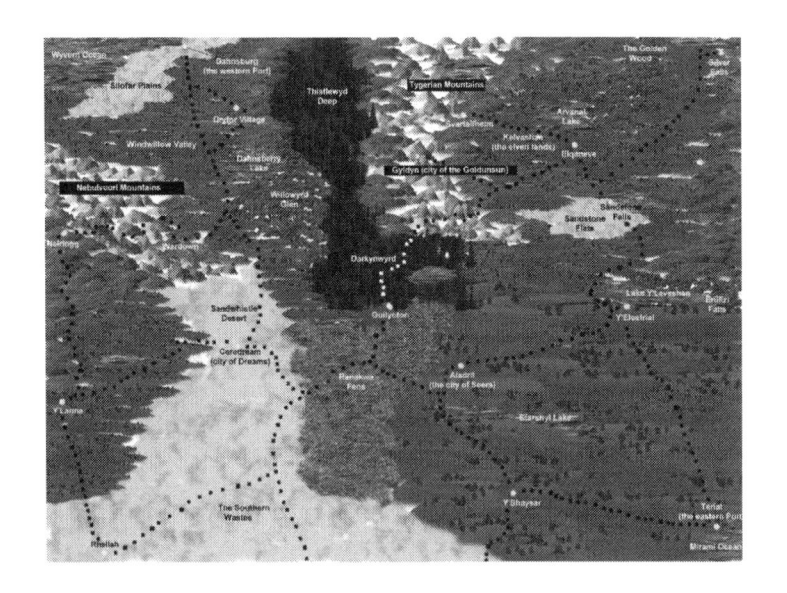

Chapter 1

"BLOCK HIM AT the pass!" I dodged out of the way, trying not to dive face first into the dirt, but I didn't see the stray tennis ball some dog had dropped under the bridge, and did a banana-peel flop onto my butt. I rolled to the side, hard, as the damned troll charged past. Or rather, *troll spirit*.

"I swear, the next blowhard who tries to tell me that spirits can't be corporeal is going to get my fist in their face," I groaned, rolling to a sitting position. *Damn it.* I had torn my skirt on a shard of glass. Well, better my skirt than my leg. At least I hadn't broken my ankle. I had long ago given up fighting in stilettos, but tonight we hadn't planned on a showdown and we were all dressed to the nines for dinner, and my heels were four-inch spiky sandals.

Delilah raced by, pausing to hold out her hand. I grabbed it and she hauled me up. As soon as she pulled me onto my feet, she was off again, trying to catch up to the lumbering ghost. Menolly was already up ahead, dangling off the troll's back like some demented monkey, only cuter. I swallowed my pride, made sure nothing was broken, and hauled ass in their direction. Thanks to regular workouts, I was faster than I used to be, but I still lagged behind. Delilah was a natural-born athlete. So was Menolly, plus she was a vampire. Me? Not so much either one.

"He's not slowing down and I can't break his neck because he's not alive!" Menolly's voice echoed from up ahead. As I watched, the troll spirit veered directly toward a massive cedar.

"Watch out for—" I stopped, wincing as the spirit skidded to a stop. In a whiplash effect, Menolly went flying over his head. She landed a good three yards ahead of him, sliding along the asphalt, cursing like a sailor. The troll turned right onto a side street and bounded away, leaving us all in the dust.

"Well, that had to hurt." Delilah shaded her eyes, watching the troll vanish.

I caught up to her and we jogged over to Menolly's side. Menolly picked herself up off the road and dusted her hands on her jeans. We had lost the troll's trail. Oh, we could go racing after him and probably pick it up again, but seeing that he was the spirit of a troll and not the actual creature, chances were we'd be off on a wild goose chase.

"What the hell was *that*?" Menolly stretched her arms over her head, then shook her shoulders out. Her eyes were glowing crimson in the pale light of dusk, a sure sign her hunting instincts had been out to play. "That wasn't like any troll I've ever dealt with before."

"That's because it was a ghost, although not your typical run-of-the-mill spook. Somehow, the spirit managed to become corporeal." I winced. The spill I'd taken was catching up to me and I was pretty sure I had bruised my tailbone. "What I want to know is where did it come from?"

We walked back beneath the overpass to stare at the Fremont Troll. A Seattle landmark, the troll was a massive sculpture that had been designed and created by a team of artists who called themselves the Jersey Devils. Formed from rebar, wire, and concrete, it was big enough to hold an actual Volkswagen Beetle in its hand. But behemoth or not, the troll was a just a sculpture. Or so we had thought. Nothing more than a neighborhood icon.

I would have been happy to remain blissfully ignorant, except Chase had called us while we were out to dinner. Someone had reported that the Fremont Troll had come to life and was rampaging around under the bridge. Once we got there, of course, we found the sculpture right where it had always been. However, there *was* a troll roaming around, only it was a confused, angry spirit.

"What do you suppose happened?" Menolly glared at the sculpture as we passed it. "Who on earth thought putting a troll under an overpass was a good thing?"

"They made this before the Supes came out of the closet." But I was right behind her in giving it a nervous glance as we passed it. Actually, the Fremont Troll was rather fun. Fans dressed him up for the holidays, and he was as much a part of the Seattle landscape as was the Space Needle. No, the troll we had faced had only hidden inside the sculpture until something set him off.

"We already knew that spirits can sometimes take on corporeal form. Something spooked this one and he's not happy. Which means our troll friend—the spirit, not the sculpture—is dangerous to anybody he happens to meet."

"I know what did it." Menolly dashed up the slope beside the troll to stand on top of his head. "Come up here."

The last thing I wanted to do was climb up a dirt

embankment in a fancy dress and corset, but I pulled off my shoes and Delilah and I scrambled up the easy rise. When we were on top of the troll, we were standing right beneath the overpass.

There we found an altar, of sorts. A makeshift "talking board" sat between two candles in Mason jars. The candles were still flickering. A quartz crystal rested to the left, a tipped-over bottle of wine to the right. The board was a rough rectangle of plywood, with the alphabet painted across it, and the words "yes" and "no" at the top corners. An upside-down paper cup rested on the board atop a thin piece of transparent acrylic, just the right size to cover one letter at a time.

"Fuck me now." I stared at the setup. "Somebody figured out there was a spirit hiding itself in the troll and decided to commune with it. Bingo, open-door policy. Idiots didn't realize that boards like this are actually portals."

"Either that, or they were just drunk off their asses and screwing around." Delilah rubbed her temples. "When will kids learn?"

"Why do you think this was a group of kids? I've met plenty of adults who don't have the sense they were born with." I toed the board. Sure enough, a sizzle sparked against my big toe. "Well, whoever they were, they opened the door, but I doubt they're capable of locking the troll back in the bottle, so to speak. Which means we have to figure out what to do with it. We can't just force it to go back inside the sculpture. That's no life for any spirit."

"I feel guilty for suggesting it, but we could call Ivana." Menolly glanced at me. Ivana Krask, or the Maiden of Karask, was one of the Elder Fae. She loved ghosts. She loved ghosts *all too much*. She trapped the nasty ones in her ghoulish little "garden of ghosts," where she fed off their energy and tormented them. But she was good at rounding up spirits, that was for sure. She'd probably salivate over the chance to nab a troll's spirit.

I stared at my sister. "While the idea of handing over this creature to her is tempting, the fact is that we don't know whether it's evil or not. And I honestly can't face myself in the mirror if we end up giving her a ghost who's just confused and unhappy."

"I thought you might say that." Menolly shrugged. "I'm out of suggestions for now. We don't know where the thing went. We don't know what to do about it if we do find it again. What do you suggest?"

"Let's head back to the car." Delilah glanced up at the sky. "We can hunt it that way. We'd better find it, though. Tomorrow night's the full moon and I won't be of any use then. I can already feel the pull in my blood." Full moons were always out when it came to any sort of plans for Delilah unless they included gallivanting around in my catnip garden, or chasing moths through the yard. They were out for me, too.

"Right. And I'll be off on the Hunt with the Moon Mother." I was swept away during the Full Moon, too, only I went racing through the skies instead of the back yard.

"So, what do we do? We can't even figure out how to contain it, let alone send it off to the happy troll gardens or whatever their afterlife is. All we've accomplished so far is a broken butt and torn skirt for you, and skid marks tearing up my leather jacket." Menolly shrugged. "Maybe we should do a little research? We may actually save time that way. We're near the station. They have computers. Chase will let us use one."

I hooked my arm through Delilah's. "She's right. We aren't going to manage anything until we figure out what we're fighting and how to combat it. Let's head over to the FH-CSI."

Delilah shrugged. "Whatever you think is right. I just

hope that thing doesn't hurt anybody while we're surfing the 'net. Come on, let's go." She held up her keys as we approached her Jeep and unlocked the doors. Without another word, we piled in the car and were off to the station.

THE FH-CSI WAS the acronym for the Faerie-Human Crime Scene Investigation unit. Over the years, it had grown from a specialty operation to a powerful city organization. Chase Johnson, the detective in charge of it, was a friend of ours. He and Delilah had been an item for a while but the gulf between them was too great. Now, he was paired up with the Elfin Queen and while they got along great, once again, circumstance had intervened.

Sharah had returned to Otherworld to take up her duty when Elqaneve and the Elfin lands had been pulverized during war. The old queen was killed, making Sharah—a niece and the only one close to the throne who was still alive—the heir. She had returned home to take the crown, leaving Chase and their daughter, Astrid, over here Earthside. It wasn't ideal, but neither Chase nor Sharah had a choice. Her duty to the throne came first for Sharah, and duty to his daughter and his own post came first for Chase.

Located in the Belles-Faire District of Seattle, the FH-CSI was on Thatcher Avenue. It was a large building with one floor aboveground, which housed the police unit and healing facilities for the Supe community. At least three stories belowground included an arsenal, a jail, a laboratory, morgue, and archives, and there was a rumored fourth level, though Chase would never confirm or deny it.

The parking lot was empty, though in thirty-six hours it would be full. A few of the jail cells were actually used as kennels during the full moon, for when some of the werewolves went careening around the city. The animal shelters sub-contracted members of the FH-CSI to round up the bigger predator types and cart them down to the holding cells until morning. Once they reverted to their human forms, they paid a nominal fee and were set free. That way, nobody got hurt and in the morning, their families could come get them, crowding the parking lot.

As we approached the building, the sound of traffic blurred in the distance. The sky was clear and the weather, balmy. June in Seattle didn't exactly fit most people's definition of *warm*, but the rain was holding off and it was sixty degrees at ten-thirty. Shirtsleeve weather to locals.

I glanced at the stars. Most of them were drowned out by the light pollution, but here and there, a bright star flickered. The sky was so different from what it had been back home in Otherworld. Here, the city lights blotted out all but the brightest stars. But there was an energy over Earthside that OW *didn't* have. And I had gotten used to that energy. I was actually grateful that I was here to stay.

I pushed through the doors. The police station was to the left, and the medic unit was straight ahead. As we entered the station, the bustle of activity hit us like a wave.

Yugi, Chase's second in command and a Swedish empath, was racing around with a clipboard in his hand. At least three officers that we could see were checking their weapons. I jumped back as Marquette—an elf who had joined the force a couple years back—hurried by. The look on her face was dour. Brooks, a full blooded human, followed her, looking just as grim. Behind *him* was Fry, another FBH. She was carrying one hell of a big shotgun.

Chase was standing at the door of his office. When he saw us, he brushed his hair back from his face and motioned us in. "Thank gods you're here. You lost the troll, didn't you?"

At six-one, Chase was Delilah's height. With dark wavy hair and olive skin, he looked Mediterranean. We had all thought Chase was human until a few months back when we discovered he actually had an ancestor from Otherworld in his lineage, giving him a touch of elfin blood. He was wearing a designer suit—Calvin Klein—and right now he looked like he was about to pop a blood vessel in his forehead.

"That's why we're here. The Fremont Troll is right where it was. What we're chasing is the corporeal spirit of a troll who was resting quietly inside the sculpture till some lamebrain decided to use a talking board. At least, that's the way we think it went down." I glanced over at his desk. His landline was ringing off the hook, three of the four lines flashing. "Your phone—"

"Never mind my phone. We have a major problem. Whatever that thing is, it's headed toward Golden Gardens Park, where there happens to be a major event going on."

Delilah paled. "What event?"

"The midnight wedding of some big-shot lawyer's kid. There are two hundred people milling around the park, half of whom are scheduled to eat a midnight supper there after the wedding. I'm sending officers over now, but we have to do something before the bride and groom end up taking their vows over a mass grave." Chase was stumbling over his words. He usually wasn't this frantic, even during emergencies.

"Slow down. We'll head out there. We just wanted to do a little research on this spirit. We aren't sure how to stop it." I frowned. "What else is wrong, Chase? It's not like you to be so panicked over a routine monster fight."

His shoulders slumping, he dropped into the chair behind his desk. "What's wrong is this: Do you know the name Brandon Rigal?"

Delilah let out a loud cough. "Yeah, he's that big muckety-muck lawyer who defends the members of the Freedom's Angels and the Guardian Watchdogs when they get busted."

The Freedom's Angels and the Guardian Watchdogs were two incredibly nasty hate-groups out to oust the Supe Community from Seattle. They had spread to other cities as well. At first the Angels were talk-only, but once the Guardian Watchdogs got involved, and with the Brotherhood of the Earth-Born backing them, now they were all violent. It wasn't a far step from shouting vile slogans to acting on the rhetoric.

"The wedding just happens to be that of Rigal's daughter. If the troll disrupts his little princess's precious nuptials, Rigal will do everything he can to rile up the Freedom's Angels and the Guardian Watchdogs. Not only that, he'll drag the FH-CSI through the mud."

Crap. That put a whole new spin on the night. We had to stop that troll spirit before he lay waste to the nuptials.

"Delilah, look up the troll on the computers. Menolly and I will head out...oh damn it, we can't. We only brought your Jeep." We had started out on the hunt for fish and chips, and later, we had planned to go clubbing. We hadn't counted on a fight. I turned to Chase. "Can Menolly and I ride with your people?"

Chase nodded. "Hurry, though. They're ready to head out. Delilah—you can use the computer in Yugi's office. He'll help you with anything you need." As we headed out the door, he called after us, "I don't care how you do it. Just get that troll or we'll all pay the price."

MARQUETTE AND BROOKS were partners and they had already left, so Menolly and I crammed ourselves into the backseat of Fry's patrol car. Fry was lean and tall, and as tough as they came. When she barked, the others jumped. *A regular Rottweiler*, Chase had said.

She glanced in the back seat as we buckled ourselves in. "Don't touch the guns and don't spill anything on the seat. Especially blood."

I glanced at Menolly, suppressing a laugh. "We aren't in the habit of grabbing guns, and I guarantee you, Menolly won't be using me as a juice box."

"Fine. Hold on. I'm cranking on the siren." And with that, the siren let out a loud alarm and we lurched out of the parking lot, gaining speed as the drivers ahead of us gave way.

Menolly stared out into the night. "You realize that by the end of this month, we won't be doing this anymore. Not like this, anyway."

My mood plunged to gloom within seconds. "I know. I don't want to think about it."

"You'd better *start* thinking about it, because Litha's coming up in a couple weeks and then..." She didn't finish. She didn't have to.

I didn't answer. There was nothing to say. Within two weeks, I'd be moving myself and my husbands out to Talamh Lonrach Oll, where I would take the crown as the Queen of Dusk and Twilight over the Sovereign Fae Nation.

MY NAME IS Camille Sepharial D'Artigo and together with my sisters, Menolly and Delilah, I came over from Otherworld a few years back. Our mother, Maria D'Artigo, was human, and our father, Sephreh ob Tanu, full-blooded Fae. They met and fell in love when he was on assignment over Earthside. He swept her off to Otherworld and they had us. Shortly after Menolly was born, Mother died from a fall off of a horse. Our father never quite recovered from her death, and we lost him a few months back.

I'm the oldest, and I'm a Moon Witch and High Priestess. And in two weeks, I'll take the throne as the Queen of Dusk and Twilight. I stand between worlds—between Otherworld and Earthside. Between light and dark. I'm married to three gorgeous men: Smoky—a dragon shifter, Morio—a youkai kitsune, and Trillian, a Svartan—one of the dark and charming Fae. They get along, mostly, and they are the loves of my lives.

Delilah, the second-born, is a two-faced werecat, able to shift into both a long-haired golden tabby, and a black panther. She's a Death Maiden, serving the Autumn Lord, and she's engaged to Shade, half–shadow dragon and half-Stradolan. Someday, she's destined to bear the child of the Autumn Lord with Shade acting as his proxy. Being the mother of an Elemental Lord—or Lady—seems a daunting prospect, but she's down with it. Delilah's very maternal.

And then there's Menolly. Menolly started out as a *jian-tu*. She could climb walls, ropes, trees with abandon. She could make it across cavern roofs, until the day she fell off into a nest of vampires. Dredge, one of the most dangerous vamps in history, caught her and the result wasn't pretty. He tortured her and then, at the last, when she could hold out no longer, he forcibly turned her and sent her home to destroy her family. I managed to lure her into our safe room and lock her in. A year of rehabilitation taught her to control her impulses, but she continually battles her inner predator. Menolly's married to a gorgeous werepuma named Nerissa, and to Roman, prince of the Vampire Nation. They make an odd little trio, but somehow, it works.

The three of us are as different as light and dark. I have hair the color of raven wings, and violet eyes that flash silver when I work my magic. At five-seven, I have big boobs and ample hips and a narrow waist, and while I work out now so I can keep up in a fight, I'm a gurly girl and I'll always be. Delilah's six-one, athletic and lean, with short blond hair in a Euro-cut, and about the only time we can force her into a dress is during special occasions. And Menolly is petite, barely five-one. Her hair is the color of burnished copper hair and hangs to her lower back in long thin braids, dappled with beads.

Our mixed blood causes havoc. Our powers fritz out at the most inconvenient times. That wasn't exactly a big selling point to our bosses at the OIA—the Otherworld Intelligence Agency—and although we worked our asses off, we were never exemplary employees. Between our lapses, and my run-in with a supervisor who got pissed when I wouldn't blow him, we were shipped over Earthside on what was ostensibly a sabbatical. Things went downhill fast.

We arrived Earthside thinking our stay would be all fun and games. A real chance to explore our mother's homeworld. We ended up at the frontlines of a demonic war and trust me, saving two worlds, one monster at a time, isn't easy. We've been to hell and back in this war, and until we find the last spirit seal and forever bind all nine away from Shadow Wing—the leader of the Sub-Realms—there will always be the chance that he'll take control of the portals, force them open, and raze both Earthside and Otherworld. We're battle weary and we've lost too many friends to this war. We just want to finish it and be done, because trust me, war wounds run deep, and we're all scarred with injuries that are mostly unseen, but always present.

WE WERE ALMOST to Golden Gardens Park when Fry suddenly veered off the road, onto the shoulder. She leaned across the passenger seat, squinting out the window. To the right was a swath of grass, and a large wall leading up to a street that ran parallel with ours. The wall was covered with ivy.

"I thought I saw something big and fast out there," she said. "Is this creature invisible?"

I glanced at Menolly. "I don't know if it can fully turn invisible, but I'd say it could camouflage itself against a background of greenery."

"Come on. Let's go take a look. Hand me the shotgun, please." She held out her hand.

I stared at the gun, not wanting to touch it. There was enough iron in that gun to burn my hands if I accidentally touched any part that wasn't wood.

"Just do it—oh." She stopped, looking at my face. "You're half-Fae. Iron thing, right?"

"Right."

Menolly grabbed the gun, letting out a faint curse as her finger grazed the barrel. She carefully lifted it over the seat. Her fingers were blistered when Fry took the gun from her, but they began to heal up quickly. Vampires healed faster than most people realized, which meant she could touch iron and—while it still hurt—it wouldn't incapacitate her.

I frowned. "That gun won't do a thing against this creature. We're fighting a spirit. Even if you have silver bullets, it's not going to make a difference."

"Then what do you suggest I use?" Fry really didn't sound happy. She gazed down at the gun, then back at the window. "He's out there—see?"

I plastered my face against the window. Sure enough, I could see his faint form against the wall, blending into the ivy. "Come on, Menolly. We'll go on foot from here. Fry, why don't you drive ahead and try to keep people from scattering. If we can keep him from making it to the park, then maybe we can pull this off without the wedding guests ever knowing what's going on. Tell them...oh, tell them you're chasing a couple burglary subjects or something that won't cause a panic."

With that, Menolly and I hopped out of the car. Fry hesitated a moment, then put the gun down and took off toward the park, which was about a quarter mile down the road.

Menolly and I headed for the stone wall covered in ivy. I had left my shoes in the car, for easier running, and as we passed over a gravel spit, my toes protested. Of course, I had to find the sharpest pieces of gravel around. I hopped across to the grass and wiped off the pebbles that were stuck to the bottoms of my feet.

"What do we do when we get there?" Menolly asked.

I kept my eye on the hulking spirit. Turned out troll spirits were as big as their bodies, which were huge. The smallest troll I had ever seen was ten feet tall, and that was a youngster. Troll parents didn't let their young go wandering until they were large enough to look out for themselves. But trolls weren't just tall. They were bulky and muscled and scary as hell.

"At least we aren't facing a dubba-troll. Two heads

are definitely *not* better than one." I paused, trying to keep track of where the troll spirit had gone. Then I saw him, up ahead, still on his way to the park. "There he is. Why he's determined to go to the park, I don't know."

"Neither do I, but let's get a move on. I'm going on ahead. You come as fast as you can." Menolly sped up. She could move in a blur, like most vampires, and before long she was keeping pace with the troll. The next moment, she was in front of him and ready to try to dropkick him backward. As her foot hit his stomach, it went right through him and she landed in a heap on the grass. The troll didn't even look back.

"What the hell? Now he's *not* corporeal?"

My phone rang as I jogged over to where Menolly had fallen. She was up and chasing him again. I stopped, leaning over to breathe, and glanced at Caller ID. Delilah. I punched the TALK button and tried to keep from panting into the phone.

"Yeah? Talk fast."

Delilah snorted. "With as many workouts as your husbands give you, I'm surprised you aren't a champion sprinter. Anyway, I found reference on the GoGargoyle search engine to a particular spirit that seems to be endemic to Earthside. Apparently, some trolls and ogres who stayed behind near the Snohomish area began to fade over the years and they've wandered around to the Seattle area. They aren't true spirits, but faded shells of the creatures they once were. They've become a form of wight, though they aren't necessarily evil by nature anymore. Some dimwit dubbed them 'vrolls'—vapor and troll mixed—and it stuck. So we're facing a vroll. Apparently, they've lost their sense to hunt, and they're more like a wild animal who doesn't understand what's happened. Poor things are just afraid, from what the reports say."

"What's he looking for? How can we stop them?"

"Vrolls are looking for one thing: shelter and a place to hide, where they eventually will fade away into nothing. But when they're riled or forcibly shoved out of their hiding spots, they turn violent. Then the only thing you can do is either find a new place for the creature to slumber, or put it out of its misery. There's no reasoning with them. What's left is pure instinct and drive for self-preservation." She paused, then added, "It's really kind of sad, isn't it?"

I bit my lip. Sad was the word, all right. But even though the vroll was a sorry creature, we couldn't let it attack a wedding. Especially a wedding being thrown by one of Seattle's most vocal hate-mongers.

"How do we destroy it?"

Delilah let out a sigh. "You have to drain it of its life force. Menolly can't. There's no blood there to drain. But magick will work. We need Vanzir."

Vanzir could drain energy. The demon had, at one time, been forcibly bound to us, but he proved his mettle and now was a good friend as well as an ally. He was a dream-chaser demon and he had the ability to feed off both the dreams and life force of others.

"Can you call him? We're at the park and I'm trying to catch up to Menolly and the vroll."

"I already did. He's on the way. Smoky's bringing him through the Ionyc Sea. He's stopping here to pick me up first. We'll be there within a couple of minutes. Oh, by the way, apparently vrolls are attracted to sparkly things." She hung up.

I shoved my phone in my pocket—thank gods for skirts with pockets. Smoky—my dragon-shifter husband—could travel through the currents of energy that separated the Ionyc Lands and kept them from colliding. The non-corporeal dimensions—the etheric, astral, and spirit realms—all formed the Ionyc Lands, and to get to them, one had to either have the ability to shift over or to travel through the great sea of energy.

The dusk was fading. We had only a few moments before it was full-on night, and it would be harder than ever to see our goal. I shaded my eyes with my hands, trying to scan ahead to see where Menolly and the vroll were. The moon was rising, though nowhere near its zenith, but its light was enough to show me the silhouettes ahead. The park was only a few hundred yards beyond. Even from here, I could hear people shouting and laughing.

Fuck. We had to keep the creature out of their path until Vanzir got here. I sent a piercing whistle through the air. Menolly would recognize it. Sure enough, a few seconds and she appeared in a blur.

"What?"

I held up my phone. "Delilah called. Vanzir is on the way. He's the one who can stop the vroll—it's not really a spirit, but a faded troll. The only way to stop it is to drain its life force. The creature's running scared and there's no way to reason with it. He's looking for a new place to hide, but if he can't find it, in his panic he'll just cause mayhem and havoc all over the place. We have to keep his attention until Vanzir and Smoky get here."

"He didn't blink an eye when I tried to smack him one. I went through him like water through a funnel. Something appears to be drawing him to the crowd. He can't eat them, can he?" Menolly glanced around, then waved to our right. "If he's looking for a place to hide, maybe the tunnel?"

I glanced over. There was a rounded archway in the wall that supported the street above, leading through to another wooded area. "Good thinking. We need to draw his attention over there somehow. If we can get him behind the wall, then maybe he'll feel safer and calm down." Then I had an idea. "Get him to look over toward me." I took off for the wall.

Menolly nodded, veering off, shouting at the vroll. I raced over to the tunnel, which was pedestrian only, cursing as the gravel bit into my feet. But I ignored the pricks and jabs of the stones, instead focusing on the area in the center of the tunnel. I could create a bright sparkly ball of energy there, hopefully long enough for the vroll to notice it and come running.

Shouts and screams echoed behind me, and I whirled around, skidding to a stop beside the tunnel opening. Oh gods, the vroll had found the wedding, and with it, the silver balloons that were attached to every chair at the event. He was headed right toward the throng of invitees, just as the bride was walking down the aisle.

Chapter 2

"**WHERE** IS HE?" Smoky's voice rumbled out from behind me as he, Vanzir, and Delilah appeared, stepping out from the Ionyc Sea.

"Over there, about to cause havoc." I waved toward the reception.

Smoky and Vanzir immediately took off sprinting. Delilah hung back.

We watched them go. I licked my lips. Smoky was one hunk of a dragon, all right, and he was all *mine*. Six-four, with ankle-length silver hair that moved on its own, he was tall, lean, and muscled. He dressed in white jeans, a long white duster, and a pale blue turtleneck.

Vanzir, on the other hand, was five-eleven, with a short platinum shag reminiscent of the late, great David Bowie. His eyes were mesmerizing. A continual kaleidoscope, they were a color beyond our perception. Vanzir was punk-chic, gaunt and lanky, and he was wearing a pair of ripped jeans and a black leather jacket over a Metallica T-shirt. Both men were scary strong, and both of them made better allies than enemies.

"I hope this works," Delilah muttered.

"Whether it does or not, I think we're screwed. The guests have noticed the vroll." As much as I didn't want to, I motioned for her to follow me and we headed over to the wedding ceremony that was quickly turning into a screaming mob. People were swarming, trying to escape. Trouble was, whoever had set up the chairs placed the rows too close together and the guests were having trouble getting out. They were tripping over each other, falling, and in one case, one man was using his folding wooden chair to beat off another man.

"Crap. We need to take control—" I stopped as Menolly raced into the crowd, shouting for order. Unfortunately, a few of them recognized her and began screaming.

"Vampire! Vampire!"

"We're being attacked, run!"

"Oh my God, we're going to die!"

Menolly was trying to make herself heard, but the screaming drowned out her voice. Smoky veered off from Vanzir to help her take control. Meanwhile, Vanzir continued directly toward the vroll, who had stopped, obviously distressed by the chaos and shouting. I stared at him, feeling sorry for the creature. He couldn't help what he was. All he wanted was a quiet place to hide and finish fading away into the mists of time.

As Delilah and I reached the mayhem, Fry came running. She stopped a ways from the crowd and, holding her shotgun in the air, let go with a round.

Oh, that would go over with Chase *really* well.

"Order! I *will* have order!" Her voice thundered above the racket. For such a tiny woman, she had one hell of a bellow.

I headed over to help Vanzir. He had positioned himself between the vroll and the crowd. The creature was studying him, cringing with fear, but also, a faint hint of curiosity.

Vanzir glanced at me. "Still want me to drain him down?" The words were callous, but his tone was not.

I hung my head. Truth was, I didn't want anything of the sort. I was firmly in the camp of the vroll now. He had been woken up by idiots who couldn't leave well enough alone, who just *had* to dabble with forces they knew nothing about. Now, he was just trying to find a safe place to live out the rest of whatever life he had.

"Yeah," I whispered. "I guess we don't have any choice. I thought I could lure him over beyond that wall, but it would just be a matter of time till someone else found him and tried the same thing. I wish we could lure him out to Smoky's barrow, but I don't think there's any way we could."

"I think you're right. Don't blame yourself, babe. He just doesn't fit in this world anymore." And with that, Vanzir turned to the creature and held out his hands. Glowing neon-colored tubes emerged from his palms and sunk into the translucent figure of the vroll. The creature stiffened, then relaxed. "I'm making this as comfortable as I can. Trust me, there isn't much life energy left in this one. He'll fade out fast and without pain."

Grateful that Vanzir actually understood, I watched, feeling that somebody ought to stand vigil over the last moments of this creature's life. Trolls were big and stupid and dangerous, true. But this one had managed to live for a long, long time, into the modern world. And now, the vroll would vanish, a frightened shell of what he had once been.

Vanzir's head dropped back and his eyes closed as he drank in the flow of life force. The look on his face was almost beatific, he was so immersed in the communion as he drained the vroll dry. There was something different, though, from the times I had seen him drain our enemies. Instead of struggling, the vroll was curled on the ground, looking for all the world as though he had fallen asleep. He was calm, perhaps for the first time since the idiots had woken him up. Vanzir was singing him to sleep for the last time, in his own, twisted way.

I wasn't going to cry, I told myself. But the tears on my cheeks still trickled down and I finally just let them fall. We had seen so much death over the past few years, had experienced so much collateral damage, and I had managed to remain strong. I had been tortured and beaten by my father-in-law and I had managed to remain strong. I had watched friends die and managed to remain strong. And I had escaped as a city fell beneath the siege of a sentient storm and managed to remain strong. Yet here, in a park at a midnight wedding, a vroll's death threatened to sweep me under.

Before I realized he was by my side, Smoky wrapped an arm around my waist and leaned down to kiss my head.

"I wish it could be otherwise," he said in that silken voice of his. "But love, when someone cannot adapt to the tides of change, they are best off in the past, where they don't have to struggle or fear. Even if you had been able to save that creature, there would be no place he'd feel truly safe. The vroll is only a shell of what he was. He's the last remnants of fear left behind. This is a kindness. He'll go to whatever afterlife awaits a troll."

I knew he was right. I had said the same thing more than once, in similar situations.

"I don't know why this one hit me so hard. I think... he seemed so childlike. Yes, we were fighting him, but then when I understood what had happened..." I paused. Maybe that was what had hit me hardest. Not that we had to send the vroll to his death, but that someone else had given us no choice. "Whoever woke him up—they're the ones I'm angry at. They meddled where they shouldn't. They didn't think of the ramifications of what they did. They just waltzed in there, deciding *Oh, wow, let's contact this spirit,* without even thinking what might happen."

Smoky pressed his hand against my lower back, his fingers touching the skin beneath the laces of my corset. His fingers worked like fire, sparking me off.

"You know as well as I do that most people—humans, Fae, even dragons—don't usually stop to think out all scenarios. Nothing would ever get done if people were that hesitant. I think this goes deeper, my love. I think you're just anticipating the changes coming up in your life, and you're scared, and projecting that anxiety. Truly, this vroll...if he was still in full form, still a troll, you'd be fighting to kill him, wouldn't you?"

I frowned, not wanting to face the reality that he was steering me toward. "Well, yes."

"You wouldn't feel sorry for him, would you?"

Again, I kicked the ground in front of me. "No."

"Then face it, you're not sorry for the vroll. You're feeling melancholy because of your own life. Granted, it's a sad thing that his spirit couldn't rest easy, but if you let him be, he'd blunder around and destroy everyone and everything he came across because of his fear."

Smoky swept me up in his arms then, a gentle smirk on his face, his ice blue eyes twinkling with just a hint of amusement. "Face it, my Witchling. Because you're heading square center toward a destiny you never expected, you're feeling trapped and afraid. Hush," he added as I started to protest. "You and I both know this is the path you need to take. I didn't say otherwise. But you're still rebellious enough to wish you had the option to choose."

A thud in the pit of my stomach told me he was right.

Feeling almost ashamed—maybe I really didn't care much about the life of a troll, given how much carnage most of them managed to wreak—I rested my head against his chest.

"You're right. I know that moving out to Talamh Lonrach Oll, joining Titania and Aeval in the Barrows, taking the crown that belonged to Morgaine—this is what I *need* to do. But damn it, can't I at least have the option of saying, 'Yeah, sure, I will do this' instead of it all just being thrust on me? I want some say in my life, damn it!" I usually loved it when Smoky held me in his arms, but right now, it just irritated me. "Put me down, you big lug. I love you, but I don't need to be carried right now. I want to stand on my own two feet."

He laughed as he set me down. "You *always* stand on your own two feet, love. No matter who might be holding you at the moment, you're always there on your own terms. And regardless of the situation, regardless of whether I—or anybody else—is there to help, you'll always take the helm. As for the crown, you may have not been given a choice, but you've told me time and again that you are your father's daughter. A soldier's daughter. I know you well enough by now to know that you'll carry through with your duties, and you'll perform them better than anybody else could. Your sense of honor is one of your best qualities, my love."

I stared up at him, mulling over his words. I could continue griping, continue letting my nerves get the better of me, or I could suck it up, move on, and make the best of the situation. I could let myself enjoy it and kick fear to the door.

Vanzir let out a faint noise and I turned. The troll spirit was fading from view, and within the next moment, he was gone. I exhaled, feeling the fear that had been coiled in my heart vanish with my breath.

Menolly was still trying to calm people, but they

weren't listening. We were dealing with a conservative group, led by someone who hated our kind and actively worked against us. And he wasn't letting the opportunity go by.

Steven Trentallon, the new star reporter of the *Seattle Tattler*—a yellow rag if there ever was one—was taking pictures of Menolly. I laughed. If he expected those photos to do him any good, he'd be mighty surprised. Vampires couldn't be photographed, but apparently he had forgotten that little fact.

Delilah was talking to Brandon Rigal, who was flailing his arms around. She was trying to calm him down, but it obviously wasn't working. Fry joined her, but Rigal wasn't listening to her either.

"Come on," I said. "We'd better get over there and sort out what's going on. Rigal is the lawyer who defends the Freedom's Angels and the Guardian Watchdogs. He's not going to let this one pass and he'll find some way to turn it back onto us that his daughter's wedding day was ruined."

"We saved their lives," Smoky said, straightening his duster. He was spiffy clean—and he never got dirty. Dirt vanished off him faster than rats deserting a sinking ship.

"Be that as it may, Rigal's going to find some way to pin the blame on us." I headed across the grass. Smoky and Vanzir followed.

Delilah was fuming. "Listen to me. We saved your asses tonight. How can you be such an idiot?"

Uh-oh. When Delilah called someone an idiot to his face, I knew it was bad. She was the gentlest of the three of us, and she never went off half-cocked. Well... seldom.

"Your kind is the reason this happened in the first place. Nobody ever had a problem till you came through the portals and stirred up all this crap. The

Supes who were already here knew better than to make waves or show themselves. You brought everything to the surface. You made it acceptable for the demons of this world to step out into the light. It's past time someone did something about this. Time to send you home where you belong." Rigal's voice was filled with veiled threats. He wasn't shouting, he wasn't railing against the wind...just speaking with calm, cold precision.

I stared at him for a moment. He wasn't a tiger, ready to pounce. No, this man was more of a snake, coiling back, watching for just the right moment to strike. Brandon Rigal was dangerous and he was going to make waves. That much I could foresee.

"Delilah, don't bother." I stepped up beside her, and Smoky followed. Menolly had joined Vanzir, standing a few yards away. The cops were reassuring people and making sure nobody had been injured. I turned to the lawyer.

"We saved your life. We could have just let the creature rampage through your daughter's wedding. And for your information, as best as we can figure, the vroll woke up because of humans—probably teenagers, screwing around. So put your blame where it belongs and be grateful your daughter's alive and in one piece and can go on with her wedding. You could have easily found yourself at a funeral tonight."

And with that, I took Delilah's arm and turned away. The others followed us.

"You'll be getting the bill for the damage!" Rigal called from behind us.

"Good luck with that." Keeping my voice just low enough for the others to hear, I added, "He can kiss my ass."

Delilah let out a snort. "I bet he'd like to. Men like that usually hate what they can't have. But do you think he'll really sue us?"

"He can try but I doubt if he's got much of a leg to stand on. But don't underestimate him. He's a good lawyer. Doesn't matter, though. I doubt if the damage adds up to much and nobody was hurt, so they can't claim injury."

As we headed back to the patrol cars, I tried not to think about what the morning headlines would say. With Steve Trentallon there, chances were good there would be a full-scale hate piece in the *Tattler* the next day and that would spur on a new round of pickets at every store owned by a Supe. Luckily, the All Worlds United in Peace organization would be out to counter-protest. They were an offshoot of the United Worlds Church, and had grown to include a number of the local churches, temples, and mosques, as well as other pro-environment, pro-unification organizations.

Delilah must have been thinking along the same lines because she said, "I should contact Neely and ask her how things are going. We haven't had much chance to do anything but sort out the aftermath of Menolly's trip to the Sub-Realms."

"Yeah, I know." I glanced over at Menolly, who was walking silently beside Vanzir. Her trip into the Subterranean Realms to rescue her wife had left her shaken and a lot quieter than normal. I wasn't sure what had shifted, but ever since then she seemed more thoughtful and less prone to fly off the handle. Maybe it was the fact that we were finally one-up on Shadow Wing, the demon lord. Or maybe it was just the realization of how close she had come to losing what was most precious in her life, but there had been a subtle change in her nature.

I glanced up at Smoky as a tendril of his hair looped up and around my shoulder. A dragon's hair had a life of its own and the tendrils could maneuver around like an arm and hand.

"Yes, love?"

"Just happy to be with you," he said.

I leaned against him, resting my head against his shoulder. As we approached the patrol cars, Smoky said, "Vanzir and I will go back through the Ionyc Sea. You girls drive home together."

"All right. We'll see you there."

He wrapped his arms around me, lifting me off my feet to meet his lips, his hair billowing around him like a cloak caught by the breeze. "Don't be long," he murmured.

"I won't," I whispered, wanting him more than ever.

BY THE TIME we found my shoes and reached home, it was nearing midnight. As we pulled into the driveway, I saw the lights were still on. That was nothing new, given how many people lived in the old three-story Victorian. Weathered and from another era, still the house stood strong. Thanks to the men, it was in good condition—freshly painted, and any damage was always immediately repaired. We had bought the mansion when we first came over Earthside, with money that our mother had put aside for us when we were young. It had grown over the years. She had opened bank accounts for us, gotten Social Security numbers for us long before Earthside knew about Otherworld, all on the chance that we would one day want to visit her homeworld.

The house sat on five acres originally, but thanks to Smoky's purse and his good will, we now owned almost ten more—four acres of wetlands, five acres of usable land, and Birchwater Pond. Otherworld had once been my home, and still was to some extent, but this house signified *home* to me. And within a couple weeks, I was going to have to leave it. I caught my breath, worrying my lip. I wasn't the only one facing a move.

Menolly and Nerissa would be going to live with Roman in his mansion. Delilah would stay here with Shade and Rozurial—one of our companions and a member of our extended family. And she would keep Maggie with her.

The thought of leaving Maggie was harder than anything else. I had found the baby calico gargoyle a few years back. She had been destined to be a harpy's lunch, but I had managed to save her and she was like the little sister we all doted on. A woodland gargoyle, she would grow slowly. She wouldn't even be out of the toddler stage for another fifty or sixty years. We all agreed that the Barrows weren't the ideal place for her, and neither was a vampire's lair, so that left Delilah to take over as her mother.

As we headed to the house my mood slipped deeper into a mire. Trying to shake it off, I paused for a moment by my herb garden, which was to the left in the front yard. I knelt, running my fingers over the spearmint, crushing a leaf under my nose to release the vibrant, sharp scent. Mint was soothing. It refreshed the mind, and I had been cultivating a particularly concentrated strain. My tears backtracked as the fragrance cleared my sinuses and washed over me with a calming effect.

"Coming?" Delilah called.

"I'll be right there." I broke off a couple of stems of the mint for some fresh tea and headed up the stairs.

As we entered the house, I could tell something was up. This wasn't a typical Thursday night. For one thing, Iris and Bruce were both at the table. Everybody else was awake and gathered in the kitchen, as well. Nerissa and Roz were poring over a sheath of papers, and

Hanna—our housekeeper—was holding Maggie, who was sucking her thumb. Chase had arrived before we had, and he was frowning as he leaned over Nerissa's shoulder, reading the page she was holding. Trillian and Morio were spreading out maps on the kitchen table.

"What's up?" I shrugged out of my jacket and hung it and my purse on one of the hooks next to the hall closet in the foyer.

"Trenyth called from the Whispering Mirror," Nerissa said, looking up as we entered the kitchen. "I took the call."

The Whispering Mirror had been a gift from the OIA when we first came Earthside, which we had modified to our own use. It was a device that allowed us to communicate with Otherworld. It was set to connect with Elqaneve—the Elfin city. We had worked with the Elfin techno-mages to modify the mirror so that we could connect with the bureau back home in OW. Voice activated, the mirror's settings were modulated so that only those with permission could take or send calls. At this point, everybody who lived on our land had that capability.

I leaned over Morio's shoulder. "Maps?"

"Yeah, maps." Morio looked up to give me a quick kiss on the cheek, then went back to poring over an area that looked to be up north a ways from Seattle.

Trillian wrapped his arm around my waist and kissed me on the forehead. "Brace yourselves for big news. Have a seat."

Hanna brought over several pots of rustlewood tea—a specialty from Otherworld—and a plate of chocolate chip cookies. "You'll be wanting this."

"What's going on?" I lowered myself into one of the chairs, and Delilah followed suit. Menolly joined us after getting a bottle of blood from the fridge, which she warmed in the microwave. It smelled like hot chocolate, and tasted like it, thanks to Morio, who had figured out how to charm the bottled animal blood into other flavors for her.

We gathered at the massive oak table that could seat twelve comfortably, fifteen if we scooched in, and every meal that we could. We also used it for war meetings.

Rozurial leaned back, a grave look on his face. "Trenyth knows where the last spirit seal is. He sent us the specifics on it."

Instantly, we all stopped talking and stared at the maps.

"So it's finally happened," Delilah said softly, breaking the silence.

We had been searching for the spirit seals for almost four years and had gone through so much pain and loss to find them. After all this time, after so many deaths, could we really be facing the final chapter?

EONS AGO, BEFORE the worlds were separated, a demon lord had risen up, intent on subjugating both humankind and the Fae. The ancient Fae Lords had fought among themselves about what to do. Some wanted to confront the demon lord directly. But others rebelled. They wanted to separate the worlds into three distinct but parallel worlds—Otherworld, Earthside, and the Subterranean Realms. A massive battle ensued and the separatists won. Using all of their magic combined, they had driven through the worlds, ripping them apart like some great juggernaut. That time became known as the Great Divide. The massive disruption had sparked off volcanoes and earthquakes, global floods and land shifts.

After the worlds were separated, the separatists created the Spirit Seal, an artifact so powerful that it was able to prevent the worlds from intersecting except for the vortexes that formed here and there—known as portals. Yet, the seal also provided the key to reuniting the worlds.

To keep the division from breaking down, the Fae Lords split the Spirit Seal into nine pieces and sent them out to the nine Greater Elemental Lords and Ladies. But even the Immortals lose track of things, and over time the spirit seals—each containing a different gem—had found their way into the world of mortals. Anyone who could reunite all nine could either unite the three worlds again—which would cause as much destruction as the Great Divide had. *Or*...they could watch over them and keep the spirit seals and the portals safe.

But the division of worlds wasn't natural. Rogue portals began to form, tearing at the threads keeping the worlds apart. Another great demon lord rose. Shadow Wing the Unraveller began sending envoys to gather the seals, intent on opening the portals to flood both Otherworld and Earthside with his armies of demons. And that's where we came in.

After a long four years, we had managed to retrieve eight of the spirit seals. Once we had the ninth, we hoped to forestall his war forever, because I was destined to be in charge of bringing together the Keraastar Knights, the guardians of the portals. But it was still a long road until then, and there was much to be done.

MY BREATH CAUGHT in my throat. "The last seal. It's been almost four years since the demonic war dropped in our laps. Where is it?"

Roz motioned to Morio, who pointed to a place on the map. "It's on Camano Island. Or should I say, in the waters surrounding Camano Island. One of the Elder Fae has it. K'thbar the Unyielding. He's sleeping in Puget Sound."

"Oh joy, the Elder Fae." Delilah's grimace spoke for us all.

The Elder Fae weren't like us. They were unique for the most part, each possessing different powers. Most of them were scary-assed and strong. We had managed to make a truce with a few like Ivana, the Maiden of Karask, but we'd been on the bad side of more than one. The Elder Fae seldom saw reason to cooperate with anybody. They were wild and feral, primal powers of the world wrapped up into freakshow bundles of not so happy-happy joy-joy.

"How do we get there? Is there a way into the lair that *isn't* beneath the water?"

Trillian frowned, tracing his finger along the coastline. "No, there doesn't appear to be. We asked Trenyth what K'thbar is like. Turns out, not so much goodness in his soul. The world is much better off when he's asleep."

"Is he a fish? I remember Yannie Fin Diver all too well, and that's one Elder Fae I don't ever want to meet again." I shuddered.

We had thought Yannie Fin Diver was one of the Meré, but when he leaped on land his tail had become legs and he had come after Delilah and me, intent on a midday snack.

"I do have the unicorn horn, if we need it. It's fully charged. I haven't used it in a while."

"That horn could knock down a wall," Delilah said. "But be careful if you use it. There are a lot of people—Elder Fae included—who wouldn't mind having it."

I laughed. "We need to create a spreadsheet to keep

track of our enemies."

"No kidding. I'll get on that right away." Delilah grinned at me, and the tension in the room began to diffuse.

When we were all breathing easier, I glanced at the maps. "Okay then, let's get this show on the road. Tell us what Trenyth had to say." The elder advisor to the Elfin throne was doing his best to help us. He had been in love with Queen Asteria and when she died, he took it hard. But he was doing his best to help Sharah and we loved him all the more for it.

"First, he said that K'thbar is powerful and big."

"Of course he is," Menolly said, rolling his eyes. "When aren't they big and powerful?"

"Right," Nerissa said. "Also, he's water-bound. He never comes onto land. So we have to meet him in his element."

"Handy, given none of us breathe water," I snarked.

"I can go." Menolly raised her hand. "Remember, I don't breathe at all."

"Yeah, but you can't go down there alone and even as strong as you are, you can't take on one of the Elder Fae by yourself," Nerissa said.

"I know who we can ask for help. Shimmer. I'm sure she wouldn't mind." Smoky spoke slowly.

I snapped my fingers. "Of course! She could be a tremendous help." I turned to Menolly. "Can you call Alex and ask him to have her contact us?"

"On my list." Menolly grinned. "I'm sure she'll be thrilled to go up against one of the Elder Fae, but hey, what are friends for?"

Shimmer was a blue dragon shifter. A water dragon, she had been sent Earthside as a punishment for some minor crime. She was soil-bound, meaning she couldn't return to the Dragon Reaches without permission, but she was okay by us. We had helped her employer,

Alex—a vampire who owned the Fly by Night Investigation Agency—rescue her when she had been charmed by one of his enemies.

"Okay, so the creature is water-bound. Does Trenyth know if he's actively *using* the spirit seal?" That would make a big difference. If K'thbar was using the spirit seal, then his powers would be magnified and we'd be in real trouble.

Trillian shrugged. "Dunno. Trenyth didn't say. He also doesn't know whether Shadow Wing is onto the location."

Vanzir spoke up. "Trytian and his father have been keeping Shadow Wing and his armies occupied in roust after roust. I'll give it to the daemons. They're tough, and they're hitting the demons where it hurts."

Trytian and his father were daemons, who were just as nasty but less chaotic than demons. They were on the offensive, attempting to dethrone the Demon Lord.

"I'm betting that Shadow Wing hasn't yet recovered from losing Telazhar, who was probably the one locating the spirit seals for him," Vanzir continued. "The current military operations should be eating up his time and focus. It's doubtful that he's had time to groom someone to take Telazhar's post."

We had managed to wound the Demon Lord on several fronts. We had taken out his best general, Telazhar. We had wiped out a number of the other sorcerers who were intent on breaking open the portals. The elves had paid dearly for it, but then the dragons had come to our aid and they were still keeping a close eye on things over in Otherworld. And we had managed to recover all the spirit seals that Shadow Wing had accumulated.

"We'll probably be facing something like a giant octopus." I frowned.

We were brainstorming ideas when the doorbell rang. I excused myself to answer it. As I opened the door, a wave of light hit me—dark sparkling energy floating in on a wave. I backed into the living room, knowing exactly who had arrived.

One by one, they took their places near the fireplace. First to enter was Derisa, the High Priestess of the Moon Mother from over in Otherworld. And then Titania, the Queen of Light and Morning. Next came Aeval, the Queen of Shadow and Night. And finally, Myrddin, the Merlin and High Priest of the Moon Mother, joined them.

"Well met, Camille." Aeval's greeting gave her away. This was a formal visit.

I curtseyed as the others filed in from the kitchen. Aeval smiled, her frost-laden eyes flashing like prisms in the ice. She was a tall and terrible beauty, with hair as black as mine, and her dress sparkled with beads, the deep indigo of the night sky.

"Do you know why we're here?"

I shook my head. "No, Your Majesty, I don't." I usually called Aeval and Titania by their first names, but tonight, it didn't feel right. With Titania, Myrddin, and Derisa in tow, I knew something big was up. "To what do we owe the honor of your visit?"

"Trenyth contacted me," Derisa said. "He told me the last spirit seal has been located and you will soon be searching for it."

I nodded. "We just found out."

Aeval straightened her shoulders. "The moment you have the spirit seal in hand, you must journey to the Tygerian Mountains and seek out the Keraastar Diamond. The time has come for you to gather the Keraastar Knights."

Chapter 3

MY HEART SANK. I knew this was coming, but I hadn't expected it so suddenly. But then again, my ascent to the throne was less than two weeks away. I couldn't show fear, and I couldn't show my dismay, so I parked my expression in neutral.

"As you will, Lady." I curtseyed again.

The formalities over with, everyone relaxed. Well, as much as you *can* relax in a room containing two Fae queens, a High Priest from antiquity, and a High Priestess of the Moon Mother.

Vanzir shyly approached Aeval. Vanzir wasn't usually shy around anybody, but the sudden blush on the demon's cheeks was both unexpected and cute. Aeval held out her hands and pulled him to her for a gentle kiss before she sat down in the rocking chair. Her pregnancy was starting to really show. He really was going to make a strange babydaddy.

The others spread themselves around the room. Merlin leaned against the mantel over the fireplace. Titania greeted Iris with a brilliant smile that told me somehow the two had managed to become a little chummy. And Derisa watched me carefully as she accepted a side chair from Trillian.

"I take it this journey's not going to be a walk down the yellow brick road?" I knew better than to expect a clearly defined route with happy Munchkins along the way, but I was hoping that for once in my life, I wouldn't constantly be in danger.

Of course, Fae nobility loved crashing hopes to the ground.

Aeval snorted. "I'm aware of that reference. First, there's not going to be any Glinda to guide you. And second, you aren't going to be linking arms with a scarecrow and a tin man, either. I also recommend you leave your pets at home." She paused, catching my gaze. I started to sweat. There was real concern in her eyes. "The problem is, we don't know the route. We only know that it's somewhere in the Tygerian mountains."

"Of course, because we need the Maharata scrolls to find out exactly where the diamond is." I frowned. The more we talked, the less fun this sounded.

"Right," the Merlin said. He held up a talisman that flashed brilliant blue. "Get ready, you're about to have more company."

"Great," Menolly said.

A moment later, the air began to shimmer. Smoky and Shade suddenly came to attention. I froze as two more figures appeared in our living room. One was a woman who stood almost seven feet tall. Her hair was the color of silver moonlight and her skin, so pale she made snow look grungy. Smoky's mother. And with her was an old friend we hadn't seen for some time. *Venus the Moon Child.*

Our home's becoming Grand Central Station, I thought. But I stood and graciously welcomed them to our house.

"Vishana, welcome to our home." I curtseyed to my mother-in-law, grateful we were on good terms. Having an MIL who was a dragon powerful enough to kill everyone in the room was enough to cow anybody. "And Venus...you wily old shaman." My smile broadened as he stepped forward to give me a warm hug.

"Camille," he whispered, his hands tight around me. Then he stood back, regarding me carefully. "So much water under the bridge, right?"

"So much water and not enough lifeboats," I said softly.

"Too true. And for so many, not enough time to reach them, even if there were." He bopped me on the nose, then turned to greet Delilah as Smoky sprang forward to Vishana's side.

"Mother! We didn't expect you." He knelt before her before rising and kissing her cheek with a light peck. She returned the almost-air kiss, but her eyes sparkled as she stared at her son.

"Derisa contacted us when Trenyth told her that he had located the whereabouts of the final spirit seal." She motioned to Venus. "It's time for Venus to rejoin you. He's the only one who knows the location of the Maharata-Vashi, the matching scroll to the Maharata-Verdi."

Menolly and Rozurial had hidden away the Maharata-Verdi in a location only they knew about. To find the Keraastar Diamond, I would need both scrolls. The Maharata-Verdi and its twin worked in conjunction, though I wasn't entirely sure how. And Venus knew the location to the latter one. Queen Asteria had entrusted him with it.

Venus turned. A fire opal, glistening and alive, hung on a platinum chain around his neck. The spirit seal glimmered in the dim light, swirling like flames caught within a glass bell. He caught me staring at it and inclined his head, a grim smile replacing the easygoing welcome. I would be his queen soon, and he would be one of my Knights to defend the portals. His life and his death would be in my hands.

I withdrew to the side as he chatted with Delilah. Venus was originally from the Rainier Puma Pride. That's how the two had met. Meanwhile, Smoky and his mother were talking with the Fae Queens. Trillian and Morio were talking to Myrddin, and Derisa was keeping her own company in the corner. Feeling overwhelmed, all I wanted to do was go up to my room and sit on the balcony, and stare at the moon.

"Too much change, too fast?" Iris crossed the room to me, looking concerned. The talon-haltija was a Finnish house sprite, but she was also a powerful priestess in her own right. And right now, I knew she was stressed out because she had twins at home, and a husband who was thousands of miles away in Ireland and the last thing she needed was to be included in our problems, too.

"Yeah. I feel like I can't breathe." I let her take my hand and lead me into the parlor where I sat on the sofa. She closed the door partway to keep out the noise and then joined me.

"I sometimes feel like that. I always wanted to be a mother. It's important in my culture, but with Bruce away and with me taking care of Chase's daughter too, it's more than a full-time job." She leaned back, resting her head on the sofa. "I'm grateful that the Duchess is here, but I always feel like I'm on display with her. She tries to be nice, but she's so used to giving orders that I never know where I stand with her. Don't let the stories fool you. Leprechauns are nothing to fool around with."

"I bet," I muttered. "Neither are dragons. Think about it—I have two mothers-in-law I've never even met. One hates my guts, and the other isn't far behind. I dread the day either decides to visit. I'm hoping that taking the crown of Queen of Dusk and Twilight will throw a bit of a scare into them." I laughed, thinking even that probably wouldn't be enough to appease Trillian's family. *Ever*. Svartans had a class structure and I didn't figure into it in any way. He had given up his family ties for me, something I hadn't fully realized until recently.

I leaned forward, elbows on knees, resting my chin on my hands. "When did things get so complicated? Four years ago, we were sorting our way out, just getting used to living over here."

"Life happens, doesn't it? That's the problem with getting comfortable. Something is bound to come along and shake you out of your complacency. Tell me something," she said, sitting down and resting one hand on my arm. "Would you give it all up? Would you give up Trillian and Smoky and Morio to have things go back to the way they were before all of this happened?"

I frowned. "Leave it to you to find the silver lining." Still frustrated, I stood and crossed to the window, staring out into the night. "Oh, Iris, of course I wouldn't give them up. And, to be honest, I'm...I don't know if *excited* is the word, but I feel like I'm walking on eggs. I never dreamed that all of this would happen. But it's going to hurt. Leaving this house, leaving Delilah and Menolly, leaving Maggie behind. I won't lie, it's not going to be easy." I stared out into the darkness, feeling tears creep down my cheeks. "Especially leaving Maggie. I'm going to miss that little gargoyle."

Iris joined me. Her hand crept into mine. "I know. When Bruce and I moved out back to our new house and when I had the twins, I had to let go of being part of your family here—at least on such an intimate level. I had to watch Hanna do the work I used to. It wasn't easy. But I have my own family and it's already expanded to include Chase and Astrid. I may complain, but I'm happy, Camille. And you will be, too. You'll still see Maggie, probably more than you anticipate. And you'll still see your sisters."

Dashing away the tears, I straightened my shoulders. "You're right. I know you're right. I just... I'm mourning the past and I'm not sure about what the future's bringing, so the loss seems more vivid and real right now."

"Excuse me." Menolly peeked around the door.

I turned, dashing away my tears.

"I don't mean to interrupt, but Vishana has to leave and wants to say good-bye." She noticed my tear-stained cheeks. "Don't tell me you're getting all maudlin."

I sniffed. "No more than you'll be when you have to pack up and move over to Roman's. Face it, we're short-timers here."

"Don't remind me. Now come on, get out here and for the sake of the gods, smile. You don't want Vishana to think you're unhappy or she's likely to try to help and that could mean a lot of trouble if she makes a move against Aeval."

She had a point. Truth was, the dragons weren't really afraid of anybody or anything. At least not when they were in force. And since I was married to a dragon, and I had the backing of Smoky's people, they might take it into their heads to "rescue" me from moving out to Talamh Lonrach Oll by sweeping me off to the Dragon Reaches to live. With that thought, I wiped my face and plastered on a smile.

"On my way."

Iris giggled. "Yeah, when the dragons say jump, we all jump." She patted my arm. "Everything will be okay, Camille. You've faced far worse fates than being queen over a Barrow full of Fae."

"Now you're just being snarky," I said, laughing as we followed Menolly back into the living room.

"It's what I do best, dear. It's what I do best." And with that, the milkmaid-pretty sprite, whose golden hair cascaded down to her feet, swung around me and headed to the kitchen.

VISHANA WAS STANDING near the fireplace, gazing at the flames. Smoky gave me a quizzical look but I shook my head and hurried over to his mother's side.

"I'm sorry I've been lax as a hostess tonight. We just arrived home from taking care of a rogue vroll whose appearance interrupted our dinner. I was feeling a little—" I stopped, suddenly uncertain where to go with the sentence. I wasn't tired and I couldn't say hungry because if that was the reason for my disappearance, I would have gone into the kitchen rather than the parlor. I usually didn't feel at a loss for words, but tonight just felt off all the way around.

Vishana took pity on me. She held her hand up. "No need to apologize. We came unannounced into your house and disrupted your evening. Venus will be staying with Queen Aeval until you have need of him—she can protect him out at the Sovereign Fae Nation. But, Camille, beware." She somberly held my gaze. "The moment you find the last spirit seal, the danger will be increased multifold. And not just from the direction of the Sub-Realms."

I frowned, unsure of what she meant. "If you mean there are demons over here—"

"Not demons," Vishana said. "Aeval, you should break the news."

I realized that they had all had a chat together before

they arrived. I didn't particularly like being out of loop, but somehow, being in on it didn't seem that appealing either.

Aeval stepped forward. "We didn't want to mention this ahead of time, because you've been dealing with so much from Shadow Wing's corner. But there are others who will not be happy to see you find the Keraastar Diamond and take possession of the Knights."

"Who?" My shoulders stiffened. Just what we needed. Another enemy.

She cleared her throat and, with a glance at the Merlin, who nodded, continued. "When the Spirit Seal was originally formed and then broken, the Maharata scrolls were written almost as a backup plan, although so much of history from then is lost. But the Great Fae Lords never intended anyone outside of their circle to be the ones to control the Knights."

"So...it would never have been either of you, even if I hadn't come along?"

"No, Titania and I were their enemies. They would have died rather than let us touch the diamond. We were prisoners by the time they made it. But we were the lucky ones. They killed the other Fae queens and great lords who fought against them. No, as far as we know, they created the Keraastar Diamond as a backup plan—the plug to pull on the doomsday device, you might say. But, like the seals, the scrolls were lost in time. And they have been forgotten until recently. You remember when Yvarr woke last winter?"

At the mention of that name, we all paused.

I slowly inclined my head. "Yes, I remember."

Six months before, we had fought a wyrm—a forerunner of the dragons. The wyrms of the earth were not shifters, but ancient beasts who were cunning and rapacious, grasping for power and wealth. The Great Fae Lords had enlisted them into the war against the Fae who wanted to keep the worlds together. When they won, they then imprisoned the wyrms, locking them away in other realms in case they might one day again need their services. Yvarr had woken and managed to free himself. And he bore the news that the Great Fae Lords themselves were waking from their own self-imposed hibernation.

"He said the Fae Lords who drove the Great Divide were waking."

"Yes, and so they are. And when they rise from their slumber, they're going to want their power back and they won't be happy to see how things have evolved, either in Otherworld or over here Earthside. They'll see you wielding the Keraastar Diamond and the Keraastar Knights...and they may decide to wage war against you to get the diamond back." At this, Aeval let out a long breath. "We will, of course, back you up if it comes to that. But you see, don't you? You *must* find the diamond and take control of it and the sooner the better. You're destined to wield it."

"And if they are waking, and they go after the diamond, they'll destroy Talamh Lonrach Oll because of you and Titania." The wheels were turning now and I was beginning to get the picture. "And if they free the wyrms still locked away..."

"They could devastate the world in their greed. They are no better than Shadow Wing, when you think about it. Neither will the wyrms be happy, if they're freed. While we dragons had already split off from their race and were creating our own society back then, the wyrms caused problems for us," Vishana said. "I remember several horrendous battles. Many of our kind were lost as we fought for our own existence. If the wyrms wake up, they'll come after us."

I suddenly felt weak in the knees and slowly lowered myself to a chair. If I found the Keraastar Diamond, as was prophesized, I'd be putting myself and all around me in danger. If I let it go, and the Great Fae Lords rose to wield it, then they'd put *everyone* in danger. Either way, it was looking like a very different but very dangerous battle might be looming in my future.

"Damned if I do and damned if I don't." I stood, turning to Vishana. "Will the Dragonkin back Talamh Lonrach Oll, if it comes push to shove against the Fae Lords and the wyrms?"

She considered my question for a moment. "If it were my decision alone, I'd say yes without hesitation. But it isn't a promise I can make. I must go to Council and persuade them. I don't anticipate much opposition, however. The battles with the wyrms may be in the past, but many of us lived through it and we fought against them, and our memories are long." Turning to Smoky, she added, "My son, I will go now and speak to the Council. You must come with me."

"But Camille—" Smoky started to say, then stopped as she held up her hand.

"Have you not yet told her?"

"Told me what?" I crossed to Vishana's side. "What should he have told me?"

"My son—your husband—is to take his place on the Council of Elders for the first time tomorrow. He should come with me now to prepare." She gave Smoky a questioning glance, then let out her breath and a puff of smoke at the same time. "Iampaatar, you mean to tell me you kept this knowledge from your wife?"

He shuffled, staring at the floor. I would have laughed if the circumstances had been less dire.

"I was going to—"

"Are you ashamed of your position and rank?" Now Vishana's attention was solely on her son, and she didn't look happy.

"No, Mother."

"Then perhaps you will tell me why? Or perhaps, you feel so lackadaisical about the Council that you cast off the privilege of being part of our future so lightly?" She was starting to rev up. I recognized all the signs in any mother who was irate with her child.

"No, not at all. I just… We were busy with other things." Smoky scowled. Being berated in front of everyone else—especially me—wasn't going to sit well. But if I butted in to take his side it would make things worse. Instead, I backed away and turned to Aeval, who was attempting to keep a straight face. Both she and Titania had that gleam in their eye that told me they were enjoying the spectacle.

"You'll take Venus home with you?" I said softly.

She nodded. "Yes, we'll go soon. But Camille, know that Titania, the Merlin, and I will do everything we can to keep you safe. Do you see why, once you find the Keraastar Diamond, you'll be safest out at Talamh Lonrach Oll? We haven't been training a military for fun out there. There's a reason Bran is in charge of it—he's crafty and cunning and powerful."

"Yes," Titania said. "We knew that when the day came that you would join us, we would need to beef up protection. The Great Fae Lords are the worst danger, aside from Shadow Wing, but they aren't the only ones who will look askance at your joining us. Some of the Earthside Fae will view your human side as a weakness."

"Didn't they feel the same way about Morgaine?"

"Yes, but she was from the old world. She walked the same forests as the Merlin. They had a respect for her that they haven't learned to afford you, yet. It will come, in time, but you'll have to earn it." She reached out to clasp me on the shoulder. "I know this all seems so daunting, but it will pass. We will manage it, and you will take your rightful place."

I considered her words for a moment, then asked, "Who was it that decided I would become part of your Court? The Moon Mother?"

With a laugh, Titania leaned closer. "The Hags of Fate, my dear. And they wield far more power than the gods themselves. Come, Aeval, we should return to the Barrows and take Venus with us."

Vishana, apparently done with chiding Smoky, motioned for me to return to her side. She leaned down and placed a faint kiss on my cheek, almost an air kiss but not quite. "Be safe. Your husband will be home in three days. I'm certain he'll bring welcome news."

Smoky, still smoldering from the scolding, kissed me, only his kiss was on the lips, and he lifted me off my feet, holding me tight. "I was going to tell you later today, honest. But now you know, and so I'll be off with Mother." He gestured to Trillian and Morio. "Keep our wife safe until I return."

"Of course, you big lizard," Trillian said with a laugh.

Smoky held out his hand and a flurry of snow blasted in Trillian's direction, catching a good share of the living room with it.

"The *lizard* bids you remember who can cause a storm with one finger," Smoky said, then laughed as he vanished along with Vishana.

"All right, we're heading out as well," the Merlin said. "I didn't come back from Ireland just to watch a spat between paramours." But his eyes were twinkling. "Come, Venus, take Aeval's hand and I'll go with Titania."

Before we could say a word, Aeval, Titania, the Merlin, and Venus were out the door and vanished the moment they touched the ground below the porch steps. I wondered how they did that. They didn't travel via the Ionyc Sea the same way Smoky and some of the others did, but I wasn't sure just what form of magic they were using.

As I turned to go inside, a noise from a nearby bush caught my attention and I quietly descended the porch steps and headed over to it, followed by Trillian and Delilah. The bushes were waving—it was a huckleberry bush—and whatever was under there was making a snuffling noise. Delilah motioned for us to wait and crouched down, cautiously pushing aside the lower branches of the bush. She caught her breath, letting out a little "O" of surprise, then reached in and pulled out not one, but two kittens. Tiny—they couldn't have been more than five weeks old—both were soaking wet and muddy, and they were mewing up a storm, but their cries were so soft I could barely hear them. One was a calico, the other was white, and they had long matted hair. They squirmed in her hands as she stood up and handed them to me.

"Let me see if there are any more. Feral litter, I'll bet you." She returned to her crouch and then disappeared, crawling under the bush.

I held the kittens close to me, whispering to them. "Little ones, shush, puss puss. You're safe. Everything's okay. I won't hurt you."

The calico snuggled under my chin, her wet fur smearing me with mud. The white one set eyes on Trillian and scrabbled to get free. I glanced at Trillian, who shrugged and held out his hands. The white kitten frantically struggled to get closer and so my strong, stalwart Svartan stood there cuddling the kitten to his chest.

Delilah came back up with two more—another calico who could have been a twin for the one I was holding, and a black kitty. With a warning glance, she nodded us away from the bushes. "I found their mother in there too. It's not pretty. Looks like a raccoon did her in, but somehow, the kittens are safe."

"They'll die if we leave them out here." I glanced over

at my sister. She had trouble having other cats in the household. It was a territorial thing, given her werecat status, but she tolerated my spirit cat that she had given me for a present just fine. "We can't put them back. I'll take them with me to Talamh Lonrach Oll, if you can handle their presence till then."

Delilah stared at the fluffballs in her arms. "They're fine. They're kittens, and I can control myself around them for a while. I haven't been as antsy about my territory for a while now." And with that, we headed back inside.

Of course, talk of the spirit seal was halted for the time it took everybody to coo over the kittens and for Iris and Hanna to confiscate them and wash them up.

"We'll make sure they're fed and safe in your suite with a clean litter box. We can't let them go traipsing around the house free in case Maggie finds them. She's not safe for small animals or babies to be around."

Maggie was a sweetheart, but gargoyles were carnivores and small animals were natural prey. She also was rough on her toys and might consider the kittens just that. The thought made me queasy.

"Yes, please. See that they're locked in my study with a baby gate or something they can't climb. That way they won't dart out when I open the door." I gave the calicoes both a smooch on the nose, loath to hand them over before Iris swept them off to the kitchen, followed by Hanna, who was clucking over the black and white ones.

"We should get back to the maps and our discussion," I said, suddenly tired. First the vroll, then the meeting with Aeval and the others had left me feeling highly emotional. "Knowing what we do about the Great Fae Lords makes it imperative that we find the final spirit seal as soon as possible. If they wake before I can control the diamond, and they wake the wyrms, everybody's going to be in trouble."

"Does anybody have any more information about K'thbar? What he's like? We need to know if there's a chance he'll wake up when we go after the spirit seal. Where's he hiding it, and how are we going to spend time under water without drowning?"

Delilah made a sudden mewing noise and I glanced over at her. She looked petrified. She was terrified of water, couldn't swim, and only took showers, never baths. Like most cats, she resisted getting wet and it transferred to her human side, as well. I made an executive decision right there.

"Tell us now if you think this one's beyond you. I know all about fear and what it can do. If you don't think you can go with us, then please say so now. We can't take a chance on you freaking out in the water, especially if there's a chance that K'thbar might wake up." I held her gaze, hoping that she wouldn't try to play the hero if she couldn't face the water.

Shifting in her chair, Delilah finally let out a long sigh. "I hate to admit it, but you're right. Any backup I can give you from the shore, I'm there. But I'm afraid if I tried to go under the water, I'd have a panic attack and then you'd have a very frightened tabby cat—or panther, more likely—on your hands and I'd probably drown. I'll go, but I'll keep my feet on land." She sounded so apologetic that I wanted to snuggle her.

"We work to our strengths," I said, smiling at her. "It's okay, Delilah. I don't do well with heights."

"Yeah, but you've fought on top of the Space Needle before. You've climbed up mountains before—and down them."

"Stop beating yourself up. I fought on top of the Space Needle because there was a railing there to keep everybody from tumbling over the side. And Chase went through hell getting me up there. As for climbing up and down mountains, well, I follow the rule of don't look down. When Hanna helped me escape from Hyto's lair, the fear of what he had done—and what he was *going* to do—outweighed my fear of going down the mountain. Torture's a good impetus to suck it up."

I tried to smile but my stomach lurched. I still suffered flashbacks and though I tried to keep them at bay, there were times when the PTSD would hit me full force. Not long ago, I had woken from a nightmare about Hyto and the only way I was able to stop the memories from sucking me down a deep, dark well was to hide in my closet. Morio had found me in the morning, and he carried me back to bed, never saying a word. We hadn't told Smoky. He was still blaming himself for what had happened.

"I'll talk to Shimmer tonight." Menolly stood. "Whatever you decide to do, I'm in as long as it's at night."

I shook my head. "Has to be during the day. Tomorrow night's the full moon, remember?"

"Damn it. Right. Well, I can't do anything about that." She grabbed her jacket and waved as she exited the kitchen.

I considered everybody's strengths. We really hadn't had much time in the water, considering all the battles we had waged. "I can swim, but I can't breathe underwater. I'll need magical help for that."

Vanzir raised his hand. "I can swim pretty damned good. I do need to breathe, but I can hold my breath for five minutes without a strain."

"Smoky's not here, or he'd be good to go with us. I can go, and in my dragon form, I don't need to breathe since I'm skeletal." Shade winked at Delilah. "So I'll go for both of us."

Trillian wasn't much of a swimmer, unfortunately. Iris was, but she couldn't risk it, given the twins. But Rozurial raised his hand.

"I'm in, too. I can swim. But I need to breathe, as well. I'll need whatever sort of magical scroll or spell you can scrape up." He paused, then hesitantly asked, "You aren't going to try to cast it yourself, are you?"

"I'd resent that, if I had a leg to stand on." I stuck my tongue out at him. "No, don't worry. I'm not that stupid. Morio, you coming with us?"

"Yeah, but like everybody else, I need magical help."

Delilah shrugged. "Tell you what, I'll research who can help us since I'm not going to be any good under the water. Meanwhile, Trillian, why don't you take on K'thbar—see what references you can find about him." She paused as my phone rang.

I glanced at the Caller ID. It was Menolly. "Hello? Anything wrong?"

"No, I'm at the Fly by Night Agency, and I just talked to Shimmer."

I didn't ask how she'd gotten there so quickly. Ever since my sister had been re-sired by Roman, the prince of the Vampire Nation, her abilities as a vampire had greatly increased. Her ability to take the form of a bat had gone from graceless to graceful—she could do more than hover a few feet off the ground and then flop around helplessly. And her speed had increased. Vampires could blur their speed to levels that put everybody else to shame. Menolly's skills had picked up significantly, even over the past few weeks.

"What did she say?"

"She's happy to help. She said just let her know when."

I decided the sooner the better. "Tell her tomorrow at noon, if she could meet us here. We'll have to find some way for us all to breathe underwater—except for her and Shade—but there has to be some witch around who can work a spell for us."

"I'll tell her. I'm going down to the Wayfarer for a

little while. I'm feeling the need to touch base with Digger and Derrick." A tinge of sadness echoed in her voice and I realized that I wasn't the only one pining for the way things had been.

Our jobs had, at first, been smokescreens to hide behind. The OIA had wanted us to remain covert. After a while, Menolly had grown to love the bar she first tended, and now owned. And I had fallen in love with the Indigo Crescent, my bookstore. But more and more we had to leave them in the hands of others as we faced the demons down. Now, with Menolly a princess in Blood Wyne's court, and me taking on the role of the Queen of Dusk and Twilight, maybe it was time for us both to face the truth and let go.

I slid my phone back in my pocket and turned to the others. "Shimmer's in. She'll be here tomorrow around noon. That should give us time enough to get up to Camano Island and take care of this before night and the full moon. But Delilah's right. We need sleep. Tomorrow morning, we have to find a way for us to breathe underwater. But for now, let's just get some rest."

As Morio, Trillian, and I slowly headed up to the second floor—where my suite of rooms was—I realized that, for once, all I wanted to do was get into bed and curl into a ball and pretend everything was just business as usual.

Chapter 4

I WOKE TO someone licking my face. And my ear. "Stop it, you two. At least until I manage to open my eyes." I tried to push them away, expecting to find two naked men, but instead, I felt two squirming balls of fluff. "Huh?" I squinted, opening one eye to find a fuzzy black face staring down at me.

I turned my head to see who was licking my ear. One of the calicoes. Laughing, I slowly rolled up, scooting back to rest against the headboard. All four kittens were on the bed, and one of them was batting at Trillian's nose. The white kitten was kneading Morio on the shoulder, making biscuits for all she—or he—was worth. I pulled the two who had attacked me into my arms and nuzzled them, waiting for the inevitable explosions.

Trillian was first, grumbling as he waved in the air. He suddenly stopped as his fingers met the kitten, and he let out a cross between a sigh and a snort. "Okay, I'm awake, you little runt. I'm awake. Quit tickling my nose."

Morio rolled over, yawning, and caught up the white kitten in his arms, pulling it to him before starting to snore again. I stared at my husbands, smiling. We were spread out in the bed that could—and usually did—hold all four of us. With Smoky off in the Dragon Reaches, we were all taking advantage of the extra space.

"What are you going to name them?" Trillian asked, shifting till he was sitting up beside me. By the look of the blanket over his lap, I could tell he was greeting the morning with all due excitement.

"I don't know yet. I was thinking of a childhood game my mother played with me. Maybe I'll name them Eeny, Meeny, Miny, and Mo." I jumped as a whisper-soft energy ruffled around me. Misty appeared. The little gray cat spirit looked at me with wide eyes, and I suddenly realized why she looked so worried. I ran my hand over her back, lightly fluffing her energy. "Don't worry, Misty. We aren't replacing you. You can play with your...well...at least two of them are girls, we know that. You'll have buddies."

She gave me a soft "mew" before bouncing off the bed and running to the window to watch the crows that were perched in the window. I could see the birds from where I was sitting. Hopefully, Raven Mother wasn't hanging with them today. That was the last complication I needed right now.

Morio finally gave up any pretense of sleep and sat up, holding up the white kitten, who was still doing his best to leave a row of needle marks along Morio's arm. "You need your claws trimmed, little one. A visit to the vet is in order, I think."

"I'll have Hanna take them in." I gathered them all in my lap and, after giving each of them a kiss, shooed them away. They bounced over to Misty and the five of them began to play. The kittens seemed confused as to why they couldn't tackle her, but it only seemed to strengthen their resolve and they darted around the room, looking like they had already acclimated to the house.

Morio gave me a smoldering look. "I think I want a morning snack before breakfast."

Trillian arched his eyebrows, throwing back the covers to show off his magnificent body. "I second that thought. What about you, babe? Are you hungry?"

A glance at the kittens told me they were occupied. We were late for breakfast but now that I was awake, I needed something to rev up my motor. Usually it was caffeine, but today, a little extra spice might be nice.

I slid out from beneath the comforter. I was wearing nothing, as usual, and my nipples had already stiffened in anticipation. A ripple of hunger raced through my body as I decided who I wanted, and in which way. I lay back, hands beneath my head, spreading my legs and bending my knees.

"Somebody say they needed a snack?" I reached down and ran my hands over the curly black hair that covered my sex. Then, sliding one finger onto my clit, I began to circle it, my breath coming in hard, short bursts. "Who's game?"

Trillian nodded to Morio. "Be my guest. I'll take care of other matters." And he leaned down, taking one of my nipples in his mouth. As his lips closed over it, he began to suck, then gave it a sharp nip. The pain rippled through me, setting off little earthquakes of desire. At that moment, Morio settled between my legs, his tongue bathing my clit as he slid two fingers inside me, stroking me until I was so wet that they slid easily in my cunt.

I moaned softly, one hand coming to rest on Morio's head as he picked up the pace, the other hand cupping Trillian's back.

Trillian rose up, his cock tight and firm, and straddled my chest. As he leaned down onto his hands and knees, aiming himself toward my mouth, I opened my lips, frantic to taste him. The stimulation from Morio's tongue was setting off a cascade of sparks, rippling through me like a net of twinkling lights.

Trillian's long, thick shaft was smooth as he entered my mouth and I tightened my lips around the head, giving him firm suction as he slowly thrust himself deeper into my throat. I had learned to take my men in deep. Now, I slid my lips along his cock, relaxing my throat muscles in the process. I used my tongue to flutter against the ridge on the back of his penis, and Trillian rewarded me with a groan as he grabbed hold of the headboard to keep his balance.

Morio must have heard him, because Trillian's excitement seemed to spark him off. He tongued me harder, swirling the nub of my clit so quickly that I had to watch my breath control—especially with my mouth full of Trillian's cock. I arched my back, pressing against Morio's tongue, as he slid a third finger inside me and finger-fucked me hard. Another moment, and Trillian let out a growl as he came. I drank him down, swallowing his cum, milking his cock as he emptied it into my mouth.

He pulled out, his eyes afire, and his cock still hard. "Tit fuck me, woman, and then I'll give it to you, hard."

As he barked out his order, Morio suddenly nipped me, just enough to send me over the edge, and I came, crying out. He pulled away and after the orgasm settled, I rose to my knees, holding my breasts around Trillian's erection, pressing them hard as he thrust between them. He grunted, squeezing my tits, and then rolled onto his back.

Still frantic with hunger, I straddled him and leaned forward as I slid down on his cock, driving him deep within me. Morio swung around behind me, and I felt him lubing up my ass, his fingers greasing me, getting me ready. He slid a finger inside my ass and I let out a cry, and then another as Trillian thrust upward, filling my vaj full with his girth and length. The jet of his skin shone against the pale shimmer of my own.

"Ready, love?" Morio's voice was harsh, telling me that *he* was more than ready.

I relaxed, falling into the sway of the chemistry that held us all bound. "Yes, please."

Placing the tip of his cock at my ass, he slowly began to drive himself inward, penetrating me slowly, moving with care so that I felt every stretch, every shift, every thrust forward as he worked the head of his penis into my ass. And then he pushed on, sliding his length in against my squirming butt as he impaled me on his shaft, holding my hips firm so I couldn't wiggle away. I let out a low moan as both my lovers took up thrusting, first Morio, then Trillian, as I became both the rider and the ridden, sandwiched between them.

Trillian's brow was covered with perspiration, his eyes lit with his passion. I gazed down into his face. He was my alpha lover, and yet, he was willing to share me with both of my other loves. That made my heart swell even more. I loved them all—all three of my men.

Too often people asked me, "But who would you pick if you could only have one?" There was never an answer, for what I loved in each one only complemented the love I had for the other two. No one man could make me complete. I was complete in myself. Yet they all added a richness to my life that I could never think of being without.

"I love you," I whispered as Trillian thrust harder. "I love you all so much."

Morio let out a loud moan from behind me as he picked up the pace, still careful to not tear me, to not hurt me. He laughed, the wildness of his kitsune nature taking over, and drove himself as deep as he could, holding me very still. At the same time, Trillian thrust upward till he could fill me no deeper, and I hung suspended between them, dizzy and awash as my breath came quicker and the energy began to build, spiraling outward like concentric ripples on a pond.

And then, without warning, I came, painfully hard, and the orgasm rolled through me like a massive wave, a tsunami of emotion that racked my heart and body. I came again and again, as Morio and Trillian joined in with their cries.

In a puddle of limp limbs and cold sweat, we lay in a tangle, exhausted and yet vibrating. I managed to slide gracefully out from between them and, standing there, covered in their cum and their sweat, I realized how lucky I was. Love was hard to find in this world—or any world. And I had been blessed three times over.

But all I could say was, "I'm taking a shower. You guys care to join me?"

Then, before I could stop myself, I raced back to the bed and jumped in the middle of the tangle. I kissed Trillian, all over his face, and then Morio. "I love you. Do you both understand how very much I love you?"

Laughing, Trillian wrapped his arms around my shoulders. "We love you too, woman. Now get in there and turn on the shower. I'll feed the cats—they're milling."

Morio just slapped me on the ass as I padded across the floor toward the bath on the other side of the hall. As I stepped beneath the steaming spray and lathered up with an amber bath gel, I lingered in the glow of our lovemaking as long as I could, not willing to face the rest of the day quite yet.

DELILAH WAS ON the phone when we clattered down the stairs. Hanna glanced at the clock, then gave us a withering stare.

"I'm not serving brunch, you know," she grumbled her way back to the stove, pulling out a pan for eggs and firing up the griddle. "Pancakes and eggs coming up, but the bacon disappeared an hour ago. You come to your meals late, you get what's left."

"It's only nine." Trillian pressed a soft kiss against her forehead. "Hanna, no bacon, even for me?"

She swatted at him, but smiled. "That might work on Iris, but it won't work on me. If you want bacon, you'll have to fetch it from the refrigerator and set it to cook yourself."

Trillian did just that, arranging twelve slices of bacon on a foil-lined pan and sliding it into the oven while I poured orange juice and then hovered over the espresso machine that Delilah had bought me.

"Hanna, will you take the kittens to the vet today? They'll need exams, nail trims, and vaccinations. Please?" I pulled four shots, adding caramel syrup, milk, and ice to the latte.

"Oh, all right. Honestly—this household gathers more strays than it knows what to do with."

"Thank you, love." Giving her a quick hug, I carried my drink over to the table. I was already feeling the pull of the Moon Mother, even though the Hunt would not ride until midnight, and it was distracting me. "We'd better find that spirit seal today."

"You think Shadow Wing may know where it is?" Delilah asked. "Remember, the full moon is tonight."

"I know. That's why I don't want to take any chances. I suppose we could wait one more day but if *we* know where it is, there's always the chance that Shadow Wing will know. We can't rest on hope that he won't. He's got one chance left to claim one of the seals and you can bet that he'll be on alert for it, especially after we destroyed his faux Keraastar Knights."

I fired up Petunia—the espresso machine—and began pulling shots. Five today would be a good start. "I use the word *we* loosely, of course, considering neither you nor I was there. Even though Menolly told us what it was like, part of me would like to see the Sub-Realms for myself."

Delilah let out a choking sound. "Not me. I'd be happy if we never heard a word about the Sub-Realms again." She was poring over her laptop. "I found some information about K'thbar but I don't know how reliable it is. I called Carter, and he didn't have much to add, though he did verify that K'thbar is rumored to be off the Puget Sound coast. He said that a number of water-born Elder Fae live on the coast lines, and most within swimming distance of a big city so that they have ready access to food. *Food* meaning people."

"Lovely. This is going to be a load of fun. So, any ideas of how we breathe underwater? Besides a scuba suit?" I accepted a stack of pancakes and three fried eggs from Hanna. Our food bill was, as usual, steep, given just about every one of us ate like a trucker. Minus Menolly, of course. As I slathered the pancakes with butter and maple syrup, Trillian and Morio joined me with their own plates, compliments of Hanna. She brought over the bacon when it was ready.

"I found a way," Roz said from the other end of the table. "A witch named Fresia. She lives up in Edmonds, and she's originally from Otherworld. She's a Water Witch and a priestess of the goddess Yemaya. She's offered to cast the spell for us if we bring her a perfect pearl for each scroll. The ability to breathe beneath the water will last for three hours."

"Perfect pearls, hmm?" I didn't want to think about

what this was going to cost us.

Shade, who was in the rocking chair near the stove, spoke up. "I can get them. Don't forget, I'm part dragon. Dragons—even half-breeds—always have a hoard of some sort. I know I have a couple strings of pearls lying around." He jumped up and put down the book he was reading. "I'll be back in a few minutes." He headed out the back door.

"Where's he going?" Vanzir asked.

Delilah lowered her voice. "To turn into his dragon self. Since he lost his Stradolan powers, he can't make the shift into the other realms in human form, remember?"

Vanzir clamped his mouth shut, nodding. We were all acutely aware of how uncomfortable the situation was for both Shade and Delilah, and did our best to make the transition he was going through as easy as possible. But sometimes, we forgot. At least Shade had been out of the house this time and not in the next room.

"Did this witch say when she'd see us?" Delilah asked.

"At eleven, so we'd better start out soon, given the possibilities of heavy traffic." Roz held up a piece of paper on which he had scribbled what looked like a shop name, address, and number.

"Good going. I guess we just gather together the pearls and our weapons and get a move on." I thought for a moment. "What weapons *do* we have that will work underwater? I don't know that Morio and I can do much in the way of magic down there. I guess we can try, but we'd better take something to back up our spells."

"Spears, swords, daggers. I'd say that hammers won't be much good, given the resistance the water will provide to our swings. Anything that can stab will work.

Poison's no good unless it's on a blade. I rather doubt we have any tridents or harpoons in stock." Roz flashed a sad look at his duster, which was hanging over the back of the chair next to him.

Roz was our walking armory. He usually carried any and every weapon he could manage to tuck inside his long coat, flashing it open like some crazed exhibitionist when we needed extra weapons. But he almost always had something that would do the trick.

"You have any of those ice bombs you carried for a while? If I recall, they could do a nasty jolt or two of frost damage. What would something like that do if you set it off underwater?" I had visions of the water surrounding the K'thbar freezing into a giant cube and him popping to the surface, one big Elder Faesicle.

Roz gave me a long, wilting look. "You really don't think we can just freeze him? Yes, you *do*, don't you? Trust me, Camille, it's not going to work. You can't freeze one of the Elder Fae into a Popsicle. I'd like to say yes, but it's not going to happen."

I deflated. "Thanks for bursting my bubble."

He laughed. "Well, you have to admit, that's a tall order. But one of those bombs could potentially shift the temperature of the water so drastically, it might shock him."

"Shock him and it would probably kill us. Remember: Those waters are frigid as it is—even in the middle of summer, they aren't all that warm. We're going to have to wear wetsuits even though we aren't officially scubanauts."

Delilah shuddered. "The thought of wearing one of those makes my skin crawl. They're skintight."

"You don't have to, remember? You get to stay on dry land." I stuck my tongue out at her. "Okay, so the ice bombs are probably not going to be a big help but I still say bring a few. What, if anything, would a firebomb do?"

"Same thing in reverse. Would heat up the water nice and toasty. Which might not be a bad idea, given how cold it's going to be. It would make it a sight easier to navigate through the water—our muscles wouldn't be so tight. So I guess I'll take a few of both, just in case." Roz was jotting down notes as we spoke.

"Claws. You ever see the X-Men movies?" Vanzir said. "We need a few of those claws. Of course, we'd have to wear them like you wear brass knuckles, but that would be bad-assed for up close and personal battle."

I blinked. "That's not a bad idea. I think there's a weaponsmith who can make them—they come with wrist and arm braces and the claws retract into the brace." I had never in the world considered getting something like that for my own use, given how prone I was to hurting myself. But I could easily see Roz or Vanzir, or even Trillian leaping around with them. "But we don't have time to order them."

"Stainless-steel garden forks. They're strong as all get out, and they are sharp," Iris said as she entered the kitchen, a basket of early lettuce and radishes over her arm. "I brought up some vegetables from the garden for you. I could hear you from the porch. You'll want to get longer ones, if you want to stay out of reach of the creature."

Trillian snapped his fingers. "Of course—and they're easy enough to get. We can stop by the hardware store on the way to Edmonds. We take daggers, short swords, and gardening tools." He snorted. "I suppose anything works in a pinch.

"I suggest we get a move on. I can't think of anything else that might be useful, given how little we know about K'thbar." I had dressed for action, but none of us owned a wetsuit, so we'd have to stop by a scuba supply store for those, too. It was going to be an interesting shopping trip, that was for sure.

As we headed out to the car, amid admonishments to *"Be careful"* and *"Don't you dare drown"* and *"Whatever you do, don't let Delilah go near the water"* coming from Hanna and Iris, I glanced up into the large oak near our house. There, on one of the branches, was a large raven. I knew exactly who it was before she spiraled down to land at my feet. In a bright flash of smoke and sparkles, there stood Raven Mother.

RAVEN MOTHER WAS one of the Elemental Lords and Ladies. She was a trickster, a lot like Coyote, and she had always had an eye for me. She wanted me to leave my post with the Moon Mother and join her ranks. Raven Mother had always been at odds with the Moon Mother, coveting the brilliant moon high in the sky, and all that the Moon Mother laid claim over, including her priestesses and witches.

But circumstances dictated that we work with her, and truth to say, she wasn't evil. It was just difficult to trust her, regardless of how much she beckoned to me. Her son, Bran, was a member of the Court of the Three Queens, and soon enough I was going to have to put up with him on a daily basis. He was head of the Fae militia out at Talamh Lonrach Oll.

Bran liked to goad me. Raven Mother wanted me to marry him, but that was the last thing on my bucket list. For one thing, I was already married and had enough husbands. For another, the thought of him touching me—regardless of how good looking he was—made me queasy. We had come to a truce but I didn't trust it to hold, nor did I trust him to keep his word. Bran was more cunning and less helpful than his mother, and he blamed me for his father's death.

Truth was, he was correct. I had killed his father—the Black Unicorn—but the Black Beast, as he was known, had instigated it.

The father of the Dahns Unicorns, he was a legendary beast, and the consort of Raven Mother. Together, they had somehow engendered Bran. Every thousand years, eight times before I had met him, the Black Unicorn had died and been reborn, shedding his horn and hide. I was lucky enough to possess a set. Only those who worked with magic could wield them, and there were plenty of people who wanted to get their hands on them, especially sorcerers.

But even though the Black Beast had engineered his own death at my hands, Bran hadn't forgiven me. And he hadn't forgiven his father for giving me the horn and hide. Bran was running some weird hate/lust relationship with me. I doubted that love entered into his emotional repertoire.

"Raven Mother, what do you want?" I knew I sounded churlish, but given the situation and the baggage behind us, I wasn't all that thrilled to see her.

"An abrupt question, and yet, no greeting? No greeting from the one who will rule her court soon? How the seedling has sprouted. How the tender young plant has become a haughty bush. Aren't you ever joyful to see your old, dear friend, Raven Mother?" As she spoke, Raven Mother began to circle me. The others stood back, wary.

"I don't mean to be disrespectful, but we need to hurry. I don't have time to talk." I stood my ground. No way was I going to tell her what our rush was. As entwined as my life was with hers, I didn't trust her and doubted that I ever would.

"Then be aware of this: Bran received a missive from

Otherworld. There are whispers that the sorcerers who survived the dragon fire have banded together and have gone back to Chimaras, the Lord of the Sun. They are very antsy, they are, to reestablish their power. They have been driven to ground and now have no thought for anyone but themselves."

My eyes narrowed. "They deserve nothing. They don't even deserve their lives."

The sorcerers had marched on the elves and destroyed their lands, and were intent on destroying everything else. They had left the order of Chimaras and thrown themselves in with Telazhar who had promised them the world if they lent him their strength. When their attack failed—and it failed in a spectacular rain of fire—the ones who had survived scattered.

"That may be, may be indeed. But they are gathering. And their first target will be not the dragons, whom they cannot hope to fight, but your beloved grove."

The Grove of the Moon Mother. I pressed my hand to my throat, catching my breath. "How soon?"

"Oh, it will not be for some time. Some time it will take them. But you should know and warn your sisters of the order. I cannot, of course, since the beautiful, shining Moon cast me out of her forest, warning me never to return. Sad is the bearer of sad tales." Raven Mother talked in circles, but I was used to it by now.

I thought about what she had said. "I have at least a few days, then."

"Oh, yes. They are not ready to move forth yet. Time it takes to gather forces and regroup."

"Thank you. I..." I stopped. I had started to say that I owed her one, but that was never a wise move with the Elemental Lords. In fact, that pretty much guaranteed a one-way ticket to enslavement. "I'll make sure that the Moon Mother gets the message."

Raven Mother eyed me craftily, then let out a soft

caw. "I still wish you would reconsider and marry my son. What a force you would be together."

"I don't doubt that," I said, giving her a long look. "But it's a force that I think the world is far better off without. Now, I have to run."

She shrugged and then, in a blinding flash of smoke infused with overtones of ruby, vanished into her raven form and winged her way south.

Watching her go, I had a sudden thought. "*The horn. Maybe I can use it under water. I'll be right back.*" I dashed back inside and up the stairs to my room, where I pushed past the clothes in my closet to a secret recessed niche that Smoky had built for me. A touch on the hidden panel and it slid back, revealing the box in which the horn sat. The hide, which had been fashioned into a cloak for me, was hanging at the back. Hiding in plain sight, so to speak. I left it in the closet. A cloak would do me absolutely no good underwater.

I opened the box and there it sat. The horn of the Black Unicorn. Crystal, with golden threads woven through it, the horn was a good eighteen inches long and so hard that even if I threw it over the edge of a cliff, it would not shatter.

Removing it from the box, I lowered myself into trance and sought for the energy. I charged it beneath each dark moon and it had plenty of juice right now.

"Camille, well met."

I opened my eyes. I was sitting in a space in between worlds. I was actually *inside* the horn. Oh, my body was in trance as far as anybody else was concerned, but *I* was here—in a room with four screens, one filling each wall. In the center of the room sat a table and chairs.

A tall man with skin the color of amber waited at the table. Sometimes he was eight feet tall, other times he was six inches. But his eyes were always sea-foam green and he was far more powerful than my sisters and me combined. He was a jindasel, an avatar of the horn. And yet, he was his own person.

In a way, he was a lot like Shade, who was both an avatar of the Autumn Lord, but also his own self. Jindasels were different than djinns, though they came from the same elemental plane.

"Eriskel, it's been awhile." And truly, it had been. While I had used the horn at Winter Solstice fighting Yvarr, I had kept it safe and hidden since then. "I need to ask you something." I explained what we were going to do. "Can the Lord of the Depths help me?"

Eriskel thought for a moment, then nodded. "But you'll need to prep the horn. The Lord of the Depths should be able to aid you, and most likely the Lord of the Winds. Perhaps the Lady of the Land. But I doubt the Mistress of Flames will be of use to you this time." He paused, eyeing me carefully. "Mistress Camille, if I might offer a warning?"

I nodded. "As always, I'm grateful for your help."

"Be very careful. Using the horn under the water? It would be very easy to lose your grasp and have it swept away before you know what's happening. Please don't let down your guard."

I gave him a quiet nod. "I thought about that on my way up here. But I think we may need the help. There's always the chance we'll get in there, find the seal, and get away without waking the Elder Fae. But I'd rather not bet money on it. Or our lives."

"Which of the Elder Fae did you say it is?" Eriskel asked.

"K'thbar."

The jindasel walked over to the western screen and held up his hands. "Lord of the Depths, come forth."

A moment later, a giant of a man swam up toward the screen. His hair was glistening with lights, and his eyes were round and glimmering. He was a merman, carrying a trident, and beside him swam a pod of dolphins. He rose out of the water that now filled the screen, against a background of crashing ocean waves, and held up his trident, inclining his head.

"Lady Camille, how may I be of service?" His voice echoed from the screen.

I gave him a quick curtsey, even though I was technically his mistress. But I believed in respect. "Lord of the Depths, I have a question. Do you know anything of K'thbar, the Elder Fae, who lies sleeping beneath the waves?"

He paused, then leaned down and whispered to his dolphins, and they turned and, with a flash of silver, streaked along the surface, away from us until they were out of sight. "I sent my servants to find out what they could."

I thanked him. While I waited, it was as good a time as any to prepare the horn. In the outer world, time passed much more slowly. We wouldn't lose more than five or ten minutes by me taking the time to prep everything before we went in.

Eriskel called up the others, and I greeted them all. The Lady of the Land was a dryad, as brown as rich, fertile earth, and she stepped from among lush bushes—tall and thick with leaves and berries. She wielded a wand made out of oak and her hair was long, the color of corn silk. The Master of Winds rode in on a giant eagle to his mountaintop, and he brought with him the lightning. He was as tall as Smoky, and pale, with leather armor. His sword was honed to a razor's edge, and freshly polished. The Mistress of Flames walked over freshly molten lava, her eyes as brilliant as the flowing rock. Her hair stretched out behind her, hardened pillow lava that flowed down her shoulders and spun out as she walked. She wore a wreath of fern and vines around her head. As they joined the Lord of the

Depths, each in their own screen, my heart welled up. They were far more primal than the Elemental Lords and Ladies. These four were intrinsically connected with the powers of earth, wind, water, and fire, and they came together in the horn to form a potent, powerful weapon.

But the horn could help, as well as harm. The Lady of the Land could make gardens grow and enrich the soil. The Lord of the Depths could summon rain and bring rivers long dried up back to life. The Mistress of Flames created new land even as she destroyed rock and stone. And the Master of Winds could call up a stiff breeze to sweep out smog and stagnant air, and he could move the ships on the waters if sailors were stuck.

I waited for a moment, then told them what we were planning.

The Mistress of Flames bowed her head and stepped back. "I'm afraid my magic has no place in this battle. I could heat the water, but that would kill the fish."

"And we could do that. Thank you." I watched as she vanished and her screen faded.

"I can help, however." The Lady of the Land smiled benevolently at me. At least, I liked to think it was benevolent. "I can shift the earth beneath the waves if need be."

"And I as well. I cannot give you the power to breathe beneath the waves, but I can extend any spells you get to that effect." The Lord of the Depths pressed against the screen. "If you need me to take action, I am here."

Just then, his dolphins returned and he held up his hand, then turned to them as they started chattering at him. He joined their conversation with whistles and clicks, and then turned back to me, his look grave.

"K'thbar isn't one of the Elder Fae. He's one of the *Primordial* Fae—the beings from which the Elder Fae originated. They live in the depths of the waters, the earth, the fiery lava, and in the upper reaches of the atmosphere. They're *big. Very* big. *So* big. And to them, the Elder Fae are as young as a newborn is to your own self. He will not understand you. Not because he's stupid, but because he is as alien to your life and thoughts as you are to an ant or a bee. All he will see is you are stealing something of his. That you are a pest come in to swipe a pretty bauble."

"Well, hell." I thought over the news for a moment, but no spectacular idea sprang to mind. "What powers does he have? Did your dolphins know?"

The Lord of the Depths laughed. "They have heard tales that he can command the waters to rise up and lash against the land. To what extent, I do not know. Nor do they. K'thbar has slept for a thousand years. Last time he woke, I believe there was some form of massive landslide into the waters, but I can't tell you more than that. The question is, Mistress Camille: is the spirit seal you seek truly important to him, or is it just a toy? I think that will decide how K'thbar reacts, should he wake when you arrive."

And with that bit of sage but unhelpful advice, the room went black and I opened my eyes. I stared at the unicorn horn for a moment, then secreted it in my pocket. I feared very much that I'd have reason to use its powers, and not just to strengthen our ability to breathe underwater.

Chapter 5

I DASHED BACK to the others, who were waiting in the driveway.

"I brought the horn. I thought I'd better, plus I can extend our ability to breathe underwater with it." Then, on a less cheery note, I told them about what the Lord of the Depths had said about K'thbar. "So, not Elder Fae. Something called a *Primordial* Fae, and far more dangerous, given that he exists outside of our frame of reference. Or rather, we exist outside of his frame of reference. I got the feeling that the Lord of the Depths was trying to politely say we're pretty much the ants of K'thbar's world."

"Yeah, and when ants annoy you, you pour boiling water on the ant hill or get out the bug spray." Trillian cleared his throat and leaned back against my Lexus. The sunlight had broken through a few lazy morning clouds, and was as good as blinding us. Life in the Pacific Northwest came at several prices, one which was the sun became a suspect ball of fire in the sky that none of us were too familiar with.

"Boiling water...I wonder if he *can* make the water boil?" Roz fumbled in his duster and brought out a couple of the ice bombs. "I decided to bring these along, along with the firebombs. If he can affect the water, then we might be able to mitigate the effects."

"Primordial Fae are big. 'They're *big. Very* big. *So* big' is an exact quote. And when a lord of the elements says that with awe in his voice, you know you have a problem." I squinted, shading my eyes. "So, yeah, I'm bringing the horn."

"We'd better make sure those gardening forks are sturdy." Vanzir let out a hiccup. "Who's driving? We can all fit in your Lexus, but not with wet suits and everything else."

I glanced at Delilah. "You and I'll drive. Morio, Trillian, Roz, you come with me. Shade and Vanzir can ride with Delilah. Where's our first stop?"

"Shimmer called, asking if we can pick her up instead of her meeting us here. So off to the Fly By Night Agency, then head up to Fresia's shop in Edmonds." Vanzir consulted his notes. "There's a scuba shop just down the street from there."

With that, Delilah and I commandeered our cars. As I eased out of the driveway, Delilah following with her Jeep, I thought about just how many times we had done this. And how long the house and land had been part of my life. I was silent on the drive north, thinking about Raven Mother and the Primordial Fae and my life to come.

SHIMMER WAS WAITING and she jumped into Delilah's Jeep without hesitation. We didn't know her all that well, but we knew she was serving time

Earthside for some fracas back in the Dragon Reaches. Smoky said she'd been dealt a raw deal and that it was better for her to be over here, and Smoky's word was good enough for all of us.

After another quick stop at a hardware store for gardening rakes, we decided to avoid the freeway on our drive into Edmonds. Instead, we wove through the city. Aurora Ave N. was a straight shot for a while. It was also known as Old Highway 99, and ran a good share of the length of the I-5 corridor. Traffic was thick, but not at a gridlock yet—it wouldn't be until later in the afternoon. Rush hour around the city was from about 4 P.M. to 7 P.M. We continued through the parade of shops on either side until we hit the area where the Evergreen Washelli Funeral Home and Cemetery spread out to both sides of the road, and then after a stretch, we were back in the city. We passed mini-malls and park & rides, salons and auto shops, through Seattle into Shoreline, and then into Edmonds with nothing denoting the difference except for signs placed strategically to tell us we had entered a new city.

Shortly after Aurora turned into Pacific Highway, I veered left at the juncture, easing us onto Edmonds Way, which curved west toward the sound through a heavily wooded residential area, then past the salmon hatchery and Edmonds Marsh, which offered interpretive walks and bird watching.

"Ferry terminals coming up on our left," Trillian said, consulting his phone. Vanzir had texted him our directions. "Shortly after we curve around the ferry toll booths, you'll make a left onto James Street, and then before we hit Third, park by the building on the left. Fresia has her magic shop there. It's called Marsh Briar Fortunes."

I kept my eyes open, and sure enough, less than a block after I turned onto James, I saw the building. I made sure there was no oncoming traffic and turned, easing into one of the parking spaces. Behind me, Delilah followed suit.

"Here we are." I turned off the ignition and glanced at the guys. "Maybe we'd better not all go in. We're likely to alarm her if we do."

Delilah must have been thinking the same thing, because she texted me pretty much what I had said to Morio and Trillian. As I stepped out of the car I could smell the brine coming up from the sound, and it sent a calm, soothing caress through my jangled thoughts. If I could change one thing about our house, it would be to move it to the waterfront.

Everybody waited while Delilah and I entered the building. The shop was filled with ocean imagery, and was a lot more open and airy than I had expected. A lot of humans seemed to feel magic had to be filled with cobwebs and spiders, but though the shadow-energy was definitely a very real factor, it didn't have to enter every aspect of practice.

The main room was large, painted in delicate shades of blue and rose and gold, reminding me of a sunrise. Besides the counter display case, there were shelves filled with books, potions, candles, and herbs, and a side table with four chairs around it. A pale blue cloth covered the table, and in the center sat a crystal ball and a flameless candle. A side door led to the back.

The woman behind the counter had golden-brown skin, and her hair was black, curling tight around her head. Her brown eyes seemed to melt with an inner warmth, and she was dressed in a flowing gown in blue, white, and tan, reminding me of waves crashing against the sand.

"May I help you?" She turned to us with a wide smile.

"A friend called earlier to ask about water breathing spells?" I rested my elbows on the counter, staring at the merchandise beneath the glass. Daggers, graveyard dust, statues, tarot decks, and wands were arranged neatly in rows.

"Oh yes, he said you'd have need of five of them? That's quite a tall order, but as it happens, I'm a priestess of Yemaya and she gives me the strength of the water." She turned toward the side door. "I'll be back in a moment. I sorted them out and put them in the back so no one else would buy them before you arrived."

Her movements were fluid and graceful, almost as though she were floating through the water. As she vanished into the back room, I took a turn around the shop.

"She has some lovely things here," I said, pausing by the table with her crystal ball and tarot cards. "I wonder how clairvoyant she is."

"She has help," Delilah said, her voice low. "There's a ghost standing by the table that looks like an older version of Fresia. I'd say it has to be a family member—maybe a grandmother or an aunt. I'm warded so the spirit doesn't know I can see her, but Fresia isn't working alone."

Just then, the witch returned, five talismans in her hands. Each was a small round beaded charm on a velvet ribbon long enough to drape around the neck. She spread them out.

"These will last a few hours—four at the most. They can be renewed but it takes me a week to recharge them. To activate them, place them around the neck and say, 'Yemaya, hear my prayer.' That will set the charm to working." She pushed them toward us. "You have payment?"

Delilah nodded and drew out a coin purse that I recognized as Shade's. She opened it and withdrew five luminous pearls, setting them in front of the woman. "Five pearls for five charms."

Fresia let out a little gasp as she picked up one of the pearls and held it up to the light. "Oh, these are exquisite. I've never seen quite so fine before." She abruptly set the pearl down, looking at us for a moment. "Wait." Sweeping the pearls into her hand, once again she vanished into the back. Another moment, and she was back. She set down a delicate shell that was iridescent white. The typical nautilus coil, it was polished, and emitted a pale glowing light.

"What's this?" Delilah asked, leaning in.

"Moon snail shell. I collect shells and enchant them. Your pearls were far more exquisite than I expected. I drive a hard bargain but I'm fair. I couldn't take all five for the spellwork—they're a quality I've never seen. So I'm giving you this as an extra. I take it you're off on some underwater adventure and, although I don't know why, I feel you're facing danger. This is enchanted. Carry it with you and it will illuminate even the murkiest depths to a radius of twenty feet. I guarantee, it will serve you better than any underwater flashlight."

"It looks so delicate." I reached out to slide my fingers over it, receiving a jolt in return. "That packs a punch."

"That it does, but only when it's out of the water. Take it beneath the waves and that jolt goes away. This only needs to be charged once a month. Place it in a bowl of ocean water under the full moon each month and it will recharge its powers. And it will serve you for hours—it will last longer than the water breathing spells will." With that, she packaged up the charms, then wrapped the shell in a bag. "It's not nearly as fragile as it looks. The magic has hardened it."

As we thanked her and then left the shop, I glanced over my shoulder. "I have the feeling we'll be returning here in the future. I wouldn't mind getting to know Fresia."

"I agree," Delilah said. Back at the cars, we double checked the location of the scuba shop, which was two blocks north and one block west on Bell Street near the thin slip of land dividing Puget Sound from the town.

"Meet you there." I waved at Delilah as I slid back in the driver's seat. Within a couple of minutes, we were off again.

The stop at the scuba store necessitated all of us except for Delilah, Shade, and Shimmer to go in to make sure we found wet suits that fit us. I really detested the snug fit—it wasn't like a corset or a bustier. It took a clerk tugging and pulling to help me into it, and the wetsuit clung to every inch of my body. It felt like my pores couldn't breathe, but I figured I could handle it for the time needed. I thought about leaving it on to drive, but that just sounded way too uncomfortable. I had no clue how I was going to get into it once we were at the beach. I'd have to ask for help.

After paying far more than I ever wanted to spend on a neoprene bodysuit and swim mask, we were off again, this time heading toward Camano Island. By now, it was nearing eleven-thirty.

The drive to Camano Island from Edmonds was a little over fifty-three miles. While there were some beautiful scenic back roads, time was a factor and so I swung over to the freeway, taking I-5 north. Luckily, traffic was light and we made good time.

We passed over the Snohomish River where it was on its last leg of the journey to meet up with Puget Sound, then into Marysville and over Union Slough, past the windswept corridor that separated the freeway from the water. By now, we were into agricultural areas where they grew mostly berries, until we reached the Highway 532 interchange. Heading west on 532, we drove through Stanwood—a town with Scandinavian roots—and finally, over the Stillaguamish River, onto

Camano Island.

Another twenty minutes saw us around the island, down to Camano Island State Park.

I glanced at the clock. "It's almost one o'clock. We have to get a move on."

"Because of the charms, we'd better plan on being out of the water by three hours at the latest to ensure our safety," Morio said. "And then, two to three hours home, given we'll be hitting rush hour. So we go now, to avoid you popping out of the car to race away on the Hunt, and Delilah turning into a tabby while she's driving."

We piled out of our vehicles. The parking strip was empty except for us. I carried the bag of charms and the shell, along with my horn. I had bought a belt to go with my wetsuit and strapped on the homemade sheath I used to carry the unicorn horn.

Camano Island was a long, finger-shaped island that looked a lot like an upside-down comma. It was heavily wooded, with about fourteen thousand people living there year round. Originally a target for loggers, it was now a haven for birdwatchers and tourists. The island boasted a beautiful state park, as well as numerous other public beaches. The Camano Island State Park was composed of 244 acres of camping, with almost seven thousand feet of shoreline. While there were plenty of people here even on a weekday, we should be able to find enough privacy for what we needed to do.

As I shaded my eyes, looking across the rocky beach, I basked in the wind that swept by us. I loved the water as much as I loved the deep woodlands. "There's a bathroom over there we can use to change in. While I'm not shy, I want to draw as little attention to us as possible."

"Agreed." Shade gave a half-shrug. "I'll get the wetsuits."

Shimmer, who was almost as tall as Smoky, lifted her chin, inhaling deeply. "The water calls to me. I wish I could turn into my dragon self and fly, but at least they left me my natural form in the water. I think I wouldn't have much to live for if they hadn't left me that." She shook her hair back, the black strands streaked with purple and blue flying as a gust caught them up. "Oh, I *am* glad I came with you, even if there's danger. I needed to be by the water today."

I joined her at the edge of the pavement. Just beyond, the beach started. In Washington State, the beaches along Puget Sound were often rocky and littered with giant trees that had washed in the water long enough to become huge, polished driftwood logs.

"You miss being in the water, don't you? It's not like my husband. Smoky's content on mountain tops or in the city, though he prefers the mountains."

"He's a mixed blood—silver and white. They aren't as tied to an element as I am, or as Shade is tied to the Netherworld. Blue dragons are connected at a core level, at the heart, with the Ocean Mother. She sings to us, she calls us, she summons us, she commands us. Every drop of rain contains her essence. Every bath, every glass of water, every snowflake. All tied to the great tides of the Earth." She looked almost starry-eyed and it hit me: she didn't just *like* the water, she wasn't just connected to it, but she worshiped and loved it like I worshiped and loved the Moon Mother.

"I think I understand. That's the way I feel about the Moon Mother. Her essence is in my soul, in my magic. I run with her on the Hunt. I hear her calling to me even in the dark nights when she's brooding and has turned her face to the earth." I shivered, folding my arms as I stared at the wide stretch of rocks between us and the water. "I'm not afraid of the water, but I respect her. The Moon Mother rules the tides."

Shimmer nodded. "You and I, we have this in common. I value the moon for her movements on the ocean. She's a powerful force. And the ocean, she sings to the moon."

After a moment, I said, "So, I'd better go get dressed. What will you wear?"

She laughed. "My skin. Well, I'll come with you. I have a bathing suit on beneath my jeans and top. I won't need the wetsuit to stay warm."

I stopped short, realizing how far we would have to swim out. We had to dive deep enough to reach K'thbar and while we had the rough coordinates, it meant going out a distance. While I knew how to swim, I hadn't been in the water for a while and I felt a pang of fear. What if my stamina gave out? What if I wasn't as good of a swimmer as I remembered?

Shimmer glanced down at me. "Don't worry. I will be there. I'm quick enough and alert enough to notice if one of you ends up in trouble. I won't let you drown, Camille."

Her words stoking my courage, I looped my arm through hers as we headed toward the bathroom.

I STARED DOWN the neoprene monster. Two attempts and I still hadn't managed to get it on. I could lace myself into complex corsets, I could manage stilettos on city streets. Hell, I could even run in them. But as I stuck my foot through the leg of the wetsuit, willing myself to try again, I began to think that maybe I *could* handle the chill of the water.

"This is worse than the one time I tried to fit myself into a pair of Menolly's jeans. It just didn't work," I grumbled, staring at the damned thing. "Can you help me?"

Shimmer giggled. "I'm glad I don't need one of those. Here, let me see what I can do."

With a tug here and a grunt and groan there, between the two of us, we managed to get me squeezed into the butt-and-boob-hugging nightmare.

"I feel like an overstuffed sausage. But they assured me this was the right size. Give me a corset any day over this." I stared in the mirror at the sleek, otterlike second skin I was wearing. It didn't look bad—it didn't cause any untoward bulges—but it was uncomfortable to have so much material binding my body.

Shimmer stifled a smirk. "Well, I don't envy you. Shall we go see how the men made out?"

"This I gotta see." I followed her out to the other side of the beach house, which contained bathrooms, showers, and an information booth that opened on weekends and served coffee and snacks. There, as the men emerged from the men's restroom, I tried not to laugh.

Oh, they didn't look bad. All the men were fit—they had to be for as much fighting as we had all been through the past years. But Morio, Trillian, Vanzir, and Roz were all covered from neck to ankle in the same form-fitting suits as I was. And it showed every curve of their body too, including their privates.

"Impressive," I said with a grin. "Very impressive." But then again, I had slept with all the men here except for Shade and Roz. I knew just how impressive they were under those suits.

"Shuddup, woman." Roz frowned as he looked down at himself. "This...is not my idea of fashion. Let's get a move on. What's the game plan?"

"The game plan is," Shade said, "that we start swimming out in that direction." He pointed in a southwest direction. "We need to swim out quite a ways. I realize that some of you might not have the stamina, so I propose that I go in, turn into my dragon self, and then you can ride on me through the water. I can change after only a few minutes of swimming. The shoal drops off quickly, enough for me to shift."

I glanced around. The beach was empty, not surprising for the time of day and the fact that it was a weekday. "All right. I'd feel better that way. I don't have nearly the stamina that the rest of you do, and I don't know how good my swimming is."

"I can change as soon as I can submerge completely in dragon form,' Shimmer said. "Shade and I can swim quicker than any of you, so we can navigate smoothly and save all of you some strength."

Morio shaded his eyes before putting on his swim mask. "Good idea. All right, let's break out the water breathing charms."

"I wish I wasn't so afraid of the water." Delilah hung her head. "I feel like I'm letting you all down."

"We need somebody up here to keep an eye on things. You just wait on the beach and keep an eye on the cars. It always pays to have a lookout, my love." Shade kissed her on the forehead and she smiled again.

I handed the others their charms. Shade and Shimmer didn't need them, of course. One by one, we each held our charm and said, "Yemaya, hear my prayer." The charms activated, emanating a gentle blue glow, and I draped mine around my neck. Immediately, I was gasping for air and yanked it off.

"Crap. I guess we put these on as soon as we submerge."

"I guess so," Trillian said, staring at the charm warily. "Let's go. Everybody armed?"

The men each had gardening forks, along with long daggers. I had the unicorn horn and my dagger. Shade and Shimmer would be using their natural talents. And Roz held up a waterproof bag of fire- and ice bombs.

As Delilah watched from the shore, we waded into the surf. The chill hit me, even through the suit, though it was manageable. Before I had gone more than a few yards, I was waist deep, and then, on the edge of the shoal. I slid the charm over my head, reassured myself both the horn and the snail shell were firmly attached to my belt, and dove below the surface.

My first thought was to breathe, but then I realized that the charm worked by suppressing that impulse. My lungs felt silent and I thought that this must be how it felt to be a vampire. It was disconcerting, to say the least. I looked around. The water was dark, but the sun was glimmering down in areas, illuminating patches.

Shade was up ahead. He suddenly dove down and then, within seconds, a skeletal head popped up. He must have reached the end of another shoal. Shimmer followed him and the next moment, a graceful neck rose up beside Shade's. Shimmer was beautiful, with her dragon's muzzle and catfish-like whiskers attached to either side. Whippet-like horns curved back, gleaming like gems, above the limpid blue eyes that flashed with sparkles. She suddenly vanished, then a moment later, reappeared just as we swam to the dropoff. I wasn't sure what to do next, but Shimmer moved aside as Shade shifted, presenting the vertebrae of his shoulders.

I knew what came next. I swam over to him and cautiously settled on the bony ridge, holding on to him tightly. The others followed suit. We were all able to fit without much of a problem. Another moment passed and then Shade began to dive, taking us with him. Shimmer followed alongside us.

We rapidly descended, then evened out. I decided to wait to bring out the shell until Shade stopped. He appeared to know where we were going. Another moment, and he settled on what appeared to be a reef.

I wasn't sure how deep we were, but thanks to the charm, I wasn't feeling any ill effects. I took a chance and cautiously swam up, then over to Shade. He stared at me, his eyes illuminating the darkness, and once again it hit me just how odd it was to realize that my family was made up of creatures I had never dreamed I'd meet. I fumbled with the bag—not so easy given the gloves of the wetsuit—and then brought out the shell.

All around us, the water lit up and we were able to see where we were. Fresia was right, the charm was a powerful help. Flashlights wouldn't have worked nearly so well. I turned to the reef and realized I was swimming right above the wreck of an old ship that had lodged there.

The entire outside of the ship was covered with barnacles, sea stars, and sea anemones with their long white tubular bodies and heads that blossomed like an inverted mushroom top. One type of sea star was a morning sun star, brilliant orange, with thirteen legs. There were several around. The other stars were more numerous, covering parts of the ship's hull. With five arms and the color of faded grapes, the purple stars made me cringe. They reminded me of the banana slugs—fat and fleshy. Yet another kind of inhabitant made me more nervous. Sea urchins, a brilliant green, were latched onto several places of the ship. Their spines were sharp and could puncture wetsuits and skin alike.

Over the side, the water plunged into darkness. I paused, registering the fact that I was hearing the roar of the tidal currents ripple past. It had never dawned on me before that I could hear under the water—but I closed my eyes for a moment and realized that there was a multitude of sounds down here. And Shimmer was making her own noise, her air bubbles rising as she blew them out her nose. I had no idea how long she could last beneath the waters, but she looked comfortable enough.

I motioned for the others to join me, and they did. Shade and Shimmer stayed in their form. They couldn't very well turn back into human form without an air breathing charm, and besides, we needed them to be our muscle should K'thbar wake up. We still didn't know what he could do. Or what he might actually do.

I pointed to the ship, then looked at Shade. He bobbed his head up and down. Figuring this must be our destination, I held up the shell and began looking for an opening, swimming rather than trying to walk on the reef. I wasn't sure how sturdy it was, or what it was made of, and decided it was better to avoid any sudden surprises.

The ship was old. In fact, I would put it at pre-1900 by the looks of it. Morio and Roz swam up beside me and I mimed looking for an entrance. They nodded and split off, as did Roz and Vanzir.

I realized that I was near a railing. The ship was on its side, by the looks of things. It wasn't a big sailing ship, but it was definitely large enough to fit a crew of ten or so. Using the railing as a guide, I swam along, looking for the bow. It wasn't long before I found it. I swam in toward the ship, and sure enough, within a couple moments, I found the entrance leading to the lower cavern. The door was gone and it looked like it had been ripped off its hinges. The wood where it had attached was splintered and raw. Holding the snail shell up, I began waving it around to attract the attention of the others. When they joined me, with Shade and Shimmer still swimming next to the boat, watching and waiting, I motioned to the door and then swam through the entrance.

The entryway led to stairs, which had become a corridor, given the ship was on its side. I swam through, holding the shell out to give me enough light to see by. I tried to avoid brushing against the sides. While I didn't think the sea stars were poisonous, the urchins were an accident waiting to happen.

Behind me, I heard a yelp of sorts and cautiously stopped, turning to see Morio wrestling with one of the urchins. He didn't look very happy, but as far as I knew, urchins in the Pacific Northwest weren't venomous. That didn't mean it wouldn't hurt like hell, but he shouldn't react to any toxins the urchin might have. He pulled it off of his shoulder and tossed it to the side.

I turned back to the passage and swam until I came to what would have been the bottom of the stairs. It opened out into a rather large galley. There were doors along what was now the bottom and top, leading into other rooms. But my attention was firmly on a pale yellow orb that surrounded the table. The orb was shimmering and I realize it was composed of energy rather than crystal. On the table, inside the orb, lay a figure that looked very much like a fish with a torso and feet. We had found K'thbar.

Chapter 6

MY FIRST THOUGHT was that K'thbar couldn't have been sleeping all that long if he was here in this ship. My second thought was, what if the orb he was in was displaced in space and the ship had settled around him? Which led to the question of whether we could actually touch him or would our hands just pass through him. He looked almost translucent.

Morio moved closer to the orb. He paused, then motioned for me to join him. As I cautiously swam over to him, I could see what he was pointing to. There, beneath the Primordial Fae, was the spirit seal. Set in a silver knotwork base, the gem was pale, pale yellow—the color of the earliest shimmer of sunrise. I could usually feel the energy emanating from the seals, but this one I couldn't, even though I knew what it was.

I gave Morio a questioning glance and started to reach toward the orb, but he grabbed my wrist, shaking his head. At that moment, a fish swam by. Without slowing down, it swam directly into the orb. The resulting zap was enough to char the fish and send it belly-up, floating toward the ceiling of the ship.

Hmm, not good. Electricity. And the wattage had been overkill on the fish, loud and crackling. The remains looked like a block of charcoal. What the energy had done to the fish, it could surely do to us, and all the underwater breathing spells in the world wouldn't save us from being electrocuted. Time to rethink our strategy.

We couldn't go in after it, but we could perhaps bring K'thbar out to us. Though yet another thought drifted into my head that he might just have more than electricity on board as a weapon. I spotted a small pebble on the floor and picked it up. Motioning for everyone to back away, I tossed the rock toward the orb and waited to see what would happen.

No zap. The rock went through and landed on the table beside K'thbar, who took no notice of it. So living things got fried, and inanimate objects could pass through. But that didn't answer the question if we could even touch K'thbar. Would the pebble have bounced off of him, or was he corporeal—would it have just landed inside his image? Realizing that the others were waiting for my cue, I looked around and found another rock.

Trillian cocked his head to the side, giving me a shake of the head. I ignored him. If he yelled later, I could always plead that I hadn't noticed his disapproval. I aimed for K'thbar and threw, just as Vanzir seemed to realize what I was doing. He lunged forward—as best as you can lunge when you're underwater—and grabbed hold of my arm, but he was too late. The rock already was passing through the orb and this time, my aim was dead on. The rock landed on K'thbar. Or rather, passed through him to land on the table below.

Automatically, I tried to catch my breath, but the charm prevented that and I almost sent myself careening to the side with the effort, I was so startled by not being able to breathe. Vanzir steadied me, but then let go and turned toward our target.

K'thbar apparently didn't need to be hit in corporeal form. Apparently I was doing a damned good job of interrupting his sleep. He stirred, and it was then that I got a good look at him. K'thbar was far larger than I had originally thought. As he shifted, the orb shifted with him and what had been about a sphere ten feet in diameter abruptly expanded like a balloon, by a good three feet.

We all backed off, watching and waiting for any sign that he was awake. Maybe I had gotten lucky and just penetrated his dreams. Maybe he was just turning over for a more comfortable position. Maybe...maybe... maybe we'd better figure out what the hell our plan of attack was, because the orb grew once again, threatening to fill the room if it continued. If it expanded to fill the ship, we were dead, given the lightning display that the fish had caused. He was cutting off our exit, though. The orb stretched to include the path to the staircase passage, and there was no way to exit the ship now without going through the energy grid around the Fae.

I hurriedly swam toward one of the doors near the ceiling. It was ajar, and I pushed it open, swimming in to frantically look for a porthole, but there was none and it hit me—the quarters were below the water, in the belly of the boat. Of course there wouldn't be portholes. I noticed that the men had scattered, and the orb was still expanding to fill the main galley.

Unable to see whether K'thbar was actually awake, or whether he still slumbered and was just having one doozy of a dream, I quickly looked around for anything that might help. I still had the shell and it gave me enough light to see by. But there wasn't anything that remotely looked like a weapon in here. I had my dagger, though, and the horn.

As I hesitated, wondering whether I should pull out the horn now or wait, I noticed that the glowing edges of the orb were starting to penetrate the floor—or what would have been the inner wall if the ship was upright. Crap, it wasn't done expanding. If that energy filled the chamber, I was toast. There was no way out except through the door, which was blocked by the orb's energy.

I pulled out the horn and held it up, focusing on contacting Eriskel.

Without warning, I found myself in the central room inside the horn again. Eriskel was looking highly alarmed, and all of the Elementals were at their screens, watching me.

"I need help. I have no idea what to do, but we're about to be a bunch of crispy critters here if we don't nullify that damned energy." Relieved to have a breather—I could think in here without wasting much time on the outside—I flopped in the chair opposite the jindasel. "What should I do?"

The Master of Winds spoke. "I can negate the lightning. But then he'll wake and you'll have a fight on your hands."

I turned to the Lord of the Depths. "If we do that, can you help us?"

"I can help you by getting you out of the ship, so you aren't trapped in there with him."

I thought for a moment. We had to retrieve the spirit seal. We couldn't chance it vanishing if the orb that was holding it near K'thbar vanished. "Can you make me immune to lightning and electricity, at least for a few moments?"

The Master of Winds arched his eyebrows. "You want to go inside the orb?"

"Just long enough to grab the spirit seal. Then I'm

out of there and you can negate the orb."

"If I give you both that immunity and *then* negate the energy, it will drain the horn and the others will not be able to help you except in the most rudimentary ways. Is this what you wish to do?"

I thought it over. If we just had him negate the orb, the chance of losing the spirit seal was very real. Right now, it was trapped inside along with the Primordial Fae. "Yes. Shimmer and Shade are in their dragon forms. They can fight K'thbar."

"Be very sure. He is not at his full power while he's in there. The orb is not a safe haven. There are reasons to keep others out—and reasons to keep someone in."

A prison. K'thbar was imprisoned in the orb, then. Double crap because that meant that somebody had considered him a big-enough danger to lock away. But I couldn't see any other way and I had to make a decision.

"Yes, I'm sure. If you could propel me near him, that would be wonderful." I had never expected to connect the word *wonderful* with the thought of cozying up to one of the Primordial Fae, but here I was, doing just that. Sometimes, life didn't work out quite like you expected it to. And that was usually okay, except this time, I wasn't going to lay odds.

Eriskel gently rested his hand on my shoulder. "Mistress Camille. Be very careful. When you exit from the horn, put the horn safely away and close your eyes. The Master of Winds and the Lord of the Depths know what they have to do. You need say nothing but do not open your eyes until you hear me whisper. You will find yourself next to K'thbar and the seal. The sphere will then be negated, so shield your eyes again. The rest, regrettably, is up to you. I will see you after you charge the horn on the dark moon. This will drain every ounce of its power till then."

As his voice faded, I was back in my body. I immediately crammed the horn back in its sheath and closed my eyes. A ripple ran through me—very unpleasant, almost like a series of minor shocks, and then I was moving, the currents sweeping me forward. I did my best to maneuver into a swimming position. Though I couldn't see, I knew precisely when I passed through the orb because it felt like a feather-light dusting of ash sprang up on my exposed skin, as though the very outer epidermis had been zapped. That should give me a rosy glow, I thought.

The next moment, I came to a halt.

"Open your eyes." The whisper was so faint I almost missed it.

I opened my eyes to find myself staring up at K'thbar. He was huge—so huge it was hard to tell where he stopped. He was far taller than the ship, which meant that the sphere existed in another realm. And he was thrashing around. Waking up, damn it. I saw the spirit seal near his hand and lunged for it. The moment my hand closed over it, he let out a roar, and I frantically tried to hold onto the seal as the world shifted.

Remembering Eriskel's instructions, I shut my eyes as tight as I could, praying that K'thbar wouldn't step on me. The flash came, then, and I found myself jettisoned sideways, tumbling through the water as I desperately tried to hold on to the spirit seal. The next thing I knew, I was slamming through the wall of the ship. Thank gods the force of the explosion preceded me, because it lessened the impact, even though I still felt like I had hit a brick wall at full speed. Splinters of wood exploded out every which way as I tried to slow myself down. At least I was in the water and not in midair, I thought. And the ship had been stationary, not moving. Two pluses. I was upside down in the water, feet pointed toward the surface—as far as I could tell—

when a gentle arm reached out to steady me. A very big, very blue arm. I glanced up to see Shimmer, in her dragon form, holding me fast.

If not for the charm, I'd be breathing in water after being so abruptly jettisoned from the ship. As Shimmer held me, I began to calm down, her steady hand—claw?—giving me the support I needed to take stock of my condition. My ears were ringing. The explosion had been loud, but I could still hear over the buzzing. I glanced down at my legs and stomach, and Shimmer must have realized what I was doing, because she lifted me up to examine me, turning me over a couple times before gently letting me go. I couldn't feel any major damage though the constriction of the suit might be dampening any pain, and apparently, she couldn't either, because she pointed toward the surface and motioned for me to swim up. I had just started to when she stiffened, her long, Nessie-like body evening out. She didn't have fins, like the Loch Ness monster, but she looked very much like an Asian dragon with smallish wings, arms, and legs.

I swam around to see what she was looking at and immediately began backing away, heading toward the surface like she had directed me to. K'thbar had shot out of the boat after me, and he was now fully awake. Now, he was the size of Shade and Shimmer—and I could fully see what he looked like. He was the color of Concord grapes, and his body was long and fish-like, with tentacles that flared out from his neck area like a squid. Also like a squid, he had a sharp, large beak, only it was hooked like that of a bald eagle. His eyes were luminous—glassy pools of black with sparkling white pupils—and he looked angry.

Holy hell, I thought. K'thbar was so big he could devour me whole. Or snap me in half with his razor-sharp beak. There was no way in hell we could fight him, not with gardening forks and daggers. Not underwater, where we couldn't move fast enough to get out of his way.

Shade and Shimmer seemed to realize the same thing, because they moved in, motioning for the others to get out of the way. I realized with relief that Trillian, Morio, Roz, and Vanzir were all okay, following me. If the blast had harmed them, it didn't show. I kicked hard, aiming for the surface with them behind me. I tried to avoid the snarling fight that was going on below. I wanted to watch, to make sure the two dragons were all right, but if we stayed in the vicinity, K'thbar would catch us.

As I hit the surface, I flipped over so I was floating on my stomach. I tried to make out anything I could below but could only see murky water. It churned as the fight continued, sending up a series of waves around us. Finally, I turned over again and took off my charm, holding tight to it in case I should need it again.

Roz and Vanzir did the same, then Morio and Trillian. We bobbed in the waves, treading water as we waited.

"I have the spirit seal. I want to get to shore as soon as possible," I said, gasping.

"Does the horn have any more power in it? Can you use it to have the Lord of the Depths send his porpoises to take you ashore?" Trillian asked.

I shook my head. "No, it's expended in full. It won't do me any good till I can recharge it in two weeks."

Roz let out a sigh. "You know how I hate taking a chance on going through the Ionyc Sea. I'm never sure if I'm going to get it right. But I can see the shoreline from here, in the distance, and I'm willing to try to take you to shore if you'll chance it."

Roz never did trust his ability to shift through the currents. But right now, my main focus had to be getting ashore securely with the seal. I had to let Shimmer and Shade take care of K'thbar in their own way.

"Let's go, then. Maybe you can come out and help the others after, if you're willing."

Vanzir shrugged. "I can shift onto the astral and head toward shore that way. That just leaves Morio and Trillian."

Roz swam over to me and slid his arm around my waist as I looped one arm around his shoulders. "Hmm, good thing Smoky isn't here," he joked.

I just gave him a long stare. Rozurial was an incubus. He was always one step away from being thrashed by my dragon-husband. In fact, at one point, Smoky had given Roz a good beating for landing a stray hand on my ass.

"Right. Let's go. Ready?"

"Yah. I'm ready." I closed my eyes. Roz wasn't as proficient at making the shift as Smoky was, and there was a jolt that landed my stomach in my throat. But then, we were in the currents.

I opened my eyes and leaned against Roz as the shifting tides of energy rose and fell around us. The sparkling mists wafted in great clouds as we flew through them, coiling with long tendrils to reach out and surround the aura Roz emanated that kept us safe. One blink…two blinks…three blinks later and we were on the shore, and I yawned. We hadn't been out there long enough for the Ionyc Sea to exert its powerful effects on me, so I hadn't fallen asleep, but I still felt the drag from it.

Delilah jumped up from where she was sitting on a driftwood log and raced over to us. "Did you find it? Are you okay? Where's everybody else?" She frantically looked around. "Don't tell me everybody—"

"Stop. Roz brought me to shore because I have the spirit seal and we didn't want to chance K'thbar grabbing it. Shade and Shimmer are fighting him right now."

"Back with Trillian." Roz vanished again.

Delilah calmed down some, but I knew she was worried about Shade. "He'll be all right. K'thbar is huge. Only the dragons can fight him. The horn's drained for this month. I used every ounce of energy to get the spirit seal, and I'm bruised and battered." Now that I was on shore, I could feel the bruises forming from where I'd blasted through the hull of the ship. I was going to hurt like hell tonight, that was for sure.

"What's he like?"

I tried to describe what I'd seen. "He's huge, and I'm not sure he's fully living on this plane—" I stopped as Roz appeared with Trillian.

"Vanzir's waiting till I go back for Morio, then he'll come through on the astral."

"Are they still fighting?" I wanted Shade and Shimmer to pull back, to withdraw. Chances were K'thbar couldn't follow us onto land, although Yannie Fin Diver had been able to, and we thought he was water-bound.

"I think so. I don't know. I'll be right back." Roz vanished once again.

Trillian hurried over to me. "Are you okay? I saw you go shooting through the side of that ship and was petrified that you had broken your neck. Or at least a leg or something."

"Nothing broken that I know of, but I'm sure as hell going to need some pain relievers and a long hot bath. I'm probably black and blue beneath this suit."

"Did you really hurt yourself that bad?" Delilah asked, turning to me. "Let's get you out of that wet suit before anything swells and we have to cut it off you."

I started to protest. How could I leave the shore until we were all back together? But Delilah wrapped an arm around my shoulder and guided me toward the bathroom. Behind us, I heard a noise and glanced over my shoulder to see Vanzir, Roz, and Morio appear. Relieved that they were out of the water, I allowed Delilah to lead me back to the bathroom.

"I hope they're okay," she said as she helped strip the wetsuit off of me.

"I do too, Kitten. I do, too." There weren't any guarantees I could give. K'thbar probably didn't have an evil bone in his fishy body, but that didn't guarantee Shade and Shimmer's safety. After all, we were the invaders in his territory, and we had stolen from him.

As my skin appeared from beneath the neoprene suit, I winced. The bruises were forming, indeed, up and down my legs and arms, and across my ass—from what Delilah said—and back, where I'd met the hull on my way out. I realized that I was starting to hurt in a major way, and let out a soft groan as she helped me back into my fighting clothes—a black Emma Peel–like jumpsuit, with belt and boots.

"I'd give anything for one of my corsets right now. I think I might have bruised a rib and the compression would feel good."

"Better you don't put any compression on it till we get you over to the FH-CSI and have you checked out. You might have a broken rib instead of just bruises." She gathered my wetsuit and carried it out to her Jeep. I followed more slowly as the stiffness began to set in.

"What's this spirit seal like?" Delilah leaned against the side of her car.

I glanced around. No one in sight, so I brought it out to show her. The pale lemon stone glistened under the flickering sun that was now playing hopscotch with incoming clouds. They were high, though, and didn't smell like rain.

"Oh, that's lovely." She let out a long sigh. "Do you realize that we've managed it? We have collected all nine seals. It's taken us four years…"

"Four years and far too many losses. But yeah, we have them now." A commotion down by the water caught my attention and I slid the spirit seal in my bag, along with the horn and the moon snail shell. "Oh hell, look."

As we watched, Shade and Shimmer came out of the waters, running as they hit the sand. They were in their human forms, and behind them, we could see a series of waves churning dangerously.

"K'thbar is chasing them. Get in your car in case we have to make a beeline out of here." Delilah shoved me toward my car and I raced to the driver's seat. The men were running toward us from the beach, and right on their heels, Shimmer and Shade. By the time they reached the car, we could see a form rising out of the water only twenty yards or so out in the sound. *K'thbar*. But he made no move to come ashore and I prayed that we were right in thinking he couldn't exist out of water. Everybody packed into the cars, wetsuits and all, and I gunned the motor, heading toward the road that would lead us out of the park. We couldn't wait around—no taking chances on losing the spirit seal.

"Do you think he'll cause problems for anybody who comes to the beach?" I asked. "We can't just run away and not deal with the aftermath, if there is one."

"I think we can contact Chase and have him talk to the sheriff or cops or whoever's in charge up here and maybe they can shut down the beach for a few days until things blow over."

"I'm going to talk to Grandmother Coyote about this," I said. "I don't want anybody else hurt if we can help it, and that sucker is now both awake and angry."

With that, I shifted gears and we headed back the way we had come, toward Seattle.

ONCE WE WERE back on the mainland, off the island, we found a service station and stopped to both get gas and give the men a chance to change out of their wetsuits. I stayed in the car, my thoughts back with the Primordial Fae. How many of his kind were out there in the world, sleeping until something startled them awake again? He was huge and deadly, but not evil. Danger didn't always wear the face of a sociopath or villain.

"You're worried about K'thbar, aren't you? That he might rampage across Camano Island?" Trillian asked me as they returned to the car. He was riding shotgun.

I eased back onto the road, maneuvering past a stalled vehicle as I slowed down to make sure nobody was hurt. The driver was standing beside the passenger door and when he saw me, he held up his cell phone and waved me on.

"Yeah, I am. I had hoped to get through this without waking him up, but I have no clue what's going to happen now. He didn't come ashore after us, so I'm hoping he really is water-bound, but I don't want to take any chances." I fell silent again.

Truth was, I was thinking about more than K'thbar. We now had all nine of the spirit seals. Everything was getting more real by the moment. Once I had the Keraastar Diamond, I had no idea what I was supposed to do about the Keraastar Knights. Everybody seemed to assume that I'd know what to do, but I had no clue. And according to legend, the Knights were supposed to go up against Shadow Wing. If that was true, then did it mean I'd be leading them into battle? There were so many variables to my near future that I wanted to curl up in my bed and just hide until it was over and settled.

But instead of telling him what I was thinking, I just said, "We owe Shimmer a big favor. She put her life on the line for us. We're going to have to figure out a way to thank her. She doesn't have a stake in this—not really. And yet she helped us out, and she probably saved my life down there by catching me when the blast shot me through the hull."

"Speaking of which, how are your bruises feeling?" Morio leaned into the front seat, catching my eye in the rearview mirror.

"Painful. I now know what a battering ram feels like." I snorted. "It's an event I could happily go through life without ever experiencing again. And I still have to run with the Hunt tonight." I had been so rattled that the energy of the approaching full moon hadn't registered, but now that I was in the car and safe, I began to feel the magnetic call of the Moon Mother.

"I, too, my love," Morio softly said.

"True."

Ever since Morio had been initiated as my Priest-Consort under the Moon Mother's eyes, he had been swept up in the Hunt with me. It was something special we shared, just like I shared a beneath-the-skin connection with Trillian that had been forged years ago during the Eleshinar Ritual, when we had been tattooed body-wide to connect our spirits. The tattoos had faded into our cells, vanishing below the surface of our skin, but the bonding ritual had drawn us together. And with all my husbands, I had been soul-bound. We had chosen to create a quartet that, should one of us be killed, we all would know. As time went on, we would also be able to find the others if they were lost or captured.

My stomach rumbled. "I'm starving. Trillian, grab me a candy bar out of the glove compartment?" I kept a variety of energy bars and candy bars around. Even with half-human heritage, my appetite was huge. All the Fae ate more than humans, and we burned it off.

He fished around in the glove compartment and brought out an Almond Joy, unwrapping it for me and handing me the pieces. I liked sweets, but they weren't my favorite—I preferred savory—but the energy would do me good and I had developed a taste for the coconut and chocolate mix.

As I ate, my body responded to the food, and finally, I was clear-headed enough to drive the rest of the way home without worrying.

FIRST THING I did was put in a call to Chase and ask him to check with Camano Island to see if there had been any incidents reported at the state park. They had responded no, and so I decided to pay a quick visit to Grandmother Coyote. I entrusted Delilah and the men to watch over the spirit seal while I was gone. I'd take care of my injuries when I returned, I promised them.

Grandmother Coyote lived out in the woods about five miles from our place. There was a turnoff where I could park, and—bruised and battered though I was—I headed through the brush and ferns toward the grove where she lived.

Grandmother Coyote was one of the Hags of Fate—the women who wove destiny into being and who cut the cords when necessary. They never played favorites, and were entrusted to right the balance when the pendulum swung too far either way. They were the female equivalent of the Harvestmen, and together, along with the Elemental Lords and Ladies, were the only true Immortals. Even the gods could fall—and did, at times. Even the gods could die. Now and then, Grandmother

Coyote would look into the future, if the time was right and the questioner had a good reason, but she never took action unless there was a necessary reason. And those reasons were known only to her and the other Hags of Fate.

The path to Grandmother Coyote's lair was through the woods, deep into a grove of cedar and fir. The field before the copse was littered with fallen branches from storms, and with scrub brush that had grown tall over the past four years since I first ventured into meet her. There was nothing pointing the way, no sign or landmark signifying this was her land, but the energy wove a net through the meadow and trees that was unmistakable. It shivered along my skin, tracing patterns up my arms and across the back of my neck like needles of light zapping me gently. Butterfly kisses of magic alerted me that yes, one of the Ancients lived in this woodland, so be very, very respectful.

I passed between two giant cedars and through a stand of huckleberry bushes, finally coming to a narrow dirt path littered with needles from the tall timber. At times, Grandmother Coyote met me in the meadow, but today I could sense she was waiting in her lair.

The early evening light was still bright—dusk came late during the summer months—and it played through the lacework of branches as I wound my way through the woodland. The sound of birdsong filled the air, their echoes ricocheting through the trees with a haunting trill. Bees were still gathering pollen, the fuzzy bumbles darting from flower to flower, their legs heavy with the yellow grains. All along the path, brambles and berry bushes overflowed their patches, blossoms white and open. Waist-high ferns sprawled across the trail, and the scent of moss growing on trees hung heavy in the forest. I stopped for a moment, inhaling deeply, the scent washing over me as it calmed my agitation from the day.

And then, I was there—at the base of Grandmother Coyote's tree. The trunk was huge, large enough to drive a semi through. I walked up to the massive cedar and placed my hand against the wood, leaning close as I whispered, "It's Camille. I need to talk to you."

A moment passed, and then another moment. Then, slowly, a doorway formed in front of me, and the next moment, Grandmother Coyote was standing beside me.

Chapter 7

GRANDMOTHER COYOTE WAS old as the hills. Old as time. The millennia of her life was etched deeply into the roadmap lining her face. She wore a long gray robe that swept around her ankles, and she carried a walking stick. Her eyes glimmered in the early evening light, and tendrils of long white hair peeked from beneath the hood that she always kept over her head. She was ancient, she was, immortal and out of the reach of any weapon. No mortal could harm her, no creature could kill her. Time itself could not touch her, for Grandmother Coyote lived outside of time. Soil-bound to the earth, she still served every realm. No power stood above her, and with her sister Hags of Fate, she was destiny incarnate.

"Camille, you seek my advice, perhaps?" With a crafty smile, she stood back and invited me into her world.

As I entered the tree trunk, the space grew, forming a tunnel with a dirt floor. She led me along the passage while eye catchers lit the way, the faerie lights sparkling and twinkling like orange-sized stars of pink and green and blue and yellow.

I knew this path. I had been along it several times and it felt oddly comforting to me. When I was here, nothing from the outside could penetrate. Nothing could interrupt. The trail led to a cavern at the end, and in the cave was an oaken table and two chairs. The chairs were covered with gnarls and burls, the knots of the wood oddly alive. A crystal ball sat on the table and a bag.

Grandmother Coyote offered me a seat and I cautiously sat down. The chairs had a habit of coming to life, and the arms could easily wrap around one's waist.

"What do you seek today?"

"Knowledge. I want to know about the Primordial Fae. About one in particular—K'thbar." I paused, then explained to her what had happened. "We woke him up, and now I'm worried he'll hurt the people on the island." I was cautious about asking favors from Grandmother Coyote. There was always a price to pay for her answers and help, but we hadn't much to go on and my instinct had insisted that I visit her to find out what I could.

She laughed, then. "You know the rules?"

I nodded. "I know."

"Then draw three bones from the bag and we shall see what we shall see." She handed me a velvet pouch.

As I took it, the energy clicked and sparked against my fingers. The first time I had been here and told to reach inside the bag, I hadn't been sure what I'd find. Now, I knew what to expect. I withdrew three bones—and bones they were. Finger bones. And I had brought Grandmother Coyote several of them as payment for other sessions.

The first one I pulled out was an elf bone. I recognized it by its energy. I set it down on the table. The second one was a bone that I couldn't place, but that felt incredibly strong and vibrant. The third was one I knew all too well. I had cut the finger off the hand that it belonged to. Bad Ass Luke's finger—the first Lesser Demon that we had faced over Earthside.

Lucianopoloneelisunekonekari. I dropped it on the table like it was a hot potato and leaned forward, staring at it. Grandmother Coyote had cleaned it of any flesh, and it was polished ivory, but it was still tingling with the demon's energy.

Grandmother Coyote smiled—her smiles were more terrifying than any glare she could give. Her teeth were sharp, needle-like, and reminded me of stainless steel.

She picked up the elf's finger. "You have a journey waiting for you in Otherworld. This reading is far less about K'thbar than it is about another matter that preys on your mind. Your travels will take you far north, well beyond the borders of Kelvashan, the Elfin Lands. There, you will find help from the men upon the mountain. You can trust them."

Grandmother Coyote picked up the second bone—the one I didn't recognize. She glanced at me quizzically. "Do you know what this is?"

"A very misshapen finger bone, but no, I don't know who it belonged to." In truth, I was guessing that it was a finger bone—it didn't really look like one, but since all the rest were finger bones I assumed that the creature it had been part of had been of an odd shape and stature.

"Bone it is, though not exactly a finger bone. This is a shard of hoof from the Black Beast to whom you delivered death."

I caught my breath, holding out my hand. She placed the bone in my palm and I closed my eyes, feeling the sweep of energy wash over me. Yes, there he was, in the current of sparks that tickled my fingers. I slowly replaced it on the table.

"He's full grown again, and runs in Thistlewyd Deep and Darkynwyrd with Raven Mother. Yet this hoof shard...tells me that you will have many dealings to come with the pair. Once you take your throne, Camille, you enter a different world. Have you thought yet about the life span a Fae Queen must have?"

I blinked. I had a much longer life span than any human, but not as long as full-blooded Fae. But the Fae Queens, they outlived even their own kind. "No, I haven't."

"You've really not considered what taking the throne fully means for your evolution and development, have you? What you will become in less than two weeks." She pulled the crystal ball to her. "How long has Derisa been alive?"

I started to answer, then stopped. "I have no idea."

"She is High Priestess to the Moon Mother in Otherworld, as you are becoming here, over Earthside. She exists outside the other witches and priestesses because she is an avatar of the goddess incarnate. You will be both an avatar of the Moon Mother as well as Queen of Dusk and Twilight, and for this...your life will no longer be the same. You aren't just moving out to Talamh Lonrach Oll, Camille. You are moving into another world."

And that stopped me cold. I sat there, barely breathing, as the weight of Grandmother Coyote's words settled on my shoulders. Of course she was right. I wasn't going to just be dillydallying around out there. Even though I had known things were going to change, the momentous shift that was taking place in my life splashed out before me like a vast panorama. There was so much I would be able to do that the thought of it overwhelmed me. And on the shadow side, there was so much I'd be expected to do that the thought of it panicked me.

I gulped back my fear. "I knew. But...I didn't."

"You needed to keep the reality at bay until it was almost time. But Camille, the time is coming and you have to walk into it with the knowledge of what you are taking on. This is your destiny. Oh, you could still cut and run, but your life would never be complete. And you would always regret doing so. Not a day would go by when you wouldn't look back and realize that—"

"I'm a soldier's daughter, and I didn't rise to my duty. I know." I stared at her, trying to sort out the explosion of feelings racing through me. "I guess this means I'll be drinking the Nectar of Life far sooner than I had planned." At some point, anyone who was half-Fae was offered the chance to drink the Nectar of Life, which would expand our life spans near to full-blood Fae's length. But I hadn't planned on facing that choice for a long while yet.

"Oh, it goes deeper than that, Camille, but that's all I am allowed to say on the subject. But you would do well, tonight, to prepare yourself. Your life as you know it has very little time left."

She picked up Bad Ass Luke's finger bone. "This bone, you brought to me."

"I remember, all too well."

"That he reappears now tells me the final showdown with the Demonkin is coming. Shadow Wing is weakened, and that makes him angry. You have the spirit seals as of today."

"Yes, we do. All of them."

"Every Great Fae Lord left in existence feels this shift. Every portal quakes from it. The fates of all three worlds hinge on what you do next. You could bring them together and watch the portals unravel. You could destroy them and see what would happen. You can raise the Keraastar Knights and do battle to keep the Sub-Realms in their place. There are so many varying futures that fracture out from this moment that I have no way to predict what will be—or what *should* be. Camille D'Artigo, you are the crux and the crossroad, and by your actions, the world will shift."

I swallowed. Hard. "Gee, put the pressure on, why don't you?" I tried to joke but the words came out thick as the panic grew. I didn't want to determine the fate of three worlds. I wanted to go play with Maggie and sit under a tree by Birchwater Pond and eat a sandwich.

"Some of us are born great..." She paused.

I nodded, murmuring, "Some are born great, some achieve greatness, and some have greatness thrust upon them." Shakespeare had it right.

"You will never know which of the three brought you to this point, and right now it does not matter. But whatever the case, Camille, you must think carefully. You must weigh the issues, and seek guidance from those you can trust. And from those you aren't sure of—sometimes the advice of a stranger can be more keen-sighted than the advice of a friend who is too bound up within your world. Now go. Do not fear K'thbar. He will rumble and roil the water, but he cannot come to land. But I advise you to not visit the waters there again for some time. He will eventually seek another spot in which to slumber, and will go to sleep once more. He was not so much injured by the loss of the spirit seal, but by the intrusion into his dreams."

And with that, Grandmother Coyote stood and motioned me to the door.

I turned back. "Will I ever get to come back to visit you again?"

"Oh, Camille. If you do not, I will be visiting you. You're bound up in my world, as I am in yours. Go and be grateful that you have the opportunity to change the world. So few have that chance." With that, she swept the bones back into the bag and I turned, finding my way out.

By the time I crossed the meadow again, my ribs and stomach were hurting and I was so glad to see my car that I almost kissed it. I slid in behind the wheel and, thoughts in a jumble, turned and headed for home.

IRIS CHECKED ME out. "No broken ribs that I can tell, but you've bruised yourself a good bit. I'll spread some salve on it, and you rest tomorrow, and the injury should be on its way to healing come Sunday."

"I can't rest tonight. I have to ride with the Hunt. But that will most likely spur on the healing rather than harm me. The energy of the rides is thick and bracing."

Iris didn't bother to argue. She knew, as well as everybody else, that each Full Moon saw me up and on the astral with the Moon Mother. Nothing could break that bond—not even death. For when I died, she'd sweep me up onto the Hunt until the day she allowed me to go to the Land of Silver Falls.

"Here, you rest for now. Lay down on the sofa and I'll bring you some food on a tray." She shooed me out of the kitchen and I knew better than argue.

Delilah was sitting in the recliner by the sofa, reading. She put down her book as I entered the room. "I wish Menolly could rise earlier during the summer."

"So do I, but you and I both know she can't. She should move to Alaska each winter. She'd almost never have to go to bed."

"Yeah, but summers would be a bear." Delilah waited until I made myself comfortable. "Shimmer's down by the pond. Vanzir's going to drive her home in a bit."

"I hope she's ready to buckle up and hang on. He's gotten three tickets in the past four months and I told him if he doesn't watch out, they'll suspend his license.

He likes to play hotshot on the road." I paused. Then, very softly, I reached out for her hand. "Things are going to change so much in the next two weeks."

Delilah squeezed my fingers. "I know. Are you afraid?"

"Yeah, I am. But..."

"But you are looking forward to this. I can hear it in your voice, behind the fear. And Menolly and Nerissa are moving. And I—I'm changing, too. We're growing up, aren't we?" She sounded almost teary.

I stared at the ceiling, trying not to cry. "I guess this time was always going to come. If we had stayed in Otherworld, Trillian would have still come back to me. And you... From what our father's spirit told you, you'd still end up with the Autumn Lord. And Menolly? Who knows what her path would have been, but she would have moved on, eventually. Life changes. It has to, or it stagnates. And that's worse than dying."

"When are you going to Otherworld? We have all the spirit seals now. It's time for you to go hunt down the Keraastar Diamond."

I bit my lip, sorting out my feelings. "Iris said my bruises would be a lot better by Sunday. I suppose I'll leave then. Menolly won't be able to come, but would you go with me?"

Delilah laughed, squeezing even harder before she let go of my hand. "Just try and stop me. Now, before Shimmer leaves I'm going to go thank her and say good-bye. I'll give her your regards."

I nodded. "I'd go with you, but right now, lying down feels like the best thing in the world."

As Delilah left, Trillian entered the room. He gave me a thoughtful look. I smiled at him and closed my eyes. I didn't feel like talking—I had too much to think about. He took the hint and tiptoed past. I didn't think I'd be able to nap, but within a couple moments, the ache of the injuries and the adrenaline of the day settled, and I drifted off to sleep.

THE WHISPERING WOKE me up. It was faint, but constant. I yawned, easing myself up with a grimace. My ribs ached like fire, and I spotted the ointment Iris had left for me. I had changed into a skirt and loose tank top when she examined me earlier, so it would be easier to reach my ribs, and now I was grateful for my foresight. I eased the tank up enough to slather a layer of salve across my ribs. The ache began to ease and I was able to catch a deep breath.

The whispering continued. I glanced at the clock. It was nearing 8:30. I had slept for ninety minutes, but it felt like more. As I pushed myself off the sofa, Delilah bounced in, her furry tail twitching with curiosity.

She was gorgeous when she was a cat—a big golden tabby, with long flowing hair. At one point when she had gotten skunked, Iris tried to get the smell out with tomato juice and she had ended up with patchwork-colored hair—from pink to icy blond. Now, her warm golden ginger colors were back, and she spied me looking at her and bounded over, leaping into my arms.

I laughed, nuzzling her head. "You love the full moons, don't you? It gives you a chance to play without guilt or care."

She licked my face, purring loudly, and I caught the same love in her eyes that was always there when she was in her two-legged form. Delilah had started off far too naive for her own good, but now, even though she had retained some of that innocent, optimistic worldview, I missed our little kitten who thought everything had a good side.

I tossed her lightly on the sofa and picked up a feather toy that I found in the corner. We played for a few minutes, me dangling the toy for her, her darting this way and that to catch it. The next moment, she danced on her hind legs as I held it up, then leaped into the air and caught hold of the feathers. I let her drag it away as I headed into the kitchen.

Hanna was there, humming brightly as she handed me a cup of coffee. "I know you'll want this before you go. And here, eat this, too." She placed a plate in front of me with honey cake on it. One of her specialties, the cake was rich with the flavor of honey and raisins and chopped walnuts. The frosting was more of a crumble, with brown sugar and oats and coconut. I bit into it, letting the crumbs melt in my mouth. It was still warm—fresh out of the oven.

"This is so good. I want a second piece."

"How about a sandwich instead? You need to be fortifying your strength for the night's run." She set a roast beef sandwich down in front of me, along with a bowl of beef barley soup. Pieces of carrots and celery and fresh peas floated in the broth, and the fragrant aroma made me salivate.

"Oh, yes. That smells wonderful. How are the kittens?"

"The vet said they're all in good shape, considering they were feral. He gave them their shots and it seems that the black and the white ones are male, and of course, the two calicoes are female. He places them at about six weeks. They're snuggled up in your suite. I put them in Maggie's old playpen—they shouldn't be able to get out of that, and they have their litter box and food and water."

"Thank you. I'll be taking them with me to the Barrow, of course." I stretched and shook my head, a rush of energy slicing through me. "I can feel the Hunt on the rise." On the nights of the Hunt, all my senses were heightened. It was as though I had smoked marijuana, or taken some shi-leaf berry tea, an Otherworld herb that provided similar effects. I dug into the sandwich and soup, my stomach rumbling as I realized just how hungry I was.

"When do you go?"

"Soon. I can feel them coming. I have to change, then I'll go out in the back yard and meet the Hunt there." I glanced over at Hanna. She and I had grown close during my imprisonment, and she understood what I went through better than anybody except Menolly. Hanna had seen me at my lowest, she had bathed my wounds and taken care of me after Hyto was spent.

Another glance at the time told me that Menolly would be up in about ten minutes. I'd have time to say hello before heading off with the Hunt.

"Hanna..." I wasn't sure how to put the question I was about to ask her.

"You wish to ask me something?" Hanna cleared away a basket of sewing from the spot next to me and sat down at the table.

I caught up my breath. "Yes, but I'm not sure what you'll think. When I move out to the Barrow, I'll need a personal maid. A lady's maid. And I thought that if you're interested..." I drifted off, almost afraid of what the answer would be.

Hanna rested her hand on my wrist. "Camille, when we first met, I was willing to let you die because it would save me and my son. Then I saw your strength. And I realized what I had become, thanks to Hyto. I had to make a choice, and I did. As much as it hurt, I made the right choice. And then you asked me to return here with you, and that, too, was the correct choice. I have a home and I'm needed. And now you offer me yet another choice."

"You're going to say no, aren't you?" It was hard to hide my disappointment, even though I had anticipated her answer.

Her eyes welled up. "Oh, if there were only two of me. But you know that Maggie will need me. Delilah will need me. You are going off to become a queen where there will be more than enough people to serve you. You will find the right woman to step up and guard over you from behind the scenes. But Delilah and Maggie, and Shade—and even Rozurial. They will need me here. And I want to be needed. I could easily be replaced out at the Barrow. But here? I make a difference. I hope you understand."

I rested my other hand on top of hers. "I understand. I truly do. I won't ask you again, because I won't put you through having to make the choice once again. But please, know that I am grateful you'll be here to care for my sister and Maggie. I think I'm going to miss her most of all."

"Then let me bring her out. Play with her till you have to run with the Hunt tonight."

I nodded, going back to my soup. Hanna brought out Maggie just as Menolly appeared. Nerissa was working late, so we sat in the kitchen and talked and played with Delilah and Maggie, who was toddling around like a pro by now, as the hours till midnight—the Witching Hour—ticked away silently.

AROUND ELEVEN P.M., Delilah raced through the kitchen, then leaped up onto the table, pilfered a piece of lamb off Maggie's plate, and then raced off.

"De-ya-ya! De-ya-ya kitty!" Maggie clapped her hands and laughed, her own fur glistening from the brushing that I had just given her.

I kissed her head, the calico fur tickling my nose. "Yes, Delilah kitty." I looked over at Hanna. My eyes widened, as another shiver of energy vibrated through my body. "I can feel them riding now. I better go change." I handed her Maggie after another kiss. "Take care of our girl."

"You know I will. Ride safely." Hanna stared at me for a moment. "I cannot fathom what it must be like."

"Riding with the Hunt...it's like a wild dream. But I've lost whatever fear I ever had toward it. Actually, Hanna, nothing has frightened me as much as my time with Hyto. I think that will forever be my gold standard for terror-inducing events. I remember that night we climbed down the mountain..." I drifted off, remembering the panic to get away, the knowledge that if he found us, the torture would be more than either of us could endure. The darkness and icy depths of the Northlands as we made our way down the glacier, with me already beaten and bruised.

"Camille, come back. You don't need to go there—you're safe now. And Hyto is dead."

Hanna's words penetrated through the sudden fog and I realized I was holding my breath. "Right. I'm going to change. And Hanna...thank you. For everything." I held her gaze for a moment, then headed upstairs.

Trillian was there, resting on the bed with a book. The playpen was sitting near the bed, but the kittens were nowhere to be seen. "Getting ready for the Hunt, love?"

"Yeah. I need to get dressed. Where are the kits?"

As I spoke, there was a loud squeak and then the calico sisters bounced up on the bed from the other side, chasing each other across it. White kitten and black kitten came bounding out of the closet, joining the fray. All of them descended on Trillian, playing with his toes as he wiggled his feet at them. He let out a yelp as one of the calicoes bit his big toe, but laughed.

"Scamp."

"You just make sure they stay in the bedroom. Delilah's changed into Tabby, and I'm not sure how she'd take to them at this point."

"I'll put them back in their pen in a bit. I just thought they might like to play for a while."

I suppressed a smile as I turned toward my closet. Trillian came across as aloof and almost rude to a lot of people, but he had a soft spot for those who were innocent and unable to protect themselves. He'd never let on, but I knew full well that he regularly made donations to a number of animal rescue organizations, along with the local food banks and the women's shelters.

I had priestess robes, but they weren't exactly the most suitable for riding with the Hunt. Instead, I shimmied into a flowing black skirt that fell just below my knees. It was full and light, but warm. My ribs were still incredibly tender, so I chose one of my acrylic-boned corsets that would compress them lightly, but not as much as the steel bones. Then, fastening the busks, I adjusted my boobs so they were positioned right, and then pulled on my kitten-heeled granny boots, tying up the laces. Finally, I attached a belt around my waist that would hold my dagger, and grabbed my staff.

Aeval had given it to me shortly before Hyto had kidnapped me, but I still hadn't learned much about it, although it contained the power of Faerie Fire. It was about five-nine—a couple inches taller than I was—and made of polished yew, fitting firmly in my hand. A crystal ball the size of my fist sat atop of it, with silver netting wound to securely keep the ball in place, and a silver foot.

Trillian set his book aside and wandered over to stand behind me as I stared into the mirror. My eyes were starting to glow with the light of the Hunt, and I felt the surge of power beginning to filter into me.

"My wild, feral witch," he whispered, wrapping his arms around my waist. "I wish we had the time for me to fuck your brains out."

I leaned back into his embrace. "You and me both." The energy of the Hunt was seductive and driven, like the rut of the King Stag in the woodlands. Trillian's breath came heavy on my neck, setting off sparks of hunger that ricocheted through me. "Oh, I want your touch. I wish you could run with us on the Hunt."

Morio entered the room at that moment. He had changed clothes as well. "Everything I needed was down in the laundry room," he said, his eyes shining like mine. "Are you ready, babe?" His voice was thick and I sensed his arousal—he was my priest and I was his priestess.

"Yeah, let's go." I turned. With one smooth move, I grabbed Trillian by the shoulders and spun him around against the closet door, pressing against him as I pressed my lips to his. My tongue met his and he moaned into my mouth as he slid his arms around my waist. Behind me, Morio let out a low growl of pleasure.

"Ready?"

I tore myself away from Trillian. "Be good. Sleep deep. Be ready for me, I'll be ravenous come the morning."

"Oh, I'll be ready. Run safe, both of you." Trillian scooped up the kittens so they couldn't dart for the door and gently placed them in their pen. "Remember, Smoky will be home tomorrow morning."

As Morio and I headed downstairs, it was almost as though I was walking on air. "This Hunt, it's stronger than in a while."

Morio placed one hand on my shoulder. "I can feel it, too. I don't know why—we passed Beltane, the high zenith of the Hunt, last month."

"Litha's coming. Perhaps it's the solstice. Whatever the case, I can barely feel the ground beneath my feet."

Hanna was waiting by the door, holding Delilah in her arms, her expression solemn. She always saw me off on the nights of the Hunt.

Vanzir joined us from the living room. "The energy is so strong tonight that I'm a live wire. Roz went out to walk the grounds and I may join him."

"It's a powerful moon. I'm not sure what's up, but keep an extra watch on the wards. Trillian will help. He's up in our room, but I'm sure he'd be glad to come down if you need him. Also, since Bruce is gone and Iris is preoccupied with the babies, you should probably do a sweep past their house, too." I stopped as a wash of energy left me lightheaded. "We have to go. They're almost here."

"Be on your way, then, and the Moon Mother be easy on you." Hanna opened the door.

Morio and I clattered down the porch stairs, stepping out into the night. The skies were clear, and we could see the moon on the rise. The Hunt was coming in from the east. I could see them in the sky, ghostly forms racing through the heavens in a long train—so long nobody knew how far it extended. I backed up, my gaze locked on the moon.

The Moon Mother was riding at the helm of the Hunt, so huge that she dwarfed the riders behind her. She sat astride a skeletal horse clad in silver armor, with crimson eyes. Steam rose from its nostrils' openings, and he was easily the size of the Black Beast. The Moon Mother's hair flowed out behind her in the astral winds and she was a silhouette of fire encased in silver form, with her bow and arrows over on shoulder. Her eyes shimmered, also silver, glowing and endless. Behind her, running fast and free in a tunic of plum, with black breeches and boots, was Derisa. Her aura crackled with lavender sparks, her magic running wild. She was the High Priestess of the Full Moon, and I was the High Priestess of the Dark Moon.

My own aura flared a deep purple as the trumpets echoed around us. The trumpeters rode to both sides of the Moon Mother, aside skeletal mounts like hers. The Hunt stopped overhead, waiting. Morio and I clasped hands and I hit the staff on the ground, thudding the silver boot so hard it felt like the earth quaked, and then we were running up a bridge of dark sparkling energy, to join the Hunt.

I threw back my head and let out a shriek, long and piercing, as the energy of the Hunt slammed into me fully, buoying me, driving me toward the chaotic and lovely strength that raced through the train of riders and runners. As the Moon Mother set off, Morio and I began to run, caught in the frenzy, beside Derisa. Behind us, all the warriors of the Moon who had fallen through time, and the priestesses long dead, raced with us. And intermingling in their midst were the spirits of bears and pumas, of elk and deer and wolves and all things wild. The winged spirits of owls and ravens were part of our chain, and hawks and eagles.

We tore through the night, a chain that encircled the worlds—both Earthside and Otherworld, brilliant in the skies of both but yet separate and part of neither. We were the fear and the shiver, the lamentations of the dead that made men cover their heads as we passed. We were the wail of the Bean Sidhe, and the jubilation of witches dancing under the moon's light. We were the ecstasy of the rut, and the march of the dead.

As we swept through the night, through the world, chasing the moon, we caught up the dead who were to join our pack. At one point, I glanced over my shoulder and—for just a moment—caught sight of my cousin

Shamas. I caught my breath as we locked eyes, and then he smiled, a fierce, joyous smile, and I knew that he was all right. I turned back to the front, my attention latching onto my Lady, and as we ran, I lost all thought except for my love of the Hunt and the Moon. With Morio beside me, we ran across the worlds, until the night was spent.

Early morn, the Hunt slowed, and the Moon Mother turned to look at me. "Well met, my Dark Priestess. Go now, and next I see you, you will understand truly what it means to walk in my shadow. Derisa will prepare you."

Before I could kneel or say farewell, Morio and I were standing in the yard. A faint light in the east shimmered. The sun was preparing to rise. And the Hunt raced away for another month.

Chapter 8

HANNA WAS ALREADY up, even though she had gone to bed late. She had a huge farmhouse breakfast waiting—bacon and eggs, hash browns and biscuits, fresh-squeezed orange juice and a compote of berries with cream. The scent of the food hit me hard and I realized just how hungry I was. My stomach let out a loud rumble. Morio snorted, but he looked as famished as I was.

Delilah was sitting there, rubbing her head and sniffing a cup of peppermint tea. Hanna started up the espresso machine and began to pull shots as we stumbled in. I was covered with the sparkles of magic that had coalesced into physical form as we came off the Hunt, and they were starting to itch.

"Take a shower, then come eat. Trillian is still asleep, so let him be. He stayed up most of the night with Rozurial and Vanzir, keeping an eye on the place. We had a fracas with a couple of goblins who decided to try to come through the rogue portal in the back yard." Hanna shook her spatula at Delilah. "Drink that tea, young lady. You knew better than to tear open the whole bag of catnip. Now you can just nurse that hangover."

I laughed as Delilah glared at her. "You mean that ten-ounce bag of catnip we bought for you the other day?"

She nodded.

"You tore open the entire bag?"

"And she ate half of it. No wonder she has a stomachache." Hanna went back to the hash browns. "Hurry up with that shower or your breakfast will get cold."

"Yes'm." I grabbed Morio's hand and we headed upstairs, tiptoeing into my bedroom to avoid waking Trillian. If he and the other men had been fending off goblins in the middle of the night, they deserved to sleep as much as possible.

Morio and I snuck into the shower without waking him up. As the hot water began to trail down my body, I slumped against the wall, luxuriating in the sensuous feel of the bath gel that Morio was lathering on my back. He slid his arms around my waist, reaching down with the washcloth.

"Spread your legs," he whispered.

I inched my legs apart. Morio slowly drew the cloth between them, lathering me with soap. He tossed the cloth to the side and then, inching down with his fingers, began circling my clit. I moaned, leaning back against him.

"Squeeze your breasts," he said.

I reached up, sliding my hands along the soap on my stomach, then rubbed my breasts, squeezing them together. I ran my hands over my nipples, pinching them and gasping as Morio chose that moment to increase his speed.

"Oh, fuck me." I raised one leg onto the side of the tub, balancing against the shower stall with my hand as the water streamed over us. Morio adjusted his stance, shoving his cock deep inside me from behind, penetrating me with his length and girth. I swiveled, a purr of delight catching in my throat as he slowly began to thrust, wrapping his arms tightly around my waist to keep his balance. Letting go of my breast, I brought my left hand down to stroke myself, my breath coming in ragged pants as he drove into me harder.

"Harder. I need it harder."

"On your hands and knees, woman." His throaty growl sent prickles up my spine and he pulled away. I immediately went down on my hands and knees, the shower spray beating down on my back. Morio was right behind me, on his knees as well, and he found my slit again, driving himself in so hard that I lurched forward. He caught hold of my waist.

I leaned my head back, letting the water splash into my face as he rode me. The feel of him inside me pushed me on and I suppressed a cry, trying not to wake Trillian. But apparently we already had, because the door opened and there he was, naked, his jet skin gleaming like polished obsidian. He was erect, with a spark in his eye.

"Room for one more?"

"There's always room," I choked out.

Morio waved him in. "The water's fine."

Trillian stepped into the shower in front of me, cautiously kneeling in the midst of the water and soap that was swirling in the bottom of the big tub. He was lined up at eye level for me, and I eagerly opened my mouth for him, taking him in, tonguing him as I drew his cock deeper into my mouth. I licked his length, tickling the ridge on the back of his shaft with my tongue, drawing my teeth along his cock with just enough pressure to make him moan.

Morio let out a hoarse laugh. "Our wife gives good head, doesn't she?"

Trillian fisted my hair, holding my head firmly as he plunged his cock in and out. I formed a tight suction around his length with my lips, gripping him with my mouth. "Oh she does, yes. That's it, babe. Take me in. Swallow me down."

Morio began thrusting again, deeper and harder, and with his left hand, he reached between my legs to finger me. Dizzy with the energy of the Hunt, swaying with the rising passion, I let out a muffled cry as I suddenly came, the orgasm hitting me so hard that I spiraled up and out of my body, then back again, reeling as the waves of climax rippled through me. Morio pounded me hard and furious, then let out a long howl as he came, holding me tight, so deep he couldn't push any further. At that moment, Trillian came, his cock pumping as he filled my mouth. I swallowed his cum, and then licked his cock clean as the shower continued to rain down on us, and the energy of the Hunt spent itself in the wash of our sexual glow.

BY THE TIME we were lathered up again, then dressed and headed down to breakfast, I was sore and tired. I felt like I'd not only run a marathon, but like my pussy had run a marathon, too. And my knees were aching from the hard tile of the shower floor. But I felt complete and the energy of the night had settled enough for me to think.

Hanna looked up as we entered the kitchen. "I kept everything warm for you." She didn't mention anything else, but a glint twinkled in her eye.

Delilah looked like she had recovered a little. "Oh man, that was one hell of a party I had myself last night."

Shade, who was sitting at the table, eating, laughed. "Yeah, and I have the pictures to prove it."

"Oh no, you *didn't?*" She dropped her fork, holding out her hand. "Hand over your phone."

"Nope. I can use them as blackmail. You should see your squirmy fuzzy little butt. Camille, I sent you one of the videos I took." He laughed, fending off Delilah's attempts to get hold of his phone. "Hey, I put up with your litter box, your toys, you pouncing on my feet, playing with my hair, so you can just allow me this one perk of being engaged to a werecat."

"He has a point." I pulled out my phone and began playing the video. Delilah was lying in the middle of the entire bag of catnip, squirming on her back, squeaking as she tossed a sisal mouse in the air. Her eyes were glazed over but she looked happier than I had seen her in a long time. "Oh, Kitten. You might want to check into CA—Catnip Anonymous!"

"Very funny." She wrinkled her nose at me, then went back to her breakfast. "So, how did the Hunt go?"

"Powerful. I saw Shamas, by the way. He looked happy."

She paused. "You okay?"

I considered the question. Shamas had been our cousin. At one point he and I had been secretly engaged, but that had ended due to his mother refusing to accept that I was half-human. And then...so much water under the bridge. But he had died, still loving me, and somewhere in my heart, I knew a part of me would always love him.

"Yeah. I am." I glanced at the clock. "Smoky should be back today. And...I guess..." I stopped, thinking that it was time to face up to the fact that I had to leave for Otherworld, to find the Keraastar Diamond. That was the next step in my evolution and one I couldn't get away from. The days till my coronation were counting down and I had to dive in and take the reins of what was quickly becoming a one-way ticket into unknown territory.

"Otherworld?" Delilah pushed back her plate. "We have all the spirit seals."

"Yes, we do. And so...the Keraastar Diamond. We'll need Menolly to go with Roz and bring back the Maharata-Verdi tonight. I'll have to take it with me. I'll contact Aeval and have her bring Venus. He'll be going." I held out my hand, trembling. "And you, Kitten. You still willing to journey with me?"

She nodded. "Of course. Who else?"

"I don't know. I thought I'd ask Aeval and Derisa. They'll be able to tell me." I thought back to Grandmother Coyote's words. "My world is about to grow so much bigger, and like Sharah, my life won't be my own anymore."

Delilah crossed behind me chair, leaning down to wrap her arms around me. "It will be all right. I promise. It will be okay."

"I know," I said, but inside, I couldn't help but wonder if she was right. Would I still be me after everything was said and done?

THE GATES OF Talamh Lonrach Oll were thirty minutes outside of Seattle on a day with moderate rain and moderate traffic, an hour if conditions were worse. Tonight, it was late so traffic was light, and the skies were clear. Smoky and Morio were with me. Delilah was driving her Jeep and Menolly and Vanzir were riding with her. The others had stayed back at the house to watch over things.

Smoky had shown up minutes before we were ready

to head out, and he hadn't had time to tell us about the council meeting in the Dragon Reaches yet. I let out a slow breath as I pressed on the gas pedal, speeding up. I was wearing my best skirt and corset—both black lace with silver embroidery—and a pair of black pumps fit to kill. They were strappy sandals, with four-inch chunky heels. I had brushed my hair till it shone, and I was wearing a silver necklace. My tattoos on my back—one from when I had first been initiated into the Moon Mother's service, and the second when I had been made a priestess—felt like they were practically glowing.

Every time I went out to the Sovereign Nation now, I had to represent myself as the Queen of Dusk and Twilight, even though I hadn't yet taken the crown. The moment I had heard the news that I would be taking the throne, I knew that I could never again appear there without being pulled together. Everything I said would be heard and analyzed by the Fae who lived there. And a number of them might not take kindly to a half-breed taking the throne. I had to hold myself up to be as beyond reproach. I was uncomfortable with the thought of being scrutinized, but I'd have to get used to it.

"What happened at the council meeting?" I glanced over at Smoky.

He looked tired, which in itself was unusual. "A lot of back and forth. There are those who are unhappy we've thrown our support behind the elves. They feel it weakens us to show any regard for anybody but our own kind. But Mother wore them down. I'll say this for her—she's got one hell of a way about her. I wish..." He drifted off, and then—after a deep breath—continued. "I wish she could have been free of Hyto earlier. But now, she's come into her own. She's being courted by several of the big Silver families, but she told me she's not interested in marrying again. I'm one of her only surviving children, but she says that's enough."

I often wondered if I'd meet any of Smoky's siblings, but wasn't sure I wanted to. Out of two clutches, only a younger brother and three sisters survived. Hyto was to thank for their mortality rate, as well.

"What was the outcome? Will they support me when the Great Fae Lords wake? Will they support Talamh Lonrach Oll?" That's what it all came down to.

"They will support you, and me. The debate was heated, but Mother pointed out that times have changed. Shadow Wing is on the fly, and the spirit seals have been found. We're already backing you in the demonic war. This is one step further. The world will change. All of the realms will, regardless of what they want. We are coming to a crossroads in history, as we did with the Great Divide."

I nodded, my eyes on the road. "Yeah, we are. And I need to pass my thanks on to Vishana. Having your people behind me means so much. As bad as Shadow Wing is, I have no idea what to expect with the Fae Lords."

"I know, my love. I know." A tendril of Smoky's hair rose and slowly stroked my shoulders.

From the backseat, Morio let out a sigh. "I confess, I have a strong fear that when you find the Keraastar Diamond and bring the Knights to bear, it will somehow trigger the path for Shadow Wing to come barreling through so the prophecy can be completed. There's no real basis for my fear, but it's there nonetheless."

"I thought of that myself," I said, turning onto a two-lane highway. We were headed into the wilds now. In the short time that Aeval and Titania had established the Sovereign Fae Nation, it was as though the land had taken new life, with trees and shrubs bursting forth with a massive amount of new growth.

Talamh Lonrach Oll stood at two thousand acres and Aeval had recently put in a bid on another fifteen hundred. The government had ordered a limit of five thousand acres for now, and I had no doubt within a year we'd be at that number. I also had the sneaking suspicion that Aeval and Titania were working magic to push the boundaries on that limit.

As we approached the ten-foot-tall silver-plated gates, I could feel the rush of earth energy. The elementals were happy, and the land was thick with life. Cedar and fir abounded, and stands of birch and maple. The Fae had planted an oak grove last year and the trees were springing up so incredibly fast. The ferns were waist high, and huckleberry bushes abounded, along with salmonberry and blackberry brambles and—unfortunately—stinging nettles. Skunk cabbage lined the stream that flowed through the reserve, and hostas and moss covered the ground.

No electricity was allowed within the borders of the gates, but magic was rife and energy itself thick and available. There were plenty of amenities, but they weren't powered by the outer world. No outsiders were allowed in without good reason, though occasionally Titania and Aeval would host days when guests could apply to visit, and a limited number of passes were granted.

I slowed as we approached the gates. Guards, ten of them, were watching the gate. The Fae militia was deadly and accurate in their aim. The guards motioned for us to pull in. The road curved toward the left, into a large parking lot. There were a number of cars here, most belonging to the Fae who lived on this land. This was as far as motorized vehicles were allowed to go. From here, it was either hoof it or take a horse and carriage.

Speaking of which, two carriages were waiting, each

drawn by a pair of gorgeous horses. Friesians, the horses were a good sixteen hands high, black as the inky night. They were strong and muscled, with a curling mane that rivaled Fabio's hair. Feathers flowed off the fetlocks, trimmed neatly so it billowed as they ran but didn't drag on the ground.

Smoky, Morio, and I took one carriage, while Menolly, Delilah, and Vanzir rode in the other. The lack of noise from the outer world—no electrical wires humming, no cars, no televisions or stereos playing—lulled me, calming my nerves. The sound of birdsong still echoed even though dusk had fallen and twilight was nearing. As I leaned back and closed my eyes, the pinpricks of magic skittered over my skin. This was old, deep magic. *Fae magic*, that saturated the land and everything on it.

Usually, when we came here, we had to borrow the carriage and drive ourselves, but from now on, that would be different. Ever since the proclamation went out about my impending ascent to the throne, I had always found a driver waiting for me, even on the visits where I hadn't let them know in advance that I was coming.

"How many do you think live out here now?" Smoky asked, keeping his voice soft.

"I don't know, but now that they are increasing the acreage to thirty-five hundred, I think that there will be quite a few Fae coming out here." I fell silent again, listening to the *click-clack* of the horses' hooves as they lightly trotted over the cobblestone path. Talamh Lonrach Oll was a wending maze of paths, with a lake at the center. The houses here were single story. No two-story houses were permitted, and absolutely no skyscrapers or apartment towers of any kind. The power that fueled the stoves and refrigerators came from geothermal energy, from the wind and the sun, and from magic.

The glimmer of eye catchers shimmered along the path, ethereal globes of pink, yellow, blue, and green lights. They were akin to will-o'-the-wisps, but without sentience. They were from Otherworld, a piece of my homeworld brought over Earthside. I wondered how long before the Fae from home and the Fae over here either got over the past and made up, or would be at each other's throats again. We weren't a gentle people, dancing around trees and kissing the earth. No matter how much we loved nature and the planet, we were also a warrior race, and not all Fae were nice by nature. Some were downright mean.

"Where are we meeting Aeval?" Morio asked.

"At the Barrow. *My* Barrow." It felt so strange claiming a palace for my own. I had been spending a lot of time out here, decorating the chambers that would be our private suite. At that moment, we curved around a large stand of fir and the Court of the Three Queens came into view. Contained within three giant barrow mounds, the palaces weren't castles in the sense of, say, Windsor Castle or Neuschwanstein, but they were palaces nonetheless, and while the barrow mounds gave some sense of size, the reality was that the courts and palaces within took up much more room. The world of Fae was like that.

Grass spread thickly over the top of the three mounds, and atop Titania's mound, a giant oak was growing, with rose gardens beneath it. Atop Aeval's mound, a huge elder tree blossomed and a garden of lilies spread out around the tree. Atop the barrow mound that contained the Court of Dusk and Twilight, a yew tree spread out in a tangle, as yew trees do, with a wide swath of bluebells beneath it. Fae were bustling around the courtyard, going about their business in the day-to-day running of the courts. I caught my breath at the beauty and symmetry of it all, and yet a wild, feral presence lurked behind the neatly trimmed grass and the carefully tended flowers.

The carriages rattled to a stop in front of what had been Morgaine's Barrow—now mine. We lightly descended, the footman who approached offering me their hand. The night was almost balmy and the magic of the land electrified the air, especially here.

"Lady Camille, Queen Aeval and Queen Titania await your presence within. I'm here to guide you." The guard was decked out in the silver and black of the Courts, and he guided us toward the entrance of the barrow. The energy around the Court of Dusk and Twilight seemed a bit muted. When Morgaine had killed herself, some of the light within the palace had died. I was smart enough to realize that it was up to me to bring it back.

We entered the palace and I was struck by just how silent it was. Morgaine may have been conniving, and she may have had ulterior motives, but she had inspired devotion in those who lived under her rule.

The Barrow itself was filled with a labyrinth of passages, all lit by a soft illumination that seemed to glow from within the walls. Our escort led us through a wide, winding corridor, past shops and apartments and what looked like government offices. I wasn't sure just how the structure of authority played out, but I knew I'd be finding out before long. There had been so little time to learn. I had only known for a few months that I was slated to take the throne, and with the battles we faced on the front with the war and trying to piece together our family and lives after our father had been killed, it felt like it had been nonstop chaos for months.

The decor here was almost ethereal, with the primary colors being in shades of blue and green and purple, black and silver. It was not so dark as Aeval's Barrow, nor light as Titania's. I stood between their two worlds, just like I stood between Otherworld and Earthside, between human and Fae. It was finally beginning to click that no, I wasn't a Windwalker—a nomad with no roots—but I had two homes, two allegiances, two worlds to which I belonged.

The underground street continued on, past another parade of shops and offices before it hit a T-junction, and there we turned to the right. The guard led us toward a set of stately double doors at the end of the corridor. A giant yew tree was etched on the heavy wood, with accents of silver and sparkling gems the size of my fist in the shades of the court. I wondered if they were real gems, or glass, but it made no difference to the beauty of the doors that led into the actual throne room and palace court.

When the guards who stood at either side of the doors saw us coming, they opened them wide, holding them for us as we passed through.

"You rate first-class service," Delilah whispered to me.

"I don't know if I will ever get used to this," I whispered back.

Menolly flashed us both a grin. "You and me both. This is the way it's going to be when I move to Roman's, though not quite so much pomp and a lot more sense of 'Screw up and you're dead for good.' Roman doesn't take mistakes well from his lackeys, although he's a fair man."

Roman, the Prince of the Vampire Nation, was definitely fair, I had to agree on that, but I'd pick living out here in the Barrows ten times over living in his court. The Fae knew how to hurt and torture, yes, but they didn't have fangs and they didn't drain blood. Generally.

As we entered the room, I caught my breath. It never failed to amaze me. The actual throne room was larger than our house, with ceilings that rose a good fifty feet. Balconies overlooked the side, and archers stood ready to take down any assassins who might make an attempt on the queen. Idly, I wondered who checked to make sure the archers themselves weren't of a nature to play drop-the-monarch.

The throne itself was handcrafted of yew, large and ornate with brass and silver fittings, and velvet cushions of the deepest plum. The throne sat up on a dais, ten steps leading up to it, against the back wall. Doors on either side were heavily guarded. The path to the throne was roped off on both sides with velvet ropes that matched the cushions, scalloping between silver-plated posts. There was an entry and exit passage from both doors to the throne itself, again roped off and guarded.

I stared at the throne, a lump rising in my stomach. The presence of the guards, the formality of the room, felt overwhelming and I pressed my lips together, assessing the rest of the room. Most of it was open, but toward the double doors through which we had come, long wooden benches lined both sides of the walkway, giving a place for people to sit while watching the proceedings of the court.

Toward the front of the benches, Aeval and Titania were waiting, along with Myrddin—the Merlin. Their various guards were keeping a close eye in every direction. We hurried up to them, Aeval motioning for the guards to let us through without searching us.

"Camille, let us retire into what will be your chambers to discuss the next step."

One thing I'd say for her—Aeval didn't waste time in small talk. We followed her out the right-hand door in back of the throne. We entered a small hallway that led to another set of double doors about twenty yards away. Once there, the guards opened the doors and checked the room, then waved us in. They shut the doors behind them and I presumed they would wait outside. Come to think of it, guards seemed to spend a lot of their time waiting.

I glanced around the chamber. A large, ornate desk sat toward the back. Bookshelves lined the walls, and two sofas—both the same leather of the chair behind the desk—sat kitty corner, facing the desk in an L-shape. The shelves were filled with books. This made me unaccountably happy. I loved books, and I loved to read.

"Working light." Aeval's command rang out, and the light quickly adjusted, growing bright enough for us to read by with no problem. I filed away the command for future reference.

Aeval motioned for us to all sit on the sofas. There wasn't quite room enough, but there were several other chairs scattered around the massive office and so Morio and Smoky dragged them over. I sat on one sofa, with Delilah and Menolly. Aeval and Titania sat on the other, with Myrddin behind them. Vanzir hesitantly took the spot beside Aeval as she patted the sofa next to her and motioned for him to join her.

"You found the last spirit seal?" It wasn't so much of a question as a statement.

I nodded. "Yes, we did. It's safe for now."

"Then the time has come for you to journey to Otherworld and look for the Keraastar Diamond. Now that all of the seals have been located, we can't possibly rest until you have established your control over them." Titania paused, then said, "Myrddin, why don't you tell them your news."

Myrddin looked decidedly unhappy. I still hadn't decided how much I liked the Merlin—he was aloof and somewhat rude, but he was devoted to helping both the Fae Queens and us.

"I received a communication from Trytian this morning. He's been keeping in touch with me, given the nature of the war." He paused.

Color me surprised. I had no clue Myrddin had connected with Trytian.

Trytian was a daemon—a subset of demons and devils. His father was leading a rout against Shadow Wing down in the Sub-Realms and he had gone to join the war. While I didn't trust the daemon as far as I could throw him, the fact was, in this war, we were on the same side.

"What did he say?" I almost didn't want to know, given how many twists and turns the war had taken over the years.

"He told me that Shadow Wing is backed into a castle on the far end of some mountain range. He's holed up tighter than a rabbit in a warren. The daemons have taken heavy losses, but things are unraveling now for Shadow Wing and he's losing members of his army. But Trytian also said to be wary. Shadow Wing has managed to enlist an ally none of us ever saw coming. One who can quite possibly manage to infiltrate Earthside even though he was long ago cast out into the Sub-Realms."

I glanced at Delilah and Menolly. We really didn't need yet another enemy at the gate. "Who? Worse than Telazhar?"

"Some might say so. Yerghan the Blade."

Menolly's eyes widened. "Yerghan? He still lives?"

"Yes. As you might know from your history, Yerghan was originally from Otherworld, but was then deported to the Subterranean Realms. He rode alongside Telazhar, and was the leader of the soldiers rather than the sorcerers. When Telazhar was captured, Yerghan managed to escape and was able to hide out for a long time before they captured him. Trytian says that Shadow Wing kept Yerghan and Telazhar apart because he feared they might topple him if they worked together."

Yerghan the Blade was one of those villains whom children in Otherworld talked about in whispered tones, hoping to avoid summoning any residue of his spirit. He was as ruthless as they came, wiping out entire villages with his rampaging hordes. He worked on one front during the Scorching Wars, Telazhar on another. I strained to remember what I could from our history lessons, but information about Yerghan was scarcer than that surrounding Telazhar.

"All I know is he was the Attila the Hun of Otherworld. Worse. You mean he wasn't killed? He was sent to the Sub-Realms? But he wasn't...Fae."

Menolly shook her head, the beads in her braids clicking against each other. "No, he wasn't Fae, but he wasn't human either. He belonged to some order, originally, like the Tygerian monks. I can't recall right offhand what it was, but he learned how to fight like no *jian-tu* ever could. We learned about him when we trained at the YIA."

Menolly had been one of the *jian-tu* before she was turned into a vampire. Elite athletes, the *jian-tu* were expert martial artists and acrobats, a lot like the Shaolin monks over Earthside.

"Unless Shadow Wing doesn't know the last spirit seal has been found, why would he try again? The only reason he could possibly have for sending Yerghan over is to hunt for it." Delilah frowned, shaking her head.

"Not necessarily. The question is: how much does Shadow Wing know about the *Keraastar Diamond*? If he knows about the prophecy, and puts enough pieces together, he might try to stop me before I can find it. Which would mean that if he *does* know we've found the last seal, he would know that my next step is to head for Otherworld to find the diamond and rebuild the Knights." I fell silent. The last thing I needed was a race against time with Shadow Wing's freaks coming after me.

I turned to Aeval. "What do you think?"

"I think it's time you left for Otherworld. And I think...that Shadow Wing may have figured out what's going on. So the sooner you leave the better." She motioned for silence as she held up a scroll and unrolled it. "This is a missive from Derisa. She says, '*It's time, Camille. Gather your things and journey to Otherworld. Do not go to Elqaneve. Instead, travel to Thistlewyd Deep and head into the Tygerian Mountains from there. The Moon Mother will be with you.*'"

And with that, the room fell silent.

Chapter 9

AEVAL LEANED BACK in her seat. "I have more news for you, and you aren't going to like it but you will listen and do what I say."

I blinked. "Nothing good ever begins with the words 'You aren't going to like it.' What is it?" There was no use arguing. I knew that—no matter what I said—I'd end up following her instructions, so I might as well just have her come out with it.

"You're taking Bran with you. He can lead you safely through Thistlewyd Deep. You will also meet Raven Mother there. Even though the Moon Mother doesn't like her, Raven Mother is definitely on our side in this." Aeval waited for my outburst, a faint smile on her lips.

I stared at her. They'd stuck me with Bran when I went in search of the Merlin, and that had been hard enough. But the look in Aeval's eyes was firm and I knew that no matter what, this wasn't up for debate.

"Fine. Any other curveballs you want to throw me?"

"Menolly cannot go, but I think that was already a given."

I nodded. "Yeah, but Delilah's coming with me. And Morio, and Smoky." I glanced over at Vanzir. "What about him?"

Aeval broke in. "The father of my child will not go tromping off on this mission. But I recommend that you take Trillian instead of Morio—you should leave someone at your house along with your sister, and Trillian has been in the mountains before. Take Shade. Venus will be coming with you, of course. And there is one more who will go with you, although you may question why. He'll need help keeping up, but you can manage."

I straightened. Who could she be talking about? I was about to ask when the door opened and Chase entered, a guard behind him.

I jumped up. "Chase? What are you doing here?" Then, suddenly understanding, I turned back to Aeval. "Are you kidding?"

"No. He must go with you and don't ask, because I don't even know why myself. But it is simply...what must be. Derisa received the same vision as well."

"But..." I stared at him, dreading the journey. Chase was in good condition for an FBH, and the tiny bit of elf blood in him didn't hurt in the slightest, but he couldn't keep up with us and we all knew it.

"It's going to happen, Camille. Accept it." Aeval let out a long sigh. "Welcome, Detective Johnson."

Chase looked confused. "I'm not sure why I'm here. You needed me for some reason?"

"Yes." She crossed to his side and inclined her head. "Detective, we are at a crossroads in history. Camille is about to take the most important journey of her life, and you need to go with her. Don't ask why—I cannot give you an answer. But I *know* that you must go with her."

He glanced at me, concern washing across his face. "Are you all right?"

I nodded, biting my tongue. I had no idea what to say to him.

"Chase," Delilah said, crossing to him. "We found the last spirit seal."

She let this sink in for a moment and as we watched, a dawning recognition crept into his eyes. He let out a loud sigh and dropped into a chair.

"It's finally over, then?"

"No. This is a dangerous time. Remember that when all the seals are found, she must search out the Keraastar Diamond and take her place as the leader of the Keraastar Knights. It's time for Camille to journey to Otherworld and find the diamond. Some of us are going with her, and Aeval says that you need to go with us."

Delilah's voice was soft in a way mine could never be—not in timbre, but in the way she phrased things. She really did have a maternal nature and though it had taken awhile to show itself, now it blossomed fully out. As she grew stronger, so did her gentle side.

"You want me... But I can't. My duties—I have to..." He stopped. After a moment, he shrugged. "This is one of those times when I really don't have a choice, do I? I do what you need me to because the Hags of Fate or the Mistress of Destiny—"

"There's no such person," I mumbled.

"Whatever. Because destiny itself has slammed down and decreed that we all get to take a ride together." He sounded a little bitter, but when I met his gaze, he smiled softly. "Yeah, I know. We do what we have to do. I'll figure out a way. Yugi can take over while I'm gone. He's my second-hand man, anyway." Then a gleam flickered into his eye. "Maybe I can catch a few minutes in Elqaneve, with Sharah."

"Um...maybe. I don't really know what the itinerary will be like, but we'll do our best. That much I can promise." I clapped him on the shoulder. "Thanks,

Chase. I was as surprised as you were, but if there's a reason you need to be there, I'd rather not fly in destiny's face."

He sobered. "Yeah, that I agree with. I've learned that much hanging out with the three of you. When do we leave?"

I glanced over at Aeval. "Do we have a day or two?"

She consulted Titania and Myrddin, then said, "One day. Today's Saturday. Leave on Monday morning, before first light. Spend tomorrow preparing. Above all, don't dawdle. Set the portal in the Wayfarer to transport you to the one near Dahnsburg Lake. You'll have to hire horses to reach Thistlewyd Deep, and then to the mountains, but that shouldn't be a problem. Bran will meet you at the bar at four A.M. on Monday." She turned to Myrddin. "Any last advice?"

"The Tygerian monks can help you, but they are deadly. Do not cross them. Be cautious of how much trust you place in them. The Order of the Crystal Dagger is a secret society, and so elusive and powerful that they are banned in most cities save for Aladril. The fact is that we don't know how they will play into this, so walk cautiously, accept help if you absolutely need it, and do not offend." Myrddin's expression was difficult to read, but his body language was wary.

"When will Venus join us?" Delilah asked.

"We'll bring him down to the Wayfarer, along with Bran. Be there, and be ready. Until then, keep your eyes open. While I doubt Shadow Wing will send Yerghan over now, there's always that chance. If Trytian is right, then you must be prepared for the possibility of attack the moment you land in Otherworld. That's why we aren't sending you to Elqaneve where they'd expect you to go." And with that, Aeval motioned toward the door. "You may leave. We'll see you on Monday morning."

As we headed out into the night, Chase accompanying us, I shivered. The temperature had dropped and a moist chill was setting in, the scent of cedars and fir drifting on the wind. I couldn't help but wonder why Chase had been added to the group, and I wasn't thrilled that Bran would be tagging along yet again.

Speak of the devil, as we exited the Barrow, I glanced to the right and there, leaning against the door, was Bran, a sly gleam in his eye. He saluted to me, in an almost dismissive manner, but said nothing. I stared at him for a moment, then turned and—without a word—crossed to the carriage.

SUNDAY PASSED ALL too quickly. I was packing for the trip—and it was difficult to pack for a trip that I didn't know the length of—trying to fit the necessities into my pack. Delilah was sitting on my bed, one leg folded on the bed, swinging the other over the side. She handed me underwear that she had rolled into a neat ball.

"Rozurial went with Smoky to retrieve the Maharata-Verdi. While Menolly went with him to hide it, there's no reason for secrecy now. At least he thought to put a Trace on it when they left it there, so he shouldn't have a problem finding it." She flopped back on the bed, stretching her arms over her head. "Enjoy your mattress tonight. It will be the hard ground after this until we find the diamond."

"I'm not looking forward to that." I didn't add that I wasn't looking forward to any part of the trip. Everything was too chaotic. I wanted to just take the crown and settle down quietly. "I wish we could just destroy all of the seals and be done with it."

"You know that's not possible. It's too dangerous."

"I know, but I can dream, can't I?" I paused, then pushed my pack aside and stretched out beside her. "Do you know why Chase is going?"

Delilah didn't even bat an eyelash. "Nope. I wish I did. It's not like we're going to Elqaneve, even though I know he's hoping for a chance to see Sharah. She hasn't told him yet, has she? That she's expected to bear a full-blooded heir."

I shook my head, staring at the ceiling. "I don't think so. If she did, surely he would have said something. The dude's got an even quicker temper than Smoky, I think." Pausing, I snorted. "Maybe not, but he's not that far behind."

"I know he took the day off to spend it with Astrid before he has to leave. I wish Menolly could come with us, but it's just too dangerous. If we got caught somewhere without shelter and she was in the sunlight—"

"Not only that, but we'll make faster time by day. More of the dangerous creatures come out at night. We have to make quick, steady progress." I paused, closing my eyes. "Delilah?"

"Yeah?"

"What if Yerghan really does show up? The history books all say there's no one to beat him at the sword. And he's had a thousand years down in the Sub-Realms. He's bound to have grown stronger. Who knows what kind of powers he possesses?"

"I don't think we can cross that bridge till we come to it, but I will tell you this: regardless of his powers, if he shows up Smoky and Shade will whale on his ass. Two dragons against one warrior? I wouldn't worry about it." Delilah stretched and yawned. "I suppose I'd better head to my room and pack. Shade said he'd do most of it, but you know men. They never know what's important and what isn't. He'll probably put lace bras in there and forget all about undershirts to keep the chill away."

At that, I laughed. I waved her off to her own room and finished my packing. Smoky and Trillian had already pulled together their packs. It suddenly occurred to me that there would only be Morio, Vanzir, and Menolly here to look over the land. But Aeval had promised to send extra guards to keep an eye on Hanna, Iris and her mother-in-law, Maggie, and the babies. That would at least give me some comfort. And Nerissa would be here.

I stuffed the last pair of panties in my pack that I had room for, and then set it on the floor next to those of the men. I propped my staff against the wall and laid out my traveling clothes—a spidersilk skirt in black, a plum tunic woven of the same material, a black cloak—though I chose not to take the unicorn cloak with me. No sense in alerting people to who I was or what I might have with me. I opted for boots with a half-inch heel and good tread that would help me while climbing up a mountain side, because the Tygerian Mountains were a huge sprawling range of peaks that rivaled the Swiss Alps. They made the Cascades look like foothills. Mount Tyger was the tallest, and about one-third of the way up was where the main monastery was for the Order of the Crystal Dagger. If we had to go there, well—I wanted to be prepared.

Finally, I placed my dagger and sheath on top of the backpack. That was all I could think of to take. The horn was depleted and I'd have to charge it under the dark of the moon. It wouldn't do me any good to carry it with me. One last thought, and I was standing by my jewelry box. The trip would be long and arduous, and we would probably run into more danger than I wanted to think about. I slowly placed my wedding rings—all three of them—into the top drawer of the armoire. I didn't want to risk losing them.

Then, as ready as I'd ever be, I clattered down the

stairs to the kitchen.

Hanna was preparing more sandwiches than we'd have room for, but she wanted to help. Iris was giving her a hand, and the twins were playing quietly in a playpen. They were around eight months old, and they had Iris's golden hair and their father's twinkling eyes. I leaned down and chucked them under their chins, then gave them each a big kiss. Next to them was Astrid, who was also eight months old. Chase was in the rocking chair, watching the babies while Iris helped cook.

"Oh, Iris, they're growing so fast. And Chase, I swear, Astrid looks more like you every day." I wasn't a maternal woman. Nothing in my body had ever screamed "Make a baby" and in my heart, I knew that path was not the right one for me. Having children wasn't anywhere near my bucket list, though I went all googly-eyed over baby animals. Baby people? Not so much. I had no clue what to do with them. But I appreciated my friends' children all the more, and I swore I'd be their crazy old Auntie Camille.

"They're near to walking, and won't that be a mess." But Iris laughed as she spread mayo on bread and arranged the slices. Hanna followed her with meat and cheese, then Iris added lettuce and ketchup. "The Duchess has turned into a surprisingly doting nanny."

"She doesn't stint on taking care of Astrid, either," Chase said, smiling softly at his daughter. "I walked in on them the other day and she was rocking her and singing a lullaby to her. I admit, the lyrics were unique, but it's the mood that counts." He laughed, then. "*'Go to sleep, little warrior, caught between worlds, Raise your banner and let it unfurl'* isn't exactly what I'd choose to sing to my daughter, but hey, I'm not complaining."

Iris burst out laughing. "The Duchess is convinced

Astrid's going to grow up to be a mighty warrior queen, Chase. I don't know why, but like you, I don't argue with her. It's not worth it because she always wins."

The Duchess was actually a duchess. Iris was married to Bruce O'Shea, or rather, Lord Bruce Golden Eagle O'Shea. His parents were a duke and duchess in the Leprechaun Court, and they were so moneyed that they made dragons look poor. The Duchess was haughty and always had the last word, but by now we had all figured out that she liked Iris well enough, and she doted on her grandchildren. She came to help Iris whenever Bruce got it into his head to take off on a research trip or whatnot. At the beginning, it had made Iris terribly uncomfortable, but now she welcomed the company.

"Well, she's going to grow up to be amazing, that I agree with." Chase lifted Astrid out of the playpen and held her up, then pulled her close to his heart and kissed the top of her head. "I love you so much. Don't you ever forget that," he whispered.

Watching Chase, I couldn't help but smile. He had started out being a lecher who was out to get in my pants, then he'd been Delilah's insecure lover. But once he and Sharah realized they had feelings for each other, he had blossomed. Now, as a father, he was hard to resist. He doted on his daughter, and he pined for her mother.

Delilah entered the room and swept up Maggie, who was securely trapped in her new, sturdier playpen. "Oh, Maggie my girl, how are you?"

"Don't let her near the babies," Iris warned.

"Don't worry, I won't." Delilah sat down over by the table. "Where's Menolly?"

"She and Nerissa are downstairs. I'm not sure what they're doing but they said to not bother with dinner tonight, they'd take care of it. What that means, I can only shudder to imagine." Hanna laughed. "Your sister, she is a fighter unparalleled but neither she nor that wife of hers can cook worth a damn."

"Well, it's rather understandable, given she can't taste any of the food she cooks. My guess is takeout." I wasn't willing to defend Menolly's culinary skills if it meant eating her food, but I felt it only right to point out why she was so lacking in the pots-and-pans department. Although, come to think of it, when we lived in Otherworld, before she was turned, Menolly hadn't been much of a cook, either. She always did her best to opt out of helping in the kitchen.

A few minutes later, the door to her lair opened. We had replaced the secret bookcase that originally led to her basement suite with a solid metal door that would be almost impossible for any wannabe vampire hunter to break through.

Menolly popped her head out. "Good evening. You didn't eat already, did you?"

I shook my head. "No, but those sandwiches Hanna and Iris are making for tomorrow look damned good. I gather you're providing dinner?"

The doorbell rang at that moment. Menolly wove through the crowded kitchen. "Yes, and that's it." She and Nerissa hushed us, making us stay where we were.

I glanced around. "Where are the others?" Smoky, Morio, Trillian, Shade, and Vanzir were absent. Roz was in the living room.

"They decided to do a quick patrol of the land. They took the new guards that Aeval assigned to watch over the place, to show them the layout. They'll be back in a few minutes."

Iris finished making the last sandwich and she and Hanna began packaging up the food, along with cookies and protein bars and apples for the road. We'd have to pick up trail rations when we got there, but that shouldn't be a problem.

"Here now, you'll have food for tomorrow and the next day, at least." Hanna set the rucksack on the counter. "Don't sit on it or you'll have flat sandwiches. I also tucked in a couple dozen hard-boiled eggs."

At that moment, Menolly and Nerissa returned, carrying two towers of boxes and bags. As they set them on the table and we began spreading them out, the aroma of barbecue filtered out.

"Ribs! From the Wayfarer?"

Menolly nodded. "I know how much you love them, so I had the new cook fix up enough for everybody. Also some slaw, macaroni and cheese, garlic bread, and a lemon cake."

Smoky and the other men trooped in right about then. There was a general chaos of washing up as Hanna and Iris set the table. Chase carried the babies into Hanna's bedroom while Roz followed with the detachable car seats that made for handy portable beds, and between the two of them, they tucked the three children in for naps. Delilah moved Maggie's playpen into the living room and she, too, fell asleep.

As we gathered around the oak table, Iris and Hanna included, and held hands, I closed my eyes and dropped my head back. "Moon Mother, watch down over us. Lady Undutar, guard this house and home. Lady Bast, watch over our felines—and watch over Maggie. Be with us, guard us in our journeys and guide us safely home again. Protect the house and hearth while we're gone, and let us rejoice in this, the family we've created."

And with that, we set to, one last night of feasting. The laughter rose, and the noise of clattering plates and silverware rang out, along with shouts of "Pass the ribs!" and "Toss me a hunk of bread, will you?" and "Is there any more salad?"

I sat back, eating, watching the people I loved the most. Tomorrow would bring the beginning of a change that would forever affect us. I wasn't sure how I felt about it, but for now, we were safe and together, and the love was flowing.

EARLY THE NEXT morning, we gathered at the Wayfarer. Nobody was there except Derrick, who had agreed to meet us. He quietly escorted us to the basement. Menolly had stayed home—it was too close to sunrise. And we had asked Vanzir and Morio to wait at home. Smoky, Trillian, Rozurial, Chase, Delilah, Shade, and I were there. Smoky took my pack from me, and Shade offered to carry Delilah's but she shook her head. Instead, he held out his hand to Chase and—without a word—Chase handed over his pack. He knew he was the weak link, and by now, his ego had evolved enough to admit it and do whatever he could to strengthen himself.

Aeval appeared with Bran and Venus, and she motioned me off to one side.

"You are walking into a dangerous situation, yes, but please do not fear. Fear is your enemy. Be cautious, watch for ambush, but remain focused on your goal. You are destined to become the Queen of Dusk and Twilight, and the Hags of Fate do not deal out destinies willy-nilly. You will find the diamond, and return, and after that..." Her voice trailed off, leaving a soft sigh in its wake. "After that, you will begin to understand the true nature of your power and your potential, Camille Sepharial te Maria D'Artigo." She kissed me on the forehead. "Go now, and return as soon as you can. Even I cannot predict where this is leading, but I'm looking forward to finding out."

She stood back and nodded for us to proceed. Derrick, who was versed in using the portal, had set the destination for Dahnsburg Lake, near Thistlewyd Deep.

"It's important you tell no one where we went. I don't care who asks." I walked toward the portal.

"I understand. Menolly explained matters to me last night. Well, I have a strong suspicion a great deal was left out, but what I don't know, I can't tell. Go and be safe, Camille." The werebadger clapped me on the shoulder. "I think whatever you're doing, it's important to more than just you. So be safe."

"Thanks, Derrick. Watch after Menolly, would you?"

He laughed at that. "Right, like Roman won't be doing that." He lowered his voice. "Digger told me that Roman's sent out some security forces to watch over your place. Menolly doesn't know because he didn't want her to, but go with a light heart. He's taking care of his Princess's family." With that, he snorted.

I flashed him a conspiratorial smile. "I know. Every time I think of Menolly as a princess, it triggers the word *oxymoron*. Okay, we're heading out. Be safe."

The portal was a spiraling vortex of energy inside of a compartment that had been built around it. The waves of energy were pulsing blue, and I steeled myself for the disorientation they caused. But it was the only way to reach Otherworld, and we had been through them time and again. With a deep breath, I turned to make sure everybody was ready, and then—before I could change my mind—plunged through the portal.

WALKING INTO A portal is kind of like walking into a bug zapper. Imagine being jolted with the most electrifying shock you've ever felt, as every atom in your body suddenly whirls apart, spreading out into the universe. Then, just as your mind seems to be hanging by a thread, the rubber band snaps and all your atoms go flinging back together with a thud and you suddenly find yourself in another place, relatively in one piece.

I stumbled through the two giant cedars that housed the portal outside of Thistlewyd Deep. To my back was the Windwillow Valley, a vast stretch of grassland and plains, where trees were scarce and the constant wind whistled through the long blades of grass, sending them in a rippling wave that traveled across the expanse.

Beyond the valley to the east, the Nebulveori Mountains rose, a swath of peaks that dwarfed anything over Earthside. The dwarves held rule there, along with giants and ogres and trolls. Goblins also, though the goblin city of Guilyoton was found between the Ranakwa Fens and the southernmost tip of Darkynwyrd.

I had been to this portal once before, coming from Dahnsburg. Now, that seemed like such a long time ago even though it had only been two years. As I reached out to steady myself, someone took my arm. With a gasp, I started to leap backward, but was startled to see Raven Mother holding tight to my wrist, her eyes gleaming.

"Camille, oh we meet again very soon, do we not? Meet again, we do. Welcome to Thistlewyd Deep. Surely you remember your last trip here, my dear?"

I glanced around, wondering if the Black Unicorn was near. "Is...*he*...here, too?"

"No, he's off running wild in Darkynwyrd, he is, my husband. But make haste and move out of the way, for another is coming through."

She pulled me out of the way as Smoky appeared. He stared at Raven Mother for a moment, frowning, but then quickly stepped to my side, putting a little distance between her and me. After that, Delilah came through, then Shade and Chase. Bran was next—and he quickly crossed to his mother's side and gave her a peck on the cheek. After Bran, Venus appeared, then Rozurial, and we were all together.

"I have your horses, I do. They are waiting for you in the glade nearby." Raven Mother motioned for us to follow her. "Derisa bade me find the fastest I could, and the ones best suited for mountain terrain. I brought in Nebulveori mountain horses, from the dwarves. These are swift steeds who can navigate rocky climes."

She motioned to the side where a team of horses stood. Tan in color, with blond manes, they looked sturdy and used to hard work. Given the dwarves love for metals, it was easy enough to figure they were used to carry ore out of the mines up in the Nebulveori range. The dwarven mountains were as rough as the Tygerian Mountains, if not worse.

"The horses should do well for us. If they can handle working for the dwarves, they can handle carrying us into the hills." I wandered over to where the animals were standing and gently patted one on the head. He whinnied, tossing his mane as he nudged me with his muzzle. His nostrils flared and he snorted warm air in my face. "Easy boy, you're a nice horse, aren't you?"

Delilah stroked the side of the horse. "I wish we didn't have to rely on Raven Mother."

I felt the same way, but glanced over to where she was talking with Smoky. "I know, but the truth is, she can help us. And as much as I don't want Bran along, there's nothing we can do about him either. We have to bring him. Aeval said so. Given that he gave me more help than I expected when we went after Myrddin, I'm not going to cause trouble."

"Hurry," Raven Mother cautioned, *tsk*ing loudly. "We are on the outskirts of the Deep, and we must make haste. There are creatures around here that would not hesitate to attack a large party, although with me at your side, they will not dare. But I must be off soon and will not be able to accompany you to the mountains."

Thistlewyd Deep belonged to Raven Mother and was far darker than even Darkynwyrd, which was a shadow land in itself, filled with primal creatures and those who lived between the light and the dark. The forest was the incarnation of magic, alive as any one of us and even more so. As frightening as it could be to strangers, to those who ran with the Hunt—like me—it fit like a glove. The energy was joyously feral, and as I watched the treeline in front of us, the shrubs and undergrowth shook as if a giant wind swept past them.

"Saddle up, my friends." Raven Mother held out the reins of a horse with a star on its forehead. "Camille, I picked this one for you. She will lead you well, and you can trust her to find her way in the dark. She is used to fell folk, and will not startle in battle. The others are also acclimated to swordplay. The dwarves have a time fending off those who would steal from them. Their beasts of burden must be stalwart as well."

I patted the horse on the head and she nuzzled me. One look in her eye and I knew we were going to get along fine. "What's her name?"

"Dwarves don't tend to name their horses," Trillian said, coming up behind me. He helped me to fasten my staff to a holder that was connected to the saddle so I wouldn't have to hold it. The horse didn't seem to mind it there, parallel to its body. "They aren't very sentimental."

"Well, everybody should have a name." I patted her muzzle again and she whinnied, as though she were enjoying it. "I'm going to call her Annabelle."

"Let me help you up onto Annie's back, then." Trillian held the stirrup as I placed my foot into it, then grasping the horn of the saddle, I swung myself up. I adjusted my skirts so they weren't trapped between my legs and the saddle and was immediately grateful I'd put on tights.

Delilah and the others mounted their horses, although as Smoky and Shade neared their mounts, the horses shifted nervously. They could probably smell dragon scent. Once we were all seated, Bran rode to the front. He turned, handling his horse like an expert.

"I know Venus needs to direct where we're to go, but for now, we need to get away from the borders of the Deep and into the forest. We don't know if we're being followed." He lowered his voice and looked directly at me. "The demons watch you and your sisters. For all we know, they could have seen you walk into the bar this morning, and not leave. We can be sure they know the spirit seals have all been found. Shadow Wing's intelligence agency is clever and cunning. Best not to take chances. We'll ride to a safe place my mother has prepared, and there the old shaman can give us our coordinates."

Without another word, he turned back to the path and led us into Thistlewyd Deep as Raven Mother watched from behind. I glanced back at her. She said nothing, but raised one hand. I decided to take it as a blessing on our journey.

Chapter 10

THISTLEWYD DEEP ENVELOPED us like a glove enveloping a hand. It sucked us in, closing away the world outside. The outskirts of the Windwillow Valley had been alive with the sound of droning bees and bird song that flickered through the air. The hum of summer reverberated through the valley, but the moment we passed into the borders of the Deep, the sounds changed. Oh, it wasn't silent here, not by any stretch of the imagination, but the birdsong changed to echoing calls, haunting and lonely. And bees still skimmed the bushes and flowers, but their hum was drowned out by that of the forest itself. The magic ran so thick here in the Deep that it tattooed its own beat, low and resonant, through the woodland.

Delilah nudged her mount over toward me, so we were riding side by side. She hadn't ever been to Thistlewyd Deep, although she had been through Darkynwyrd, which could easily be a wooded nightmare of its own.

"The forest makes me uneasy. I feel we're being

watched," she said in low tones.

"That's because we are. We have a couple days' ride to get through this part of the Deep so you might as well get used to it. This is where I felled..." I stopped, glancing ahead at Bran. If he could hear us, he made no indication. "The Black Beast. Within this wood."

"The forest practically reeks with Raven Mother's energy. Everything feels chaotic and topsy-turvy. I wouldn't want to live here." She shuddered, but when Bran gave a quick glance over his shoulder, she fell silent.

"Watch what you say here. And watch what you think. As deadly as the goblins and their ilk are, this is probably one of the most dangerous places in Otherworld." I used my knee to nudge my mount to quicken her pace. The sooner we were through the Deep and into the mountains the better. But I was curious about the safe place Bran had mentioned. The words "safe" and "Thistlewyd Deep" didn't exactly go together.

We rode in silence for some time. I wasn't sure how long—watches didn't work very well in the Deep, and I couldn't wear one anyway. My aura stopped them like... well...like clockwork. But the morning gave way to noon before Bran motioned to a side path off trail. He *tsk*ed at his horse and turned to the left, heading northwest into the thicket of undergrowth that carpeted the forest floor. Foliage grew knee high here, ferns and brambles, shashka bushes and ivyvine. The forest was a lot like those of the Pacific Northwest over Earthside, coniferous and ancient. The oak groves tended to grow in the Elfin lands, but here, conifers ruled, tall fir and spruce, sequoia and cedar.

We followed Bran for a couple of miles to the edges of a large pond. Once there, he swung off his horse and motioned for us to follow. As we dismounted, a thick fog began to rise up around us, encasing us in a ring of mist.

"The mist will protect us from prying eyes and ears for a while. We'll rest and eat here, and Venus can tell us what he needs to tell us." Bran led his mount to the water, letting the animal drink. Delilah and Trillian gathered the rest of the horses and did the same.

Meanwhile, Bran settled by a ring of stones that had been used as a fire pit at some time in the past, although it looked like it had been a while, judging by the state of the charred wood within. He knelt and struck a match to some kindling, settling in to make a tidy little fire. "We won't be here too long, but the forest will soon grow damp and chill the further we go, so if you want some hot tea or something, I suggest you make it now. After this, we ride until sunset and that's at least another seven hours."

"I'll make the tea," Shade said. He brought out a pan from his backpack. "I've also got a skillet, for when we run out of Hanna's sandwiches. Which, given the number of us, won't be long in coming." He settled in to heat water, while the rest of us formed a makeshift circle around the fire. The ground was damp, so Smoky and Rozurial found several downed trunks and dragged them over for us to sit on.

Chase was looking around, his eyes wide. "I've been to Otherworld several times now, but I never expected anything like this." His voice was hushed. "It's...beyond words. I can feel the forest. It's like an animal crouching around us."

"Wait until we're in the thick of it, Detective." Bran walked over to stand by him. "At the heart of the Deep, the magic is so thick it makes those who are head blind nauseated. It's intoxicating and heady, and very, very deadly if you don't watch your step."

Chase shuddered, just enough to tell me he was afraid. But he took a seat on one of the logs and held out his hands to the fire. "I don't know why I had to come, but I suppose I'll find out in good time."

Venus cleared his throat. "Let's get this show on the road. I'm here because Queen Asteria entrusted me with the location of the Maharata-Vashi. The Maharata-Verdi contains the incantation to awaken the diamond. The Maharata-Vashi contains the location to find the—" Here, he paused, glancing around. "Safe haven or not, I will not speak the actual name aloud here. You need it to find the gem you seek. The reason we came this way is because the Maharata-Vashi rests in a cavern where the foothills of the Tygerian Mountains kiss the edge of Thistlewyd Deep."

"Do you know what cave? There must be an abundance of caverns in the Tygerian range." Smoky reached in his pocket and pulled out a pipe, which he filled and began to smoke. He never smoked in the house because smoke bothered both Delilah and me, but when he was out at his barrow, and when he was outside for some time, he indulged. I wasn't sure what mixture it was that he smoked—it definitely wasn't tobacco—but he seemed to enjoy it.

Venus snickered. "If I didn't know, I wouldn't be much use to you, would I?" He arched his eyebrows. "The answer is yes. Queen Asteria, rest her soul, taught me a riddle that will lead to the scroll."

"Let's hear it," Rozurial said. "I have the Maharata-Verdi with me, safely tucked away among my weapons. I suggest that when we find the other scroll, someone else carry that one so that if we're ambushed, we have a chance of keeping them from both being stolen."

Accepting an aluminum mug of tea from Shade, Venus leaned forward, resting his elbows on his knees. "Here's what I was taught." He cleared his throat, and then in a low voice, began to sing.

Where bridge crosses a stream that winds like a snake,
There find the juncture, the north path you will take.
Trees that blossom white, even in the snow,
Signal that you're on the path, where you need to go.
By a boulder wide, that's giant as a troll,
Bend to your right, bewaring rocks that roll.
Follow the song of the martingeese,
It will lead you to the cavern that you seek.

I frowned. "So we need to find a bridge over a winding stream. Then take the north path at the juncture... Trees that blossom white, even in the snow?"

"Canaberry trees. They blossom during the winter. The white flowers fall off in early spring and return in late summer, so right now they will be just budding. But I know what to look for." Bran snorted at my look. "So surprised I know my flowers?"

"No, but—well. Yes." I held his gaze for a moment and then laughed. "Do you blame me? Anyway, so we find canaberry trees and continue along. Then, we look for a gigantic boulder as big as a troll and there, we listen for the sound of the martingeese. I assume they're thick around that area. The cavern should be near there."

"Well, it's not exactly a map, but it's better than nothing and should serve as a general guide." Smoky handed out sandwiches from the pack to everyone. "Eat hearty. You'll need the energy. Riding a horse may not seem that difficult but I guarantee that you'll be sore by the end of the day, and hungry enough to eat your mounts. I promise that Shade and I won't eat ours." He laughed. I groaned at the bad joke.

"I hope you don't or you two will be walking the rest of the way."

Chase bit into the hearty beef and cheddar sandwich. "So the second scroll gives the location of the diamond itself?"

I nodded. "Yes. But we need both scrolls for me to claim it. I've got no idea what goes into the process and frankly, I'm not looking forward to finding out. These things are never as simple as *Grab object, state claim, bingo it's done*. Especially with something of this magnitude."

Venus swallowed a bite of his food and then wiped his mouth on his sleeve. "Do you realize, you'll be my boss, so to speak. I'll be in your service, as will Luke and Amber."

I ducked my head, thinking of Tam Lin and Benjamin, two lost souls who had carried the spirit seals, and died because of them. When Telazhar had razed Elqaneve, he had managed to scatter the Keraastar Knights. Tam and Benjamin died, while Venus, Luke, and his sister Amber had managed to escape. Three knights out of nine, which meant six slots that I had to fill. And it couldn't just be anybody—the person who wielded the spirit seal had to mesh with the energy, and a bond was formed that—if the seal was forcibly taken from the Knight—would kill them.

"I can't even imagine what it's going to require to find matches for all of the gems. I can't just hold open tryouts, like casting calls." I accepted a couple of cookies from Delilah, then polished off an apple after that.

"I think the seals will take care of that, once you're in possession of the diamond," Bran said. At first I thought he might be making fun of me, but the expression on his face wasn't a smirk, like usual. "I think your biggest problem will be fending off those who would see you dead because of your new positions. Camille, you bear the hide and horn—of my father. You're taking the throne as one of the Earthside Fae Queens. You're the Earthside High Priestess of the Moon Mother. I don't mean to be alarmist, but you should be wary. Not everyone is going to be all happy-happy joy-joy about this. And once you claim the Keraastar Knights? It's no longer simply a demon lord that you have to fear. There will be others only too happy to slap you back into what they deem your place in life."

"Until recently, you seemed to be one of those," I said. I wasn't letting him off the hook that easily. Bran had been a thorn in my side for too long.

He slowly stood, tossing his napkin in the fire as he stared me down. "You know why I feel how I do. But my mother has a special place in her beady little heart for you, and I kneel to her wisdom on this. She would see us wed, if at all possible." Smoky jumped to his feet but Bran held out one hand. "Back, lizard. I am not out to steal your wife."

"See that you aren't," Trillian said, also rising.

"My mother would see us paired off. If you were amenable, I would accept her decree but trust me, you may have three husbands but I doubt if even you could satisfy my carnal nature. I enjoy variety, and I also prefer my paramours to be as crafty as I am. You're too soft-hearted for me." He was speaking without guile now, intent and focused on me. "We might as well clear the air completely. I bend to my mother's will because she could unmake me as easily as she bore me. My father dotes on her. And now that he's returned, I'm no longer overly anxious to see you in the grave that you thrust *him* into."

I tried to calm my breathing. Bran grated on me. He was too damned handsome for his own good, and too dangerous to ever consider courting even in friendship.

"Then understand this: I don't trust you and I probably never will. But I work with you because destiny seems to have thrown our lots together and I'm not willing to fly in the face of the Hags of Fate, or of Aeval and Titania. And they both want you along on this journey. I am grateful, however, that you are guiding us through the Deep. So let's find a civil middle ground and stay there, shall we?"

"As you will," he said, then turned back to his horse. "Everyone, finish your meals, attend to any needs you may have, and let's be off again. We ride until sundown, which should put us close to the bridge. If I have my bearings right, we should reach the area where the cavern is by noon tomorrow."

And with that, Delilah and I cleaned up and found a private place in the woods to use as a restroom. After we washed our hands and faces in the pond, we returned to our mounts and Bran led us back to the trail, and we set off again, into the depths of Thistlewyd Deep.

***

SUNSET CAME LATE and my lower back and butt were aching as I swung off the horse. I brushed her down and led her to a patch of grass where the other horses were eating. It felt like I was walking with bowed legs for the first few minutes until I did some toe-touch stretches and shook myself out. I unhooked my staff from the saddle and propped it near the area where Trillian spread out both his bedroll and mine.

Bran kindled a fire, making certain to ring it with stones so it wouldn't flare out of control.

We were near a stream, and the trees were so thick in this area of the Deep that they blocked out most of the remaining light. A chill began to fill the air, a sour tang of moisture that never left the forest, retained within the mulched carpet of detritus that covered the forest floor. Delilah motioned to me and I joined her as she began to set out more sandwiches and cookies.

"There's enough protein bars left for breakfast, but we'll have to find food after that." She portioned out the sandwiches—two per person. "I wish we had something hot to go with this. Even though it's June, it's going to be chilly tonight."

Bran leaned on a tall branch he had found near one of the trees. "We can make a fish broth, if someone catches a couple fish. The stream is jumping with samracks. In fact, I'm willing to give it a try if you gather a basket of handover roots, which are near the edge of the water. Do you know what they are?"

I nodded. "Lethe used to have me gather them when I was little. I know what they look like. Delilah, grab a flashlight and let's go see what we can find."

Handover roots were common and easy to spot—hence their name. Travelers gathered them hand over fist on journeys since they were easy to identify and didn't seem to have any counterparts that were poisonous and easy to mix them up with.

Delilah fished through her backpack until she found a flashlight, while I retrieved a light muslin sack. We always took several of them on trips because there always seemed to be something we needed to gather. As we crossed through the glade, over to the stream's edge, we saw that Bran was already on the rocks that provided a path across the stream, kneeling and intently watching the water. He was carrying a long, wicked-looking dagger. Before we could say a word, he lunged, still managed to keep his balance, and brought the dagger up with a fat, wriggling fish on it. He dropped the fish into a bag that was on the rocks next to him.

"He's got balance, I'll say that for him." I led Delilah away from the area where he was fishing, not wanting to scare the fish. "I couldn't do that."

"I might be able to, but it wouldn't be easy. Menolly could manage it, though." Delilah glanced around. "I remember eating handover roots, but I don't recall what they look like."

"Here, let me show you." I hunted around for a moment, bidding her to point the flashlight this way and that. After a few minutes, I spotted a large spike of green with yellow flowers at the top.

"There. During the summer, they have spiky yellow blossoms. Here, let me dig one up."

I knelt, unsheathing my dagger from my belt. I brushed away several inches of mulch—fallen needles and decaying leaves—from the base of the plant, then dug around the handover root, about two inches from the stalk all the way around. I grasped the stalk and gently rocked it, easing it out of the ground. There was a tearing sound as the root tendrils gave way and the root came out, long and fibrous, about three inches in diameter. It was about the size of a large potato.

"Those over there, they're handover roots too?" Delilah pointed to a small thicket of the plants.

"Yeah, those are handovers."

We moved over to the patch and dug up eight more roots before washing them off in the stream and carrying them back to the fire. Bran had managed to catch five of the samracks—each the size of a medium-sized trout—and he had scaled and gutted them.

I handed Delilah the bag of handovers. "Here, start chopping these for the pot. You don't need to pare them. The skins make good eating, too. I'm going to look for some wild parsley and a larabay plant."

Larabay was a wild herb that tasted very much like a leek. They, too, grew wild through the forests of Otherworld, especially the northern climes near water. It didn't take me long before I found five of them, which should do well for seasoning. I washed them in the stream and carried them over to Delilah. She cut them up and added them to the soup. Bran had diced the fish into the pot along with the handover roots. Trillian dug a box of salt out of his pack and added a spoonful of it to the pot and before long, the rich aroma of broth filled the camp.

We ate the sandwiches as Bran ladled out the soup for us. We had each brought our own enameled camp mug. They were light and easy to carry. I pulled out my spork—another implement we had added to our gear— and began spooning up the hot broth and food.

"Mmm," Delilah mumbled, her mouth full. "I'm so glad we took the time to make this. I needed something hot."

"It's good," Chase said. "I want to help out. What can I do?"

Roz clapped him lightly on the back. "We'll wash the dishes after everyone's done."

The evening passed quickly, or perhaps I was just tired enough to make it seem so. Shortly after dinner, I found myself yawning. While Roz and Chase washed the dishes, and Delilah and Shade snuggled off to one side, I wandered over and sat down by Venus. He sprawled back against a log, sitting on his bedroll near enough the fire to stay warm. As I joined him, he glanced over at me, a crafty smile on his face.

"The journey hasn't been difficult so far," he said, returning his gaze to the fire. "Too easy, perhaps."

"Don't say that. I want it to be easy. The mountains aren't going to be a picnic. They're harsh, Venus, and filled with danger." I shivered. The Tygerian Mountains were wild and so were those who lived in their peaks. The Order of the Crystal Dagger had fortified their monastery, but that protection didn't extend to travelers.

"Easy is as easy does. I'm not saying we're walking into a trap, my dear. But I've found that when great things come too easily, they aren't appreciated for what they really symbolize." He paused. "You know the diamond will change you, just as the seals have changed those of us who bear them."

I hugged my knees to my chest. Nobody could ever accuse Venus the Moonchild of being comforting. "I thought as much. I don't know what I'm getting into, Venus. I don't really want this honor, if it's that. But nobody can ever say I shirk my duty. I grew up fast. My father expected things to be done right. He, himself, grew up under the same expectations. I think I inherited his devotion to duty. In some ways, I'm probably best suited to this."

He considered my words. "I think you are. Delilah doesn't have the patience to put up with it, and Menolly, well...I think it's safe to say she can walk away from things easier than you can. When you put that gem around your neck, be prepared. I had no clue what would happen when I actually took on the spirit seal for my own. It's like one door closes and another opens, and you find yourself part of history in a way you never expected to be."

I glanced over at Delilah. "She's growing. And so is Menolly. Both have come so far from where we were when we arrived Earthside. I don't know about myself. I feel the same, and yet, I'm not. I'm tougher. I'm also letting go of always having to take care of them. They don't need me so much now, and that's a good thing, given what's coming up for all of us. I guess we've all grown up a lot."

Venus nodded, a sage look on his face. "You ventured Earthside expecting something totally different than what you ended up with. It's bound to be a shock, but you're adapting and you're not fighting it. That's the key—to go with the flow. To ride the current of your personal destiny and surrender to what it means to you. I'm not saying you don't ever make new goals and try out something that seems foreign to you. But it means that you quit trying to control the universe, because nobody can do that. In the long run, we're the sum total of where our journeys have led us. If you fight the journey, you end up stagnant or backtracking."

The conversation was leaving me with the distinct feeling that I had entered territory a little too existential for my own peace of mind. At least right now. I touched his hand lightly, smiling.

"Thanks, Venus. I guess I'm just nervous."

"There are ways to take care of that nervousness."

Venus entwined his fingers through mine. The wily old werepuma winked at me, holding my hand as he rubbed his thumb against my palm. I suddenly realized just why Nerissa had found him so enticing. He might be a bit grizzled and scarred, but Venus put out a scorching hot energy and right now, it was tickling me in ways I knew that I shouldn't be thinking about. Especially with Smoky around. Trillian would probably just laugh it off, but Smoky? Not a good idea.

I gave his hand a firm squeeze, then jumped up as quickly as my inner thighs would let me. They were protesting the ride in a most vehement manner, and I worried that I'd be too sore to move the next morning.

"Well, I need to turn in. I'm beat and I think I'd better stretch before bed or I'm going to be terribly sore tomorrow." I couldn't believe that I was stumbling over my words, and I was grateful that it was dark so he couldn't see me blushing.

He let out a soft laugh, low and throaty, and waved me off.

I hurried over to my sleeping bag, motioning for Delilah to join me. The men were gathered around the fire talking.

"What is it?" she asked as I dragged her over to my sleeping bag, where I gently lowered myself to the ground, spread my legs, and started stretching, leaning over to grasp my foot and hold the stretch.

"Venus. Did he ever come on to you?" I lowered my voice, making certain no one could hear me.

Delilah stared at me for a moment, then adopted the same pose and began to stretch out as well. "No," she said, glancing around at the fire. "They're talking so loud I don't think they can hear us. Why, did Venus just...?"

"Yes, he did. I managed to backtrack without being rude but holy hell, I can tell why Nerissa trained under him. Literally. All her talk about him teaching her how to transfer pain to passion? I believe her. I mean, it wasn't that I didn't believe her but I really do believe her now. I didn't know what to say." I groaned as I hit a point where my inner thighs decided to rebel. "I hope to hell I can walk tomorrow morning. It never occurred to me that we were going via horse. I thought I was in shape but apparently I was wrong."

"I'd say give them a good rub, but somebody might get the wrong idea if he saw you." Delilah stifled a snicker.

I smacked her lightly on the arm. "Smart ass. Honestly, if I were single, it would have been hard to resist. He's got some heady fire, I tell you that."

We finished stretching and Delilah had me turn around. "Take off your corset. You have a shirt under it. We need to check on your ribs."

Trillian meandered over. "What are you doing?"

"Checking Camille's ribs and her back." Delilah handed the flashlight to Trillian. "If you could hold this while I check under her shirt. I should put a good layer of the salve on, too."

Between the two of them, they slathered me up with salve and Trillian reinforced the padding on my sleeping bag with an extra blanket. I wasn't looking forward to sleeping on the ground, but there was no help for that. As I slid into my sleeping bag, Delilah returned to hers. Trillian settled down beside me, leaning over to kiss me good night.

"I know that old scoundrel put the make on you, but he'll respect your space if you say no. Don't tell Smoky about it or the lizard's likely to use Venus as an asswipe."

I coughed. "I thought nobody else noticed."

Trillian stroked my face, his hand soft against my cheek. "If you think I don't keep an eye on you, you're very much mistaken. I watch out for my wife. I'm your alpha…you're my love. I consider it my job to know what's going on."

Smoky joined us and we fell silent about Venus. "Shade will be taking first watch. He'll wake Trillian and Bran in a few hours, and you will in turn wake me shortly before dawn. That way we'll have a full night's rest."

As they both slid into their sleeping bags and the camp fell silent except for the hiss and crackle of the bonfire, I realized once again that I couldn't ask for better protectors. I fell into a deep sleep, interrupted only by the occasional rustle of brush as some animal wandered past.

THE NEXT MORNING, I was almost as sore as I had feared I would be. Smoky carefully helped me up, but then took the unusual stance of making me stretch out, helping with his hair as he gently pushed and pulled my limbs in a variety of ways they didn't want to go. He was careful to avoid my ribs, and he made sure nobody saw anything they shouldn't, but by the time we were done, I'd privately labeled him as bad of a drillmaster as the one we'd had in training when we first went to work for the Y'Elestrial Intelligence Agency. The first year had been spent divided between classes and physical training. I'd graduated from Basic Core near the top of my class on the intellectual side of things, but barely scraped by on the physical side. After that, I'd given up any semblance of gym and confined my athletics to walking and the occasional sprint.

"Dude, I am not Gumby. I'm not that bendy!" I limped over to the morning fire. Delilah was dividing up the protein bars. She, too, was walking with a hitch.

Bran snorted. "You think this is bad? Wait till we're riding rough terrain. *If* we're riding rough terrain. I suppose it all depends on what the scroll tells you once you find it." He motioned to a pan on the fire. "I thought to bring coffee, seeing how all of Earthside seems to be addicted to it."

"Oh, bless you." I leaned over, wincing, and held out my cup. As he poured my coffee, I noticed he had a mug of the same right next to him. "All of Earthside, huh? And what's that?"

With a soft laugh, he said, "I didn't claim to be immune to its effects. Especially given that I'm primarily living over Earthside now."

As I gingerly lowered myself to sit on one of the logs, Trillian brought me a couple protein bars and a bowl of blueberries. "Here, eat these. I went out and found a scattering of early berries. The men agreed to divide them up between you and Delilah."

I gratefully took the fresh fruit. The protein bars would help but they weren't exactly the heartiest of breakfasts and I was thinking about Hanna's waffles with regret.

The sun was starting to peek through the eastern timber line, scattering its rays through the dense foliage. While it was shaping up into a warm day, the chill in the air was still nippy, and dew covered every branch and leaf. I inhaled deeply, sucking in a lungful of the clean air, and held it for as long as I could before slowly exhaling. The air was bracing and tasted clean, unlike most air over Earthside. There was always an odd flavor that settled at the back of my throat back home, though I was getting used to it.

"How long before we reach the place where we're thinking the scroll is?" I cupped my coffee mug, warming my hands, again grateful that Bran had good sense to bring it. Better sense than the rest of us, given we'd all forgotten about it.

"I think we'll be riding till a little past noon. Maybe two o'clock? Three? We have to pass a series of ponds first—the Seven Grottos. I warn you, be cautious. I've heard tell that some kelpies have set up home there, and there have been disappearances. My mother has been meaning to check into it, but she gets distracted easily." His tone slipped, just enough for me to hear the mild vein of contempt behind it.

I knew that Raven Mother treaded lightly around her son. At one point, she had indicated to me that he didn't listen to her. Most children rebelled against their parents but Bran was unpredictable. Which brought to mind another memory. Bran had been holding something over Morgaine's head before she died. I had never figured out what that was, but they had been at each other's throats on our trip to find Myrddin. Mistletoe, the pixie attendant to Feddrah-Dahns—the Prince of the Dahnsburg Unicorns—had also confided in me that, at one time in the past, Bran had wanted Morgaine and she had rebuffed him.

On that trip, we had also learned that Bran was in debt to Beira, the Mistress of Winter and the mother of the *Bean Nighe*. I had witnessed her threatening him for payment by the Winter Solstice. Given that had passed, he must have found a way to pay her off because he was still standing. They might both be Immortals, but she was far stronger than he was.

"We'll be careful," was all I said. I didn't like bog Fae, in general. The kelpies and will-o'-the-wisps were dangerous and all too happy to lure people to their death, be they human or Fae or anything in between. The Elder Fae who haunted the boggy marshes were far worse. Jenny Greenteeth, the Black Annis, Bog-Mother, all spawned a legacy that turned traveling through marshland into a dangerous journey.

As we saddled up again for the day, I dreaded the coming ride. Or rather, my thighs dreaded it. Trillian helped me back astride the horse and as I patted Annabelle's head, she whinnied.

"Take it easy on me, would you? I'm a newbie at this." I fumbled in my pocket for one of the apples I had confiscated and leaned down to hand it to her. She took the fruit, giving a little shake of appreciation. Laughing—my experience with horses was limited and I hadn't realized how pleasant they could be—I clucked to her and she started forward as I steered her into the train we had formed. I rode behind Trillian, who was behind Bran.

As we passed deeper into Thistlewyd Deep, I began to realize that the entire forest was actually a giant hive-mind. I could feel it on every side of me—above and below, too. It throbbed with activity and as I tuned in, I realized that every being that entered the forest became a part of the whole. We were, too—simply by being here, we had become part of the Deep.

Delilah rode up beside me. The path was wide enough, though it wouldn't have handled three abreast. She let out a long breath. "Now I understand why Father warned us against this place. We've been on some odd journeys before, but I've never felt any place quite as...alive...as this woodland. It makes Panther want to come out and play, and it makes Tabby want to run for her life."

"I understand. I was just thinking about how Thistlewyd Deep is one gigantic organism. We've become part of it simply by crossing the borders." I glanced up at the sun. "We're halfway to noon, I think—" I stopped.

"What's wrong?"

"Can you hear that?" I could hear the faintest of voices, riding the wind like distant chimes. Closing my eyes for a moment, I let Annabelle lead the way. But a sudden jerk jolted me out of my thoughts. My eyes flying open, I saw that Delilah had grabbed hold of my reins. Annabelle was stopped in the middle of the path.

"What's going on?" I glanced around. "Why did you stop me?"

"You were starting to veer off trail, that's why. I can hear the voices too, they're calling us." Delilah shouted to Bran and Trillian, who backtracked. "You said there were kelpies near the Seven Grottoes. Are we near there?"

Bran glanced around, contemplating our surroundings, then nodded. "We are, actually. Just through those two bushes to the right lies the path into the ponds."

I was about to say something when a loud noise crashed off to our left. Annabelle whinnied in fear, then bolted onto the path toward the Seven Grottoes. I glanced over my shoulder just in time to see two large creatures crashing through the forest directly toward our party, and they looked angry, mean, and hungry.

Chapter 11

I GRABBED THE reins, trying to calm Annabelle as we careened through the undergrowth, but she was on a one-way mission to put as much distance between us and those creatures as possible. I gave up trying to stop her and instead focused on holding on for dear life. While I had ridden horses in the past, I had never had any inclination to be a show jumper or any such thing.

Shouts from behind told me that a fight had ensued. I prayed that whatever those things were, they wouldn't manage to damage anybody in the process. As for me, the last thing I was worried about was getting involved with them. Right now, I'd actually welcome it. Annabelle was careening around rocks and jumping over fallen logs, and I just held tight, trying to gather enough energy to project a calming aura, but it was hard to cast a spell when my main focus was on keeping my seat. I had the feeling if I fell off at this speed, I'd break something—quite possibly my neck. In fact, this was how my mother had died. That sobered me even further.

"Hush, hush, it's okay." My words were choppy

thanks to the bumps and jolts that accompanied me. *Ms. Camille's Wild Ride*, I thought. Toad had nuthin' on me.

Then, the soft cadence of song hit me again. Oh great, we were nearing the ponds and the kelpies were singing. Annabelle responded, beginning to slow. I tried to ignore the summons. As soon as my horse was trotting instead of galloping full speed, I grabbed out a tissue from my pocket and tore it in two, stuffing the halves into my ears for makeshift earplugs. While it didn't fully mute the singing, it distorted it enough to where I wasn't totally entranced. I felt the pull, but was able to force my attention away from it.

I was finally able to gather up my energy. I needed to keep Annabelle from being lured in. Kelpies ate horses, as well as people. While I wasn't sure of my ability to cast a spell to mute out their singing, there was nothing to do but give it a try. I focused my attention on the area around us.

Kelpie's song and siren's lure,
Fade into a general blur.
Silence those who would charm,
Keep them from doing harm.

As the magic shot out from me, every which way, there was a sudden burst of light ahead of us. I shielded my eyes from the flash. *Great.* What the hell had I done now? I cautiously opened my eyes as the flare faded away and I squinted, trying to see what was going on.

Holy fuck. The entire area ahead of us was one massive blur. I couldn't quite see the path—couldn't quite see the ponds that I knew were there. The copse rippled like a distorted wall. What on earth?

Annabelle whinnied, shaking her head as if she was just waking up. I also realized that, except for birdsong and the croaking of frogs, the forest ahead of us was silent. I had muted them, all right. *Fade into a general blur.* Crap, I had also blurred them too, whatever that meant. I wasn't sure if the blurriness was an illusion or if I had somehow thrust them into a slightly different reality. As I sat there, cocking my head from one side to another as I puzzled over what had happened, a noise behind me shook me out of my thoughts.

"Camille? Camille?" Smoky was running hard and fast through the trees. He made better time than if he had been on his horse. The hem of his jacket was flying behind him, and I wondered how it managed to avoid being caught on anything. But then again, as one of his dragon attributes, he never got dirty so it made sense that extended to more than cleanliness.

I held up my hand. "Over here."

"Are you all right?" He skidded to a halt, his duster settling around his legs as he slowed.

"What?" His words sounded muffled until I realized it was due to my makeshift earplugs. I pulled the tissue out of my ears.

"I said, are you all right?"

"Oh, yeah. Annabelle just led me on a wild ride." I pointed ahead. "What do you see?"

He frowned, squinting. "I'm not sure, but it looks like a blurry... Camille, what did you do?"

"How do you know *I* did anything?" As silly as it sounded, I was suddenly on the defense. My magic backfired so much that my family assumed any mishap could be attributed to a misplaced spell.

"Do I really have to answer that?" He laughed, but then turned back to the still-blurry glade. "What happened?"

I told him about Annabelle sprinting because of the creatures and how we had raced through the woods till the kelpies began luring us in. "So once she began to calm down, I was able to cast a spell. Which backfired. Maybe. Just a little."

"You blurred them out? Are they in a different dimension or did you just mangle everybody's vision?" Smoky headed over to take a look, ducking away from me before I could smack his shoulder for teasing me. As he neared the glade, I realized he was staying perfectly clear against the background.

"You're not blurry."

"Good. I don't want to be." He reached out. "Tree trunks are still here. I think you just cast a general obstruction spell."

It was then that I remembered the creatures who had chased me here in the first place. "Wait—what were those beasts and is everybody okay?"

"Everybody is fine. Shade, Delilah, and I managed to take them down. They're some form of overgrown carnivorous rodent. Gigantic rats." Smoky was still focused on the trees. "I think we should take a look at the ponds. It's off our itinerary, but kelpies prey on others."

I didn't want to go hunt down the kelpies and I didn't want to chance having to fight them. But I knew he was right. They were a danger to anybody passing through, and the next group of travelers might not be able to fight them off, let alone know the kelpies were a threat.

"All right. Giant rats, you say?"

"Not exactly but close enough." He returned to the side of my horse. "Wait here. Put those earplugs back in. I'll summon the others. They're only a ten-minute ride—run—away, but I can go through the Ionyc Sea so I'll be right back, and they'll follow." Before I could say a word, he vanished, blinking out of sight.

With a sigh, I replaced my makeshift earplugs, stuffing the tissue inside my ears again. Sighing, I decided that the kelpies were going to pay for this distraction.

SMOKY WAS GOOD to his word. He returned a couple moments later, and told me the others were on the way. I stayed astride Annabelle at his request.

"Where's your horse?"

"They're bringing him. I didn't want to scare the poor beast by bringing him through the Ionyc Sea. It's hard enough for a horse to handle a dragon rider, but the Ionyc Sea? That would probably give the creature a heart attack."

We waited for another ten minutes, Smoky relentlessly patrolling the area while he insisted I stay on Annabelle. I liked the horse, but was aching to get off her back. Literally, my legs felt like they were one accidental contraction away from going into spasm.

Finally, I ignored what my dear dragon had ordered and slid off of the saddle in a somewhat less than graceful manner. But at least I was on the ground. The cramps hit the moment I tried to walk over to Smoky's side. I groaned, bending to place my hands on my knees as I tried to breathe through the wave of charley horses that rippled along my legs.

"Crap. Why didn't I plan for this and take some time to get in shape. We could have rented horses and built up stamina but no, I didn't even think about how we might be traveling to find the Maharata-Vashi." I grumbled on, pretty much a broken record, until we heard voices as the others broke through the foliage, joining us.

Delilah took one look at my face and was off her horse. Although the aches and pains were also hitting her, she was a lot more fit than I was. A lot more fit than I'd ever be. She hurried over to me.

"Camille, are you all right? Smoky told us you're fine, but I don't think you are."

"I'll be all right once the damned leg cramps settle down. I'm okay, really." I eased out of the stretch and slowly stood. My legs were still aching but the cramps had eased off. "Damn, though. When we go home, we're taking riding lessons and keeping it up, just in case."

She laughed. "I think I'd like that, actually." Sobering, she turned toward the wood. "Smoky says you made it blur."

"I made it blur, all right. Spell misfired, but at least it quieted the kelpies down so we can't hear them now."

"I don't know if that's a good thing or not." Delilah contemplated the forest ahead. "If we can't hear them, they could sneak around and ambush us."

I pressed my lips together. I hadn't thought about that. I had meant just to quiet their songs, but what if I had managed to give them a blanket silence spell? That would be just about the way things worked, given my history.

"Maybe you're right. I guess I should negate the energy." I wasn't sure if I could manage that—spell reversals were harder than actually casting the spell in the first place—but I closed my eyes and searched through the repertoire in my head. Finally, I remembered the Reversing spell that I had been taught as a child. I cast it, wording it as cautiously as I could, and stood back, watching as the entire area began to shimmer. The energy cleared, and we were staring at the forest as it should be. But I could hear the kelpies singing again.

I tried to ignore them, stuffing the tissue back in my ears. One look at Chase and I knew he would be in big trouble. "Trillian, you and Shade take Chase back to the path. Get him away and don't let him answer the call."

As they led Chase away, I detached my staff from Annabelle's side and walked over to Smoky. "Let's go. But be careful. How do kelpies affect dragons?"

"We're mostly immune to them. But..." He stopped to listen, then shook his head. "There's something different about these particular Fae. I can't explain it but they sound stronger than their Earthside kin."

"That's because they come from the Deep," Bran said, crossing to our side. "They were probably born in Thistlewyd Deep, and that strengthens their abilities." His angular jaw was set, his eyes dark and flashing. "If you are serious about taking care of them, then we go on foot, because they can lure our horses in and make a bloody meal off of them. I won't chance my steed to a painful fate. So, decide, and one way or another, we move. The longer we stand here, the better their chance to lure us into their snare."

Delilah looked about as overjoyed as I was, but she merely drew her long dagger after she dismounted. Lysanthra, her weapon, was sentient and had occasionally sparked with an unexpected power or two. We all knew there were other abilities locked within the blade, but they would come out in their own time. Rozurial withdrew his magical stun gun, smiling grimly. Venus surprised me by drawing a wicked-looking dagger. It was curved and the curves were sharp, barbed with what looked almost like stingers. Plunge that into anybody's flesh and it would rip them to hell when you yanked it back.

We were all on our feet, and we tied the horses to trees to prevent them from bolting or running off. I motioned to Bran as he drew his sword. "I guess we're ready."

He gave me a nod, and we headed into the thicket that separated us from the ponds.

THE FOREST SUDDENLY seemed to mute except for the piercing notes of a very vocal bird and the steady drone of bumblebees. The undergrowth began to thin as we approached the ponds, and the trees here were tall birch, white bark gleaming under the flickering sun. The temperatures had climbed into the low seventies, and I began to feel slightly off-center. I shook my head as we silently proceeded, trying to snap out of the beckoning daze. It wasn't the kelpies' song—the tissue provided a fairly good buffer. But the warmth and the lack of sound and the anticipation created its own form of trance, and I was sliding fast.

Smoky's hand on my shoulder startled me out of my reverie. I glanced up at him. He flashed me a grim smile and once again, I realized how much I loved him. My dragon lord. My prince of the skies. He had forced himself into my life and captured me with his passion and his devotion.

I caught my breath, realizing that there was no place I'd rather be than with my three men, whether it was in the bedroom or on the battlefield. We played together, and we fought together, and together we would navigate the storms that befell us.

"I love you," he mouthed.

I blew him a kiss, and then turned back to the path. We were nearing a breach in the trees and through it, I could hear the breeze playing against the currents of the pond. I steeled myself, and glanced over at Delilah. She had followed my lead. I could see the tufts of tissue poking out of her ears. *Good.* The last thing we needed was one of our party being held hostage by the kelpies.

As we neared the clearing, I could see the glimmer of water rippling under the sunlight. The scent of flowers—I couldn't place which type—floated by on the light breeze. Intoxicating, they made me want to run toward the ponds, to lose myself in their heady aroma, but I forced myself to stand still.

From where I was standing I could see the ponds—they ranged from hot-tub size to big enough to swim in, and seemed to form a chain against a terraced hillside, the smallest at the top pouring into the one below and so forth, like a naturally tiered fountain.

The bottom one was as large as six Olympic-sized swimming pools, and on the other side of it, lounging against rocks, were the loveliest men I had ever seen. Kelpies could take the form of any fantasy you might have. Sometimes they even mimicked horses, leading weary travelers who thought to catch a free mount into the bogs.

I tried to clear my sight, to see them as they were, but it was difficult. Their charm was a powerful aphrodisiac. But then, something inside clicked—it was as though my own glamour rebelled against theirs—and I caught a glimpse of one of them in his true form. I decided it was a *he*, because as he stood he resembled the Swamp Thing, with a penis that rivaled the biggest I'd ever seen. The kelpie was covered with a layer of bog mulch, with branches and sticks poking out from the slather of stinking mud.

He leaned his head back and let out a single, crystal clear note, which seemed so out of character with his form that it was hard for me to put the two together. His teeth were neon white, glowing under the sun, sharp, ragged needles filling his mouth. A breeze gusted by and I barely restrained an impulse to gag. The scent of flowers had turned to decay.

"I can see them." Apparently, once I managed to break the charm, it broke the charm for all of them because I was staring at a group of at least six of the creatures. A pod—nest—whatever they called their groupings. There were three males and three females, by the looks of them, and they were all lounging at the edge of the pond.

"What do you want to do next?" Bran said. "I can see them as they are."

"I can't," Roz said, "but it doesn't matter. I can feel their energy from here and it's dangerous and deadly."

"I guess we engage. If you see someone toss down their weapon and head toward the kelpies, intervene. We all run the risk of being charmed, though I doubt Smoky will have much trouble keeping away from them."

I glanced at the kelpies, trying to decide if I had any magic that would stand up to them. Turning to Roz, I held out my hand. "Give me ice bombs. Or firebombs. That pond isn't very large. If we bombard them with ice or fire, it's going to become mighty uncomfortable and force them out. Once on land, they won't have as much power because their magic comes from the water."

He fumbled in his duster, pulling out a bag of the firebombs. "Just don't fall into the pond while it's boiling. That's a small-enough space that even just five or six of these will bring the water almost to boiling and anything in there's going to fry." He paused. "You're sure? This will kill off the fish, too."

"The fish are already dead," Bran said. "The kelpies will eat them all, if they haven't already. Either way, they're dinner for somebody."

"I'll take them." I held out my hand for the bag. "I don't think my magic will be much use here, and with these, at least I can chase the kelpies out of the pond and you guys can be ready to take them on. I don't know that my bruised ribs are going to allow me to help with the fighting unless you're desperate. I'm more of a hindrance that way."

"Then you need to get over to the pond's side without being seen, because they'll come out of that water in a heartbeat the moment you set foot into the clearing." Roz handed me the bag of bombs. "And as much as I like you, I am not going to wax enthusiastic about your ability to lob the firebombs from here. I've seen you throw."

"Yeah, yeah. Technicalities." I stuck my tongue out at him, but he was right and I wasn't about to argue the point. I'd never sign up to be a pitcher in a game of softball. I glanced around. The trees encircled the clearing, so if I worked my way through them, keeping quiet and out of sight, I should be able to make it over behind the pools. But that still left enough distance for the kelpies to move.

Smoky tapped me on the shoulder. "Simple. Ionyc Sea. It's easy enough for me to pop you in, then out. I can see exactly where we're aiming for even though I haven't been there before. We step out, you throw the bombs, we vanish again."

"That would work," Bran said. "How long till those things heat up the water?"

"Drop the entire bag in there and within five seconds, it's going to be one hell of a hot tub. That many bombs? Will take it from cool shaded bathing pond to boiling lobster pot within less than a minute. They won't have time to get out before they're burned. Now, it may not kill them, I honestly don't know, but at least they won't be able to retreat into the water to recharge for a while. That hot? Will take at least ten minutes to calm down to unpleasantly warm." Roz motioned to Smoky. "Go, while they still haven't noticed us. We'll engage the moment you vanish away from the pond."

Smoky held out his arm and I snuggled into it. "This will be quick. Try to keep alert."

"All right. The drift doesn't take hold of me that fast if we aren't traveling a great distance." When traveling through the Ionyc Sea, if we were journeying farther than a few miles or between worlds, the massive churning of energies lulled me to sleep. Delilah encountered the same effect, though it was less now that she was getting used to journeying through the alternate realms as a Death Maiden.

I held tight to the bag of firebombs as we faded, focusing all my thoughts on what I had to do. The currents had barely taken hold of us, the mist swirling like nebulous ghosts, when we stepped off the Sea again, right next to the pond. The kelpies were gathered on the other side, near the cascading water from the upper tiers. I didn't stop to think, just tossed the bag of firebombs into the water, and Smoky swept me into the Sea again. The next thing I knew, we appeared at the treeline.

The others had already charged out, and I hurried to look at what our handiwork had wrought. The kelpies were screaming, high-pitched whistles of pain that hurt my ears. They were struggling to reach the eastern edge of the pond where they could climb out, but the waters around them were churning. I wished at that moment that we had long-distance weapons with us. A good bow and quiver of arrows would solve a lot of our problems right now.

As it was, the others were on the shore, ready to meet the kelpies. The females shifted direction, heading instead for the western side. Bran and Delilah raced around to meet them. One of the males broke off from the others, swimming toward the south point, but Roz and Venus were there. Smoky and I took the eastern edge. I pulled out my dagger. One of the males still heading in our direction vanished from sight, sinking in the boiling water. He then bobbed up again, floating, his skin blistered through the layers of mud. I grimaced. Not the prettiest way to die.

Smoky pushed me behind him as the other kelpie approached the edge of the pond. I moved back, glancing over to see the one heading to the south—toward Roz and Venus—also vanish below the water. They raced around to bolster Delilah and Bran's presence. One of the females had reached the water's edge. She was trying to dodge Bran's attacks, but he was deadly with his sword. Delilah moved around back of her, lunging with Lysanthra.

The other two females pulled themselves ashore, one managing to evade Roz's stun gun. But the other met Venus head-on. He was swifter with his dagger than she was with her claws, and he plunged it into her heart with dead-center accuracy. She convulsed as blood pulsed out around the blade. Venus pulled, hard, and the barbs on his dagger ripped the surrounding flesh as he yanked the blade out of her. An explosion of blood saturated her chest, splattering the old werepuma as well, and she stumbled back, falling to her knees. He brought the blade across her throat, and that put an end to any life she might have left in her.

The one who had evaded Delilah's attack staggered as Bran sliced through her arm, cutting it cleanly off. She managed to dodge them, heading back to the pond, but stopped as she eyed the still-boiling water. As Bran jogged toward her, she made her choice and threw herself in the pond, sinking beneath the surface.

The third female was headed in our direction. Smoky charged forward, his nails lengthening into claws, and in a blur of movement, he slashed across her chest, neatly opening her up. My husband was good at eviscerating his enemies, I had to give him that. She looked down, a confused expression in her eyes as she watched her organs tumble out. Another moment and he sliced her throat, and she went down, quivering for a few seconds until her body stilled.

I gave one glance back at the pond, counting the

floating bodies. Yes, we had managed to kill them all. "I guess...we're done."

"Not quite," Bran said. "There were three pairs in there. I'm guessing there might be eggs."

"Kelpies lay eggs?" Delilah looked confused. "I had no idea."

"A number of the water-based Fae do. But there's no way they could survive the boiling water. If there are any in there, they've been hard boiled." Roz shrugged.

I wasn't so sure. Something about the upper tiers of ponds caught my attention. "Up there. Chances are they kept their eggs in a protected spot. Want to make a bet if they do have a nursery it's in one of the upper ponds?"

Bran flashed me a look that was almost approving. "Good thinking." He hoisted himself up the rocks that led to the upper tiers, followed by Smoky.

Sure enough, a few moments later, they held up half a dozen large eggs that were each about the size of a small eggplant. I wasn't sure what they did to them—and I really didn't want to know—but when they returned, it was sans eggs.

"They won't hatch now," was all Smoky would say.

Delilah gave me a quick look, shuddering, and I grimaced in reply. It wasn't exactly like unfertilized chicken eggs. There had been baby kelpies in there. But we weren't dealing with a nature versus nurture argument. Kelpies grew up to feed on others, regardless of who brought them up. In fact, chances were foster mama and papa would be their first feast.

Delilah was washing the blood off of her hands in the pond, well away from the floating bodies. "Hey, it's still nice and warm."

Roz, Venus, and Bran joined her. Smoky, as always, was clean as a whistle. I hadn't been close enough to get any blood spray or debris on me. We were about to head back to our mounts when Bran stopped us again. "They've been making a meal off of travelers for some time. My guess is that, in the water there, probably in a hollowed-out chamber in the rocks, there's a tidy stash of money and valuables."

"We don't need the money," I started to say, but Bran let out a snort.

"You may not, but I'm not quite set up with three sugar mamas to support me. One of which happens to be a dragon. I might be an Elemental Lord—"

"Minor Elemental Lord. Your mama's the biggie," Delilah broke in.

Bran narrowed his eyes. "I remember slights." But then he seemed to think the better of it and shrugged. "Given your alliance with the Autumn Lord, however, I'll let it go. However, as I said, my mother chooses not to gift me with her baubles, and she does love shiny trinkets. So I must make my own way as I can."

"Then go ahead, take a quick look." Smoky waved him toward the water.

"I get first pick." Bran stripped off his clothes right there, and I had to admit, he cut a handsome figure. I tried to avoid staring at his cock, especially when Smoky gave me a smoldering look. Delilah grabbed me by the shoulders and led me away.

"Better we take a rest over here." She guided me toward a fallen log. Whispering, she added, "We don't want Smoky to turn Bran into chunk chicken, do we?"

I stifled a laugh. "I can't help it—I may not have any interest in touching, but looking is second nature."

"Trust me, he doesn't have anything you want." But she broke out in giggles then, and we sat snickering and making bad jokes until Bran surfaced.

"Hey, you cackling hens," he shouted. "I'm decent again."

"You're never decent," I called out. I glanced at Delilah. "You look. Is he dressed?"

"Yeah, come on."

We returned to the men where Bran, soaking wet but back in his clothes, was kneeling by a chest the size of a small ottoman. He eagerly pried it open, refusing Roz's offer of checking the chest for traps. The rest of us backed away, not wanting to get caught in the crossfire of any explosions or magical spells. But there was only a soft click. Bran cautiously opened the lid.

The chest was filled with gold and silver coins looking to be from all over Y'Eírialiastar—the proper name for Otherworld. There were pendants and rings inside, a sparkling chalice, a dagger that was probably enchanted to some degree. There were other knickknacks and doodads as well. Not a king's ransom by any means, but a good chunk of change.

Bran paused, staring up at us. "How will we divide this?"

Smoky shrugged. "I'm a dragon. I have my own treasure and have no need for a handful of coins. Keep it."

Roz glanced over at us, and I gave him a shrug. It was up to him what he wanted to do. As for me, I didn't want to be beholden to Bran in any way.

"I'm out. Camille, too," Delilah said.

Venus shook his head. "I have no need."

Roz gathered up a handful of coins. "This will serve me well to replenish the firebombs and whatever else we might use of mine on this trip."

Bran slowly stood, then walked over to me. He held up a necklace that looked to be of obsidian beads, pearls, and a sapphire pendant. "I would gift you with this." He held it out. "Consider it my repayment for my churlish nature."

I wasn't going to take it, but that would probably make him irritating and difficult to work with. "Thank you," I finally said, accepting the necklace. "It's beautiful." I tucked it away in my pocket until I could put it in my pack.

He held out the dagger to Delilah. "You like blades, I can tell. This, I have no need of."

She started to say no—I could see it on her face—but then she must have reached the same conclusion I had, thanked him, and gracefully accepted.

Bran made gifts to Smoky—the chalice, to Venus—a ring, and to Roz, another bag of coins before filling his saddlebags with the rest of the treasure. I wasn't sure what to think, but maybe we were rubbing off on him. One could only hope.

Bran tossed the chest back in the pond, where it sank within seconds, and then we mounted the horses. Having disposed of the kelpies, we set off again, back to Shade, Chase, and Trillian.

As we rode through the forest, the enchantment that the kelpies had woven around the area was broken, and now the trees loomed dark and chaotic around us. We were in an area of Thistlewyd Deep where it would be unwise to stray from the group. The energy was restless, and I could hardly wait until we were through to the mountains.

Chapter 12

WE HAD SPENT more time than I wanted to on the kelpies, but Bran hastened the pace and we began to make up the miles. He assured me this would only put us an hour or two behind and that we would still reach our destination before night.

"That's a good thing," Trillian muttered. "We're going to need to find food for dinner, because there isn't much left in the way of cookies or protein bars."

I didn't say anything but I was in full agreement. Our midmorning snack was a single granola bar and frankly, that wasn't enough to sustain my good mood. I had no intention on going to bed without dinner. If nothing else, we should be able to find some handover roots, and some of the early berries were in season. It would take some foraging but we could have some sort of meal for dinner, but we couldn't see to forage in the dark.

We wound further into the Deep, taking a secondary path shortly after our fight with the kelpies. "It will save us time," Bran said, "even though the trail is a rougher ride."

"Rougher ride" was correct. We bounced along, our horses steering around the roots and stones that littered the narrower path. The trail felt closed in, the trees looming closer on either side. While I loved being in the woods, I was starting to feel like we'd never find our way through. The mood was oppressive, weighing heavily like a stone around the neck. When I glanced over my shoulder, I saw that Delilah looked just about as overjoyed as I felt, her mouth set in a grim line.

I nudged my horse to the side, swinging in again beside her. "This part of the Deep feels dangerous."

"Oh, we're being watched, all right. Panther is right at the surface, very close to making an appearance, which wouldn't be a good surprise, given I'm astride a horse. I'm doing my best to rein her in, but I won't guarantee that when we stop, she won't appear and run off to find out who's following us. Because we *are* being followed."

I closed my eyes, reaching out to try to sense whoever was out there. But there were so many things—so many sensations that muddied the energy. I could tell there was definitely somebody trailing us, but I couldn't pinpoint the source. Just a general sense of watchfulness.

"Yeah, we are. I'm going to tell Smoky. I don't trust telling Bran. He just waves me off when I voice concerns."

"That's because he's still pissed at you. And I think he's attracted to you and he doesn't want to be—and it makes him all the more angry." Delilah gave a little shake of the head. "I know we need to accept his help, but Camille, keep one eye open around him. Always. He's a lot like Shamas, only with a twisted bent."

"You're right about that, actually." I hadn't made the connection before, but now that she mentioned it, I realized that Bran did remind me of a petulant, perpetually angry Shamas. And Shamas had been petulant enough. Bran just multiplied that entitled mentality ten times over.

I dropped back to Smoky, who rode near the back of the group. He gave me a quizzical look. "Tired of the Raven Master's company?"

I let out a soft laugh. "Always. But there's something else. Delilah and I were talking and both she and I sense that we're being followed."

"We are, my love." A tendril of his ankle-length hair rose to extend itself across the distance between our horses. It wrapped around my shoulders, then the tip rose to stroke my face. "I have been aware of that for some time now. But I can't go off hunting them because whoever it is, they're crafty. I've lagged back a couple times, and once even backed off the road to wait, but the moment I do, they seem to notice. So they're watching us with a keen eye, and me in particular. Methinks whoever it is can sense that Shade and I are dragons."

"Lovely, that's just what we need. Well, if they're afraid of you, that's a good sign. Do you think it's some animal hunting for food? The sensation I had was one of curiosity and wariness. But I couldn't pinpoint it in the wash of activity that's running through the Deep."

He cocked his head for a moment, then he withdrew the strand of hair, his hair lifting to divide itself into three sections, which then plaited themselves into a long braid. Smoky often braided his hair before a battle, so I sat up straighter in the saddle. If we were headed for an altercation, I wanted to be ready.

But rather than shout a warning, Smoky simply said, "Halt. Wait up a moment."

Everyone stopped and rode back to us. The trail wasn't wide enough to gather in a group, but Smoky held up his hand and said, "No worries. I smell pixie dust."

Bran started to growl, but I knew what that meant. Or at least, I knew what I *hoped* it meant.

"Mistletoe! Are you out there?"

Another moment and the bushes near us parted and out flew Mistletoe, the pixie attendant to Feddrah-Dahns, Prince of the Dahnsburg Unicorns. Mistletoe was about as big as a Barbie doll, with pale, almost translucent skin. He sparkled like a glitter bomb, with little lights twinkling around him. His wings looked like those of a dragonfly.

I clapped. "Well met, old friend." My gloom lifted and I held out my hand.

Mistletoe flew over and landed on my palm, tickling me as he settled down. He glanced over at Bran and scowled. "Lady Camille, I bid you welcome from my master, Feddrah-Dahns."

He spoke in Melosealfôr, which meant he didn't want the others to understand. I knew that Delilah, Roz, Venus, and Chase didn't understand the high language, although I wasn't sure about Smoky, Shade, or Bran. Neither dragon let on whether they could understand, but Bran just looked confused.

"Are we speaking in the high tongue for a reason?"

"Yes, because I do not trust the Raven's son, simply because of his craftiness. Camille, I warned you last winter that someone was looking to steal the horn and hide from you. And then Feddrah-Dahns gave me a name to check out."

"Yes, a sorceress named Iyonah. Have you found out anything?"

"I have. It took me much research and I had to make a number of trips, but she hearkens from the south— from the Southern Wastes."

I frowned. That wasn't good news. The sorcerers who inhabited the Southern Wastes tended to be those who followed Chimaras, the sun god who was intent on destroying the Moon Mother. "I hadn't heard that Chimaras boasted priestesses. I thought his followers were always male."

"They are and she's not. I found several people who have met Iyonah, most of whom were from Rhellah. They say she came out of the desert one day, that she walked out from the empty dunes. She told one traveler that she hearkens from a city that lies beneath the sands down in the Southern Wastes—a city forgotten by time that only appears when conditions are right." He frowned, shaking his head. "We had not heard of such a city so I did some research on it."

I hadn't heard of it either. "What did you find?"

"There is a tale—most think it a child's bedtime story—of a huge city that existed down in that area before the Scorching Wars. It boasted a beautiful palace and the city was known as Kyradream."

"Ceredream, you mean?"

"No, not Ceredream. It was named *Kyradream*, and it was a major stopover on the way to the End of the World, where the Uriami Ocean takes over. During the beginning of the Scorching Wars, the land was laid waste beginning in the south realms, and from what I gather, this city was caught in a magical dust storm and it vanished."

The End of the World...it had been a long time since I had heard that term. The Uriami Ocean was said to meet up with the Mirami Ocean somewhere in the distant south. Nobody knew what was on the other side of the oceans, as far as I knew. But the End of the World was supposedly an area to where travelers, hoping to navigate the waters, would journey. Few ever returned, and those who did were usually so out of it that they couldn't—and wouldn't—talk about their travels.

"I wonder—Could Kyradream be the origin of

Ceredream? Did those who survived whatever happened move north and rebuild, and eventually forget that the city ever existed?" I glanced over at Smoky, who was watching intently. Bran, on the other hand, was shifting impatiently on his horse.

"That could be. However, Iyonah specifically told the people I talked to that she was from Kyradream. That she had come out of the sands, searching for the horn and hide of the Black Unicorn." Mistletoe shifted and his wings grazed my fingers.

I laughed. "You tickle me."

"I'm sorry, my Lady Camille." But he grinned back at me and I realized how much I missed him and Feddrah-Dahns. I had grown fond of both of them, and wondered if when I took the throne, I could visit more often.

"So did you find out why she's looking for the horn and hide?"

He shook his head. "No, just that she says her city is in need of it."

My thoughts ran through the possibilities. The horn was incredibly powerful as a weapon, but there were other ways in which to use it. "I have some thoughts on why, but I'd rather not discuss them here. Will you tell Feddrah-Dahns I'd like to visit with him as soon as possible?"

Mistletoe jumped to his feet and, with a deep bow, said, "Of course I will. I've delivered my message and should go now. But you should also be aware that your journey to Otherworld is common scuttlebutt among certain circles. It is known you are here, although few understand why. I know, of course, but rumor has it that you are here to visit with Tanaquar and with Sharah about your upcoming coronation."

"Spread that rumor as widely as you can. It will serve me well in the coming days as I continue on my real mission."

Mistletoe nodded again. "I will. Be careful, Lady Camille. I would have you come to no harm. And I will talk to my master and tell him you have been apprised of the situation." With that, he fluttered up, zoomed around Delilah with a laugh, which she returned heartily, and then vanished back into the undergrowth.

With relief, I watched him go. At least our stalker had been a friendly one, and with some valuable and interesting information.

"What did the pixie want?" Bran asked. He either didn't know who Mistletoe was, or chose not to reveal it if he did.

"Nothing much. He just had a message for me that has nothing to do with our journey." I cast a veiled look at Delilah and she gave me a short nod. "Let's be off. I want to find the Maharata-Vashi today, and I don't want to wait until dark."

We headed back along the path, picking up the pace again. Two hours past midday and I was beginning to wonder when we were going to find the stream that would lead us to the juncture. But just as the thought crossed my mind, the sound of rushing water filtered through the trees from up ahead, and another two minutes' ride abruptly brought us into a clearing. A stream crossed our path, cutting through the land in a deep, narrow channel. A bridge stretched over the stream, and even from here I could see that the waterway bent and curved to the left, and to the right.

"*Where a bridge crosses stream, that winds like a snake, there find the juncture, the north path you will take.*" I shaded my eyes as a sunbeam splashed across my face, blinding me. "Where's the juncture?"

"Across the stream. We cross the bridge and we'll find three paths. We take the left one. It will lead us northeast. After we're on the path, we should have another eight miles to reach the vast stand of canaberry trees." Bran still sounded grumpy, but he also sounded relieved. "Let's go. We can stop to eat when we reach our destination."

"What about food, though? Should we take half an hour to fish here?" Delilah waved off my protest before I could even open my mouth. "In other words, is there anything in the mountains to eat or are we just going to hope that we find something there?"

"There are small mammals and deer."

"Right. We're going to take down a deer and then dress it before sundown? I don't think so." She wrinkled her nose. "Camille, I'm hungry."

"We continue on," I said. "There are bound to be handover roots there and we can roast them in the fire. I have to reach that scroll before dark. We had good reason for taking care of the kelpies, but every moment we spend out here means another moment for Shadow Wing to figure out where we are and come after us." I realized my voice was growing sharp, but the moment we had emerged into the clearing, with the bridge and the stream, and the paths on the other side, I had felt exposed. It was as though the claustrophobia of being cloistered in the thick of the Deep brought with it a sense of protection. Out here, there seemed to be far more potential for unwelcome strangers to stumble in on our party.

"Okay—don't get upset." Delilah *tsk*ed to her mount and rode up beside me. "We'll go now. I'm just being a pain."

"It's not you, Kitten." I bit my tongue. I had always hated snapping at her. Even though Menolly was the baby of the family, Delilah had always been the most sensitive and easily hurt. "I just feel exposed here. It's probably two P.M. now. If we have eight miles to ride before we reach the trees, then we'll be pushing toward dusk by the time we find them. How far beyond that we need to travel, I don't know."

"Good point. All right. Let's stop for a quick drink and then head on."

I couldn't argue with the need to refill our water canteens or to water our horses, so we picked our way down to the river's edge and spent twenty minutes resting and letting our horses drink and eat grass. While we were waiting, Bran hauled out his dagger and, once again, balancing on a rock, managed to snag five samracks that were quite a decent size. They wouldn't provide all the food we needed for dinner, but it was better than nothing.

The moment I saw what he was doing, I began to hunt handovers. Delilah helped me. The movement stretched us out from riding. I was still sore but was getting used to Annabelle's rolling gait. Between the two of us we netted a solid ten pounds of the roots. That would see us two meals, at least. I also found some watercress and wild onion. Smoky vanished into the undergrowth and when he returned, he had four good-sized loopers, birds in the duck family.

"Well, we have dinner tonight and breakfast," he said.

"A bit more for breakfast," Trillian called from a nearby huckleberry bush. "Early berries. Still a little sour but they'll add good flavoring to the birds." He returned with a small sack of the somewhat under-ripe huckleberries.

We filled our canteens and divvied up the food to carry, then Bran motioned to the bridge.

"Let's ride."

As we crossed the bridge and took the left fork in the juncture, I spotted a house in the woods, on the path that we had turned away from. I wondered who might live here at the crossroads, but then decided that was a path we didn't have time to explore. At one time, I could have had a little house out in the forest, if I had continued to live in Otherworld. But just like the fork in the road we had just left behind, that life was one of the many paths that I'd never walk. Life offered so many possibilities to start, but as we continued, our choices winnowed down. There were paths we'd never see, and others we'd catch a glimpse of but wouldn't have time to explore. And still others that would be barred from our journeys.

As we picked up the pace, heading toward the canaberry tree stand, I thought of all the possibilities that I had left behind and how many more were waiting for me. Ones that I knew nothing about.

THE SUN WAS well into the western side of the sky by the time Bran stopped on the path, pointing up ahead. We were reaching the edge of the treeline, it looked like, and the trees were thinning here. The stream met up with us again, winding this way and that, flowing from the northeast, from the hills. A bridge led over to another path that looked far more worn than the one we were on.

"We're near the foothills of the Tygerian Mountains." Bran rode back to my side. I was riding beside Trillian.

"How far are we from Gyldyn?" Trillian asked.

Gyldyn was the city of the Goldunsun Fae—a branch that had originated in the southern climes. They had uprooted their city when the Scorching Wars roared to life and moved to high in the Tygerian Mountains. While they had a lot of snow, they were open to the sun during the summer, and they had grown used to the altitude and solitude their position brought them.

"If you ride on flat land, a good four or five days' ride south. But with the mountain passes? A week or more at best." Bran motioned for us to continue and we rode out of the Deep into a rolling expanse of grassy knolls and hills. The hills gained a good altitude—three to four thousand feet at their peaks. Beyond the foothills, the brooding crags of the Tygerian Mountains rose, cloaked in mist and fog near their bases. It was amazing that people managed to navigate through them, but there were multiple passes. Rocky and frightening passages, yes, but during the summer they were traversable.

I stared at the vast panorama. The mountains stretched farther than we could see, north and south, slicing across the horizon with a jagged silhouette.

"They're so beautiful." Although the thought of working our way into them frightened me, the expanse was breathtaking.

"They are. Beautiful, deadly, and the source of our rivers." Trillian reached out his hand and I took it as we sat astride our mounts. "But you've been to the Northlands. They make the Tygerian Mountains look like a hike in the woods."

I nodded, silent. The Northlands were like the Himalayas—the tallest mountains in Otherworld and they led to the Dragon Reaches. The Tygerian Mountains led into the Northlands to the far distant north.

"The canaberry grove is across the stream, to the left." Bran dismounted and led his horse down to the water. "Water the horses and take a short break. We'll reach the stand within thirty to forty minutes and the stream runs past it, but I'd rather not force our mounts to wait that long."

I groaned as I slid off the horse. I was getting used to mounting and dismounting and could manage it myself without help by now, but that didn't mean my legs appreciated the workout. As I led Annabelle down to the water, I noticed a bush covered with hedgeberries.

"Somebody bring me a container and I'll gather the berries for dinner."

Delilah brought over a quart-size plastic tub and we proceeded to fill it within minutes. "I'll see if we have another. We won't find a lot of berries once we head into the mountains, if that's where the scroll tells us to go."

"True that." I popped a handful of the fruits in my mouth. The succulent globes burst with rich juice that tasted a lot like elderberries, and the taste lingered on my tongue. Delilah managed to find two more tubs, and she had enlisted Roz to help us. By the time the horses were watered and ready to go, we had managed to pick three quarts. She fastened them securely in the saddlebags on her horse and we mounted our horses again, following Bran over the bridge and out of the Deep.

The trail here was easier going and we made good time without the constant profusion of roots and rocks to watch out for, although the grade began to slope upward and the stream vanished into a deepening ravine to our left.

Within half an hour, the rich green leaves of the canaberry trees appeared. They were distinctive trees, and when I saw them, I realized why I hadn't recognized the name. They were the same trees I had grown up calling boxwood. Boxwood was known for its hard wood and for the orange fruits that ripened during early spring. The trees were an odd conifer, with leaves instead of needles. Their flowers blossomed out in the winter, the fruit ripening by the spring equinox.

"Too bad it's so late in the season." Delilah pulled up beside me. "I love boxwood fruit." She licked her lips.

I grinned at her. "Me too. It's been a long time."

"The boulder, Camille—is that it?" Roz pointed out a tall standing stone near the middle of the thicket. It was huge, as big as a troll, for sure. And there was another fork in the path, to the right, leading through the trees toward the mountains.

"The path directly beyond it turns to the right. We go that way, I assume, and listen for the martingeese." I didn't like the nebulousness of the directions, but we had found the way so far. I turned around and asked Venus to ride forward. The path here was wide enough for us to all gather around the gigantic stone.

Venus approached, staring up at the stone. "That's it, I know it is."

"What do martingeese sound like?" I had never heard of the birds before.

"They make a *whoop-whoop* sound—a little like a loon, in a sense," Bran said. "It's so distinctive that when you hear it, you'll notice it. They're loud, and their calls echo for miles."

We turned onto the right path, which immediately sloped in an upward grade. This path was narrower, but we could still ride three abreast, and so Bran, Trillian, and I took the front, while Delilah, Chase, Venus took second row. Shade and Smoky and Roz brought up the rear.

Chase, who had been quiet for a long time, suddenly spoke up. "Something about this area speaks to me. I've never been here, never been anywhere quite like it, but something about the approaching mountains seems to be calling to me."

Chase's psychic abilities had opened up when he was fed the Nectar of Life to save his life, and I had learned to pay attention. His hunches and instincts had played out more often than not, and he never mentioned them unless they were strong enough that he couldn't ignore them.

"Do you think it could be related to the elf in your blood?" Delilah asked.

"No," he answered after a moment. "This feels like something else. I don't know what, though, but I can't shake the feeling."

We must have been approaching five o'clock when a sudden swishing sound startled me, and I jerked to my right. The path was overlooking a large pond, with a narrow trail leading down to it. On the surface of the pond were hundreds of white birds, and the *whoop whoop whoop* that echoed from them filled the air like muffled propellers.

"Martingeese," I said softly, as the impulse to head toward the pond overwhelmed me. It was as though a homing button had just activated, driving me to turn off the main path and head toward the pond. "This way. We have to go to the pond."

The others said nothing, just caught up to me. I took the lead, because the trail leading down the grassy slope was only passable by one horse at a time. Annabelle picked her way down carefully, through the dust of the path. The hill was steep, and my horse didn't seem to trust walking through the grass, so I gave her the lead, guiding her gently and allowing her to sort her way down to the clearing near the pond. On the opposite side, I could see as we got closer, were more foothills, buttressed against the other shoreline.

"The cavern—it has to be there. I know it." And I did—as sure as I knew my name, I knew that the cave hiding the Maharata-Vashi was on the other side of the pond.

The birds flocked into the sky as we rode toward the pond, and I became acutely aware of how exposed we were from the air and the sides. I pressed Annabelle to a trot, wanting to be out of visibility's range as soon as possible. We came to the shoreline and I immediately began trotting around the edge, taking the quickest route to circle the pond.

"Camille? Camille, is something wrong?" Delilah galloped up to my side.

"We need to be out of sight, and we need to get to the other side of the pond as quickly as possible. There's something out there, trying to get a fix on us. I don't know *how* I know it, but I do know it. Trust me, please."

Whether it was Shadow Wing tracking us, or some wayward sorcerer who was after the horn and hide, I had no clue. Or maybe it was one of the Great Fae Lords, waking, who didn't want me to interfere with the running of the portals. Or perhaps just a hungry ogre, looking for lunch. Whatever the case, it was imperative that we got out of sight as soon as possible.

The others didn't argue, just followed me toward the opposite shore. We managed to circle the pond without anything happening, but I was still uneasy. But we reached the edge of the foothills without incident and I tried to focus on looking for the cavern. The scrub brush was thick between the shore and hill, but it was low growing. I shaded my eyes as we rode along beside it, searching for the opening.

"Where is it? It has to be somewhere along here. How hard is it to spot a cave? It's still daylight." I was starting to feel frantic. "We need to find the cave, *now*."

"Calm down, Camille." Smoky tapped me on the shoulder. "We'll find it."

"I know, but we have to find it. Please, trust me. We can't screw around." I pushed Annabelle forward, trying to get around him, but he said something under his breath and the horse stopped. Great, he had to be a horse whisperer, too?

"Camille—what's gotten into you? You sound terrified."

By now the others were starting to gather around me. Venus rode up and cocked his head, staring at me closely. After a moment, he nodded and said, "Tagalong."

"What the hell is a tagalong?" Delilah was squinting at me.

"A spirit has latched on to her. She's not possessed, but she's feeling their impulses. Camille, tell us exactly what you're feeling."

I stared at the old shaman, trying to listen to him. I knew he was saying something important, but his words seemed drowned out in the thundering fear that raced through me. I focused on the feeling of his hand on my wrist. It was real. Solid. Warm. Comforting. As I poured my attention into his grasp, into the touch of his fingers against my skin, the panic began to subside. It was still there, but at a lower ebb, no longer reverberating through every cell in my body.

"I feel panic." My words felt like they were coming from somewhere distant, outside of myself. "I have to hide the scroll. I have to hide it or something horrible will happen. I have to seal it away to know it's safe. There's something looking for it, to destroy it. To prevent me hiding it for the queen to find." Even as the words came out of my mouth, they sounded jumbled up, a mix of my thoughts with someone else's. "No. I mean—I need to *find* the scroll."

"Yes, a tagalong but one, I think, that has a reason for choosing you other than looking for a psychic happy meal." Venus motioned for me to get off my horse, and he did the same. "Close your eyes, Camille. Close your eyes and take a deep breath."

I didn't want to close my eyes. We were out in the open and they were coming. They would ride into our midst and strike us down. But Venus's voice was so soothing that I couldn't help but obey.

"Camille, take another deep breath and tell me what you see. Keep your eyes closed. Let your mind drift."

I followed his directions, and images began to flood my mind. "I see...warriors fighting—they're Fae. I can tell by their eyes. They're wearing purple and silver—and they have vicious-looking swords. It's a battle—" I stopped. Someone came into sight whom I recognized, even though she was clearly far younger than I remembered her. Queen Asteria, creeping with Trenyth through the shrubs, watching for the soldiers who were all around the area. It was then that I realized whom the Fae were fighting. It was the elves. *The Fae versus elves?*

Queen Asteria looked so young, younger than I'd ever imagined. She was dressed in a simple dress, spidersilk and the green of the surrounding land. But even though she wasn't wearing her crown, I could tell she had already taken the throne. There was a regal quality to her, even in her haste. Trenyth, dressed in a tunic and trousers and a simple cloak, barely looked old enough to shave. My heart hurt as I watched them. I missed her—she had become such an integral part of our lives that it was still hard to accept that she was gone. She hadn't exactly been a mother figure to us, but perhaps, a grandmother figure.

I mouthed her name as I reached out, but I could only watch as she and Trenyth pressed up against the hillside behind one particular oddly shaped rock. I took note of where they were in relationship to the pond, watched as the soldiers swarmed the area. But for some reason, the Fae warriors didn't seem to notice the two of them were there.

Queen Asteria turned to Trenyth, holding her finger to her lips. Then, she motioned to him and he reached in the pocket of his tunic and brought out a small metal disk. I couldn't tell what it was, or what it was made of, but he pressed it against the side of the hill and there was a soft hiss—I could actually hear the noise—and the dirt vanished. In its place was a door.

A barrow mound. The hill was a barrow mound. I recognized it immediately as that, once the doorway had been exposed. Trenyth stood back as Queen Asteria reached out and knocked on the door. *Once. Twice. Three times.*

The door slowly opened. I could hear it in my mind, easing open with a cavernous silence that echoed through me. They slipped inside and I followed them, watching. Once inside the barrow mound, Queen Asteria crept over to the far wall of the chamber, a veritable repository of scrolls. There were small holes, the size of a scroll tube, covering the vast wall. Thousands of them. Perhaps tens of thousands. She stopped, then turned to stare straight at me.

She can't see me, I thought. *She's dead.*

But she looked at me as I gazed into her eyes. Then, reaching up, she pointed to one of the symbols painted on the wall. It was in Melosealfôr, and it was the symbol for eighty-one. Then, she slowly poked her finger against the side of a column of scroll holes. I counted carefully. At twenty-three she stopped and pulled out a scroll from her pocket. She glanced back at me, holding my attention, then slid the scroll into the hole in the wall. And then, before I could see anymore, she and Trenyth and the inside of the barrow mound vanished, and I was blinking, standing there with Venus.

Chapter 13

"CAMILLE? WHAT DID you see?" Venus was holding me by the shoulders, and I realized he was holding me up while keeping Smoky at bay. Apparently I had been so deep in trance I couldn't stand by myself.

I let out a long breath. "I know where the scroll is. This is a barrow mound. I'm not sure if we can get in, but I know where to look for the entrance. And I know who hid it." I turned to Delilah, my eyes wet. "Queen Asteria and Trenyth hid the scroll away. She was terrified that the Fae Lords would find her. It must have been near the end of the Great Divide. I think the legends have it wrong. I actually think the Spirit Seal was created by the enemy of the Fae Lords who wanted to divide the worlds, as a way of bringing it back together again in the future."

Delilah caught her breath. "So you think Aeval and Titania know?"

I thought about it for a moment. They would have had no reason to lie to us, or keep the information from us. After a pause, I shook my head. "No, they were trapped by the Great Fae Lords before this happened. I think Queen Asteria carried on the work. She hinted to us more than once that she wasn't in favor of the Great Divide. I think she worked on the side of the opposition. She was in the resistance, so to speak."

"Do you think she actually created the seal?" Delilah's eyes widened. She had loved the old Elfin Queen just as much as I had.

I shrugged. "I doubt we'll ever know. But she hid the scroll, so I wonder if she also hid the Keraastar Diamond. The veils of time blur things together, and she had her reasons for keeping silent, I'm sure." I paused, hesitating for a moment before adding, "I think she knew I was there. I mean, how could she? But yet, she looked directly at me. I can't help it. I believe she knows—knew—I'm here to get the scroll."

"Stranger things have happened," Venus said. "Remember, magic exists outside of time. So do many beings and creatures."

Bran, who had been standing to the side, suddenly came to attention. "Queen Asteria was cagey and cunning. She always had reason for doing whatever she chose. She was one of the few in the Elfin kingdom that my mother respected. And one of the few I've ever felt the desire to be gracious to. I'm not keen on the elves, but Queen Asteria wasn't nearly as complacent as others thought her to be."

I knew that was true, from experience. But a glance at the sky told me that the light was starting to wane, bringing with it the first chill of evening. "Come on. I want into that barrow before nightfall."

"Where's the opening?" Venus asked. "You said you know?"

I stood back, eyeing the pond, then turned in the direction where I had seen them enter the mound. It took only a moment to figure out where they had found the entrance. I pushed through the scrub toward the side of the hill, the others following me. Once there, I stood at what I thought was the exact spot where Queen Asteria had been standing.

"The problem is, she had a metal disk she pressed against the side of the hill—right about here." I touched a stone that I remembered seeing next to where she had touched the metal to the hillside. Nothing happened. "I don't know how to make the door appear, but it's right here."

"Did you say 'metal disk'?" Venus stepped forward.

I nodded. "Yeah, it was about the size of a silver dollar. Maybe a little bigger."

"Like this?" He reached up to his neck and withdrew a chain that had been hidden below his tunic. "Chain" wasn't exactly the right word. I recognized it as spider-silk—so strong it would be extremely resistant to being cut. As he drew it out from beneath his shirt, a metal disk was hanging from the end. It looked a lot like the one I had seen Trenyth had Asteria.

"Like...that." I slowly held out my hand. "Where did you get this?"

"Queen Asteria gave it to me when she told me about the Maharata-Vashi. She didn't say why. She just said don't lose it and that I'd know when it was needed. I've worn it ever since, just as I've worn my spirit seal." He slipped it off from around his neck and handed it to me. "I've learned to act on faith over the years of my life."

I took the medallion. It had an antiqued look, and as I held it, I flashed back to seeing the queen firmly press her disk to the wall. I followed suit, slamming the metal against the compacted wall of dirt and grass. The metal flared as it hit the wall and I almost dropped the disk, but managed to hold onto it as a door appeared in the hill. I knocked on it three times, and it slid open, letting out a long hiss as stale air rushed out. I stared at the mound, suspecting that no one had entered this mound since Queen Asteria and Trenyth, though there was no way to know.

"We found it. We actually found it," Delilah whispered.

"Is it safe?" I wanted to rush in, but had enough sense to hold myself back.

Bran peeked inside. "There's light in there. It seems to be a natural illumination. As long as the door stays open, we should be able to breathe."

"Maybe somebody should stay outside with the disk, just in case it decides to shut on us." I turned to Roz. "Will you wait here?"

He nodded. "Chase can stay with me."

"Thanks, dude. I really don't feel like wandering into a mountainside right now." Chase was staring at the opening with a faint look of terror in his eyes. "It's nothing against you or your search, but frankly, I know my limits and who the hell knows what's in there after all these years? I'm not Pandora and this isn't my box."

That broke the tension. I cracked up, relaxing for the first time in a while. "Good thinking. Who's going with me?"

Smoky and Trillian stepped forward, as well as Delilah and Venus. Shade opted to stay outside in case Roz and Chase needed help. I handed them the medallion.

"You can open the barrow that way if it closes on us. Don't lose it. We may need to come here again." I turned to the others. "Ready?"

They nodded, but this time, Smoky and Trillian hung back, waiting for me to take the lead. I looked over at Venus and he gave me the slightest of nods. *This is it*, a soft voice said inside. *The turning point. You're going to be calling the shots soon. And here's where you start*. Shoulders back, head held high, I took a deep breath and entered the barrow, flanked by Smoky behind me to my left, and Venus to the right. Behind them were Delilah and Bran.

The barrow felt like a freshly opened tomb and indeed, it was very much an ancient repository. Catacombs for scrolls, rather than mummies. The chamber was vast—so vast I couldn't begin to estimate how many thousands of scrolls lined the walls, each in a narrow hole, hundreds of rows and hundreds of columns. The ceiling of the barrow had to be a good fifty feet high, and the chamber itself was at least two hundred feet wide. I wasn't sure how far back it went, but as I pressed inward, the illumination grew from a dim glimmer to a bright sparkling light. It wouldn't match a fluorescent light, but it was bright enough to see into the corners, and it emanated from the walls, the ceiling, and the floor.

"What magic is this?" The very air felt charged to the point of making my skin jump. I had no idea what had gone into the making of this place, but whoever had crafted this barrow had to have been incredibly powerful. "It wasn't the Great Fae Lords who made this place. I can tell you that. The magic here is even more powerful than they could wield."

Smoky let out a faint huff. He sounded mildly perplexed. "No fires here. Fire magic, natural fire, it won't work here."

I didn't ask how he knew, but I trusted his word. As I cautiously approached a gap in the back wall, I realized it was a passage, and then it hit me full force. "We're in a library, I think. There are more scrolls back here."

In fact, there were rows of the natural stone shelves, much like library stacks carved out of the ancient mountainside. And each held row after row of scroll tubes.

"Who created this?" Delilah asked in a hushed voice.
"Welcome to the Akashic Library."

The voice took us all by surprise and I spun around. Behind us, a dark vertical line appeared in the air, and out from that line—as though stepping through a gate—a woman appeared. Dark skinned, she was dressed in a flowing dress the color of eggplant, with a silver shawl around her shoulders, the color of moonlight. A diadem encircled her head, with a droplet of lapis lazuli marking her forehead. Her hair was deep black, as were her eyes, her pupils twinkling stars.

"I am Sesarati, the Keeper of Lore. What do you seek?"

"Sesarati?" Bran's eyes went wide. "I've heard of you." He turned to me. "She's one of the Hags of Fate, like Pentangle, the Mother of Magic."

I had heard of the Akashic Library, as had a number of humans. But I had always thought it was a myth. I glanced around, realizing just how much knowledge and wisdom had to be contained here. I could spend lifetimes reading and learning. The desire to sit down, grab a scroll, and start studying hit me so hard that I could taste it.

Sesarati smiled, aloof but not unpleasant. "I can sense your hunger to learn. But the eternal scholars hoard knowledge like a miser hoards gold, seldom using it wisely. Don't let yourself be caught up in the hunger. Learning is good, but what you do with it is even more important. Now, what have you come for?"

I cleared my throat, forcing myself to focus on her. "I come for the Maharata-Vashi."

She held out her hand expectantly, and I stared at it, not knowing what she wanted.

"If you require payment, I'm afraid I'm not sure what currency you use." I was all too aware of what some of the greater beings like the Elemental Lords and the Hags of Fate required, and I wasn't about to pledge it without first knowing what I was offering.

"What I require is your hand so I can know that you are authorized to take the scroll." She cocked her head, giving me a look that was almost...human.

I let out a soft laugh. "Sorry, I'm new to this."

"So I can tell. Give me your hand, please."

I glanced at Smoky. He inclined his head. Apparently, he was aware of who she was and seemed to feel it was all right. I trusted him, especially when he agreed with an action rather than immediately jumping to attack.

Cautiously, I held out my hand, placing it in hers. She felt almost shimmery, as though she were a flicker of energy rather than a corporeal being, and for all I knew, she was. The Hags of Fate were beyond our scope. Even Grandmother Coyote, who seemed far more approachable—I instinctively knew on a gut level just how powerful she was and I never overstepped the boundaries I could sense were in place.

Sesarati closed her hand over mine and prickles of energy raced through me, like an army of ants marching across my body. I shivered, trying to shake it off, but then she let go and stepped back. "You are who you are. I will get the scroll for you."

"I saw...I had a vision of the woman who originally brought the scroll here. I didn't see you in it." It wasn't exactly a question, because I didn't know if she'd answer, but I wanted to see what she would say.

"That is because I never leave this library, even in visions. This is my home. It is where I've always been, and it's where I'll always be. I'm only visible to those who enter the library. I can neither be summoned nor called upon. To enter, you must possess one of the talismans—and those are not given lightly. See that you never let your key out of your possession again. It will be safe for the moment, but when you re-enter the outer world, you must keep it with you forever or it will be destroyed." Sesarati vanished then, stepping into her personal portal—or whatever that dark line of energy was.

I let out a sharp breath. I hadn't even realized I'd been holding it. "This library could be worth..."

"It's priceless," Bran said. "The wisdom of the universe lies in here."

"And to think that the Akashic Library is in Otherworld." Delilah folded her arms, shaking her head. She looked just about as stunned as I felt.

"This isn't Otherworld," Venus said. "Nor is it Earthside. The moment we walked into the barrow, we ceased to be on any planet. We're somewhere tucked away in the depths of the universe, I'll wager."

"He's right," Trillian said. "The Akashic Library is universal. My guess is that Sesarati wears many guises, depending on who visits."

The thought of where we were kept washing over me like waves. *Boom. We're in a universal library. Splash. We're in a room that contains the wisdom of the ages. Whoosh. We're standing outside of time and space. And probably outside of our galaxy. And I have a key to the library.*

I searched for something to say but once again, found myself speechless. I still felt the desire to pull up a chair and read forever—to just keep searching through the scrolls to learn everything I could possibly learn, but Sesarati was correct. Knowledge without application wasn't the most useful path in the universe, and what good was anything I learned if I couldn't apply it to my life? To my loved ones' lives?

Another moment—we were all lost in our thoughts, it seemed—and the line reappeared, and Sesarati stepped out of the narrow portal. She had a scroll in hand, which she held out to me.

"This now goes into your possession. Use it wisely.

The knowledge contained within the Akashic Library is never given lightly. Results are expected, if continued use of the library is to be allowed." With that she motioned toward the door.

I glanced at it. At some point in the past few moments, it had shut behind us. "How do we get out? I left my key outside with friends in case it was a one-way situation."

"Oh, there are no problems leaving the library. It's the getting in that's the hard part." As she spoke, the door began to open, and—scroll in hand—I thanked her and led the others back toward the outer world.

WE EXITED THE barrow and the door slammed shut behind us. I immediately took possession of the key, and then held up the scroll tube. "I supposed I'd better make certain this is the right one."

"You didn't look while you were in there?" Chase asked.

I shook my head. "You'll understand when I tell you about what happened. It wasn't anything that I expected, either." I glanced at the sky. Dusk was approaching and I was tired. "We need to make camp and rest. I'm hungry and tired."

Bran pointed toward a small copse of trees a few hundred yards away to our right. We'd have the lake between us and the other side of the clearing, and a clear sight line to the barrow mound, although the door had vanished the moment we exited.

Delilah immediately began hunting for firewood. "We need to roast up the loopers and handover roots. It's going to be chilly here by the pond. We're at a higher elevation than we were last night."

I tucked the scroll in my pocket as we made camp. I wanted to read it, to yank it out and unroll it, but it felt as though we should bivouac before doing anything else. We found a good spot, with enough rocks to ring a campfire, and while Delilah and Shade built the fire, Trillian made quick work of dressing the loopers while Chase washed the handover roots and berries. Bran went fishing again—he said that the fish bit better at dusk. Venus, Roz, and I laid out all the bedrolls, and Smoky carried fallen logs over to sit on. Within twenty minutes, we were encamped and resting beside the crackling fire, while the birds roasted on a makeshift spit, and the handover roots bubbled in the pan that Shade had provided. Another few minutes and Bran returned with a string of fish—enough to roast up for breakfast, as well. Cold fish in the morning didn't sound all that appealing, but it definitely sounded better than an empty stomach.

I spied a flowering shrub nearby and quickly gathered some of the leaves and blossoms. "I haven't had fresh kettle-nap tea in years." The tea was good for soothing the nerves. Speaking of soothing, my ribs were aching, although the pain was less than it had been the day before. I'd have Delilah apply salve to the bruises before bed.

Shade brought out a second pan—smaller than the other, but it would work for several cups of tea—and Chase obligingly filled it from the pond. Movement on the pond's surface indicated that it was fed from an underground spring, and the ripples of current prevented stagnant water from accumulating. The result was no algae on the surface and no swarms of mosquitoes or other biting insects had gathered over it.

I crushed the blossoms and leaves and dropped them into the water, then sat back, gazing into the fire. It was time. I could feel it, like a pendulum slowly swinging.

I withdrew the scroll from my pocket and motioned to Venus. He crossed to me. Roz handed me the Maharata-Verdi, which, unlike its twin, was encased within a magical leather tube. I asked Venus to unroll it, as I slipped the cap off the ivory scroll tube of the other. The ivory was from some ancient animal, long extinct. As I ran my hand along the tube I felt the impression of a huge beast—probably a mastodon.

"The magic within the tube itself is extremely powerful," I whispered. It seemed counterintuitive to speak in normal tones. I cautiously shook out the scroll within and gently unrolled it. The paper crackled, but it held together, bound by magic and time.

As Chase shone a flashlight beam over it, the image of a map came into view. It was easy enough to read. There was Thistlewyd Deep, and the Tygerian Mountains. The lettering below the scroll was in the same ancient Melosealfôr as the Maharata-Verdi, which I could pick out a word or two of, but the fact was, right now we didn't need to know what it said. An "x" on the map marked a position in the Tygerian Mountains, near the monastery belonging to the Tygerian monks. Which meant that the Order of the Crystal Dagger had been around for thousands of years.

"I'm guessing the monks might be able to read this," Roz said. "If you want to consult them. I think we'll have to, anyway, given the position of that 'x.' If that's the diamond, then it's on their property and we'll never get past them to hunt for it without permission."

"I think you're right," I said, staring at the drawing. "That's near the monastery, which means it's probably on their mountain. I doubt if it's in the monastery itself." I wasn't sure how approachable the monks would be. Rumors put them as incredibly helpful, or a pain in the ass.

"So, how far from here to the monastery?"

"Four days by horse, without any issues."

"A few hours by dragon," Smoky spoke up. "I can fly you there. I can take several of you on my back. Shade can take the rest. Now that we know where we're going, it's a lot easier and we won't even have to go through the Ionyc Sea which, given the circumstances, is best. I've been to the monastery before. I know the way."

I glanced at Annabelle. "What about our horses?"

"I will stay to watch them," Roz said. "I won't be welcome at the temple, anyway. They don't tend to like my kind there. We seem to insult them, for some reason."

"Lack of control. You take away their control and not much can do that." Bran turned the handle of the makeshift spit. The loopers were beginning to smell really good and my mouth watered. "The monks, while not celibate, prefer to keep the upper hand with everything, including their sexuality. You remind them that they don't always have control over their personal responses."

He turned to the rest of us. "One thing you must understand about the Tygerian monks is that they are incredibly disciplined. Their martial arts, their diet, everything down to the way they dress, brush their hair—it's all regimented. They train from a very young age. Only boys who haven't hit puberty yet are accepted into the order, and even then, the younger the better. They spend their lives devoted to the teachings of the temple."

Chase leaned forward, resting his elbows on his knees as he held out his hands toward the fire. "Sounds like the Shaolin monks."

"I know who you speak of. Yes, there are some similarities although the Tygerian monks haven't had to make concessions to a modern age. They're still as deadly and as fierce as their ancestors. They are true fanatics."

"Are they all boys?" Chase asked.

Bran shook his head. "There's a women's division, but their monastery is deeper into the mountain range and they seldom come in contact with their male counterparts. Both branches are deadly. Both branches are almost chaotic in their relentless drive for order."

"They sound—unpleasant." Chase was mincing his words.

I nodded. "Generally, although Menolly knew a priest from the Temple of Reckoning in Aladril. He was a priest of Great Mother Dayinye, and he was originally from the Order of the Crystal Dagger. But I had the feeling he had left the monastery for good, although he never said anything about it. At least as far as *I* know. He was pleasant enough, but intense." He had helped save Menolly from Dredge by cutting her link to him—the link all vampires have to their sire. That seemed so very long ago, though it had only been four years.

"The loopers are ready," Bran said, poking the birds.

Trillian had dressed them in a way that took less time over the fire. The fish were also ready. Bran set aside enough for breakfast before parceling out the rest of them. Trillian carved the loopers, while Delilah used a sturdy campfork to spear the handover roots, which were soft and tender in the water. Soon, we were all busy with food and tea. The buttery flavor of the birds melted against my tongue, and I mashed my handover root, swirling the juices from both bird and fish into them to produce a creamy puree. Delilah handed around the salt, and I sprinkled some of that onto everything. The roots were almost as good as mashed potatoes, although they could have done with a little milk.

"If Roz stays to keep watch over the horses, somebody should stay with him. Shade and Smoky can't, if they're going to fly us up there. Bran, you seem to be familiar with the order. Are you coming along?" I couldn't stay, and neither could Venus. For some reason, I had to take Chase with me, and the two dragons had to go.

"I should. I know their ways. Trillian can stay here. Delilah, you might want to stay as well."

She shook her head. "As much as I'd rather just play campout, I'm going if Camille is. I won't let her go into this alone."

Trillian frowned. "I'd rather go, but Rozurial should have someone else with him. All right, I'll stay here. But be careful up there. I've had some dealings with the Tygerian monks before and I'm not comfortable with you heading into their territory."

I didn't want to say anything, but that didn't surprise me. Svartans didn't get along well with anybody too rigid. The entire Svartan race had a knack for chaos, and if the Order of the Crystal Dagger eschewed it, there were bound to be some sparks flying when the two got together.

"Smoky will be with me, love. And Shade and Delilah. You stay with Roz. You're more comfortable in the woods than he is."

He nodded. There wasn't much he could do to stop me, and he knew it. "Guard her well, you big lizard. Or I'll chase you down."

For once, Smoky didn't answer. He, too, looked pensive.

"We leave in the morning? Or should we go tonight?" Even though I was tired, I was anxious to get moving now that we knew the location.

"Morning. If there's trouble, we all need to be on the top of our game," Delilah said. "Tonight, we rest. Let me look at your ribs."

She led me off to the area where I had laid out my sleeping bag. I stripped off my shirt, shivering in the cool evening air. The day had been plenty warm, but here, out in the open, the moment the sun went down, the temperatures started to fall.

"Your bruises are fading. You're healing up pretty fast. How do they feel?"

I tentatively did a few chest stretches, wincing as the ache set in. But it wasn't nearly as bad as it had been. "I should be back to normal in a couple of days. Whatever *normal* is."

After a moment, during which we sat hand in hand, Delilah nudged me with her shoulder. "I miss Queen Asteria. But at least I got to see her when she was young, too. When I—" She paused, then bit her lip. Delilah had been given the task of escorting Queen Asteria out of her life, onto the next leg of her journey. She had seen the Elfin Queen in various stages of her life and had come to understand her in a way none of the rest of us ever could.

"She and Trenyth were so young. The world was so different then. And yet, they were caught in a war. War's always with us, isn't it? None of us can live in peace, can we? I used to wish for the world to be a peaceful place. Now, I just hope it survives." My mood was rapidly spiraling and I wasn't sure how to stop it. I needed to pull myself out of the depression that had settled around my shoulders.

"Do you think we'll have to face Shadow Wing? I'm hoping that Trytian's father can take him down. At least we have a connection with the daemons."

"We may have a connection, but I will never trust them." I shook my head. "It would be easier if we didn't have to face him. Without the spirit seals, he'll have a far harder time breaking through the portals. But with the rogue portals cropping up, and the entire system breaking down, I won't rest easy until he's dead."

Delilah wrapped her arms around her knees as I

unzipped my sleeping bag. I took off my bra, pulling an oversized flannel sleep shirt over my head before I slipped out of my skirt. Folding my clothes, I slipped them into the pack and closed it tightly to prevent creepy-crawlies from nesting in it. There were venomous spiders and snakes in the mountains and while we hadn't seen any yet, I knew they were around. Secretly, I was grateful we wouldn't be hiking our way up to the monastery. Even with the horses, it was all too easy to meet a nasty critter who would have no qualms about taking down a large enemy—or anybody it thought was an enemy.

I slid a rolled-up travel pillow under my head and yawned. "I'm glad you're here. This isn't an easy journey, and every step brings me closer to the Summer Solstice."

"What are you afraid of?" Delilah pushed herself to her knees, getting ready to go back to her sleeping bag and Shade.

"I guess...I'm afraid of not being good enough. Of being found wanting." But that wasn't the only thing that I feared, and I knew it. "If I'm honest, I'm afraid of leaving you and Menolly. I'm afraid of the fact that—for the first time in our lives—we'll be on different paths, living apart. It's always been us against the world. Now, everything's changing."

Delilah leaned down to kiss my forehead. "I think we're all afraid of that. But as you've told me so many times, we have to grow. We have to accept change. If we stay together and ignore our futures just because we're afraid, then we'll stagnate and eventually we'll resent each other."

I knew she was right—and truth was, I had told her that very thing so many times. "Thanks, Kitten. Thanks for being with me. For helping me meet my destiny. I love you."

Delilah stroked my arm. "You'll always be my big sister. You'll always be the one who took over when Mother died. Never forget that, Camille."

As she headed back to her own sleeping bag, I stared up at the stars. The moon, fading toward crescent, was a brilliant glimmer against the backdrop. "I hope I can do you justice," I whispered to the Moon Mother. "I hope I make you proud."

And the moon, being the moon, only answered with a pregnant silence.

Chapter 14

AS WE STOOD in the clearing, we could feel the sun on our backs as it glimmered through Thistlewyd Deep. We had chosen a space where, when Smoky and Shade shifted form, they wouldn't go toppling into the pond or smash themselves up against the hillside.

Roz and Trillian moved the horses well out of the way, tying them securely to trees far enough away so that when two dragons appeared, they wouldn't be too terribly panicked. Dragons ate horses, and horses knew that.

I worried my lip. We had eaten breakfast, gathered only what we thought we might need, and there was no more reason to stand here. Excuses: done.

"It's time." I motioned to Smoky and Shade, who were standing a good distance from us. "Go ahead. Make with the wings."

Delilah let out a snort. "In Shade's case, that's bones."

"Yeah, but it seems impolite to point that out."

Within a slow blur that gathered speed, first Smoky

shifted form, and then Shade. The dragons stood there, side by side. I thought that Shade looked like what Smoky did on the inside. He was older than Smoky, and a little bit bigger, but without flesh, he seemed almost like a pteranodon or a pterodactyl.

I motioned to Venus. "You and Bran come with me. Chase, you can ride with Delilah."

Chase gave me an odd look and I suddenly realized how odd it might be for him. He had dated Delilah and now he was going to ride on her fiancé's back. But he said nothing, just followed her over to Shade's side.

Bran and Venus escorted me up to Smoky, who obligingly knelt for me to climb on his arm, then scramble up on his shoulder to his neck. Tendrils of his mane fluttered back, coiling around my waist to keep me in place. In some ways, riding on Shade would be easier, because there were more crevices where the bones met to grab hold of. But either way, riding a dragon was fun, if potentially dangerous. I had tied a sturdy leather thong to both ends of my staff, and now I looped it around one of the spines that rose along Smoky's neck. They weren't as sharp as bone, but some sort of rigid cartilage. I doubled the loop so that if Smoky had to tilt sideways, the staff wouldn't go sailing off into the air.

Venus and Bran situated themselves behind me, and Smoky pushed off, leaping into the air as his wings caught an updraft. He soared over the pond, followed by Shade, and as we gained altitude I was able to tell just how lucky we were to be riding on dragonback.

The foothills were a good climb, but they were dimples compared to the Tygerian Mountains. Within minutes, we were soaring over a vast array of peaks and crags. The mountain range below us stretched out farther than we could see, the mountains growing in height to the north. The range widened as well, and the snow-covered array looked terrifyingly jagged, although memories of the Northlands flashed through my head. These mountains would kill you if you ventured into the wrong areas. The Northlands, on the other hand, would hunt you down and eat you on toast for breakfast.

I shivered. At this height, even my cloak didn't do much to keep me warm. I leaned back to find myself snuggling against Venus. He was shivering too, and he wrapped one arm around my waist, pressing against me to keep warm. The shaman was burly, and I rather wished he could turn into his puma self here so I could cuddle with the big kitty. But that wouldn't be practical, and so I settled for the warmth that our bodies could manage. I didn't know how Bran was faring, and I decided to refrain from asking.

The miles passed by quickly. Dragons were fast and they were big, and in this area, they weren't unexpected. We swooped past the tree level but still close enough to the ground that there was plenty of air to breathe, although I kept my head down, not wanting to get any bugs or birds in the face. I tried to stare at Smoky's neck. Watching the dragon scales of my husband was a lot better than looking over the side at a drop that could easily kill me.

We had left at the first blush of dawn, and by noon, we were flying around some of the taller peaks rather than over them. The temperatures had dropped dramatically, and I was shivering, even with Venus's added warmth. I tried to position myself so the sunlight could fall on me, and even though it was nearing the Summer Solstice, at altitudes like this, the chill was daunting.

I was about ready to thump on Smoky's neck to get his attention when we began to descend toward one of the taller peaks. Breaking my firm don't-look-down rule, I saw the shape of a structure on the side of the mountain, which meant we were circling Mount Tyger and the monastery.

As we spiraled down, the monastery got larger. It was simple, but beautiful in its minimalism. Built out of stone, the temple was gray, with windows around the outside that contained no glass, but a translucent, flickering energy. I wondered if it was a form of force field that kept people out as well. The temple was two stories, about as large as a typical Denny's restaurant, and it was surrounded by a stone fence that matched the walls. The temple was on the edge of a cliff, with a large clearing to the side, which was where we were headed.

We were high enough that the only trees here were scrub, bent sideways from the constant wind. Grasses and wildflowers dotted the high tundra, along with lichens and moss. There was little here to eat for animals, but somehow, wildlife managed. We were probably about ten thousand feet up, but the peak of the mountain was much higher than we were.

As we landed, a wave of dizziness hit me, doubling me over as I climbed off of Smoky's back. I slipped and hit the ground with a thud. Thankfully, I didn't have very far to fall. Venus knelt beside me, as did Bran, and a moment later, Smoky pushed through the pair and lifted me up.

"The air is thin here. You are used to living near sea level," he said.

Shade, Chase, and Delilah joined us, Shade helping Chase walk. "It seems we forgot what an abrupt rise in elevation can do."

Delilah was rubbing her head. "I've got the headache from hell."

I tapped Smoky on the arm. "Put me down, please. The monks are coming."

And sure enough, they were. Three monks from the temple were walking our way. They were dressed in silver gowns, with blue sashes and blue hats that reminded me of fezzes. Silver tassels hung off the side of the hats, and each monk wore an exquisitely embossed leather sheath by their side, holding a long dagger. I knew immediately what kind of daggers they were carrying—the famed crystal blades that gave the order their name. I felt myself jonesing to get a look at them. I wasn't necessarily a blade aficionado, but they were heavily steeped with magical energy and I'd probably never get another chance to see one up close. It seemed rude to ask, though.

Smoky set me down and I straightened my skirt. Then, a little woozily, I stepped forward and inclined my head, holding up my hands in the universal sign used throughout most of the northern cities and lands in Otherworld to symbolize respect. Palm forward, bent up at the wrist, with the other palm crossing it. *Open hands, open heart.* The others followed suit, even Chase, once he saw the rest of us doing it. He was good at picking up things quickly, I'd give him that.

One of the monks stepped forward. He eyed us, his gaze slowly moving from person to person. At Bran, he did a double take. And when he came to Chase, he frowned slightly. Then, in Melosealfôr, he said, "You are on our lands, in our territory. You indicate you come in peace. We honor your intent, as long as you hold it. Come, eat, and rest."

There was nothing to do but accept. One just did not wander into the monastery and demand to be let loose to go after a diamond that was hidden on their land. To refuse food and drink, or at least their hospitality, would be a faux pas that could end in bloodshed.

"We are on your lands, in your territory. We come in peace. We hold our intent, and accept your generosity." I turned to the others and translated what we had said.

"We can trust them?" Chase asked.

"We have no reason not to. Plus, this is their land. We can't just go barging around without their permission and I'm not going to do anything to get us on their bad side. Besides, it's lunch time, and a hot meal would be welcome." Smiling, I turned back to the monk, who was watching us carefully.

He motioned for us to follow, and they turned and headed toward the temple. Right then, I knew we were right to follow protocol. If they were comfortable enough to turn their backs on us, they could easily defeat us. I wasn't sure how much they knew, but by the looks they had given Smoky, Shade, and Bran, they understood exactly who they were allowing under their roof.

We crossed the barren courtyard and by the time we got to the temple doors, I was so weak-kneed that I could barely manage. I didn't want to show any vulnerability but the truth was that I needed help if I wanted to make it any farther. I looked around, motioning to Smoky. He moved closer to my side and held out his arm. I wrapped my arm through his and he subtly brought a tendril of his hair up to wrap around my waist. While I was still walking, he was mostly supporting me.

Delilah, on the other hand, was doing fairly well. But Chase was still looking woozy and so Delilah scooted over to him and wrapped her arm around his waist. Shade merely smiled, and Chase looked extremely grateful.

As we entered the temple, a deep resonance echoed through me that almost knocked me out. It wasn't a sound—not audible, but more an internal shifting, a pulsing of energetic waves that rolled through me. I caught my breath, so startled that without Smoky's support, I would have been knocked to the ground. Behind me, Shade grunted too, as did Bran. Venus just let out a laugh and rubbed his hands together.

The temple was as ornate on the inside as it was sparse outside. Rich tapestries covered the walls, mandalas in brilliant blues and silvers, punctuated with red. The patterns on the woven rugs seemed to be moving, but when I looked again, they were still. Optical illusions, perhaps. Or maybe it was magic. By now, I wasn't that sure of anything.

The benches were carved from blocks of stone that looked like they had been hewn directly out of the mountains. Glassy black spheres ornamented the walls, and flickering out of the dark orbs were etheric blue lights. But even from where I was standing, I could tell there was no heat. Weapons lined the walls—silver staves, wooden sticks, silver daggers, shuriken, and wickedly curved swords that were so ornate they looked like they should be in an art museum.

The hall we entered was long and wide, with the ceiling at least twenty feet high. At either end were large fireplaces, with massive fires crackling away. Doorways led to halls along the back of the chamber. In the center of the hall was a large statue, of a goddess that I didn't recognize. She rose to the ceiling, and around her spiraled a long, curving staircase, leading to the second story. The stairs were narrow and steep. Running those several times a day would keep me in shape, I thought.

The monks passed by the staircase, leading us toward a hallway that was center against the back wall. The hall was narrow, but not long, and opened out into yet another chamber, this one containing a door against the back, a door to the right, and a long table, in the center of the room. Like the benches, it was carved from one giant piece of stone, each of its legs at least twelve inches square. It would take one hell of a disaster to move the table, let alone destroy it. It occurred to me that had this table been in the throne room at Elqaneve, Queen Asteria and our father might have survived if they had been able to duck beneath it.

The lead monk—or at least, he seemed to be the lead monk—motioned for us to take a seat at the table. The long benches were also carved in stone, but at least they were padded with a thick cushion. Still dizzy, I gratefully slipped onto the end of one of the benches and braced my elbows on the table, trying to shake off the altitude sickness.

Another moment and a fourth monk joined us. He was wearing the same outfit as the others except there was an insignia of some sort on his left shoulder. The others parted for him as he slowly approached the table, and I was pretty sure he was either the head honcho, or as close to it as we were going to meet.

He looked us over, then took a seat opposite. "We welcome you into our temple and bid you rest and eat. But first, we would ask your names."

He spoke in Calouk, the common tongue. Everyone at the table could understand him, save for Chase. Delilah translated what the monk had said.

I cleared my throat. "We value your offer, and accept. My name is Camille Sepharial te Maria, and these are my comrades. My husband Smoky, my sister Delilah Maria te Maria, her fiancé Shade, Venus the Moonchild, and Chase Johnson, who cannot speak the common tongue."

The monk nodded to each in turn. When I had finished, he said, "My name is Keth and I am the Speaker. I ask that you direct all your questions to me. I will be at your disposal while you take rest with us. My brethren are only allowed to speak to strangers when there is a need and I am not around. I will have food and drink brought to you. Do you eat animal flesh?"

My stomach rumbled at that moment, and I blushed. "Yes, we do, all of us. Although we have a few animals we will not eat of. Cats and dogs, big cats." There was no way Delilah and Venus were going to play cannibal.

Keth nodded. "Then we will bring food." He turned to the monks behind him and gave an order in a language I didn't recognize—it definitely wasn't Melosealfôr or Calouk—and they left the hall.

I wanted to dive in and ask him if we could search on the property, but it would break tradition and protocol to do so before eating. Instead, I said, "Your temple is beautiful. We appreciate your gracious invitation. We weren't sure how you felt about visitors."

"Generally, we're wary. But we seldom have dragons visit, and the few times they've come in the past, it was a congenial affair. Indeed, for dragons to approach our compound, there must be something important afoot, so we chose to greet you rather than warn you off."

I realized that of course they knew we had two dragons with us. They had to have sentries watching and they would have seen us land. That they weren't afraid of dragons and had a favorable view of them boded well for us.

Keth turned to Chase. "You are not from Otherworld, are you? But yet, you are not fully human. Your aura tells a story of mixed parentage from long ago."

That he spoke in English surprised the hell out of me—and Chase. I kept quiet, though—it wasn't my question to answer, and since he had directly asked Chase, I figured it better to let the detective answer on his own.

Chase glanced at Delilah, then at me. We both nodded. "Yes, I'm from Earthside. And there is elf in my lineage. I didn't know about it until recently."

"You are also going to live a very long time, given the proper circumstances. The Nectar of Life flows through your veins, and your aura as well. There is a story there, but perhaps for a different time." Keth studied him for a moment and then, seemingly satisfied, turned back to me. "Here is your meal. Eat, and after you finish, we will talk further. Until then, the door to the right will lead you into a chamber where you can clean up and refresh yourselves. I'll return when you're ready." With that, he abruptly stood and left the chamber as two other monks brought in great trays of food and filled the table.

The food was hearty and there was a lot of it. Roast bird—what kind I couldn't tell, except it had been turkey-size in life given the size of the drumsticks—and a side of ham, cheeses and breads with their yeasty, warm scent, a tureen of vegetable soup, a crock of butter and one of honey, and three large pies that smelled suspiciously like apple all spread across the table. A regular smorgasbord. The monks brought in large pitchers of fresh creamy milk, and ale, so frothy with head that it smelled like yeast and hops.

Chase waited until we were alone again before asking, "Is it safe to eat?"

"You mean are they trying to poison us? I'm going to say no on that. And the food here is bound to be good. You don't train as hard as they do on empty calories or subpar quality." I helped myself, stabbing a large slice of the bird breast, a hefty chunk of ham, and a couple of the rolls. The hot food was welcome. Though we'd eaten on the road, there was nothing like a tramp through the woods to stir the appetite, and the altitude may have made me dizzy and lightheaded, but the food seemed to be calming my symptoms.

Smoky poured me a glass of milk—somehow, I didn't think alcohol would make a good complement to the dizziness—and Shade served bowls of the soup, which had been cooked in a rich meat base, and was filled with chunks of carrots and handover roots, along with wild chervil and cress leaves. As everyone set to, a comfortable silence rose around us as the tension began to fall away. After about twenty minutes, we pushed back our plates. Delilah and I ventured into the washroom and—sure enough—it also contained a bathroom, to our relief. We took care of business, and washed our hands and faces.

As we returned to the table, the servers were carrying away our plates, and Keth had also returned. He had brought with him a bottle of what looked like brandy, and was pouring cordial glasses for us.

"Dwarven brandy, straight from the Nebulveori Mountains." He handed me a glass.

The scent was almost intoxicating, and I felt grounded enough to take a sip. It was like grape honey on the tongue, rich and full-bodied. As I murmured "Thank you," he offered the others their glasses.

"Now, then, while the food sets, tell me why you have come to visit our temple." He spoke in English this time.

Chase cleared his throat. "May I ask a question—without meaning to be rude?"

"Ask. You cannot find answers if you do not seek them out." Keth seemed in a generous mood, or perhaps he was always this good-natured.

"You call this a temple, but also a monastery. Which is it?"

"A sanctuary can be one and still be the other. This is our monastery and it is also our temple. Either word works." Keth leaned forward, his elbows on the table. "Remember, constraints provide only limitations. Expand the definition, and you expand the potential."

Chase grinned at him. "I see what you mean. Thank you."

"Then, let us proceed. Lady Camille, I feel you are the one to answer my question. Tell me, why are you here?" The monk turned back to me.

I swallowed my nerves. This was it. How they reacted would be the difference between whether we had to find a way to sneak around behind their backs—quite possibly causing a political schism that could mar future relations between the Order of the Crystal Dagger and just about every city or group I belonged to—or whether we'd have them as allies.

"I am Camille Sepharial te Maria, High Priestess of the Moon Mother and soon to take the throne of Dusk and Twilight. I've come for the Keraastar Diamond, to gather and lead the Keraastar Knights into the coming battle against Shadow Wing, who rails against the portals and seeks to break through and devastate both Earthside and Y'Eírialiastar. It was Shadow Wing who drove the armies of Telazhar against Elqaneve."

Keth didn't jump, or start, or show any of the reactions I had expected him to. Instead, he merely leaned back in his chair and folded his hands across his stomach.

"You don't seem surprised."

"Surprise? We're taught to anticipate but never expect. We're taught that surprise is our enemy. It leads to being caught off guard. I have long learned to moderate my reactions, Priestess. Your news is not something we expected, but neither am I surprised. We knew that Shadow Wing was behind Telazhar—the Order doesn't merely sit up here on the mountain and hide out from the rest of the world. But we have little to do with the goings-on. All things pass in time. So, you come for the Keraastar Diamond? Why do you think we have it?"

"I don't think you have it here in the temple, but the Maharata-Vashi led me here and points to the gem being on your land." I withdrew the scroll and spread it out to show him the legend. "Can you read ancient Melosealfôr? I can only read a few words."

He leaned across the table, gazing into my eyes. "Do you trust me to read it *correctly*, that should be your question?"

I held his gaze, peering into the deep brown pools that seemed to go on forever. After a moment, I realized that yes, I did trust him. His energy was clear. He wasn't on our side, but he wasn't against us, either. He was playing Switzerland in a world of opposites.

"Yes, I think I do. I also need the incantation on the Maharata-Verdi translated."

"That, I can also do." He studied the map. "First, the map. It reads thusly: *The Keraastar Diamond is found in the Cavernica Redal.* There's a cave system that begins on our land. The Cavernica Redal isn't far—a day's journey up the mountain side behind the monastery, but a dangerous trek, and whatever guards the Keraastar Diamond, you will have to vanquish."

"How long has the diamond been here?" Venus asked.

Keth shook his head. "The cavern has remained untouched since long before my time—it goes back generations of monks, and guarding it has only been one of our duties, but one we have taken seriously. But there are servants along the way who will challenge you. We can give you no help. You must face and defeat them, or you will die on the crag."

I didn't like the sound of that. Dying was not part of the plan, and given the elevation, chances were that trolls or ogres wandered the mountains around here. Possibly giants as well. Even if they were half-giants, they'd still be trouble.

"We'll leave as soon as possible. I have no choice. We'll have to face whatever is waiting for us."

He took out a piece of parchment. "Then I will translate the incantation for you now. I'll write it in modern Melosealfôr, as well as write a pronunciation guide to say the words in the ancient form. You may need to do that instead."

I turned to the others. "Chase, I hate the idea of taking you up there with me, but every instinct I have is screaming that you must be a part of this. Venus, you have to go, too."

Chase set his lips in a thin line, but nodded.

I was beginning to sense something unfolding that I really didn't want to think about, because it would shift so much in our private world, but the feeling wouldn't leave me. Chase had to be there. Chase was part elf. And Chase had drunk the Nectar of Life. I wasn't clear on what was going on, but whatever it was, it was going to be yet another wide bend in the journey.

Delilah seemed to sense the same thing too, because she placed her hand on Chase's arm. "We'll be there to help. Whatever this is."

Venus shrugged. "You are going to be my queen, Camille. I will do anything I can to help you. But what are we going to do about Rozurial and Trillian? We left them back at the edge of the foothills."

"That's over a week's journey on foot. They have to know we aren't coming right back. I guess…we have to trust that they'll be all right until we find the diamond. There's no way we can go back for them now, unless we're willing to leave the horses to fate. They're not used to running free."

Bran shook his head. "No, without someone to watch over them, they'd be lunch for some monster within days. Predators abound in the Deep, and in the foothills. Although I suppose you could give them to one of the families that live along the river, but even that much travel would put us a day behind."

"And we don't know that they'd be well treated. Though frankly, I don't think the dwarves are all that concerned about their well-being either. No, we climb the mountain without them. I wish our cell phones worked over here." Whispering Mirrors were all well and good, but they weren't portable and they didn't make up for the lack of a good communications system.

"If you like, when you return, one of the dragons can fly two of my monks down to where your friends and horses are waiting. We will take care of the animals and bring them up the mountains to our monastery, while the rest of you fly down to Svartalfheim, the closest city from here." Keth shrugged. "Otherwise, it will take you over a week to make your way out of the mountains if you go on foot. And if you're to take the throne at midsummer, you can't afford that much time."

I nodded. "He's right. All right, we go to the cavern, find the diamond, and then Smoky, you can fly two of the monks down to the horses, then bring back Roz, Trillian, and our gear. Then we fly to Svartalfheim, and go through a portal to the Wayfarer."

Keth glanced over to the wall. There was a clock of sorts, though it ran on Otherworld time, which was very much like Earthside time but counted in longer increments than minutes.

"During the night, the dangers on the mountain increase. Be prepared. The ghosts come out at night. The Cavernica Redal is a day's climb up the mountain. If I were you, I'd start out at sunrise. Your dragon wings will not take you there. The peak has been off limits to dragons for many many years, through a treaty, and that treaty is magically reinforced. A dragon who flies too close to the mountain top will fall out of the sky. You're lucky you didn't attempt it on coming in."

Smoky looked at me. "It's up to you. Now, or sunrise? This is your journey, Camille. We're just here to back you up."

I didn't want to face monsters. I didn't want to travel in the dark. But an urgency inside pushed me to make haste, to hurry up and get on that mountainside before dusk fell. Whether it was my own insecurity or a premonition, I didn't know. But I did know that the more I followed my gut, the better off my life went, even if it wasn't the easiest choice.

"We go now." I stood. "We head out now, and climb as far as we can, as fast as we can. I can't give you a reason other than my intuition tells me that the sooner we get there, the better. I've had this feeling that we've been watched all along, and I still have it. I don't want to wait and give whoever might be out there a chance to catch up and perhaps wait to ambush us."

"Then we go now. Can you give us any guidance as to where we'll find the cave?" Delilah asked.

Keth smiled—faintly, but it was a genuine smile. "I can do that. It's going to be hard for you to miss, actually, but without our permission, you'd never make it there. Anyone who attempts to scale the mountain from here on up either has our permission or they never return." He held out armbands—silver strips of material with a blue tip.

"You each will wear this. That signifies you've been given our blessing. Many have attempted to forge the material, but we make this weave ourselves and it possesses an auric energy that reads true only to itself. We can tell a forgery a mile off, and that is one factor intruders don't count on. We read energy from a distance. So keep these tied to your right arms at all times. It won't give you a free pass with the guardians of the mountain, but it will prevent any of our monks you might meet along the way from destroying you."

I cringed, waiting for Smoky or Shade to say something all blustery, but neither said a word, simply accepted the bands without comment. We tied them around each other's arms, making certain they were firmly bound.

"What happens if somebody tries to cut this off of us?" I asked, fingering the material, which seemed deceptively fragile.

"Try. You, Delilah, try cutting the band off her arm." Keth pointed to Delilah's dagger.

Delilah frowned, but obliged, sliding her blade beneath the material and attempting to cut through it. But nothing happened. The material resisted the blade, even though I knew she kept it honed to a fine edge.

"Why won't it cut?"

"We charm the bands. No blade may cut them save for our own crystal daggers. So go and be safe. Return if you can. And when you find the diamond, remember—you may take it, and only it. Anything else in the mountains belongs to our order." With that, Keth motioned for us to follow him, leading us out of the other door that exited the room. "We never allow true guests to exit by the front door. Only those who are cast out leave that way. You come in the front door, and exit through the back. That means you've been accepted by the Order and may return in the future."

Their customs didn't seem very different than those of a number of cultures in Otherworld. In fact, the monks didn't seem nearly as fearsome as I had originally expected them to. But as we left through the back door, we entered a yard where several of the monks were training.

As we watched, they circled one another, feinting and throwing in turn as though they were tossing a ball back and forth. When they hit the ground, their bodies left imprints in the hardened soil—the force they were using was so great. Yet they each stood, never diverting their focus, never crying uncle or even showing a flicker of pain on their faces, although I saw enough blood and bruises to convince me that broken bones had to be involved.

Keth led us beyond the training, to the end of the enclosure that circled the monastery. He opened the gate and pointed to a dirt track cut into the mountain that began a long, lazy spiral up toward the peak. It was steep and narrow, and there were no guard rails or handholds. The track made me dizzy just looking at it, so I turned away, trying to keep my balance.

"It's a long way up. You'll climb the mountain through the night till morning. By the first crack of dawn, you should be near the Cavernica Redal if you encounter no dangers and take only moderate breaks. Whatever you do, take nothing other than the diamond, and dragons—do not shift into your natural forms. I have had sandwiches prepared for you, and I wish you well."

I hoisted my staff. It was time to put it to use. Shade took the bag of food and draped the strap over his shoulder. We accepted fresh canteens from Keth, and then, he stood back.

"May the gods see you safely up and back. There's nothing more my Order can do for you—not until you return. Your armbands will keep you safe from any of the monks on the mountain." And with that, he turned and walked away, not looking back.

I sucked in a deep breath. "Smoky, will you go first?"

He nodded. "If you are sure?"

"I'm sure. Let's climb."

And so, we did.

Chapter 15

SMOKY LED THE way, and behind him came Venus next, then me, then Bran, Chase, Delilah, and Shade brought up the rear. I was immediately grateful for my staff. The path was a scant two feet wide, the winding trail cut right into the mountain. It was compacted dirt—the rains up here would not come for another few months—but there were enough stones and loose rocks to litter the way and make it hazardous. And while the mountain did slope, the dropoff was steep. It would be all too easy to go tripping over the side. One misstep, one slip, and it would be a long step down.

The vegetation was scarce—a few scrub bushes, most looking prickly and full of thorns, and scant grasses that were parallel to the ground given the perpetual wind. Mountain goats could exist up here, and rodents and a few predators, but anything else that lived on the mountain had to be creatures we really didn't want to meet.

The sun was slowly lowering itself to the west, but

from here, we'd see the last rays unless the clouds rolled in. Thinking about climbing the mountain at night started me second-guessing my choice. Had I made the right decision? Keth said that the mountain's ghosts came out to play and I wasn't sure if he was being poetic or if he really meant actual spirits on the mountainside. And what if we couldn't see the path? We had flashlights, but still...

I tapped Smoky on the arm. "Do you think I made the right choice to start at night?"

He glanced back at me. "I think you made the choice your instincts told you to make. We'll be all right. We're strong together. We have two dragons, an Elemental Lord, a shaman, a Death Maiden and...a Faerie Queen witch. Just keep alert, watch your step, and don't drift off."

We made good time for the first hour—as good as we could headed up a steep winding grade. But by the time the sun began to set, the temperatures were beginning to drop and I realized it was going to be a chilly night for everybody. At least the hike would serve to keep us warm. I wanted to chat, to break the silence, but then thought that might not be a good idea. If there were ghosts or monsters on the mountain, then our voices would only alert them. Better to walk in silence and keep as low-key as possible.

Another hour and Chase softly asked for a break. There wasn't a good place to spread out, so we did our best to rest on the path, cautiously leaning back against the slope behind us. Smoky and Shade stayed standing, facing front and back respectively, to watch for anything that might be creeping up on us.

Delilah passed out sandwiches that the monks had given us—it was nearing dinnertime and my stomach was rumbling. The bread had a tender crumb, and the meat was succulent and moist. We left enough for breakfast, because a day's climb up the mountain meant a day's climb down. When we finished eating, we took off again, winding our way around the peak. My guess was that the cave was only a few miles from the monastery, but the grade of the peak and the narrowness of the path would be what slowed us down.

As we climbed, the waning crescent of the moon rose into the sky, and her pull on me echoed through my body. The magic of the mountain was beginning to thicken, too, like a mist creeping around us that we could feel but not see. It was ancient, as old as Otherworld when it first divided off from Earthside. At times I wondered what those days had been like. The disasters that the Great Divide had caused had rocked both worlds. Earthquakes, volcanoes, floods—the land had screamed in protest as the Great Fae Lords drove the parting of the worlds. Like some juggernaut, a behemoth monster, the Great Divide tore land from land, parting the world into three realms. How many millennia had passed since then, nobody knew, but it had been tens upon tens of thousands of years. The thought of what might happen if the portals ripped apart and the three worlds slammed back into one another was a terrifying possibility. And that was exactly what Shadow Wing was trying to bring about.

I gazed up at the mountain beside me. The Keraastar Diamond would help me prevent that from happening. The weight of three worlds pressing down on my shoulders, I suddenly felt very small and vulnerable, and terrified that I wasn't the right choice for the job. If I screwed up...

I caught my breath, my head reeling with the thought of what could happen if I fucked up.

"Are you all right?" Bran asked, reaching forward to steady me. For once, he didn't sound sarcastic.

Smoky turned. "Pause," he said, holding up his hand

so everyone would stop. "What's wrong?"

I shook my head. "I just fell into a spiral of thoughts. I'm all right. I'm sorry." I didn't want to tell them what I'd been thinking. For one thing, I wasn't looking for their reassurances. This was more of a fight with myself, a battle with my own confidence, and I was smart enough to recognize that I was the only one who could shake off the doubt.

"Be cautious. We're nearing some rock fall up ahead and while it might be a good place to stop for a moment, there could be creatures hiding up there as well." Smoky turned back to the path and motioned for us to start again.

Bran leaned forward to whisper, "You wouldn't be here if Aeval and Titania didn't think you were the right person for the job. Queen Asteria, as well. Remember that."

I glanced back at him, giving him a quick nod, and tried to keep my thoughts focused on the climb.

As we approached the pile of rocks that littered the side of the mountain and tumbled down below the path, I reached out, trying to sense if anything was there. Smoky had slowed, and was cautiously approaching the first pile of rubble, when a massive, dark figure rose from behind the opposite end of the rocks. Even in the fading light of dusk, it was obvious that we were facing a dubba-troll.

Crap. Dubba-trolls were the worst. Two-headed, they also had twice the strength and half the brains of other trolls. They were immune to bullets and any bladed weapons not made of silver. Hammers, mallets, maces—all worked well against the creatures, but we were sadly lacking in the blunt-weapon division. And far worse, we were on a precarious mountainside with a one-way ticket to an early grave if we fell off.

Smoky immediately called for Shade to join him.

Which meant, of course, some jostling. "Camille, Venus, Chase, get to the end of the line. Bran and Delilah, behind us."

We shuffled around, trying not to knock each other over as we shifted positions, all the while the dubba-troll was grunting, forcing his way through the rocks. The best possibility we had was for Shade and Smoky to tip him off balance and send him over the side.

Delilah drew Lysanthra. The blade would be able to pierce the troll's skin, at least. And Bran brought out his own sword, which glowed faintly in the dim light. A magical blade as well.

I motioned for Chase to work his way back to the end of the line. "Keep your eyes open. We don't want anything to surprise us from behind, so if you see anything that looks like it might be a danger, give a shout out. Venus, watch with him. I'm going to call on the Moon Mother's power. We have a clear sky so I doubt I can find enough energy in the air to call down lightning, but there are other ways to kill a dubba-troll. Damn, if Morio was here, we could cast some form of death spell his way."

Venus joined Chase without a word, keeping watch over the trail behind us. Meanwhile, Smoky and Shade quickly conferred, with Smoky taking up position first and Shade close behind him. As Smoky engaged the dubba-troll, I turned away. It was best for my magic if I didn't watch—it was too distracting.

I raised my arms to the sky, summoning the Moon Mother's power. She was waning, moving into her shadow phase, which was my power. I had started out focusing on the full moon's energy and my spellcasting had always been wonky, with a good chance of backfiring. But once I had learned that I worked best under the dark moon, my magic had grown stronger and I was less likely to screw up my spells.

The crescent was rising just over the horizon, visible from where we were on the mountain. I gazed up at the Moon Mother, closing my eyes as I reached out to her. I could feel her power crackling around me, the power of shadow and veils, the power of dusk and twilight and the night sky. The wind rose as I called her down into me. What had been a steady breeze strengthened into a stiff squall, buffeting against us. I could hear fighting behind me but brought my focus back to the Moon Mother and her energy.

Give me your strength. I call down your force and your might. Help me, my Lady of the night sky.

As I silently mouthed my prayer to her, the wind turned into a wild whirl of gusts, and the clouds began to gather, racing in from the distant east. They drove forward, huge and luminous, and the sky took on an ominous green tinge. I could feel the rain heavy within them, and the crackling touch of ozone—the smell of lightning—began to build. She was with me, my Lady, in her waning light. She tickled my fingertips, sending trails of prickles along my arms so that the hairs stood straight up. Then her light vanished as the clouds covered the sky, and my stomach tensed. The lightning was there, the energy at my fingertips.

I turned, slowly, holding onto the power, and focused on the dubba-troll as the electricity began to surge into my hands. Holding out my palms, I aimed the fork of lightning at the troll, doing my best to avoid Smoky and Shade, who were launching their attacks at him.

Smoky saw the bolt coming first and jumped back, knocking Shade to the side. They landed against the hill behind them. The dubba-troll paused, then turned my way as the shriek of the lightning hurtled toward him. The brilliant light lit up his face and I could see first the confusion, then the terror as he stumbled back, trying to get away from my attack. But it was too late. The lightning hit him square on the chest, then ricocheted off to blast into the stones on the slope of the mountain below us.

The entire rock face gave way, thundering down the mountain, shaking the upper rocks loose. Smoky and Shade scattered, racing back toward us to avoid the sudden avalanche. Shade grabbed Delilah as he came to her, and they managed to clear the rocky area just before the entire deposit gave way and roared down the mountain below us. As the rocks cleared away from the path, taking the troll with them, I caught my breath. My hands were still tingling.

The clouds burst then, drenching us with a cool rain, and the lightning began to play against them, thunder echoing behind. My heart was racing as Delilah pressed against me, her eyes glued to the storm that I had called in. I knew what she was feeling because I was feeling it, too. Ever since we had been caught in the massive sentient storm that had destroyed Elqaneve and killed both our father and Queen Asteria, we had both been leery of thunderstorms. But this one, I had caused. And all I could do was hope that it played out quickly and then departed.

The downpour soaked us within less than a minute. My cloak helped deflect some of the water, but it still managed to get through. I shaded my eyes to stare up at the play of lightning against the clouds.

"Might want to put away weapons." As I spoke, it occurred to me my staff had a metal tip, and I lowered it, holding it so that it was horizontal rather than vertical.

"Troll's dead," Bran said. "Rocks are gone."

"And we're all going to catch our death in this," Delilah grumbled. But even as she spoke the sudden squall vanished and the clouds started to part, heading off again for whatever climes they had hailed from.

Smoky snorted. "Nah. I may not be able to transform into my dragon shape, but…" He motioned for us to back away, then in the next moment, launched something toward the ground. It hit and the temperature suddenly soared, along with a brilliant flash. "I stole one of Rozurial's firebombs," he said with a grin. "Crowd in and the heat should dry us out in a few moments."

The air around where the bomb had exploded was toasty warm and there was a tidy fire burning. It was almost too warm, but right now that was good for taking the edge off. The heat radiated into our clothing and while it didn't dry us out all the way, we were a lot warmer and drier. We stood there until the heat began to dissipate, then Smoky motioned for us to fall in line again.

"Let's get moving, and hopefully anybody else along the path will have seen what played out and will think twice before attacking us. Because there's no way they could miss all of that."

He set off again, and we followed suit. We marched on for another hour, gradually making headway up the mountain. According to my computations, we were halfway there. Another pile of rocks littered the way, although smaller and easier to see around. There was enough room to crouch behind, but Smoky checked out the rock fall closest to the mountain and gave us the thumbs-up.

"Nothing here, and the rocks down the slope are too far to worry about as long as we keep an eye out." He glanced at me. "I suggest we stop and if you need to relieve yourselves, take advantage of the rocks for privacy."

He had a good point. We couldn't march all night without going to the bathroom. We'd reach the Cavernica Redal around two in the morning, by my calculations, and we had all eaten and drunk plenty of water.

I motioned to Delilah and we headed to the back of the rocks. She kept watch while I made use of the makeshift privy, and then I stood guard for her. Thank gods somebody had thought to bring toilet paper on the trip. Leaves weren't all that comfortable, nor were they plenty in this area.

The men took their turns while I pulled out a bottle of hand sanitizer, then handed it around. "You know, I used to think about what I'd miss when we returned home from Earthside, after our stint was up. I guess that's a moot concern now. Now, I have to think about what I'll miss about not making the rest of my life over here in Otherworld. At least we can visit, though." I paused, then looked at Delilah. "You still don't know where you'll end up, do you?"

She ducked her head, frowning. "No, the Autumn Lord hasn't given me a clue. Shade, do you know?"

He shrugged. "I'm about as clueless as you are, to be honest. I don't know where he'll want his child raised. *Our* child."

I thought about her path. Delilah was slated to become the mother of a child by the Autumn Lord, with Shade as the proxy father. Given the choice between her fate and mine, suddenly ruling the Court of Dusk and Twilight didn't seem so intimidating. Kids were never on my "must-do" list. But Delilah was suited for motherhood, and I suddenly hoped the Autumn Lord would keep her Earthside. I wanted to know who my niece—or nephew—would be. I wanted to play auntie and buy them outrageous presents that she would never agree to.

"What are you thinking about?" Smoky wrapped his arm around my waist. "You look so far away. So wistful."

I leaned my head against his arm. "I guess...destiny. The Hags of Fate. Where we started and where we're all ending up. If anybody would have told me when I first came Earthside that I'd end up marrying a dragon… or a youkai-kitsune…I would have laughed them out of the house. If I had known Trillian was going to be coming back into my life, I would have been terrified. The thought of taking my place with Aeval and Titania would have sent me running back here to Otherworld. Now, it all feels so right, even though it's still a little scary."

"Destiny doesn't usually look the way we imagine it," he said. "Destiny has a way of waiting till we turn our backs and then rolls in like a whirlwind, throwing all our plans to the wind. But when they settle down again, changed—sometimes beyond recognition—we realize that what we thought we wanted wasn't really what we needed at all."

"You two are very philosophical tonight," Chase said. He had been standing close enough to hear us talking. "I never dreamed my life would become what it has. I still don't know where I'm going to end up. And I've decided that, as long as Astrid and Sharah are safe, I'm okay with that."

"You've come a long way from the Chase we first met when we came Earthside." I patted him on the shoulder. "I'm happy you found your love."

He paused, looking like he was going to say something, then shook his head, pressing his lips together. But the look on his face wasn't altogether happy.

"Is something wrong?"

For a moment, I didn't think he was going to answer, but then he let out a long sigh. "I know that Sharah's expected to produce an heir—one who is full-blooded elf. I've known for a while but I couldn't talk about it, while I processed what the implications were. Astrid can never take the throne, and I'm actually happy about that. I think ruling a kingdom is too stressful for most people." He stared at me and I couldn't help but wonder if the comment was also pointed at me, but this wasn't a conversation about my journey.

"How do you feel?"

"Angry. Sad. Resigned." He shrugged. "I've come to realize that in the end, it doesn't matter what I feel or think. Sharah's the queen of Elqaneve. They have traditions going back tens of thousands of years and they aren't going to change them just because I want them to. Nor is she an empress or dictator. She can't just abruptly tell her people that everything they've grown up with is being tossed aside because she wants it to be."

"Unfortunately, you're right. I'm sorry, Chase. But that doesn't mean you and she can't still be a couple."

"No, but it means that my idyllic vision of a happy little family, just the three of us, is blown apart. Smoky, you talked about destiny not being what we always want it to be. I think I'm finally realizing that. And I'm learning to accept that it will be what it needs to be. I'm not in control of the universe, but I'm in control of how I react."

The detective looked and sounded so much older than when we had first met. He was also, sadly, wiser in the way that the world worked. That was one thing I missed about both him and Delilah. Both had been idealists. Delilah had been naive in so many ways, and Chase had been so resistant to doing anything other than the way he been taught was right. Now, the pair of them had both grown and evolved, but a certain innocence had fled with the shedding of their skins.

"Everything works out as it must. Maybe not how we would like, but usually, there's a reasoning to life's currents, even though we can't always see the big picture." It was pithy advice, I knew, but the only thing I could think of to say at the moment. "Come, we've got to keep moving."

Smoky took up the lead and once again, we set out. The sky was once again clear, and the path had grown steeper. I was extremely grateful that I'd brought my staff because it gave me leverage as we climbed up the dirt trail, so hard in places it was almost slick. The rainstorm had been isolated, and the further we distanced ourselves from the dubba-troll's hideout, the steeper the climb became.

About thirty minutes into the fifth hour of climbing, I began to hear whispering on the wind. The voices blew past me, impossible to catch, but the susurration echoed in the back of my mind, as though the winds themselves were trying to tell me something. I fell into the rhythm of the hike, focusing on putting one foot in front of the other. A few minutes later, Delilah worked her way up past Bran and Chase.

"The spirits that Keth talked about? They're here. I can see them. The mountain is cloaked in a shroud of ghosts." She was looking a little green around the gills. "I'm blocking out their ability to know that I can see them, but they're calling out for us, trying to lure us off the path. Be cautious if you hear anything. They don't have our best interests at heart, I can tell you that."

I shivered. "I can hear them, although I can't hear what they're saying. I can just hear the whispering of their voices."

"I can hear them too," Shade said, surprising both of us. Ever since he lost his Stradolan powers thanks to an energy-leech that had invaded our house, his abilities to work with spirits had drastically decreased except when he was in his actual dragon form. "Something is happening to me as we climb the mountain. I didn't want to say so before, because I thought it was my imagination, but there is heavy magic here and it's affecting me. I'm not sure what's going on."

Delilah, looking worried, turned to him. "Honey? Are you okay?"

He nodded. "Yes, but it's as though…it's almost like if I just tried hard enough, I could reach out and snatch my powers back. I want to try, but I'm worried that it might be a trick the ghosts are playing on me. That it's actually something set up to harm me."

Delilah glanced at me. I shrugged, not sure whether or not his assessment was right. If he had a chance to reclaim his powers, we needed to give him the leeway to do so. But what if he was right and it was a trick? What if the spirits were trying to trick him into doing something that would harm either him or us, or both?

I turned to Bran. "What do you know about this mountain? Anything?"

"All I know is that Pentangle has been spotted around this mountain way too many times. The Mother of Magic doesn't usually show up unless there's something incredibly powerful about a place or event." He frowned, staring up at the peak that was dimly illuminated against the backdrop of the night sky. "I think we have to walk softly and keep our eyes open lest we fall into any number of traps and tricks."

"Good advice," I murmured. Turning back to Shade, I asked, "What do you want to do? What's your gut instinct?"

He frowned, closing his eyes. "Whatever it is, if there is a chance for me to regain my powers, it's farther up the mountain."

Smoky nodded, then motioned for us to start in again. "Onward, and ignore the voices around us. We can't afford to be led on any wild goose chases."

We climbed through the hours following, one hour, two. When we were—by our reckoning—an hour away from the cave, we paused for a snack. Delilah handed out apples and cookies that the monks had given us, and we ate in silence. I was feeling the power of the mountain pressing down on me. The immensity of the magic here was wearing, and it was giving me a headache because my magic didn't mesh all that well with the innate magic of the Tygerian monks and their mountains.

When we finished, we took up again and at this point, I kept my attention carefully focused on my feet. We were all carrying flashlights. The light of the crescent moon wasn't strong enough to illuminate our way.

Another thirty minutes and Smoky held up his hand, slowing. "I think I see it. Up there." He nodded toward a fork in the path that led to a dark blotch against the mountain. The opening to the cavern.

As I stared at it, something inside resonated deep and loud. There it was. And I knew that the diamond was in there.

"Let's go," I said, focused only on the end point now. Every instinct inside was screaming to get there before someone came along to interfere.

We were nearing the turnoff when a deep rumbling like an earthquake raced along below our feet. I threw myself to the side of the hill, trying to keep from slipping off the edge of the trail, which was slanted at a highly uncomfortable angle. The trail flattened out again ten yards ahead, but here, it was more vertical than horizontal.

The others followed my lead, and we clung to the side of the hill as a large mound of dirt began to form ahead of us, pushing up from below the ground from deep inside the mountain. I pressed hard against the hillside, holding on for dear life.

The dirt rose up, clinging together rather than scattering. It formed into a large, hulking creature, its body rounded like a barrel while its arms and legs were trunk-like columns of soil and rock all mixed together.

The golem had no eyes, no mouth, but reminded me of an artist's mannequin created out of dirt rather than wood.

"Elemental!" Smoky pushed me behind him, his hair keeping me steady as it wrapped around my waist. "Earth Elemental."

"Crap." Shade squeezed past the others till he was near the front with Smoky.

I turned to Bran. "Do you have anything to counter an Earth Elemental? Because I don't."

He was staring beyond me at the growing mound of walking dirt. "Uh, no. Frankly, I have never dealt with one and even though my mother would, no doubt, have some ace up her sleeve, I'm afraid I don't. I wish to hell she'd left me out of this."

"I wish she had, too," I muttered, trying to think of what I might have running around in my magical bag of tricks. I had my doubts if a lightning bolt would do much against the Elemental, considering that the ground just absorbed lightning. Rain might turn it into mud, but it would have to be a downpour that would wash us off the mountain, too. Fire? I didn't even want to go there. And earth would just strengthen it. Death magic wouldn't work, even if Morio had been here. "Without the horn, I'm useless in this fight."

Venus shook his head. "My magic works differently, and I don't think there's much I can do either."

That left the two dragons. Smoky and Shade couldn't turn into their natural forms, but they were both far stronger than the rest of us put together. They approached the Elemental, who seemed to be following their movements with its head, even though it didn't have any eyes or ears. I had no idea how the creature worked, or who had set it to guard the mountain, but right now wasn't the time for speculation.

Smoky glanced over at Shade. "The Ionyc Sea."

Shade shook his head. "Could be suicide and I can't shift there unless I'm in dragon form."

"I can drop the creature off in the Sea. Leave him out there. There's nothing else we can do. We can't turn form and attack him. We can't fly around him. We can't just climb the mountain. We have to do something." Smoky called back to me. "Camille, I'm going to grab hold of it—well, some part of it—and shift over into the Ionyc Sea."

Before I could stop him, Smoky raced ahead toward the Elemental. I clasped my hand to my mouth, trying to keep from screaming at him to stop because the truth was, I couldn't see any other way. Even if we turned around and headed away, we had activated the creature and I knew enough to understand he was a guardian. Once awake, he'd pursue us until either he was dead or we were. I wanted to curse the monks for not telling us what to expect. Logically, I knew that wasn't fair, but right now my husband was about to body-slam a giant walking ball of mud and attempt to stay alive long enough to transfer it into the Ionyc Sea, where he would then do his best to shake the creature off before it killed him.

Smoky raced toward the Elemental, his duster flying behind him. Delilah put her arm around my shoulders, holding me as I watched, unable to drag my gaze away. The Elemental turned toward my dragon, rearing upward. The creature was a good twelve feet high, and as Smoky aimed for one of his legs, grabbing hold, the Elemental echoed a thundering rumble that shook the ground below our feet. Without another word, Smoky vanished, taking the creature with him. I collapsed to my knees, unable to move, waiting to see if my husband would return alive.

Chapter 16

"IT WILL BE all right. He'll be back." Delilah leaned down and, holding my shoulders, helped me stand up. I huddled against her, staring at the last spot the Elemental had been standing. "Breathe, Camille."

It was then that I realized I was holding my breath. I let it out in a burst, gasping.

"How long does it take? He wouldn't have to go far, would he? The creature couldn't get back here on its own, could it?" I turned to Shade. "You know the Ionyc Sea. Is what he's attempting even possible?"

"Oh, it's possible. I imagine he's just making sure the creature's far enough away." But Shade looked worried, even as he spoke. "There *are* potential complications, though."

"Don't say that!" Delilah smacked him on the arm.

He blinked at her. "But..." Turning to me, he said, "Please don't worry. Smoky's experienced. He's not all that young, even though he's quite a bit younger than me."

I slowly moved forward until I was staring into the

gaping hole from where the Earth Elemental had appeared. "This mountain is far more dangerous than I thought."

"It's even more dangerous further up, beyond the cavern. I've heard tales of massive birds—rocs, they call them—big enough to tangle with dragons. And still other horrors that lurk in the depths of the mountains." Bran stared up through the night sky at the mountain next to us. "Do you want to go on and let Smoky find us when he returns?"

I pressed my lips together. Was he just *trying* to antagonize me now?

Delilah moved between us. "Bran, can you go help Shade? He's exploring around the hole where the Elemental came from."

As Bran moved off, Delilah glanced at him over her shoulder. "Don't mind him. He's an annoyance, but I don't think he's deliberately trying to goad you. Remember, Raven Mother dotes on him and she doesn't rein him in. She's like a lot of parents, Elemental Lady or not."

I shrugged. "Whatever. But once I'm living out at Talamh Lonrach Oll, I'm setting some limits. He may be welcome in Aeval's court but he's not setting up residence in mine." I glanced up at the mountain, my nerves playing me like a harp strung way too tight. "Where *is* he?"

"Give it time—" Delilah stopped as the air nearby shimmered and Smoky stepped through, looking no worse for the wear.

"You're back!" I raced over to him, grabbing him around the waist as I planted my face firmly against his chest. "I was so worried." I didn't care who knew it. I tried to keep a brave front but even I had my limits. Standing back, I then placed one hand on his chest. "If you ever do that again, I swear I'm going to kill you when you get back! You understand me?"

His nose twitched and he gave me a wry grin. "What? Save the group?"

"Yes. *No.* You know what I mean." I tried to glare at him but couldn't manage it. "Oh fuck it. I'm just glad you're back. You scared the hell out of me. So tell. What happened?"

"That Earth Elemental knew how to hang on. I had to go deep into the currents to shake him. Luckily, it seems that once away from solid ground, Earth Elementals have a way of turning back into the inanimate matter from which they're made. You know how you fall asleep?"

I nodded.

"Well, he fell...to dirt. I was able to shake him off then, but it took me longer than I expected. He'll never wake up there."

"Good information to have." I contemplated this for a moment. "Would this work on all the elements?"

"Maybe not air, but then again, grabbing hold of an Air Elemental would be a feat almost impossible to master. I don't really want to try it." He gazed down at me, tipping my chin up. "I promised you I'd come back. I will always keep my promises, love. You know that, don't you?"

I reached up to stroke his cheek. "I know you *mean* what you say, Smoky. But there are forces in this world that could devour both of us without blinking. One of these days, I'm afraid you'll run into one and it will strike you down before you realize what's happening."

"Then I promise to be more vigilant." He leaned down and brushed my lips with a kiss. "We'd best get a move on now, my Fae Queen in waiting."

I nodded, and he motioned to the others. "I don't know if we'll encounter anything else till we reach the cavern—it's right along the fork—but stay alert." And with that, he led off again.

We skirted the hole that had contained the Elemental and continued toward the fork, where we turned to the left, edging along an even steeper path toward the Cavernica Redal. All the way—which was short but slow going—I felt like we were being watched, but nothing else came popping out to try to stop us. Fifteen minutes later, sweating from the harrowing climb, we reached the ledge in front of the cavern. It was wide enough for us to gather on without crowding, and for the first time since we had started up the mountain, I felt like I could breathe without fear of toppling over the side.

I stared at the cavern. Here I was, not quite at the top of the world, and inside lay the key to my destiny. I wasn't sure what I was supposed to be feeling—wonder, thrills, fear…but mostly I felt queasy and I was sick of being on the road. I was tired, and I wanted to climb into a warm bed and sleep for a couple days.

"You want all of us in there with you?" Chase wandered over to where I was standing.

"Might as well. It's cold out here, maybe it will be warmer inside." I flashed him a weary smile. "Mostly, I just want this done and over with."

"I hear you on that one." He winked at me. "Remember when life was so easy? When the good old days when I'd come into the store and flirt with you and you'd threaten to kick me in the balls if I didn't stop?"

That broke the tension. I coughed, then snorted, then laughed so hard my voice echoed through the night. "Oh gods, I know I shouldn't be so loud, but I can't help it." Wiping tears away from my eyes, I draped my arm around his shoulder. "Chase, I'm glad you're here. You've always been here for us. Thank you."

"Don't get maudlin on me, woman," he said, but his voice was cracking rather than stern.

Shaking my head, I wiped my eyes and let out a soft

breath. "All right, let's go meet my destiny. I have to go in first—I know that. Chase and Venus, you're behind me. Then the others as you will." Sobering, I straightened my shoulders and, taking the lead, entered the cavern.

THE CAVERN WAS vast that I couldn't see the back. As soon as I entered, my flashlight switched off. But in its place, a flicker of illumination began to glow from the walls—faint swirls of blue, green, and purple light. From the entrance, I could see a narrow path of smooth stones leading in. They, too, glowed softly in the same colors. The stone path led forward to what appeared to be a deep square pit.

I motioned for Venus to walk behind me, and for Chase to walk behind him.

"The rest of you, stay back along the edge, or you'll be in danger." I wasn't sure where the knowledge came from, but I was running on instinct. From here on, I realized that it was all up to me—to my intuition. I took three deep breaths, letting them out slowly, before beginning my walk along the stone path. I kept my attention focused straight ahead. There were demons hanging out in the shadows to the sides. I could feel them waiting for the chance to jump in, to cause havoc.

"Camille? We're being watched." Chase sounded uncertain.

"I know. Ignore them. Focus on Venus's back. Don't look into the dark. Don't doubt. Simply trust me. Put your life in my hands." Surprised by the strength in my voice, I straightened my shoulders and, the heel of my staff marking each step, I continued toward the edge of the pit.

A low rumble began to vibrate the floor of the cavern, rippling through my feet. It was like a heartbeat of some long-dead goddess waking to life. With each step, the lights of the cave grew brighter.

"It's so beautiful," Venus whispered.

I glanced up to see the patches of color blending and moving, swirling like the aurora borealis, sparkling with each pulse. The swirls spread, linking up with each other, until the entire ceiling was a rippling vortex of light.

Turning my attention back to the path, I stopped at the edge of the pit. We were halfway into the giant cavern and I was entranced by the energy. It was familiar, like a song I'd heard long ago and forgotten until one day, the chords suddenly began to play in my mind again.

The pit was square, created out of bricks of the colored stone, terracing down to a center point about ten feet square like an inverse ziggurat. A dizzying set of steps led to a bare-leafed tree in the center. The tree was short—only about six feet tall, and it was cloaked in shadow—a mere silhouette. A swish of movement danced around it. *The guardian.* I wasn't sure where the thought came from, but whatever was down there was guarding the tree.

The demons hiding in the shadows let out a howl, but I ignored them. They were there to frighten me off and I hadn't come all this way to turn around and run. I knew that if I gave them any attention, they would come out of those shadows and be on me before I could take another breath. Instead, I focused on my mission. Behind me, I could feel Venus's trance, the waves of his energy reaching out to surround both Chase and me. He was steady, an anchor negating some of the tension, binding all of us into the trance.

As I put my foot on the first step, the entire stair running around the pit lit up. Then the second. The third. Each step shimmered to life as I descended, Venus and Chase following me. And every step locked me into what I was doing. The world fell away as I descended into the pit, and the only thing that mattered was the tree in the center. The stairs continued to light, the pit flaring to life, and I lost track of how far down we had gone. Thirty steps...fifty...until we were finally at the bottom. Chase moved to my right side, Venus to my left, standing a step behind me.

As I stepped into the center circle, the howling of the demons grew louder and the entire floor was glowing. I ignored the demons, focusing on the tree and the shadows of the guardian surrounding it. As I approached the swirling mass of shadows, they gathered itself in front of the tree and took form into one, brilliant, shining figure. I paused.

She rose up before me like a sunburst of dark jewels, with wings that reminded me of those of a feathered, tattered bat. Spreading them wide, she tilted her head to look down at me, and her eyes were a glimmer of ice and snow.

"I am the Guardian of the Keraastar Diamond. Only the true Queen of the Keraastar Knights may claim it. All others will die. Do you wish to begin?"

I swallowed. *Hard.* I knew that I was supposed to claim the diamond. The question was, did *she* know? And if she did, how would I prove it to her?

"Don't doubt," I heard Venus whisper to me from somewhere far distant.

"I'm ready." I kept my eyes on the Guardian at all times, trying to remain focused. Then it crossed my mind that—whatever she was about to throw at me—it couldn't be worse than some of the things I'd already been through.

"Come closer." She motioned to me, crooking her

finger.

My feet moved on their own, even though my head was arguing that this wasn't exactly the best idea. But in my heart, I knew that I had to go through with it. There was no turning back, no changing my mind. Whatever waited for me at this dark faerie's hands was the next stage in my journey.

As I approached her, she enveloped me in her wings, embracing me in a shroud of cobwebs and faraway wind chimes, of spiders spinning out their webs in the dark of the forest, and that indeterminable space between twilight and starlight, when the Queen of Dusk gave way to the Queen of Night. Birdsong echoed in my ears, lonely and haunting, calling home for the evening. I felt the rivers of time pass by, the cycle of life moving in a spiral. Midnight to morning, morning to noon, noon to twilight, and twilight back to midnight—time marched ever onward and yet, always came back to the same place.

As I tried to sort out the emotions racing through my heart, the eons flashed by in a parade of images. The rise of Fae, the flight as a grandeur of dragons rose into the air, the wars of men laying the ground waste with blood, the scent of death rising. And yet, always life sprang from death and rose once more, and then—as do all things—fell into decay. Through all of this the gods kept watch, and the Immortals—the Elemental Lords, the Harvestmen, and the Hags of Fate—dealt out the hands that decided destiny and fate.

I had scarcely caught my breath when the sparkling guardian of the diamond spun me around, dancing with her in a macabre waltz as the ghostly strains of violin music echoed around us. We danced on the web of life—our feet lightly landing on thread after thread. We danced until I could barely remember my name, or why I had come to this place. I was no longer on a journey, but I had *become* the journey. I was the end goal—and I was the traveler. I was the Fool of the tarot, seeking my path through the wild wood, and I was the Universe at the end of the road, looking back on what I had been and looking now on what I had become.

"Why do you want the diamond?" the Guardian asked me as we waltzed.

I didn't need to think. I just answered from deep within my heart. "I don't, but destiny bids me to take it and raise the Keraastar Knights in order to defeat Shadow Wing. So I accept the responsibility."

"You will rise to be a fearsome queen. Will you accept what this brings into your life?"

Then I saw. This was the end of dillydallying. The time had come. I saw the raging of demons, as I led the Knights into battle. Blood spilling on the ground like water over the falls. A harsh and terrible light and then, the image of Shadow Wing filled my mind. I had never seen him—none of us knew what he looked like. But there he was, rising like a winged demon, taller than a giant, with coiling horns and ruddy-red skin and flaming eyes. He wielded a sword and he was looking right at me.

I could barely breathe. Evil bled off him like sweat, and everything that he touched became tainted and vile. I tried to break away, tried to hide but there was nowhere to go. He could see me, as clearly as I could see him, and he knew what I was doing. He knew I had come for the diamond, and soon he would have a rival he never expected. I would be flanked by my Knights, but still—when it came time to face him down—I would be there, on the front lines, standing between him and the world.

"Do you still wish to take the diamond?" The Guardian's voice penetrated the fog of fear that had banked around me.

I wanted to say no. I wanted to say *Forget about it, I'll be moseying on home and thank you very much for your time.* But I did neither. I was my father's daughter. I straightened my shoulders. Sure, there were places I could hide, but if he broke through, the worlds would burn. And I could help prevent it from happening.

I found my voice. "Yes. I will take the diamond."

"Once the Keraastar Diamond goes around your neck, you will never be able to free yourself from it. Are you ready?" She sounded almost sorrowful.

"I'm ready."

"Then, Queen of the Keraastar Knights, I bestow upon you the Keraastar Diamond. What is about to be done can never be undone. Only the will of the gods, or your death, will sever the ties about to be made."

She led me to the tree. There was nothing else in the room—not Chase, not Venus, not the demons in the shadows. I only had eyes for the Guardian. She backed away and motioned to a hole in the crotch of the tree.

I stared at the black hole, knowing that once I placed my hand inside, anything could happen. But I reached in the crevice, sliding my hand into the inky blackness. I was prepared for something to grab me, or for some creepy-crawly to clamber up my arm.

The space inside the tree was cool and dry and shallow. And there, right below my fingers, was a smooth, icy stone. Taking hold of it, I withdrew my hand. In my palm, the size of a tangerine, rested a brilliant, round, faceted diamond set in platinum with a long chain, also made of platinum.

The light in the chamber hit the facets and set them blazing like a prism. I stared at the massive diamond. It must have been almost one hundred carats, and the energy was spinning off of it, reverberating through me, racing in rivers up my arm. I wanted to recognize this diamond, though I had never before laid eyes on it. But something inside wavered. Something was wrong. I held it out, shaking my head.

"No, this—this is wrong."

"Put on the necklace, Camille Sepharial te Maria. Put it on now."

Something wasn't tracking. "Why the rush?"

"Don't ask questions. You must put on the diamond now, or it can—and will—destroy you. You must wear the necklace." The Guardian's wings rippled, as she moved toward me. "Put it on. *Now*."

I stared at the necklace. Everything felt so odd. I had thought there would be more...pomp and circumstance. More ritual. But instead, a winged faerie was pushing me to toss the diamond over my head before—*wait*.

The diamond began to slowly turn in my hand, moving on its own. At that moment, everything became clear. This wasn't the Keraastar Diamond. As it began to edge toward my wrist, where it grabbed hold with the chain trying to slither up my arm like a snake, I threw it long and hard toward the other end of the pit, where it exploded in a puff of smoke.

"No. That's *not* the Keraastar Diamond! Give me the real gem." I turned to face the Guardian, hand out.

The Guardian backed away. "Read the incantation, if you have it."

Of course—the Maharata-Verdi's incantation that the monk had translated for me. I pulled it out and read it, my voice dancing over the Melosealfôr words.

The Guardian paused, looking hesitant. I tried again, using the ancient form, cautiously following the pronunciation guide Keth had prepared.

As soon as the last word left my mouth, the Guardian shifted form into a ball of blinding light. She flew up and out of sight. The tree began to shudder, quaking as though the earth rumbled beneath it. It let out a wheezing cry as it crystallized, then shattered into a thousand shards. I quickly dropped, covering my head so the glass wouldn't slice into my face. A moment later, the cavern lit up as though it were filled with sunlight. Venus rushed forward, offering me his hand as I stood, Chase right behind him.

I slowly turned. Where the tree had been stood a simple dais, and on the dais sat a black velvet box about the size of a paperback. The pulsing heartbeat of the cave seemed to be concentrated within that box. I could feel it clearly now. Slowly, I reached out and picked up the case. The demons in the shadows began to fade.

Venus and Chase stepped up to flank my sides. I glanced at Venus and he nodded for me to go ahead. I sucked in a deep breath and slowly cracked open the lid, pushing it back. Inside the case, on a black velvet cushion, rested a diamond necklace. The stone was similar in size to the fake one, but this gem was a fantasy cut—with hundreds of facets making up the circular cabochon. Set in a black metal that I didn't recognize, the pendant was on a velvet black ribbon.

Mesmerized by the stone, I lifted it out of the case, setting the box back on the dais. As I held it up, the energy resonating off the stone sang to me and I realized it was singing a song I knew in the core of my heart. I turned to Venus and handed him the pendant, then slowly knelt in front of the old shaman.

With tears in his eyes, he whispered, "I'm so sorry, Camille. I know what this will do to you—it's a double-edged sword. It makes you the mistress, and yet, the slave." And then, he placed the necklace around my neck.

As the stone touched my chest, the demons gave one last howl and then vanished forever from the cavern. I slowly reached up to finger the pendant and I knew in that moment, I'd never be able to remove it. For good or ill, I was the Queen of the Keraastar Knights, and I would wear the diamond until the day I died.

THERE ARE MOMENTS that define the rest of our lives. Crossroads in the path of destiny, as it were. As I stood, I wasn't sure how I felt—there were changes going on, I could sense them, and yet this chapter would have to play out for a while before I knew what was going on. I sucked in a deep breath and forced a smile to my lips as Venus knelt before me.

"My Lady of Twilight," he whispered. "I am your servant."

I lightly touched his head, stroking his hair. "And I accept your service."

Then, as I turned, I saw Chase standing there and I knew why he had come. "And you, my friend." Even as Venus had wept while he placed the stone around my neck, my heart echoed with sadness. I gazed into the detective's eyes and he let out a choked sound.

"I-I can't be. Can I?" He looked caught like Bambi in the headlights.

I reached out and traced his cheek with my fingers. "You will join my Knights. The amethyst seal belongs to you." I could see it as clearly as though I were holding it—the seal belonged with Chase, and he would wear it and take his place among my Keraastar Knights.

"But I'm FBH—" he started to say.

"So was Benjamin. And Tam Lin, or at least he was at one time. You also have elf in your background, and you have taken the Nectar of Life. There's no choice, my friend. This is your destiny—you're going to be the leader of my Knights. When we return home, I will summon the dragons and have Vishana bring you the stone. You and your daughter will move out to Talamh Lonrach Oll and live in my Barrow."

"What about my job? My life I've built?" But then he stopped short, and knelt beside Venus. "I know," he whispered. "I think I've always known that something like this waited for me."

I smiled then, suddenly feeling gleeful as a rush of joy began racing through me. The stone was softly pulsing against my heart and I gazed up at the ceiling, where the rippling lights spread out like the aurora against the horizon.

"Stand, my friends."

They stood.

"Tell me, if I have to be queen of an army, who better to lead it than the two of you?" I looped my arms through theirs and—quite giddy—began to laugh. "We'll take Shadow Wing down."

Even as I spoke, I could see that I would form a powerful circle with my Knights, and the seals would be linked through the diamond so that we would all be stronger than the sum of our parts. I wasn't clear on how yet, but it would come to me. The Keraastar Diamond was a living, sentient entity. In a flash of vision, I could see the Spirit Seal before it had been broken. It had been nine seals, all right, but they had all been linked at the center with the diamond I was wearing. That, no one ever spoke of when repeating the legend.

I was taking my place in history, as were Chase and Venus, as were Luke and Amber. And as would Tanne Baum and still others yet cloaked from my sight. Reeling from the diamond's energy, I slowly began the ascent up the stairs to where the others were waiting. I was grateful I hadn't realized until now just how deep this transformation was going to be. If I had, I might never have had the courage to go through with it.

THE OTHERS WERE waiting topside for us. As we emerged from the pit, Smoky stepped forward, then stopped, waiting for my cue. I swallowed hard. At least I still had my loves. And I would need them in the coming months.

I touched the diamond around my neck. "It's done." I didn't want to tell them about Chase yet. That was his news to tell and the others would know soon enough. "We need to go home. I want to leave this mountain behind and never return."

In fact, now that I had the diamond, the only thing I could think of was to get home and get away from this barren land. All the stress and strain from the trip was overwhelming me, and I couldn't face another day of hard walking. Not with the shifts and changes going on. "Can you take us back to the monastery through the Ionyc Sea?"

Smoky considered the question, then nodded. "I know where it is, and I know where we are. I can take you two at a time."

Bran cleared his throat. "I can go on my own."

Smoky motioned for Delilah and me to join him. "I'll take the two of you, then come back for Venus and Chase, then Shade."

The giddiness vanishing as fast as it had come, I wearily leaned into his arms and closed my eyes. Delilah joined me, and—in the blink of an eye, or the expanse of a lifetime, depending on how you looked at it—we vanished from the cave and a deep sleep pulled me under.

I WOKE TO find myself in my bed, the comforter tucked over me. Delilah was sitting beside me, looking worried, and Smoky was standing behind her.

Struggling to sit up, I squinted, trying to figure out what time it was. "How long have I been asleep? Are we home?" For a brief moment, I felt very Dorothy-like. Was it all a dream? Had it been one long, extended potato-chip and chocolate-induced vision? Instinctively, I reached for my neck. There was the pendant. It was real, all right.

"You fainted in the Ionyc Sea and you've been asleep ever since. We decided to follow through with the plans we had in the first place, and Shade and I transformed into our dragon selves and went back for Trillian and Roz, taking the monks with us so they could lead the horses up to the monastery. When you still weren't awake by the time we got back, we decided just to fly down to Svartalfheim. We came through the portal there last night and when we got home, we called Mallen. He examined you and said you were just exhausted. That your body was adjusting to the energy of wearing the diamond and was pretty seriously confused."

Mallen was the head of the medic unit at the FH-CSI. If he thought I was all right, I trusted his judgment. "What's today?"

"The seventeenth. You've been asleep about thirty-six hours." Delilah handed me a glass of water, which I eagerly downed. She paused, then said, "Chase told us what happened. I'm not sure what to say."

I handed the glass back to her. "Remember how we always felt there was something slightly different about Chase? And then when he drank the Nectar of Life, he started to change, and we found out about his heritage? I think...this was meant to be all along."

Touching the pendant around my neck, I could sense

the gentle pulse of energy. It had aligned to me and I had aligned to it. I could never give it away, or remove it. "I understand now, a lot that I didn't. I can't put it in words, but there's this sense I have that destiny has been playing into all of our lives since the day we were born. We know it has with you—with the Autumn Lord claiming you from birth. But I think all of us—we all have parts to play in this world. Menolly does with Blood Wyne and the Vampire Nation. We're being drawn apart not because we shouldn't be together, but so we can fulfill our fates."

For the first time in a long while, I felt at ease with the thought of moving to Talamh Lonrach Oll. It was what was meant to be. I couldn't stay here and run the Court from our house. I couldn't lead the Keraastar Knights to whatever fate they might have from around the kitchen table. I still ached to think of moving away from my sisters, but the ache was muted by the realization that we would still be close, and we'd be growing into the women we were meant to be.

"So...what now?" Delilah glanced up at Smoky, a look of resignation on her face.

"We ask Vishana to bring Luke, Amber, and the seals to the coronation. I finish packing. And then...come Summer Solstice...I walk into the twilight."

And with that, I pushed back the covers to step into my coming life.

Chapter 17

ON THE AFTERNOON of June 19, I stood in my bedroom, staring at the pile of boxes. Menolly's lair was pretty much in the same condition. Tomorrow, our rooms would be cleared as she and Nerissa moved into Roman's house, and Smoky, Trillian, Morio, and I left for my Barrow. And then, tomorrow night I would go through an all-night ritual that would culminate at just past midnight with my coronation. We would greet the sun on Litha with a party like none I'd ever attended before. I folded my arms across my chest as I walked over to the bed and sat down, silently assaying the room. So much had happened in this house, but it was time to let go and walk away.

Delilah peeked into the room. "Are you ready? Iris and Hanna are finishing the baskets for tonight."

We were going on a walk, Delilah and I, down to Birchwater Pond. I nodded, still conscious of the weight of the diamond around my neck. The energy had muted itself—or rather, I was used to it—and I no longer was acutely conscious of the thrum and sizzle of it, but the fact that I was wearing a gem worth probably at least four million dollars was taking me awhile to adjust to. The one thing I had discovered, for which I was incredibly grateful, was that I could mute the visibility of it. To the outer world, unless I chose for them to see through the glamour, I could shift the stone to look like fancy costume jewelry.

I was wearing a leaf-green skirt and a plum-colored bustier, and I had slipped into my granny boots. Draping a black shawl embroidered with gold and silver metallic threads around my shoulders, I joined Delilah and we clambered down the steps and into the kitchen.

Iris and Hanna were cooking up a storm and I hugged both of them, kissing them soundly on the cheek before Kitten and I headed out the back door. The back porch smelled like freshly turned soil. Hanna had been taking clippings from my witch's garden for me and potting them on the long plank table that we used for gardening. They, too, would travel to Talamh Lonrach Oll.

Once we were free of the porch, I dropped my head back, enjoying the feel of the summer sun on my face. Summers in Seattle were generally pleasant, with only a handful of days climbing into the nineties. It was about seventy-five degrees with a light breeze, and the fresh air did me good.

I grabbed Kitten's hand as we headed toward the trailhead and wound our way into the forest that divided us from the pond. The scents of cedar and fir were thick, and even with the summer sun there was a perpetual feel of moisture in these ancient forests, with the moss and lichen trapping the dew from early morning.

"I wish Menolly could be with us." Delilah frowned. "I know she can take all the walks she wants during the night but it seems so unfair that she can't ever again see the sun."

I shrugged. "It is what it is, you know? I know she misses sunlight, but the stars have their beauty and the moon shines down. It's *all* lovely. I wonder, do you think there's anything like a reverse-vampire somewhere? A person who cannot walk abroad in the night, where the moon will scorch them cold?"

Delilah gave me a funny look. "I don't know, but that seems just as painful in some ways. Give me a balance any day."

We rounded the curve leading to the clearing bordering our pond. As we entered the glade, the lapping of the currents on the pond were like music to my ears. We had been busy over the years, decking out the area with picnic tables and benches, with built-in grills and a stone circle in which to hold our rituals. I wandered over to the edge of the pond where we had placed a low bench that was perfect to sit on and think. As I sat down, Delilah joined me, cautiously edging onto the seat.

"You're still afraid of water, aren't you?"

She laughed. "You can take the girl out of the cat but you can't take the cat out of the girl. Water will always spook me, I think."

I picked up a smooth, flat stone and sent it skipping across the pond's surface. "I think...I think I'm glad I'm staying over here, Earthside. I love Otherworld but somehow, Mother's home feels comfortable to me."

"Chase is going to have one hell of a transition to make." Delilah leaned forward, elbows resting on her knees as she stared at the water. "Did you know when we went after the diamond?"

I shook my head. "Not really. Maybe I did, but if so—I can't pinpoint any real thought about it. I just knew that Chase had to go with us. I wasn't sure why."

"How do you think this will affect his relationship

with Sharah?"

"I think perhaps it will make it better. Maybe the elves will accept him as a Keraastar Knight more than they would as an Earthside detective? I don't know. He'll be living out at the Barrow, so he can soak up a lot of cultural mores that way."

"Elves aren't the same as Fae, remember. Except maybe for the Svartans. Everybody tends to forget they started out as a branch of the Elfin race." Kitten shrugged. "I hope that it helps. It can't make it worse, I think."

"He knows about Sharah needing to bear an heir to the throne—a full-blooded elf child. He told me. I think he's resigned to forever living separately from her. But somehow, I don't think that will happen. When everything shakes out and is done, in the end, I believe they'll get their happily-ever-after. Call me a romantic if you like, but I don't think that the Hags of Fate will keep them apart."

We sat there in silence, soaking up the sun, until Delilah suddenly leaped up and turned into her Tabby self. She bounded into my arms and I snuggled her, realizing this was her way of saying good-bye. Of acknowledging the changing seasons of our lives. I tickled her tummy and played with her paws, then let her down and she raced through the clearing with me after her, playing a game of tag. For a moment, we were children again, tossing our cares to the wind as we raced and romped. Finally, I gave up, flopping down on a patch of grass. Delilah shifted back, joining me.

"That was fun," she said, laughing. "We should do this more often."

"We still can, you know. I'm just moving a half hour away." I rolled on my back, staring up at the sky. "Can I tell you something?"

She flipped over too, resting her arms beneath her

head as she gazed at the clouds that lazily drifted overhead. "What is it?"

"I'm happy. I'm excited. Sad, yes, but Delilah, we're growing up." I rolled up to a sitting position, wrapping my arms around my knees. "We're growing up and we're really, truly, taking control of our lives. You'll be getting married in a few months. We'll all have our homes and families. Whatever children you have will know their crazy Auntie Camille and Auntie Menolly. And Auntie Iris. We're lucky. Despite Shadow Wing and all the pain of the past few years, we'll always have each other. Nobody can ask for more."

And sitting there, basking in the sunlight, my Kitten could only agree.

THAT NIGHT WE gathered around the kitchen table. Everybody was there—all of our wonderful, goofy, extended family. Iris and Hanna had covered the table with a feast, and we reminisced over the past few years, nobody wanting to mention that tomorrow, everything would be different. We avoided talking about Shadow Wing, and in the space of a few hours, we held a wonderful wake for the life we had been leading.

Menolly and Delilah and I stayed up late, gathering in the living room to watch movies and play with Maggie. Everybody else gracefully found an excuse to leave us on our own. Without a word, Menolly turned on the Jerry Springer show and I brought out the Cheetos.

As the night wore on, Maggie fell asleep in my arms and I handed her gently to Menolly, who was sitting in the rocking chair. As she gently rocked our calico wonder, we all fell into a comfortable silence, watching an old science fiction movie, cheering as Patricia Neal faced down Gort. We chimed in when she stopped the robot from wreaking havoc with *Klaatu barada nikto*, and then cheered as Klaatu gave his final speech. *"Your choice is simple: join us and live in peace, or pursue your present course and face obliteration. We shall be waiting for your answer. The decision rests with you."*

Menolly quietly tiptoed into Hanna's room and put Maggie in her crib, then returned. "I wish we could face Shadow Wing and tell him the same thing."

"We could, but I don't know if he'll listen." I yawned and stretched. It was two A.M. "I suppose it's time for bed. Menolly, what are you doing?"

"I carried all our boxes out to the porch earlier tonight. Nerissa and I will be leaving in a few minutes. We're moving into Roman's house now."

At our looks, she shrugged. "There's no use putting it off. You'll be gone tomorrow. We'll be out at Talamh Lonrach Oll for your coronation tomorrow night. Aeval even invited Roman."

Delilah was starting to tear up. I felt the tears welling, but pushed them down as hard as I could. There was no use making this even more difficult than it was.

"Then, I suppose...this is it. I'm going upstairs now to bed. Delilah, you should, too. Menolly..." I paused. "Be happy."

She nodded, her face rigid. She hated crying because her tears always came out as blood and stained her clothes. "You too, Camille. And Kitten...we'll see you tomorrow night."

At that moment, Nerissa appeared in the doorway. "They're here to take our boxes."

I kissed Menolly on the forehead, then embraced Nerissa. Delilah followed suit, though tears raced down her cheeks. Without another word, I turned away and raced up the stairs, unable to stand another moment.

Smoky, Trillian, and Morio were there, waiting.

Trillian opened his arms and I slid into them, weeping. Morio slid in behind me, and Smoky snuggled up on the other side. He was carrying the kittens, and he tumbled them into my lap. Misty pounced on the bed as well, and we rested in silence, the kittens falling asleep as I stroked their fur. An hour wore away, with my beloved husbands simply holding me, brushing my hair, massaging my hands and feet.

Finally, Morio gently disengaged the kittens from my lap and tumbled them back in their playpen, as Trillian helped me undress. Then, with Smoky on one side, Morio on the other, and Trillian resting behind him, I fell asleep in our communal bed, safe in the protection of the men who loved me most in the world.

THE NEXT NIGHT, I stood naked and alone by the edge of the lake out at Talamh Lonrach Oll. My tears of the past few days were dried, and all I wore was the Keraastar Diamond and the two tattoos that marked me as the High Priestess of the Moon Mother. We were headed toward the dark moon, the time of her power that was my power, and I could feel her riding on my shoulders. This was her will, and I would always bend my knee at her hem.

The land was rife with members of the Sovereign Fae Nation, but here—on this night—the only ones with me at the lake were Aeval, Titania, and Myrddin. The coronation would come at just past midnight, but first, I had to pass through the fire that would turn me into the Queen of Dusk And Twilight.

The echoing calls of owls filled the air, and a murder of crows circled overhead, watching. The trees sang an incessant litany cloaked in the wind, their boughs creaking and shaking. Overhead, the sky was clear and the night was slowly gaining on us.

I had disrobed by the side of the lake and now, I waited as Aeval and Titania approached me. Aeval carried a silver chalice, and Titania, a flask of glowing oil. They motioned for me to take my place on a square stone in front of them. As I did, my feet began to tingle and I realized it wasn't any ordinary boulder, but rife with the magic of the land. Pinprick needles raced up my legs, tickling me and burning at the same time.

Aeval set down the chalice on another stone and held out a long dagger. She cast a Circle as Titania kept watch.

Beneath Litha's summer moon, beneath the stars and jet-black sky,
I weave this Circle with magic's rune, all unwelcome flee or die.
To this sacred space we come, To this night of summer's height,
To the ancient charms we turn, to the ancient charms and rites.
Hags of Fate, hear me now, to your will we bend our knee,
Come to us, your faces show, come to bestow destiny.

As she spoke, a great mist rose up by the water and out of the mist stepped a figure that I had met once before. She was regal, buxom, and barely skimmed my height by an inch. Wearing an ivory corset beaded with silver and a long flowing skirt the color of the mist, she looked more ethereal than real. Her hair cascaded around her, to her knees, the color of ice floes and winter snow. Atop her head, she wore a headdress of silver. Crystal antlers rose up from the headdress to tower over her. Her eyes were jet, with faint silver flecks, and she was a most fearsome and beautiful sight. She was wielding her wand—a thin birch branch with silver winding around it that sparkled in the night.

Pentangle...the Mistress of Magic. Pentangle, one of the Hags of Fate.

Aeval and Titania bowed to Pentangle. I felt awkward—standing on the stone, I was taller than she was and kneeling would be precarious. I tried, but she stopped me.

"So we meet again, Camille, as your destiny plays out." She turned to Aeval. "Are you ready? Is *she*?" And I knew she was talking about me.

Aeval nodded. "I have the Nectar. And Titania carries the elixir."

"Then we proceed." Pentangle turned to me. "Before you can ascend to your throne, you must go through death and rebirth. Morgaine went through this same ritual, as did Aeval and Titania in their beginnings."

I glanced at them. It had never occurred to me that they would have had to go through a ritual to take the throne. Somehow, in my mind, they had been born Fae Queens, rolled out of bed, stepped up to the throne, and taken their crowns like I might roll out of bed and make coffee in the morning.

Pentangle let out a soft smile. "No, child. Everyone who ascends to great power had to begin somewhere. You do not become great by the name you are born to, but by the destiny you are offered. And even then, you have to accept your path and fulfill it."

That she could read my mind made me just as nervous as the first time I had met her, walking on the shore of the Ocean of Anger in the Netherworld.

"Are you ready?" She held my gaze. I couldn't have lied to her if I wanted to.

I summoned a deep breath and let it out slowly. "I'm ready." And in my heart, I was.

Pentangle turned to Aeval. "The Nectar?"

Aeval handed her the chalice and Pentangle stirred the contents with her wand. "The hands of time slow and still, as I charm, so be my will." She pointed to my feet with her wand. "Make certain your feet are firmly planted on the stone of ages."

I glanced down, wiggling my toes to make sure they were flat against the rock. I had never heard of the term "stone of ages" but now wasn't the time to ask questions.

Pentangle handed me the chalice. "This is the Nectar of Life. Drink deep, and your years will stretch on for eons. Drink deep, and you will live as long or longer than any of the full-blooded Fae folk. Drink deep, for without the Nectar of Life, you cannot take the throne."

I held the silver chalice in my hands, my stomach rolling like I'd eaten too much sugar or had too much caffeine. *I can't be scared of this*, I thought. *I always knew I'd drink this one day. Chase took the Nectar and he's fine.* But Chase hadn't drunk Nectar empowered by Pentangle, and he wasn't taking a throne.

But he is becoming one of your Knights. And his life is changing in ways he can't even fathom. Be brave. Step into your future.

At first I wasn't sure where the thought had come from, but then I glanced up. Pentangle was smiling at me—faintly, yes, but there it was, at the corner of her lips—a slight upturn.

You know I can read your thoughts, Camille. I see your heart, and I see your fear. But let fear pass away. You no longer need it.

I raised the chalice to my lips. No words were necessary. No formal proclamations. All that was required was for me to drink the Nectar of Life. I sipped the golden liqueur, and it was like fiery honey on my tongue, racing down my throat like the oldest brandy ever known, smooth and yet with a fire so deep that it worked its way into every cell of my body.

I drank the Nectar in one long swallow and handed Aeval the goblet, reeling as the magic began to seep into my cells and my blood, changing my DNA as it went, twisting me inside out and then inside out yet again. My thoughts were scattered like a flock of startled birds, winging away as the Nectar waged war on the cells that wanted to age. It hurt, as though I were being sliced, diced, and twisted like a licorice whip. I cried out and would have fallen except for Aeval, who grabbed my hand to keep me steady. Forcing myself to see through the haze that was running rampant in my body, I once again planted my feet firmly on the rock.

Pentangle motioned to Titania. "Next, the elixir."

Titania handed her the vial of oil and Pentangle took it, motioned for me to kneel. I was holding onto the corners of the stone with my hands, my knees firmly against the smooth surface. Pentangle opened the elixir and held up the dropper.

"Open your mouth, Camille, and stick out your tongue."

Even though I knew this was a solemn rite, I let out a half-crazed giggle. If she was holding a tongue depressor, this couldn't be any weirder. I felt like I was undergoing one of the most bizarre physical exams ever. But I stifled my laughter and held out my tongue.

Humor is an important attribute for any member of royalty to have. Again, Pentangle's voice echoed in my head. *I think you'll find it brings you closer to your subjects than Aeval and Titania are with their own Barrow halls.*

Now I did stifle my laugh, hoping neither of the Fae Queens had caught that remark. The last thing I needed was to be held up to comparison to them before I had even gotten to wear the crown.

Pentangle held out the dropper and let one single drop of the glowing oil fall on my tongue. It absorbed into my skin quickly, tasting like blackberries and cream. The next moment, my back began to itch and then—sharp pains burrowed deep below my shoulder blades, twisting like a drill bit boring into my body.

"Don't scream," Pentangle cautioned.

I bit my lip, drawing blood as the pain increased. What the hell was happening to me? But as I knelt there, squeezing the rock so hard that I cut the skin on my fingers and blood raced down the sides of the stone, I happened to glance over at Titania and Aeval.

They stood there, the same as always, but now I could see a deep sparkle of color around them—their auras stood out as clearly as if they were illuminated by Morio's Faerie Fire spell. And from their backs, I could see massive wings unfolding, sparkling with color, transparent and yet luminescent. I realized I had never seen anything like *this* before. And then, I realized what was going on with my back.

"Wings? I'm growing wings?"

Pentangle nodded, a soft smile on her face. "All Fae Queens wear wings. The Guardian of the Keraastar Diamond? She was the spirit of the stone, a Fae Queen who gave her life to protect the gem until the rightful owner came along so many thousands of years later. And now you, too, bear the mark of a Fae Queen."

"I saw *her* wings."

"She allowed you to. You'll have that choice as well, but guard wisely who you allow to see them. There are reasons we hide them and you will learn as you go along."

At that moment, the skin felt like it split wide on my back. I groaned, stifling the shriek that came to my lips. The next moment, the pain was gone and I felt the gentle waving of wings behind me. I shifted, and they moved in the wind. As I weakly sat back, they moved along with me, but weren't impeded by the ground or plants or the stone itself.

"Your wings are visible only to other Fae Queens and various beings of such sort. You will see them in the mirror, but your loved ones won't. Your wings mark you as royalty in the Fae world such as no other heads of state."

"Does Tanaquar have them?" I asked. "And Lethesanar?"

"No," Myrddin said. "They may rule Court and Crown, but they are not Fae Queens such as Aeval or Titania. Or you, now." He had been standing back, watching all of this unfold, and now he crossed to Aeval's side. It was then that I saw that he—too—bore wings.

"You, too?"

He nodded. "I may be the Arch Druid, but I am also of the Fae realm and Fae nobility."

Aeval held out her hand. "Come, stand. Then walk into the lake and rinse off, and then, we have a coronation to attend." She was smiling kindly. So was Titania.

"I remember getting my wings," Titania said softly. "So very long ago. I was so afraid."

"I was too." Aeval glanced over at me. "I think what marked Morgaine as different...was that she wasn't afraid. She was cocky and too certain of her entitlement. It was her undoing in the end."

I didn't want to talk or think about Morgaine at this point. I was having a hard time even processing what had occurred already, so much had happened. Aeval and Titania led me to the edge of the lake—only a few yards away—and I cautiously walked into the water until I was waist deep. I ducked my head under, immersing myself. My wings felt light and shimmering as I waved them in the current, shaking off what was basically their amniotic fluid. And then, a similar rush of joy to what I had felt when the Keraastar Diamond was placed around my neck hit me and I rose from the water, feeling reborn into a new strength. As I stepped out from the water a glow centered in my heart, and it reverberated through the diamond.

I glanced around. "Where's Pentangle?"

"She'll meet us at the Barrow. Now come, dress."

Standing next to Aeval, Titania, and Myrddin were two attendants. They dried me off and then there, under the waning moon, they dressed me. Afterward, they bade me step into a pair of lace panties, then brought out a shimmering skirt the color of twilight. It floated down around my waist, flowing out, so sheer it was almost weightless. Next, they fit a dusky blue corset with accents of silver and black around me, lacing me into it. The corset pushed my breasts up, spilling out the way a good corset worked. As I lifted my feet, they slid leather boots on my feet and laced them up to my knees. They fastened silver arm bracelets around my upper arms and, of course, I wore the Keraastar Diamond.

I turned to Aeval and saw myself reflected in her eyes. She gave me a sad smile.

"I knew from the first time we met that one day you'd be standing here. You freed me from my prison, and I'm about to consign you to your own—albeit more pleasant. But Camille, it *is* a prison, and as the centuries roll on, you'll understand more what I mean. Thank you for stepping up to take the crown. For voluntarily giving yourself over to our world." She sounded so resigned that I wanted to cheer her up.

But what she said rang true. It resonated with a deep knell that sounded the end of my freedom. To wear any crown brought with it responsibilities and formalities, and while I expected to still love my life, it would never again feel freewheeling except when I was running with the Hunt.

"It's who I am, Aeval." As I said it, I knew that it was true. I wouldn't be happy if I turned away.

"Then come, and join us in Talamh Lonrach Oll and take your place as one of our own."

Chapter 18

TITANIA SNAPPED HER fingers and the undergrowth rustled as another attendant led four horses through the trees.

Decorated with ribbons and pennants, in the colors of the Barrows, the stately Andalusians came trotting in. A white one bore the flag of the sun, and his ribbons were green and gold. He stopped by Titania's side, as if they were old friends. The second, a black stallion, bore a flag was that of a silver star against the black background. He dipped his head to Aeval. The third, a bay stallion—golden brown with a dark mane—sported ribbons of red and white, and he came to stop by Myrddin's side. The Merlin patted his muzzle lovingly. And the fourth—a gray horse—stepped up to me. The pennant on my horse had a deep blue background with a silver crescent moon.

We mounted the horses, the attendant helping me up. I had learned to be comfortable on the horses in Otherworld, and this horse seemed even more compliant than Annabelle. The saddles were thickly padded, for which I was grateful, considering my underwear consisted of a thin lace panty. Titania took the lead, then Aeval, then Myrddin motioned me in line and he swung in behind me.

As we rode onto the path leading back to the Barrows, an escort of armed guards fell in and I realized they had been waiting for us. Eight rode at the front, another eight swung in behind Myrddin. Everything was surreal. I had wings that almost nobody could see unless I let them. I had drunk the Nectar of Life. Everything that I had been building up to the past few months was suddenly very real and happening now.

The forest buzzed with life. Frogs were croaking, insects clicked and snapped, the owls were softly hooting, and everywhere, the undergrowth rustled and rattled with the movement of small animals. The trees themselves were awake and watching, and I understood now just how alive and vibrant this sovereign land was. Aeval and Titania had established not just the Fae Nation, but they had enlivened the land as well. Everything was aware and listening.

As we rode out to the main trail leading to the Barrows, the knot in my stomach began to dissolve. The path was lined with members of Talamh Lonrach Oll and they cheered as we passed, waving ribbons and flags at us. A number of the flags were the same standard as the pennant on my horse, and I realized that these people would be living in and around my Barrow. I would actually be holding Court. Another giddy wash of emotion slammed through me and I struggled not to laugh.

Solemn occasion, Camille. Suck it up and don't let your nerves win. Consider it payback for all the times you teased Menolly about being a princess. Put your game face on and stop smirking. I finally managed to calm myself and fell into the solemnity of the moment.

We reached the courtyard in front of the Barrow of Dusk and Twilight and I flashed back to Summer Solstice two years before, when Aeval and Titania had established Talamh Lonrach Oll and reclaimed their thrones. We had been here for their coronation, and Queen Asteria had given them their crowns. Our father had been here then, and with a swift stab to the heart, I wished he could see me now—that he could be here to witness me taking the throne.

The land sang with their energy, with the energy of the Earthside Fae and a crazy dance of joy and celebration filled the air, the currents of energy rippling through the crowd as we entered the courtyard. Eye catchers lit the cobblestone square by the hundreds, faerie lights sparkling in the night.

Three massive barrow mounds comprised the palace of the Court of the Three Queens, each signified by the flags flying from each mound. They were covered by a thick, luxurious carpet of grasses and roses. A large dais rose in front of the palace and there, standing next to it, were my sisters and the rest of my extended family except for Hanna, who was home babysitting Maggie. Vishana was there, as well, with Amber and Luke standing beside her. Chase and Venus had joined them.

Derisa was waiting on the dais, and Trenyth and Sharah were there as well. I could see the longing in her face as she glanced at Chase, who was holding Astrid, and my heart went out to all of them. How things would change once Chase took the spirit seal, I didn't know, but maybe, somehow, it would be better.

As we rode through the crowd, all eyes were on us. I began to shake, ever so slightly, and I struggled not to cry. I had made sure all of my makeup was waterproof, but the last thing I wanted was to look a mess or look vulnerable during the ceremony.

We reached the dais and the guards encircled us as

attendants moved forward to help us off the horses. I patted my horse, realizing she would probably be mine from now on, and that thought took the edge off my nerves. I had come to like horses more than I ever thought I would in the past week. They were smart, sensitive creatures. If I could keep focusing on small things, like friendly horses, instead of the fact that I was in a courtyard mobbed with people, I could make it through.

Aeval motioned to me to get in line. Once again, Titania ascended the steps, followed by Aeval, then I came next, and finally—the Merlin. Myrddin had put on his antlered headdress and it hit me that *that* was *his* crown. He wasn't all that friendly, in fact I found him aloof and rather snobbish, but right now, he was being supportive and that was all that mattered.

We approached the center of the platform where Derisa, Sharah, and Trenyth waited. I gave a quick, nervous glance toward Smoky and the others. Delilah raised her hand slightly and wiggled her fingers at me, smiling. I winked at her, wanting to establish that connection. Regardless of where I was headed, she and Menolly would always be my anchors in this world.

Sharah inclined her head. She was dressed in all the Elfin finery that Queen Asteria had worn, and the crown on her head seemed to fit more every time I saw her. Her eyes flickered as she whispered, "Congratulations, Camille."

Derisa stood tall, a proud look on her face. "I'm so glad to see this day," she said in a low voice. "Lyrical sends her salutations."

I broke out into a dizzying smile. That was code for: Lyrical was pissed as hell and was being forced to eat crow. One of the elders of the Coterie of the Moon Mother, Lyrical had been the bane of my life back in Otherworld when I was in training. She had tried to block my initiation, calling me a half-breed and scorning every suggestion that I join the Order. Now, I had my vindication.

"Please tell her I value her support." Stifling a snicker, I happened to glance over at Aeval, who was staring at me, her mouth set in a stern line. But her eyes were laughing.

Aeval turned to the crowd. "Good people of Talamh Lonrach Oll, we gather today to witness the coronation of a new Queen of Dusk and Twilight. Listen well, and remember this day, for you are all part of the living history of this sovereign land."

The crowd roared in return. *"All hail the Queen of Shadow and Night! All hail the Queen of Light and Morning!"*

Aeval held out a long silver blade, the tip touching my breast, pointing directly at my heart. Myrddin moved behind me, blocking any chance I had of getting away. My wings twitched and I realized this was what it felt like to be a cat and sense things with whiskers.

Then the questioning began, Aeval beginning.

"Know that it is better to fall on the tip of my blade than give false answers, for if you knowingly bear falsehood, we will strike you down. Do you understand?"

I straightened my shoulders, my mood sobering. She meant every word, and would have every right.

"I understand." I almost jumped as my voice echoed through the courtyard along with hers. Apparently someone had cast a Projection spell so that we could be heard all the way through the heart of the Fae nation.

Titania spoke next. "Camille Sepharial te Maria D'Artigo, listen well to our words and answer from the truth of your heart. Have you been through the ritual to drink the Nectar of Life?"

"I have."

After that, they alternated questions. Both Aeval and

Titania seemed to rise up to tower over the crowd, and I felt like I was mirroring them. Their eyes were flashing dark and brilliant.

"Have we taken you through the secret rites to bestow the mantle of Fae Queen upon your shoulders?"

My wings twitched at that question. "Yes, you have."

"Have you, in your heart, given yourself over to Talamh Lonrach Oll and its people? Will you live for your people? Will you die for your people?"

In my heart, I was flashing back to my initiation during that wild night when I was accepted by the Moon Mother. And now, she had bid me move into yet another realm, enlarging the scope of my work for her.

"I do so pledge my life and will, under the guidance of the Moon Mother herself."

"Will you take the crown of the Court of Dusk and Twilight, and pledge yourself to it until the day you die? Will you take the mantle of the Queen of the Keraastar Knights and lead them into the coming battles as so prophesized?"

I felt like I was vibrating. This wasn't simply a swearing-in ritual. This was a binding magical pledge, and the gods themselves were listening. The Moon Mother might as well be standing here to take my oath.

"I do so pledge. I will take the crown and wear the mantle."

"Kneel before me."

I slowly sank to my knees as Aeval sheathed her dagger. Titania was holding a crown and they moved forward. Myrddin put his hands on my shoulders and it felt as though I could barely breathe, sandwiched between the three of them.

Aeval turned to the crowds. "Then let the people hear and take note: Camille Sepharial te Maria D'Artigo has pledged her life to this land, and to you, its people. She has pledged to rule over the Court of Dusk and Twilight. She has pledged herself to the Keraastar Knights. Let nothing put aside her pledges but death, and may death seek her out swiftly if she reneges on her oaths."

Again, a wild cheer went up.

Titania waited till the crowd was silent again. "Then, by the will of the gods, by the will of the Immortals, we do so crown you Camille, Queen of Dusk and Twilight, Queen of the Keraastar Knights. Join us in leading Talamh Lonrach Oll and her people into the future, where the Sovereign Fae Nation will once again rise strong over the land."

As Titania placed the crown on my head, a dizzying wave rushed through me, and I realized that—for good or ill—I had just moved onto my new path and aligned myself with the Earthside Fae for the rest of my life.

I ROSE, HELPED by Myrddin, surprised to find that I was crying. Aeval and then Titania embraced me, kissing me on the cheek. Then Aeval whispered, "You should give Chase his spirit seal now and officially declare ownership of the Keraastar Knights."

I had little to no idea of what I was supposed to do, and I was grateful for the coaching. "I'm not sure of what words to use..." I paused, feeling stupid.

"Use words that people will understand. We don't stand on pomp and circumstance except during official business. This will be most of our people's first impression of you, even though most of them have heard you mentioned. Think about what impression you want to make."

I nodded, thinking quickly. Then, I turned to the crowd. "Thank you for welcoming me into your hearts, and this beautiful nation. In my first official act, I claim my Knights under my protection. Chase, Venus, Luke, Amber, please join me. Vishana, if you will?"

Vishana led the others up to the dais. She handed me an embossed case and a shock raced up my arms. I could feel the spirit seals within. They were separated from touching by their individual boxes, but they were resonating. One slip, one chance of letting them all touch, and I could destroy the world as we knew it. The overwhelming power that rested in my possession was terrifying—and a little heady.

I opened the case and immediately gravitated to the one I knew was the amethyst. I locked up the case and handed it to Vishana again. "You must keep this in the Dragon Reaches until I call for it. We can't take the chance on the unattached ones being stolen."

She nodded. "As you will...*Queen* Camille." A faint smile escaped her lips.

"Chase Johnson, step forward."

With a desperate glance at Sharah, Chase moved into position in front of me, bending down on one knee. "Your Majesty."

I wanted to tell him to knock it off, but he was right—in public, that was my title. He was following form.

"Do you swear yourself to me and to the Keraastar Knights? Do you willingly take this seal and vow to protect it with your life, and to lend yourself to its will?"

"I pledge my oath to you and to the Keraastar Knights. I forsake my former life." His voice was thick with tears, though his eyes were dry, and I knew all too well how hard this was for him. As I placed the spirit seal around his neck, there was a hush as it settled against his heart, and then, his aura flared and I knew the match was right.

Chase rose, bowing, and then I embraced them all and took their pledges to me as their queen, and the coronation ended with a massive fireworks display, thanks to Vanzir and Rozurial, as the feasting began.

Before joining my family and all of the Supe nobility who had attended for the feast, I retired to a private garden with Derisa. An entourage of bodyguards accompanied me and I realized this was one more thing I'd have to get used to.

The garden was off my bedroom, deep in the Barrow. I had opted not to use the bedroom Morgaine had occupied. Somehow, the Barrow mages had managed to build me a private garden space even in the midst of the Barrow Mound. Small but open to the sky, the scent of roses hung heavy, and here were my seedlings from my witch's garden. I slowly eased myself down onto a stone bench, all too aware of my wings. They weren't uncomfortable, but they tickled and I could feel them moving softly in the astral wind.

"Did you know?" I asked Derisa when she joined me. "Did you know this would happen?"

She shrugged. "Who knows what might happen? I had visions…this was one possible future. You do know that all your advisors voted that you shouldn't be offered initiation. But when you came before me, the Moon Mother sang to me. She alone rules my actions. And so I took you under my wing and initiated you. And…here you are. Where you are supposed to be."

I hesitated to tell her what was weighing heavy on my heart, but I needed to confide in her. "What if this Court…what if it conflicts with the Moon Mother's will?"

Derisa shook her head. "Don't worry your head, my love. She will not let you fall into that position. What else worries you?"

I paused again, searching through my thoughts to make certain I spoke clearly. "What if I can't find the other Knights?"

"Again, you would not wear the diamond if you

weren't destined to renew the knighthood. You will find them, probably where you least expect."

The High Priestess reached out and took my hand. "Camille, you are one of the chosen. Some have lesser journeys to walk, some even more powerful ones than you have been given. But those whom the Hags of Fate choose to invest the future in, well...this is a gift, though at times it may seem like a curse. You will help create history. You will not simply witness it, but you will *forge* it. Be grateful for the chance to leave your mark."

And with that, she stood. "You should attend your guests. Enjoy the night. Celebrate now, for I have the feeling the coming days will be rife with learning the ways of your court."

And with that, she led me back to the great hall, and the night passed in a blur of music and food, and as morning light brought the beginning of the waning year, I called my husbands to me, and retired to my bedroom.

Chapter 19

TWO WEEKS LATER, Menolly and I were sitting on the porch steps with Delilah. The house felt so empty, and a part of me longed to move back, but I knew that time was gone forever. The night sky sparkled overhead, and I stared up, realizing how much clearer it was out at Talamh Lonrach Oll. There were some perks to living in a Barrow city.

"So...how's Chase doing?" Delilah bit her lip. "Yugi's been promoted to chief, but I don't think anybody at the FH-CSI understood why he resigned so quickly. We can't tell them, of course, but it really left a hole there."

I shrugged. "He's adapting. The spirit seal is beginning to work on him. He's more confident, and a little more aloof. Astrid is enjoying the attention, though. She's in the equivalent of the Fae daycare out at the Barrow and she has lots of playmates there, and loving nannies. Sharah stayed for two days to visit him. I'm not sure what went on between them, but both seemed happier by the time she had to leave." Pausing, I motioned to Menolly. "And you? How goes it at Roman's?"

Menolly gave me a shake of the head. "I've never had to deal with so much formality in my life. But I will say this, living among vampires has helped me. I don't feel so—alien. Nerissa is adapting. I think she could adapt to just about anything. And she has a way of winning people over. I think they like her more than me." With that, she laughed. "Oh, trust me," she added, leaning back against the steps and folding her hands under her head, "it's a drastic change, but I think we'll be okay. I'm able to spend more time with Erin, too. I have a feeling about her...she's going to make a mark on society one day."

"Grandmother Coyote predicted as much, early on." Delilah handed Maggie to me and I snuggled her to my chest.

"I think the guys miss Rozurial. But Vanzir's out there. He's probably having the hardest time adjusting. He's not only a demon among Fae, but the babydaddy of Aeval's child. That was quite a bomb when she told her court that she was expecting." I winced, rubbing my head as Maggie tugged on a strand of my hair. The damned crown gave me a headache.

"Ingz...Cammy got ingz like Maggie." Maggie pointed over my shoulders.

I stared at her. "You can see them?"

She giggled.

"See what?" Delilah asked, sitting up. "What's she talking about? You have wings? Where?"

I let out a slow breath. I had yet to tell them about my wings, though Smoky, Morio, and Trillian knew. Finally, I handed Maggie to Menolly and clambered down the stairs, turning my back to them.

"Watch." I closed my eyes. I had been spending twelve hours a day learning the ways of the Court, and one of those lessons had been about my wings. I willed them to appear, shedding the glamour that kept them cloaked.

"Oh. My. Gods." Menolly and Delilah were by my side immediately, examining the huge curling wings that draped off my back.

"When did this happen?" Delilah held out a finger. "Can I touch them?"

"During the ritual before my coronation and please don't. They still feel incredibly awkward and I'm not sure how I'd react."

But Maggie wasn't listening. She reached out and poked one of my wings and I jumped, feeling her tickling finger right down to my core.

"I guess that answers that," Delilah said. She slid her arm through mine and began to walk around the house. Menolly followed, carrying Maggie. "So, you have wings. I guess that trumps any news I've got. Except that Shade and I have decided on where we want to get married."

"Where?" I was dying to talk about something other than the changes in my life. I wanted to talk about something normal for a change.

Menolly smiled. "I bet I can guess, but I'll let you tell us."

Delilah smiled. "Yeah, I imagine you do know. I thought—down at the pond. A simple wedding, just immediate family and friends. I found a green sheath dress that will be perfect for a wedding dress. I want both of you to be my bridesmaids, please? And Nerissa, too. I've asked Iris to be my matron of honor."

"Oh, that sounds perfect." I slid my arm around her waist and hugged her. "Tell us more. What flowers? Who will perform the ceremony?"

As we headed toward the pond, discussing wedding plans, the glowing moon rose. She was nearing the full stage and soon I'd be running with the Hunt again. Delilah would be bounding through dandelions in her

Tabby form. Menolly had promised to come out and help Shade kitty-sit her during the shift, not out of need but out of the desire to reclaim some familiarity with what had been our lives up until recently.

The birds were singing as we passed into the woods, on the trail toward Birchwater Pond, and the night seemed to stand still for us, pausing to give us the chance to catch our breath. I wasn't sure what was going to happen in the coming weeks, but they were bound to be interesting.

We hadn't heard from Trytian in a while and were trying to contact him, but the battle in the Sub-Realms was raging on, that much we knew. I was toying with whom to deed the Indigo Crescent. I couldn't very well run a business and be a Fae Queen as well.

Menolly retained ownership of the Wayfarer, but she had withdrawn from working there now, given her new position in the vampire community. And Delilah had let her PI license lapse. She had never been passionate over the job to begin with, and now her life was moving in a new direction as well.

Yes, I thought as a breeze wafted by, filling my lungs with the scent of cedar and moss, of warm summer flowers and the leftover haze from the day. Things had changed. And they would be changing even more. I was about ready to contact Tanne Baum, our friend from the Hunter's Glen Clan, and see if my hunch was right about him. Smoky, Morio, and Trillian were making themselves useful around the Barrow, and as Titania joked, at least Smoky and she could share the barrow space without threatening each other now. I had first met Titania when I was whisked away to my dragon's barrow.

As we approached the water, echoes of past celebrations reached out to touch my heart. So much of our joy surrounded this land, this pond. Whatever was coming, we'd always have this time and place to return to in our memories.

Menolly seemed to pick up my thoughts and she carried Maggie over to the bench near the water and sat, singing softly.

I've wandered so many trails,
Some dark, some light, some bleak,
My heart today feels old and frail,
As solace I do seek.
But one bright light shines ever on,
Within my soul and heart,
And gives me hope to carry on,
Though our paths may part.
You will always be there,
My anchors and my loves,
My family, my sisters dear,
Wherever I may rove.

As her voice rang out into the night, Delilah and I built a fire, and we sat there, watching the moon rise, holding onto our past even as we knew that, come the dawn, we would return to our homes and move onward into the future. We accepted the paths the Hags of Fate set before us. And that was right and true. Because all life evolves, and even though we were no longer living together, we still had battles to fight, and dreams to live, and love to embrace.

~End~

If you enjoyed this book, know that the next Otherworld book—HARVEST SONG—will be out May 2018.

Meanwhile, how about getting acquainted with my new characters—the wild and magical residents of Bedlam in my Bewitching Bedlam Series, about fun-loving witch Maddy Gallowglass, her smoking-hot vampire lover, and their crazed cjinn Bubba (part djinn, all cat). Read BLOOD MUSIC, the prequel, and BEWITCHING BEDLAM—the first in the series, while waiting for MAUDLIN'S MAYHEM to come out.

Or, if you prefer a grittier series, try my post-apocalyptic paranormal romance—the Fury Unbound Series. The first two books—FURY RISING and FURY'S MAGIC—are out, and the third will be out in June 2017.

You can also read my entire Chintz 'n China paranormal mystery series, including HOLIDAY SPIRITS, the holiday novella I wrote to wrap it up.

For all of my work, see the Bibliography at the end of this book, or check out my website at Galenorn.com and be sure and sign up for my newsletter to receive news about all my new releases.

Upcoming releases

June 2017: Fury Awakened (Fury Unbound—Book 3)
July 2017: Maudlin's Mayhem (Bewitching Bedlam—Book 2)
August 2017: Re-release of the Bath and Body Series
August 2017: Fury Calling (Fury Unbound—Book 4)
October 2017: Siren Song (Bewitching Bedlam—Book 4)
October 2017: Taming the Shifter (Anthology)
November 2017: Fury's Mantle (Fury Unbound—Book 5)
December 2017: Silent Night (Otherworld Holiday Novella)

Playlist

I often write to music and I always try to put my playlists in the book so you can see what music influenced me.

Air: Playground Love, Napalm Love, Moon Fever
A.J. Roach: Devil May Dance
Al Stewart: Life in Dark Water
Android Lust: Here and Now, Saint Over
Arch Leaves: Nowhere to Go
The Asteroids Galaxy Tour: Sunshine Coolin', Heart Attack
AWOLNATION: Sail
Beck: Nausea, Qué Onda Guero, Emergency Exit, Farewell Ride
The Black Angels: Always Maybe, Don't Play With Guns, Young Men Dead
Black Mountain: Queens Will Play
Blue Oyster Cult: Godzilla
Boom! Bap! Pow!: Suit
The Bravery: Believe
Broken Bells: The Ghost Inside
Buffalo Springfield: For What It's Worth
Crazy Town: Butterfly
Chris Isaac: Wicked Game
Cobra Verde: Play with Fire
David Bowie: China Girl, Fame '90, Golden Years
Death Cab For Cutie: I Will Possess Your Heart
Dizzi: Dizzi Jig
Don Henley: Dirty Laundry
Eastern Sun: Beautiful Beaing
Eivør: Trøllbundin
Elektrisk Gønner: Uknowhatiwant
Fatboy Slim: Praise You

Faun: The Market Song, Hymn to Pan, Iduna, Oyneng yar
FC Kahuna: Hayling
Fluke: Absurd
Foster The People: Pumped Up Kids
Gabrielle Roth: Raven
Garbage: Queer, #1 Crush,
Gary Numan: My Breathing, Walking with Shadows, I Am Dust, Cars (Remix), Petals
Gorillaz: Dare, Last Living Souls, Demon Days, Clint Eastwood, Fire Coming Out of the Monkey's Head, Kids With Guns, Stylo
The Gospel Whiskey Runners: Muddy Waters
Hedningarna: Ukkonen, Juopolle Joutunut, Räven (Fox Woman), Grodan/Widergrenen (Toadeater), Drafur & Gildur
Huldrelokkk: Trolldans
Ian Melrose & Kerstin Blodig: Kråka
In Strict Confidence: Silver Bullets, Tiefer, Snow White
Jessica Bates: The Hanging Tree
The Kills: Sour Cherry, You Don't Own The Road, Nail In My Coffin
Kirsty MacColl: In These Shoes?
Lady Gaga: I Like It Rough, Paparazzi,
Ladytron: I'm Not Scared, Paco, Ghosts
Leonard Cohen: It Seemed the Better Way, You Want It Darker
Lord of the Lost: Sex on Legs
Lorde: Royals, Yellow Flicker Beat
Low with Tom and Andy: Half Light
Marilyn Manson: Tainted Love, Personal Jesus
Matt Corby: Breathe
Nine Inch Nails: Deep
Orgy: Social Enemies, Blue Monday
Puddle of Mudd: Famous
The Pussycat Dolls: Don't Cha
Queen: We Will Rock You, Another One Bites the Dust
Roisin Murphy: Ramalama (Bang Bang)

Saliva: Ladies and Gentlemen
Screaming Trees: Where the Twain Shall Meet
Shriekback: Dust and a Shadow, Underwater Boys, The King in the Tree, The Shining Path, The Big Hush, Intoxication, Go Bang, Now These Days Are Gone
Simple Minds: Don't You (Forget About Me)
Stone Temple Pilots: Atlanta
Strawberry Alarm Clock: Incense and Peppermint
Styx: Renegade
Sweet Talk Radio: We All Fall Down
Talking Heads: I Zimbra, Burning Down the House, Girlfriend Is Better, Moon Rocks
Tamaryn: While You're Sleeping, I'm Dreaming, Violet's in a Pool
Toadies: Possum Kingdom
Tuatha Dea: Tuatha De Danaan, Long Black Curl
The Verve: Bitter Sweet Symphony
Warchild: Ash
Zero 7: In the Waiting Line

Cast of Major Characters

The D'Artigo Family:
Arial Lianan te Maria: Delilah's twin who died at birth. Half-Fae, half-human.
Camille Sepharial te Maria, aka Camille D'Artigo: The oldest sister; a Moon Witch and Priestess. Half-Fae, half-human.
Daniel George Fredericks: The D'Artigo sisters' half cousin; FBH.
Delilah Maria te Maria, aka Delilah D'Artigo: The middle sister; a werecat.
Hester Lou Fredericks: The D'Artigo sisters' half cousin; FBH.
Maria D'Artigo: The D'Artigo Sisters' mother. Human. Deceased.
Menolly Rosabelle te Maria, aka Menolly D'Artigo: The youngest sister; a vampire and *jian-tu:* extraordinary acrobat. Half-Fae, half-human.
Sephreh ob Tanu: The D'Artigo Sisters' father. Full Fae. Deceased.
Shamas ob Olanda: The D'Artigo girls' cousin. Full Fae. Deceased.

The D'Artigo Sisters' Lovers & Close Friends:
Astrid (Johnson): Chase and Sharah's baby daughter.
Bruce O'Shea: Iris's husband. Leprechaun.
Carter: Leader of the Demonica Vacana Society, a group that watches and records the interactions of Demonkin and human through the ages. Carter is half demon and half Titan—his father was Hyperion, one of the Greek Titans.

Chase Garden Johnson: Detective, director of the Faerie-Human Crime Scene Investigation (FH-CSI) team. Human who has taken the Nectar of Life, which extends his life span beyond any ordinary mortal and has opened up his psychic abilities.
Chrysandra: Waitress at the Wayfarer Bar & Grill. Human. Deceased.
Derrick Means: Bartender at the Wayfarer Bar & Grill. Werebadger.
Erin Mathews: Former president of the Faerie Watchers Club and former owner of the Scarlet Harlot Boutique. Turned into a vampire by Menolly, her sire, moments before her death. Human.
Greta: Leader of the Death Maidens; Delilah's tutor.
Iris (Kuusi) O'Shea: Friend and companion of the girls. Priestess of Undutar. Talon-haltija (Finnish house sprite).
Lindsey Katharine Cartridge: Director of the Green Goddess Women's Shelter. Pagan and witch. Human.
Maria O'Shea: Iris and Bruce's baby daughter.
Marion Vespa: Coyote shifter; owner of the Supe-Urban Café.
Morio Kuroyama: One of Camille's lovers and husbands. Essentially the grandson of Grandmother Coyote. Youkai-kitsune (roughly translated: Japanese fox demon).
Nerissa Shale: Menolly's wife. Worked for DSHS. Now working for Chase Johnson as a victims-rights counselor for the FH-CSI. Werepuma and member of the Rainier Puma Pride.
Roman: Ancient vampire; son of Blood Wyne, Queen of the Crimson Veil. Menolly's official consort in the Vampire Nation and her new sire.
Queen Asteria: The former Elfin Queen. Deceased.
Queen Sharah: Was an elfin medic, now the new Elfin Queen; Chase's girlfriend.
Rozurial, aka Roz: Mercenary. Menolly's secondary lover. Incubus who used to be Fae before Zeus and

Hera destroyed his marriage.
Shade: Delilah's fiancé. Part Stradolan, part black (shadow) dragon.
Siobhan Morgan: One of the girls' friends. Selkie (wereseal); member of the Puget Sound Harbor Seal Pod.
Smoky: One of Camille's lovers and husbands. Half-white, half-silver dragon.
Tanne Baum: One of the Black Forest Woodland Fae. A member of the Hunter's Glen Clan.
Tavah: Guardian of the portal at the Wayfarer Bar & Grill. Vampire (full Fae).
Tim Winthrop, aka Cleo Blanco: Computer student/genius, female impersonator. FBH. Now owns the Scarlet Harlot.
Trillian: Mercenary. Camille's alpha lover and one of her three husbands. Svartan (one of the Charming Fae).
Ukkonen O'Shea: Iris and Bruce's baby son.
Vanzir: Was indentured slave to the Sisters, by his own choice. Dream-chaser demon who lost his powers and now is regaining new ones.
Venus the Moon Child: Former shaman of the Rainier Puma Pride. Werepuma. One of the Keraastar Knights.
Wade Stevens: President of Vampires Anonymous. Vampire (human).
Zachary Lyonnesse: Former member of the Rainier Puma Pride Council of Elders. Werepuma living in Otherworld.

Glossary

Black Unicorn/Black Beast: Father of the Dahns unicorns, a magical unicorn that is reborn like the phoenix and lives in Darkynwyrd and Thistlewyd Deep. Raven Mother is his consort, and he is more a force of nature than a unicorn.
Calouk: The rough, common dialect used by a number of Otherworld inhabitants.
Court and Crown: "Crown" refers to the Queen of Y'Elestrial. "Court" refers to the nobility and military personnel that surround the Queen. "Court and Crown" together refer to the entire government of Y'Elestrial.
Court of the Three Queens: The newly risen Court of the three Earthside Fae Queens: Titania, the Fae Queen of Light and Morning; Morgaine, the half-Fae Queen of Dusk and Twilight; and Aeval, the Fae Queen of Shadow and Night.
Crypto: One of the Cryptozoid races. Cryptos include creatures out of legend that are not technically of the Fae races: gargoyles, unicorns, gryphons, chimeras, and so on. Most primarily inhabit Otherworld, but some have Earthside cousins.
Demon Gate: A gate through which demons may be summoned by a powerful sorcerer or necromancer.
Demonica Vacana Society: A society run by a number of ancient entities, including Carter, who study and record the history of demonic activity over Earthside. The archives of the society are found in the Demonica Catacombs, deep within an uninhabited island of the Cyclades, a group of Grecian islands in the Aegean Sea.
Dreyerie: A dragon lair.
Earthside: Everything that exists on the Earth side of

the portals.
Elqaneve: The Elfin city in Otherworld, located in Kelvashan—the Elfin lands.
Elemental Lords: The elemental beings—both male and female—who, along with the Hags of Fate and the Harvestmen, are the only true Immortals. They are avatars of various elements and energies, and they inhabit all realms. They do as they will and seldom concern themselves with humankind or Fae unless summoned. If asked for help, they often exact steep prices in return. The Elemental Lords are not concerned with balance like the Hags of Fate.
FBH: Full-Blooded Human (usually refers to Earthside humans).
FH-CSI: The Faerie–Human Crime Scene Investigation team. The brainchild of Detective Chase Johnson, it was first formed as a collaboration between the OIA and the Seattle police department. Other FH-CSI units have been created around the country, based on the Seattle prototype. The FH-CSI takes care of both medical and criminal emergencies involving visitors from Otherworld.
Great Divide: A time of immense turmoil when the Elemental Lords and some of the High Court of Fae decided to rip apart the worlds. Until then, the Fae existed primarily on Earth, their lives and worlds mingling with those of humans. The Great Divide tore everything asunder, splitting off another dimension, which became Otherworld. At that time, the Twin Courts of Fae were disbanded and their queens and the Merlin were stripped of power. This was the time during which the Spirit Seal was formed and broken in order to seal off the realms from each other. Some Fae chose to stay Earthside, others moved to the realm of Otherworld, and the demons were—for the most part—sealed in the Subterranean Realms.
Guard Des'Estar: The military of Y'Elestrial.
Hags of Fates: The women of destiny who keep the balance righted. Neither good nor evil, they observe the

flow of destiny. When events get too far out of balance, they step in and take action, usually using humans, Fae, Supes, and other creatures as pawns to bring the path of destiny back into line.

Harvestmen: The lords of death—a few cross over and are also Elemental Lords. The Harvestmen, along with their followers (the Valkyries and the Death Maidens, for example), reap the souls of the dead.

Haseofon: The abode of the Death Maidens—where they stay and where they train.

Ionyc Lands: The astral, etheric, and spirit realms, along with several other lesser-known noncorporeal dimensions, form the Ionyc Lands. These realms are separated by the Ionyc Seas, a current of energy that prevents the Ionyc Lands from colliding, thereby sparking off an explosion of universal proportions.

Ionyc Seas: The currents of energy that separate the Ionyc Lands. Certain creatures, especially those connected with the elemental energies of ice, snow, and wind, can travel through the Ionyc Seas without protection.

Kelvashan: The lands of the elves.

Koyanni: The coyote shifters who took an evil path away from the Great Coyote; followers of Nukpana.

Melosealfôr: A rare Crypto dialect learned by powerful Cryptos and all Moon Witches.

The Nectar of Life: An elixir that can extend the life span of humans to nearly the length of a Fae's years. Highly prized and cautiously used. Can drive someone insane if he or she doesn't have the emotional capacity to handle the changes incurred.

Oblition: The act of a Death Maiden sucking the soul out of one of their targets.

OIA: The Otherworld Intelligence Agency; the "brains" behind the Guard Des'Estar. Earthside Division now run by Camille, Menolly, and Delilah.

Otherworld/OW: The human term for the "United Nations" of Faerie Land. A dimension apart from ours that contains creatures from legend and lore, pathways to the gods, and various other places, such as Olympus. Otherworld's actual name varies among the differing dialects of the many races of Cryptos and Fae.

Portal, Portals: The interdimensional gates that connect the different realms. Some were created during the Great Divide; others open up randomly.

Seelie Court: The Earthside Fae Court of Light and Summer, disbanded during the Great Divide. Titania was the Seelie Queen.

Soul Statues: In Otherworld, small figurines created for the Fae of certain races and magically linked with the baby. These figurines reside in family shrines and when one of the Fae dies, their soul statue shatters. In Menolly's case, when she was reborn as a vampire, her soul statue re-formed, although twisted. If a family member disappears, his or her family can always tell if their loved one is alive or dead if they have access to the soul statue.

Spirit Seals: A magical crystal artifact, the Spirit Seal was created during the Great Divide. When the portals were sealed, the Spirit Seal was broken into nine gems and each piece was given to an Elemental Lord or Lady. These gems each have varying powers. Even possessing one of the spirit seals can allow the wielder to weaken the portals that divide Otherworld, Earthside, and the Subterranean Realms. If all of the seals are joined together again, then all of the portals will open.

Stradolan: A being who can walk between worlds, who can walk through the shadows, using them as a method of transportation.

Supe/Supes: Short for Supernaturals. Refers to Earthside supernatural beings who are not of Fae nature. Refers to Weres, especially.

Talamh Lonrach Oll: The name for the Earthside Sovereign Fae Nation.

Triple Threat: Camille's nickname for the newly risen three Earthside Queens of Fae.

Unseelie Court: The Earthside Fae Court of Shadow and Winter, disbanded during the Great Divide. Aeval was the Unseelie Queen.

VA/Vampires Anonymous: The Earthside group started by Wade Stevens, a vampire who was a psychiatrist during life. The group is focused on helping newly born vampires adjust to their new state of existence, and to encourage vampires to avoid harming the innocent as much as possible. The VA is vying for control. Their goal is to rule the vampires of the United States and to set up an internal policing agency.

Whispering Mirror: A magical communications device that links Otherworld and Earth. Think magical video phone.

Y'Eírialiastar: The Sidhe/Fae name for Otherworld.

Y'Elestrial: The city-state in Otherworld where the D'Artigo girls were born and raised. A Fae city, recently embroiled in a civil war between the drug-crazed tyrannical Queen Lethesanar and her more level-headed sister Tanaquar, who managed to claim the throne for herself. The civil war has ended and Tanaquar is restoring order to the land.

Youkai: Loosely (very loosely) translated as Japanese demon/nature spirit. For the purposes of this series, the youkai have three shapes: the animal, the human form, and the true demon form. Unlike the demons of the Subterranean Realms, youkai are not necessarily evil by nature.

Biography

New York Times, *Publishers Weekly*, and *USA Today* bestselling author Yasmine Galenorn writes urban fantasy and paranormal romance, and is the author of over fifty books, including the Otherworld Series, the Fury Unbound Series, the Bewitching Bedlam Series, and many more. She's also written nonfiction metaphysical books. She is the 2011 Career Achievement Award Winner in Urban Fantasy, given by RT Magazine.

Yasmine has been in the Craft since 1980, is a shamanic witch and High Priestess. She describes her life as a blend of teacups and tattoos. She lives in Kirkland, WA, with her husband Samwise and their cats. Yasmine can be reached via her website at Galenorn.com. Be sure to sign up for her newsletter to find out about new releases.

Books by Yasmine Galenorn:

Fury Unbound Series:
Fury Rising
Fury's Magic
Fury Awakened (May 2017)
Fury Calling (August 2017)
Fury's Mantle (November 2017)
Fury Unchained (2018)

Bewitching Bedlam Series:
Blood Music (prequel novelette)
Bewitching Bedlam
Maudlin's Mayhem (July 2017)

Siren Song (October 2017)
Witches Wild (2018)

Otherworld Series (in order):
Witchling
Changeling
Darkling
Dragon Wytch
Night Huntress
Demon Mistress
Bone Magic
Harvest Hunting
Blood Wyne
Courting Darkness
Shaded Vision
Shadow Rising
Haunted Moon
Autumn Whispers
Crimson Veil
Priestess Dreaming
Panther Prowling
Darkness Raging
Moon Shimmers
Harvest Song (2018)
Blood Bonds (2019)

Otherworld: E-Novellas:
The Shadow of Mist: Otherworld novella
Etched in Silver: Otherworld novella
Ice Shards: Otherworld novella
Flight From Hell: Otherworld--Fly By Night crossover novella
Earthbound
Silent Night: Otherworld Holiday Novella (December 2017)

Otherworld: Short Collections:
Tales From Otherworld: Collection One
Men of Otherworld: Collection One

Men of Otherworld: Collection Two
Moon Swept: Otherworld Tales of First Love

Chintz 'n China Series:
Ghost of a Chance
Legend of the Jade Dragon
Murder Under a Mystic Moon
A Harvest of Bones
One Hex of a Wedding
Holiday Spirits

Whisper Hollow Series (in order):
Autumn Thorns
Shadow Silence

Lily Bound Books:
Souljacker

Fly By Night Series (in order):
Flight from Death
Flight from Mayhem

Indigo Court Series (in order):
Night Myst
Night Veil
Night Seeker
Night Vision
Night's End

Indigo Court: Novellas:
Night Shivers

Bath and Body Series (originally under the name India Ink):
Scent to Her Grave
A Blush With Death
Glossed and Found

Misc. Short Story Collections:

Mist and Shadows: Short Tales From Dark Haunts

Anthologies:
Winter's Heat (novelette: Bewitching Bedlam)
Taming the Shifter (novelette: Bewitching Bedlam)
Once Upon a Kiss (short story: Princess Charming)
Silver Belles (short story: The Longest Night)
Once Upon a Curse (short story: Bones)
Never After (Otherworld novella: The Shadow of Mist)
Inked (Otherworld novella: Etched in Silver)
Hexed (Otherworld novella: Ice Shards)
Songs of Love & Death (short story: Man in the Mirror)
Songs of Love and Darkness (short story: Man in the Mirror)
Nyx in the House of Night (article: She is Goddess)
A Second Helping of Murder (recipe: Clam Chowder)

Magickal Nonfiction:
From Llewellyn Publications and Ten Speed Press:
Trancing the Witch's Wheel
Embracing the Moon
Dancing with the Sun
Tarot Journeys
Crafting the Body Divine
Sexual Ecstasy and the Divine
Totem Magic
Magical Meditations

Printed in Great Britain
by Amazon